FULL CIRCLE

TENTH BOOK IN THE BRIGANDSHAW CHRONICLES

PETER RIMMER

This book is dedicated to all the men, women and children who lost their lives on both sides of the conflict.

The Rhodesian Bush War, July 1964 to December 1979.

ABOUT PETER RIMMER

Peter Rimmer was born in London, England, and grew up in the south of the city where he went to school. After the Second World War, aged eighteen, he joined the Royal Air Force, reaching the rank of Pilot Officer before he was nineteen. At the end of his National Service, he sailed for Africa to grow tobacco in what was then Rhodesia, now Zimbabwe.

The years went by and Peter found himself in Johannesburg where he established an insurance brokering company. Over 2% of the companies listed on the Johannesburg Stock Exchange were clients of Rimmer Associates. He opened branches in the United States of America, Australia and Hong Kong and travelled extensively between them.

Having lived a reclusive life on his beloved smallholding in Knysna, South Africa, for over 25 years, Peter passed away in July 2018. He has left an enormous legacy of unpublished work for his family to release over the coming years, and not only they but also his readers from around the world will sorely miss him. Peter Rimmer was 81 years old.

ALSO BY PETER RIMMER

~

STANDALONE NOVELS

All Our Yesterdays

Cry of the Fish Eagle

Just the Memory of Love

Vultures in the Wind

~

NOVELLA

Second Beach

~

THE ASIAN SAGAS

Bend with the Wind (Book 1)

Each to His Own (Book 2)

~

THE BRIGANDSHAW CHRONICLES

(*The Rise and Fall of the Anglo Saxon Empire*)

Echoes from the Past (Book 1)

Elephant Walk (Book 2)

Mad Dogs and Englishmen (Book 3)

To the Manor Born (Book 4)

On the Brink of Tears (Book 5)

Treason If You Lose (Book 6)

Horns of Dilemma (Book 7)

Lady Come Home (Book 8)

The Best of Times (Book 9)

Full Circle (Book 10)

Leopards Never Change Their Spots (Book 11)

Look Before You Leap (Book 12)

THE PIONEERS

Morgandale (Book 1)

Carregan's Catch (Book 2)

FULL CIRCLE

First published in Great Britain in January 2021 by

KAMBA PUBLISHING, United Kingdom

10 9 8 7 6 5 4 3 2 1

PART I

MAY 1967 – "THE STORYTELLER"

1

Katie Frost received her proposal in the mail. The landlady had given her the letter with its Rhodesian stamps when she came home from work. The first line sent her dull London day screaming into excitement. He wanted to marry her. She was going to be a farmer's wife. No longer the drudgery and boredom of working a comptometer for Sedgewick and Biggs, adding, subtracting, feeding in the figures of a London auditor day after day in a row of girls just making a living. She had the chance to get out. Bobby had given her the first chance in her life to break the ties of monotony. At twenty-three, finally, she was going to get a life.

Hugging herself with excitement, Katie went to the window of her room. Outside it was raining. The slate roofs of the houses were grey and wet. A pigeon on the roof opposite sat motionless in the drizzle. She was going to escape.

Dear Katie,

This may come as a surprise but will you marry me? We didn't know each other long during my two trips to England but I think of you often. A bachelor's life on a Rhodesian farm gives a man time to reflect on his future. You see, they have allocated me a four thousand acre Crown Land farm, the last of a few the

Rhodesian government are offering to qualified farm managers for seven shillings and sixpence an acre, which sounds good until you realise how much money has to go into turning virgin bush into a productive farm. The farm is in Centenary East, near the small village of Mount Darwin (one tarred road in the middle, two hundred yards long). I am writing this letter to you from my tent on my own farm. Out the flap, high up like some portent, I can see Mount Darwin, the mountain that broods over this part of the bush. The locals say the mountain has a mystical importance to them. Something about the ancestors. There's a cave at the bottom of the mountain where an old Sangoma lives (witch doctor we would wrongly say in English). He is a holy man of medicine with great knowledge and wisdom. Before I signed the agreements at the Land Bank (I have borrowed five thousand pounds to add to the five thousand I saved from my bonuses working for Jeremy Crookshank and Callum McFay) I visited the Sangoma with Sekuru to make sure I was doing the right thing. Sekuru was assistant bossboy at World's View when I worked for Jeremy Crookshank. With Jeremy's blessing he has joined me in my venture as bossboy of Hopewell Estate. How do you like the name? If you hope well in life everything turns out fine. I gave the Sangoma one of our new Rhodesian dollars (when the British government applied sanctions after UDI we changed our currency from Rhodesian pounds to Rhodesian dollars – we were out of the sterling block so it didn't matter, I suppose.) And he blessed my venture. You should have seen the smile on Sekuru's face. He's now building himself a mud hut further down the river. Well, not really a river, more of a stream. I am going to stay in a tent until six tobacco barns are up. The first job we are starting tomorrow is stumping out the trees from thirty acres, land enough to grow tobacco for six barns. If I have time this year I will build a small house from the timber we cut. Raw bush timber but it'll last for a couple of years. There are plenty of reeds down by the river to make a thatched roof. We'll build a brick fire-place and chimney in the middle of the one-roomed house so we can be warm in the cold winter evenings... In this part of Rhodesia we make our own bricks, from ant hills... Can you believe it being cold in Africa! We're at five thousand feet above sea level in Salisbury and three thousand on the farm. When you get to the Zambezi escarpment, twenty odd miles from where I am writing this letter to you Katie, it drops straight down into the Zambezi Valley where it's hot the whole year round. It's going to take a few years to pay off my debt but I think it's worth it. A man has to be independent. Can't work for somebody else for the rest of my life. Never get anywhere that way.

Look, Katie, I can't offer you much right now but when we get up to a hundred acres of tobacco and twenty-four barns we'll get rich like my old boss Jeremy Crookshank. Having worked in Centenary West for five years many of the farmers will help me. Sanctions have reduced the price of tobacco on the auction floors but the crops are still selling. We grow the best Virginia tobacco in the world in Rhodesia. At a tenth of the cost of the Americans. A couple of years ago when they were still openly buying our tobacco, an American buyer on the floors told me we grew as good tobacco as anything he had seen in Virginia. I had breakfast with him that day, just before the auction started. After seven years with Jeremy and Callum I know what I'm doing. So will you marry me, Katie? You'll have to write to Private Bag 9, Mount Darwin. The RMS truck drops off a mail bag every week at the Dax turnoff where the road from Bindura and Mount Darwin crosses the road to the village of Centenary. If you want to come, write to me. I'll send you the money for the boat fare. You can have a holiday coming out and sail to Beira in Mozambique and catch the train to Salisbury where I'll fetch you from the railway station. Despite sanctions our banks here have ways of sending out money to England. If I don't hear from you in a month I'll know you don't want to marry me. Send the letter by airmail. I'll be waiting at the Dax turnoff for the RMS truck every Thursday.

Love from
Bobby

> *PS. If you agree I'll write to your father asking for his permission to marry you. We'll be married in the Salisbury Cathedral though we won't have a honeymoon until the end of the first season. I don't think I can afford two fares for your parents to get them to the wedding as all my money is going into the farm. Tractors, ploughs, discers, flues for the barns, workshop equipment, a one-ton truck – it never seems to stop.*

With her excitement at boiling point Katie just had to tell someone. At first she thought of phoning her mother to tell her the good news but decided against it. On Bobby's two trips to England her mother had discouraged their friendship. Katie's mother had thought Rhodesia was an island off Madagascar. When Katie told her it was the British colony that all the fuss was about her mother had changed the subject.

"Oh, don't get involved with a man who lives in a place that's in a mess. Find some nice boy from England, Katie. Now I want you to help me with the church bazaar next Saturday. Your father wants to play cricket so you'll have to help. Did I tell you, Katie?..."

At that point, Katie had switched off. Not that it mattered. She had not so much as kissed Bobby Preston. But she had liked him. Most of the boys her own age were boring. All they wanted to do was drink and have sex.

With the letter from Bobby in her handbag she put on her coat. Linda lived just down the road. At the door of her friend's rooming house, Katie rang the bell.

Up in the room, Katie gave Linda the letter to read and sat on the bed. By the end of the letter, Linda was crying. They had been friends for ten years, ever since they met at school.

"What's the matter?"

"You're so lucky. Four thousand acres! That's so big I can't even imagine it. Oh, Katie. Give me a big hug."

"So what must I do?"

"Say yes... Does he have any friends? I can come out on the boat with you and be bridesmaid at your wedding. I've saved a little money. We can share a cabin... You're so lucky. So you slept with him, you little minx."

"I only kissed him at the end of his second visit."

"Oh, that's so clever. No wonder he wants to marry you. I always say don't let them have it until they put a ring on your finger. And he wasn't bad looking."

"But what will happen in Rhodesia?"

"Who cares? You're going to be married. Live on your own farm. To a man you only kissed. Most of my other friends have to get themselves pregnant. You want to go down the pub to celebrate? It's Friday. You got all weekend to write him a nice letter. So when are you going? I'll have to resign from Sedgewick and Biggs. So will you. I'm sick of sitting in that big room with all the other comptometer operators. You remember how at school we dreamed of marrying a rich man who would look after us? When we get to Rhodesia I'll come and stay with you."

"He lives in a tent."

"What a giggle. Plenty of room for another tent on four thousand acres. Anyway, who knows who we'll meet on the boat?"

"You really want to come too?"

"Why ever not? You're only young once. In ten years the best of your looks will be gone. Come on. Down to the Pig and Whistle. We'll celebrate. We're going to Rhodesia."

"Don't you need a coat?"

"Who cares? I'm warm inside... I've never lived in a tent. I wonder what they use as a bathroom. I was so bored when I heard the knock on the door. Now I'm as happy as a cricket. Down the pub they all work for someone, never going to get anywhere. Stuck in the same old rut year after year. Getting up, going to work and coming home again. In the pool where we sit with the typists there aren't any men. Anyway, who'd want to marry an accountant? So boring. How much do you think the boat fare will be to Beira? Where the hell is Beira? Can't you get from Cape Town to Rhodesia by train? Might be cheaper. Dad might give me a bob or two. He always says I'm going nowhere with my life. At last some excitement. And if your Bobby changes his mind when he sees you again we can check out the local talent. England's so grey and boring. It's May but it's still cold and raining. I hate being stuck in this room but what else can I do, Katie? Live at home? Be driven round the bend by Dad and Mum. It's an hour's journey from Dorking to London... They must need comptometer operators in Rhodesia. They must have auditors."

"Aren't you cold without a coat?"

They had walked out of the rooming house and down the road.

"Just lucky it isn't raining. In we go, Katie. What you having? The usual?... Fred, give us two halves of mild and bitter. Katie and I are going out to Africa. Where the sun shines. Hello, Dave. Hello, Eric. How was your week at the office? Mine was bloody awful. Everyone listen. My best friend Katie is going to be married to a Rhodesian. Live in a tent surrounded by wild animals. And I'm going with her. Cheers. To your wealth, to hell with the rest. Anyone else want to come with us?"

"Don't be daft, Linda. Rhodesia's not going to last."

"What you know about it, Dave?"

"You're right. Bugger all. You two enjoy yourselves. You only live once. If it doesn't work you can always come back to England. Sounds like a good adventure to me. Who's the bloke, Katie?"

"Bobby Preston. He's English. Went out to Rhodesia seven years ago when he was eighteen. Didn't have to do his National Service that way. Came over to visit his parents. Met him at a party, Eric. All the girls from the typing pool had gone to the pub on a Friday. Someone was having a bottle party. Got invited with the rest of the girls."

"I wish I had somewhere to go... Oh, well. Enjoy the moment. It's Friday night and I just got paid. I'll miss you girls. The old Pig and Whistle won't be quite the same."

"Don't start getting sentimental on us. You can come and visit us."

"I'd never leave England for a foreign country. Where'd I get a pint of bitter? You want me to buy you a drink seeing I just got paid?"

"Don't mind if you do. Need all my money for the boat fare."

On Saturday Katie wrote Bobby the first letter she had written a man. It was short. She didn't know him that well. It was easier for him to talk about his farm than for her to talk about her room in Notting Hill Gate. Or write about the girls in the typing pool. Her parents in Dorking. She said 'yes' to his proposal and made the excuse she was in a hurry to post the letter. When she thought about it she found it hard to conjure up his face. They had gone out four times, or it might have been five. At the time it had not seemed so important. Bobby had done most of the talking, all about his life in Rhodesia. She had kept quiet, not having much to say. Talking about the office would have sounded so trivial. She had listened. Men liked to talk about themselves. Her mother had said that if she wanted to catch a man she had best be a good listener. Only when she was married would she get her word in edgeways.

"Flatter them, Katie. Listen with big open eyes to every word they say."

"Do you do that with Father?"

"It was during the war. Didn't know if he was coming back from Burma. We were in a hurry in those days. Living in the present. You won't understand. War makes you behave differently. You tell each other what you're feeling a lot more quickly. We got married on your dad's home leave. He was still in Burma when you were born. Didn't know he'd ever see his daughter. All worked out when the Americans dropped the bomb on Hiroshima and the war came to an end. We were lucky, you and I, Katie. He came back."

"You ever regret getting married in a hurry?"

"Not for a second. You look at a man and know." Then her mother had sighed.

THE TRAIN PULLED into the railway station at Dorking just after lunch. Katie walked the ten minutes home.

"What's wrong, Katie? What you doing here?"

"I'm getting married, Mum. To Bobby. You remember Bobby Preston? That man I met from Rhodesia. He's got his own farm now and wants me to marry him. Four thousand acres. When he gets up to growing one hundred acres of tobacco he says we're going to be rich. Sending me the boat fare. Linda is coming with me on the boat. We sail from Tilbury to Cape Town and up to Rhodesia by train through Botswana. Went to the travel agent with Linda this morning. Booked our passage in eight weeks' time... What's the matter, Mum?"

"It's so far. You barely know the man. What about me and your father?"

"The wedding is going to be in Salisbury Cathedral. You can come out for the wedding. Have a holiday. We're going to be living in a tent."

"Oh, my God!"

"Be happy for me, Mum."

"You'd better go and tell your grandmother. How far away is Rhodesia?"

"Seven thousand miles."

2

While Katie was going into her grandmother's room where the old lady was lying in bed, a broad smile on her wrinkled face at the sight of her granddaughter, Bobby Preston was sitting under the shade of a msasa tree drinking a cup of tea. They had finished stumping out trees for the day, and Sekuru and the thirty labourers were back in the small compound of thatched mud huts further down the small river. The kettle, hanging from the tripod over the open fire, was still letting off a thin whiff of steam as the wood in the fire burned down. Bobby, well satisfied with the week's work, was thinking of Katie. By now his letter would have arrived. With luck next Thursday at the Dax turnoff he would find her letter of reply. Tired from working all day with the gang helping cut down the trees, he could only hope her answer was yes. He needed a wife. A man with a four-thousand acre farm needed a wife and kids. He needed a family. His own family. People to belong to. People to give him purpose in life. To make all the hard work worthwhile. To give good reason for taking the biggest gamble of his life building a farm out of the African bush.

Far away Bobby could see Mount Darwin, rising high above the bush. In front of him the tent flapped in the breeze, the fly sheet banging softly on the second layer of canvas underneath. By the time the rains broke in October he would have started a house. In five months he would have cleared the thirty acres, ploughed and disced the land, planted the seed beds, built six barns and started his house. Smiling to himself, Bobby stretched out his legs from where he was sitting in his canvas chair and finished his tea. Building a home and a farm was deeply satisfying, a challenge that would take up years of his life, making what he wanted from life grow before his eyes. With the open tent flapping in the breeze, Bobby got to his feet, put on his bush hat and walked round the tent to his truck. He needed some company. From the compound the smoke from the cooking fires was being pushed across the river by the breeze. He could hear someone talking in Shona, the sound too far away for Bobby to understand. It was Saturday afternoon. Time for a drink in the club. They would be playing tennis. He would sit on the veranda of the Centenary East Club and drink a cold beer. Watch them play tennis. Talk to his friends… All the way to the club he was thinking of Katie. Of what she would think of life in Rhodesia.

"We'll be happy, Katie. That's what counts."

"HELLO, Bobby. You want to make up a four for tennis?"

"I want a cold beer, Hammond. How's your new farm progressing?"

"Much the same as yours. We're halfway through the stumping. Stumping out trees is a bugger. You got to go down so far to get out the tap root. Have you started building your barns?"

"The builder boy is making bricks. We found big ant hills close to where we want to build the barns. All that nice red earth. He's going to fire the first kiln next week. Why is it the saliva from the ants makes such good bricks?"

"I have no idea. I'm building a house first. You still in a tent?"

"What's wrong with a tent?"

"You heard from your girl in England?"

"Not yet."

"I hope you didn't say you lived in a tent."

"I did, as a matter of fact. Farm buildings come first. Can't cure tobacco in your house, Hammond. The idea of farming is to make money. Lots and lots of money."

"I wish I could find a woman. It's lonely on your own."

"Don't tell me."

"There are so few single girls in Salisbury."

"Why I'm bringing one out from England."

"She hasn't agreed to marry you yet, Bobby... Let's have a beer. The tennis can wait. Wouldn't it be nice for such close neighbours to both have wives? The wives would become friends. We'd all be friends. Eat dinner together on the weekends. Go into the bush together looking for game. You ever been down the escarpment into the Zambezi Valley?... An ideal life. Good food. Good company. Good sex. What more could anyone want?"

"The kids would be friends," said Bobby wistfully.

"You got it. I'll get a girl if yours accepts."

"I'm probably dreaming."

"We all have to dream. What would life be without dreaming? Anyone else in the club we know?"

"We know them all."

"You know what I mean. Chaps our age. This new Centenary East club is better than the Centenary West. In your old club, when you worked for Jeremy Crookshank, they're all over forty. One foot in the grave. Have you seen your old boss?"

"Came over during the week to offer me help."

"My old boss is helping me. Brought some fresh butter from his cows. Fruit and vegetables. It was the moral support I liked most."

"It's nice when people help. Stops some of the panic in the stomach... Are you buying or am I?"

"Haven't paid for last month's booze."

"Then Morris had better put the beers on my card. Good to see you, Hammond."

"Good to see you, Bobby. Without a house, how do you get a bath? There are crocodiles in the river. One big bastard I saw just yesterday. Gave me the eye."

"I have a pulley up into the tallest tree by the river. Fill a bucket with water and haul it up to the top of the tree. There's a hose pipe from the bottom of the bucket with a tap and a rose at the other end. When the bucket's up high in the tree and the rose just above my head I turn on the tap. Best shower I ever had."

"Well I'll be buggered. Who dreamed that one up?"

"Chap I met on one of my safaris into the bush. He was an old prospector. Been in the bush most of his life."

"Did he ever find anything?"

"Not much. He was always following the rainbow. Shared most of his food. Lived in a tent. Showered from a bucket under a tree down by the river. One of the happiest old codgers I ever met. Had to buy him drinks, of course, when I met him in Salisbury. The conversation was worth the price of every beer. He could tell a tale or two that old man."

"What was he looking for?"

"Emeralds and diamonds."

"Maybe one day he'll strike it lucky and buy all the drinks. Mine's a cold Castle. What was his name?"

"Koos Hendriks. He's an Afrikaner. An old Boer. Said I was the only Englishman he had ever liked."

"I'll bet he says that to everyone who buys him a drink."

"At least I get a shower every morning. On cold days I leave the bucket full of water out in the sun before hauling it up into the tree. That way the water is hot. At this time of year it's cold first thing in the morning. Twenty minutes in the sun to heat a bucket of water and you get a hot shower. All because of Koos Hendriks."

"Can you remember why we fought the Boer War?"

"I have no idea what it was all about. Wars are so damn silly."

"There's a rumour of terrorists infiltrating the country. Lying low. That one day they're going to attack us."

"You can spend your life worrying about the things that never happen... Morris, give us a couple of ice-cold Castles."

"Coming up, Boss Bobby."

"Did you see how Morris looked at me?" whispered Hammond. "He knows. I heard the Russians are training blacks in Zambia to attack us whites so the communists can take over the country. All part of the cold war. There's big shit in Vietnam. Thank God the British government kept us out of that one. The Russians use surrogate armies to fight the Americans, training insurgents and supplying them with arms to fight the war against capitalism. So I heard. Some chap from England was rabbiting on in the men's bar at Meikles Hotel. Said it was just another form of empire building. Through communism, the Russians want to control the world. Who knows?"

"I'm more concerned about getting my barns built before the first crop of tobacco ripens."

"So am I… Cheers, old boy."

"Ah, there you are, Hammond. As club chairman, I have to remind you about your outstanding bar bill. If you haven't got your cheque book go and get it. Bad form not to pay your bar bill. Be a good fellow. How are the new farms coming along?"

"Just fine, Mr Quinton."

"Now, off you go for your cheque book, young fellow."

"Yes, sir. May I finish my beer?"

"Who paid for it?"

"Bobby Preston."

"Then drink up."

"My cheque book is in the truck."

"Of course it is. Bring me the cheque before you go back into the bar."

The chairman of the club handed Hammond his bar bill, huffed once and left.

"Good," said Bobby. "The next round is on you."

"Would he have thrown me out of the club?"

"Damn sure he would."

"Better go. He's watching me from the veranda. When I come back I'll tell you about Mrs Wells."

"What about her?"

"When I make up a mixed four for tennis she gives me the eye and touches my arm."

"She might be nearer forty than thirty. Too much hard tennis and sun."

"Any port in a storm."

"Better go, Hammond. Old Quinton is glaring at you and stroking his moustache. You know he was Indian army before he came to Rhodesia. Sticklers for paying their bills in the officers' mess."

"You just want me to pay my bill so I can buy the next round."

"Of course I do. Hasn't Mrs Wells got three young children?"

"Doesn't stop them looking. Her husband's much older than her."

"Be careful. It's a small community. People talk. What you need is a young wife."

"Don't we both?"

While Hammond went to get his cheque book from the glove compartment in the front of his truck, Bobby took his beer outside onto the veranda. Standing alone he looked down on the tennis courts where Mrs Wells was playing tennis. Hugh Quinton was still waiting for Hammond to give him the cheque. The two tennis courts down below were made from the same clay that came out of the ant hills Bobby used to make his bricks. Like the clubhouse behind him, the tennis courts were new, the tall wire-mesh fence able to stop the tennis balls before they ended up in the bush. The clubhouse was on a hill overlooking the dry countryside that went on and on into the distance, nothing but trees, grass and wild animals, the few farms pinpricks in the endless wilderness. From where Bobby stood, looking directly out to the hills thirty or more miles away, he could barely make out these tiny signs of human habitation. Until the white man came to grow his tobacco there had been nothing but bush for all the centuries. The sound of the tennis rackets hitting the small white balls echoed out into the distance. Watching Mrs Wells run after a ball made Bobby think back to Katie. Katie liked playing tennis. She had told him so.

On his last trip to England, Bobby had hired a car at the airport to drive to his parents' new home in Surrey. Like Hugh Quinton, Bobby's father had been a regular officer in the army, retiring as a brigadier general six months before Bobby arrived back in England on leave. Luckily for his father his mother's family had money, the old man's army pension after thirty-nine years' service just one thousand pounds a year. Once retired, all the perks had gone: the free car with the driver, the free house in the officers' quarters, staff to look after the chores. From living the good life Bobby's father was poor, lucky his wife's inheritance had bought the house. It was small, suburban, not far from the High Street of Epsom. Bobby's father hated the place. So did Bobby. From being someone, Bobby's father was nothing. The sight of his father, now irrelevant, made Bobby even more determined to make his own money in farming and have something to show for his life at the end.

On his last weekend in England Bobby had driven with Katie into the country. He had bought a small picnic basket he would take back to Rhodesia and asked his landlady to fill it with food for the picnic. Instead of staying in a cheap hotel, Bobby had taken a room in a boarding house in London, close enough to the West End to take in the shows. From playing the records on his wind-up gramophone in the middle of the African bush, Bobby had spent most of his money in London going to the shows, building up memories for all those lonely nights on his own back on the farm just listening to their music. Twice he had taken Katie to see a musical.

They had found themselves in a wood not ten miles from his parents' new house, Bobby thinking it too presumptuous to take her to meet his family. Under an old oak tree on a perfect spring day Katie had told him she liked playing tennis. In the picnic basket they had found hard-boiled eggs and sandwiches made from newly baked bread. Bobby had put in a bottle of wine. For hours, lying on their backs under the spreading oak tree, they had told each other the little stories of their lives, the blue sky above just visible through the oak trees. It was a perfect time. A perfect picnic. They were happy together alone in the woods, both of them content. Under that tree Rhodesia had seemed so far away. Now, he hoped, Katie was going to join him in Africa and live in a tent under the tall, riverine trees that were just as beautiful as the oaks.

"She's got nice legs, hasn't she? Just don't look at the face. I've given Quinton my cheque."

"What are you talking about?"

"Mrs Wells. That's her playing tennis."

"Sorry. I was daydreaming."

"Want another beer? Your glass is empty. Let's go back into the bar."

"I think she's waving at you."

"I rather think she is... You know, her husband never comes to the club."

"What about her children?"

"Leaves them at home with the nanny. She's only been out from England ten years. Met her husband in London when he went back on leave. She was lucky to find a husband. So, what do you think?"

"Leave her alone, Hammond. She's got a husband. Don't bugger up her life."

"What else can I do?" Mrs Wells was still looking at them as the players changed sides for the serve.

"You can stop waving and smiling at Mrs Wells. You'll have the whole block talking."

"That's not my problem."

"It will be if Stanley Wells gets hold of you. He's a tough old bastard. Wouldn't want to get on the wrong side of him... Are you buying?"

"Come on. I'm just kidding."

"Oh, I hope you are. What's her first name?"

"Elizabeth."

"Don't you find it weird us few English stuck in the middle of nowhere playing tennis as if we had never left England, imposing our way of life?"

"We've done it all over the world. We expect everyone else to change. You know in India they're fanatical about cricket... Ah, Morris. You can start a new card for me. I expect Mr Quinton mentioned it."

The clubhouse had filled up with farmers and their wives sitting in groups at the tables. When Mrs Wells and her doubles tennis partners came into the bar she deliberately sat next to Hammond, touching him briefly on his bare arm. Bobby recognised Hammond's instant arousal. No one else seemed to notice. After two more drinks, feeling out of it, Bobby drove home to his farm. His tent camp was twenty minutes on a dirt road from the club. Outside the tent, under a tree, the gas-operated refrigerator was faintly humming, the big gas cylinder next to it providing the power. Inside the fridge with its top-compartment freezer, Bobby found his meat for the night. A half-finished salad would go with the meat. The fire, under the tripod that hung the kettle, was already laid by the cook. The sun was beginning to set, the red glow reflected in the gently flowing surface of the river. It was the end of May with no rain expected until November. From further down the river Bobby could hear the gang enjoying their well-earned Saturday evening. Like Bobby, they still had no women. Just a keg of white maize beer Bobby bought for them every weekend. The sound of them all enjoying themselves was comforting. On Saturday nights, his night off, the cook stayed away from Bobby's tented camp. Bobby put a match to the fire that would cook his meat on the *braai* grill. The sound of splashes echoed up from the river. There were animals drinking and birds going up to roost in the trees. Bobby wound up his gramophone player and put on the original cast recording of *Hello, Dolly!*, one of the London shows he had seen with Katie, bringing back pleasant memories.

In the comfort of his canvas chair, the light from the flames rising higher into the canopy of the trees as the sun went quickly down, Bobby took the top off a beer and drank straight from the bottle. The beer was pleasantly cold. He was content. The week's work had gone well. When it was pitch dark, with the smoke from his fire keeping off the mosquitoes, the frogs calling from the river, the cicadas from the long grass that ran back through the trees, Bobby grilled his meat. He had put two potatoes in tinfoil in the fire before he sat down. The half-finished salad stood on the folding camp table next to his canvas chair. Far away a buck barked, one short bark and then silence. Bobby ate, enjoying every mouthful of his food.

After his supper Bobby took the single hurricane lamp into the tent and closed the flap. A mosquito net hung from the centre pole of the tent. With the light out, Bobby lay down in his camp bed. Sekuru and the gang were still singing further downriver; the maize beer having done its trick. They sounded happy. Bobby closed his eyes and fell into a dreamless sleep.

A squeal of dying agony woke Bobby from his sleep making him instantly reach for the gun by the side of his bed. The gun was a .358 calibre Winchester that close-up would take down an elephant. He got out of bed and opened the flap of the tent. The dying animal had been not more than fifty yards from his camp. Above the trees were millions of stars in the clear night sky. A small sickle moon was shedding colourless light over the bush. The river down behind the trees was in pitch dark. For a long while, gripping the rifle after having pushed forward the gun's safety catch, Bobby looked and listened for the predator. There was not a sound. The lion, leopard or hyena had carried its prey back into the bush from the river to its lair far away. His workers' camp was quiet. Death had come and gone into the night. Looking up, Bobby could see three layers of the stars. He could make out the Southern Cross with its north-south pointer that guided men like Koos Hendriks through the bush, giving them direction as good as any compass. Bobby's heartbeat had slowed back to normal.

Back in the tent with the flap closed, the gun by his side, Bobby tried to go back to sleep. He was wide awake. England and all his upbringing seemed far distant from his present reality. His father's last tour before Bobby left England to farm in Rhodesia had been in Germany with the British Army on the Rhine. During his father's five-year tour in Germany Bobby had been sent to boarding school in England. By then, his two sisters, older than Bobby, had left school, both working as secretaries in London, living in digs. Bobby had been a late surprise for his mother and father, making his upbringing solitary and lonely. The two older girls thought him fun but there was no real communication. No help growing up from either of them. His father was always involved with the army, his mother not quite sure what to do with so young a son. If his mother had been younger it would have been easier for her. The war, with his father away for three years fighting the Japanese, had been difficult for his mother. Bobby had been born during the war. Nine months after his father had come back from Egypt where he had been stationed. Now the British, Germans, Italians and Japanese were friends again. It had all been pointless, killing each other for the sake of killing, unlike the night's predator that had killed by the river to eat. Bobby hoped Africa, his part of Africa, would stay peaceful for the rest of his life. Bobby hated arguments, let alone fights.

He lay awake for a long time. There was no more sound coming from the river. Outside, the night was quiet. The frogs and cicadas had also gone to bed.

When Bobby woke for the second time the birds were calling to the dawn. The temperature had dropped during the night. He pulled up his blanket and lay on his back smiling, listening to the birds. There was not one false out-of-tune note from any of them. All the birds were in tune.

Putting on a sweater, Bobby went out of the tent. He had picked up the gun just in case. The dawn was beautiful. With the bucket in his right hand, the gun pointed at the trail in his left, Bobby walked down the steep bank of the river to the water and filled the bucket. There was a kudu and a family of warthog on the other side of the river. The kudu took no notice while the warthog, small animals much like pigs, ran away, having seen his gun. With the bucket full, Bobby walked up the slope to his tent and put the bucket in the morning rays of the sun. After breakfast, he would haul the bucket up into the tree and have his morning shower, compliments of Koos Hendriks. It was Sunday, the gang's day off. Bobby had told Welcome, the cook, to take the day off with the rest of them. On Sundays, Bobby liked to be on his own. He was at peace with himself, never lonely except for his need of a woman.

Bobby understood Hammond. He just hoped Hammond, in his need, would not make a fool of himself with Mrs Wells.

"Please come, Katie. You'll love this place. All you can hear is the sound of birds and the odd splash in the night." Bobby was happy, smiling, pleased with the day.

He got to hoping, as he made the fire to cook his breakfast, that a letter would come in the mail bag on Thursday.

"All this and a woman. What more could a man want?" The kudu looked back at him from across the river, not moving. The family of warthog were back again, drinking at the water's edge. There was no sign of the predators that had killed in the dark of the night.

The big frying pan was just perfect, big enough for two. Three bangers, as Bobby liked to call his sausages, went in with the bacon. Next he sliced open three tomatoes and put them in the pan. The hot fat from the pork sausages and bacon sizzled the tomatoes. A mound of Friday night's leftover mashed potatoes went in next. The kettle, now hanging from its tripod above the frying pan, was just below boiling, steam seeping from its metal spout. The coffee cup with a spoonful of instant coffee was ready next to four slices of bread he would toast on the grill when he took off the frying pan. When everything was ready, Bobby cracked four eggs into the frying pan and basted the eggs with the hot fat using a spoon. The big breakfast plate stood next to the fire, keeping hot. Only during the week, when Bobby worked from sunup to sundown, did he need the help of Welcome to cook his food and keep the camp clean. Welcome spoke a smattering of English. Mostly they spoke in Fanagalo, the bastard language from the mines of South Africa that was used by the diverse tribes to communicate. Welcome was Shona from Rhodesia, three of the gang were from Nyasaland, two from over the eastern border in Portuguese Mozambique. None of them understood each other's language and, like Bobby, had learnt the simple Fanagalo, a mix of Zulu, bits of English, Afrikaans and Portuguese.

"Where did you get the name Welcome?"

"My mother had five girls before me. My name in Shona means Welcome. She was pleased to have a boy."

"You got the job, Welcome. Welcome to Hopewell Estate. Can you cook?"

"Yes, boss."

"Then you will be my cook and run my camp."

The young black man had smiled, showing a row of white teeth. The conversation had been in broken English mixed with Fanagalo. They had slipped into each other's lives without any problem. Welcome had built himself a mud hut on the river next to the rest of the gang. Welcome said he needed a woman.

In the shade of a tree, Bobby ate his breakfast, wiping up the remains on his plate with a piece of bread. He was full. Content. Happy.

"It's not all bad," he said to himself.

The sky was powder-blue with light fluffy patches of clouds. The clouds were motionless. With the kettle above the fire, boiling gently, Bobby stripped himself naked. The bucket of water he had pulled from the river was now warm. Bobby had filled the shower bucket to the top with the hot water and hauled it up into the tree by the rope, the hose pipe snaking up behind the bucket. Tying the rope to the trunk of the tree when the bucket reached the top, the hose above Bobby's head, the tap just above the shower rose within reach, Bobby stretched up and turned on his shower. The water gently soaked his face and body.

"Koos, you old genius. This is bloody perfect." He was laughing with happiness.

Letting the sun dry his body, Bobby poured himself a second cup of coffee from the water-kettle into his mug. During the week, Welcome brewed him coffee from ground coffee beans. Only on Sundays did Bobby drink instant coffee. It reminded him of England and his mother. When the sound of a distant truck caught his attention he put on his shorts.

"A visitor. I'll be buggered. Lucky I finished breakfast."

Five minutes later, a truck Bobby recognised drove into his camp. The truck belonged to his old employer, Jeremy Crookshank, who farmed in Centenary West half an hour from Hopewell Estate. The man getting out of the truck was Jeremy's manager, Vince Ranger.

"Am I too late for breakfast?"

"Just missed it, Vince. Ten minutes earlier you'd have caught me in the act. How are you? How's World's View?"

"Jeremy sent me over with some supplies. He knows you don't yet have a vegetable garden. There's fruit and vegetables, meat and eggs. Well, it was more Bergit's idea."

"How are the kids? I miss those two boys."

"Four children now. You know the old saying in the Centenary. The kids are the only crop that never fails... I'll have some of that coffee."

"Only instant coffee on Sunday."

"The fire's still hot. Where's Welcome?"

"Gave him the day off."

"Is she coming?"

"Don't know yet. Maybe Thursday. Maybe she won't reply. Maybe she got married."

"Wish I had a girl I could ask to marry me. I love farming but it's lonely on your own without company."

"I'll cook you some breakfast."

"That's my boy. My, the place is beautiful."

"There was a kill during the night. Probably a leopard. They hunt at night."

"See anything?"

"Not a thing. After the death call the bush went deadly quiet. No carcase this morning... This is a pleasure having company. Please thank Bergit. Those boys must be so glad to have a new mother. Bergit thinks of everyone. I can't imagine my own mother killed by lions. Those poor boys... What a perfect day. I'll get another folding chair from the tent. You sit in that one... This is a pleasure. My old assistant. How's it going, being manager of World's View?"

"Jeremy still makes most of the decisions. I'm getting five per cent of the gross this year as my bonus."

"You'll make more than me. Takes years here to make a profit. The first five years, everything you make goes back into the farm."

"I'm happy being a manager. Less responsibility. Less risk... You really going to cook me breakfast?"

"Of course I am. Sit yourself down. Make yourself comfortable."

"What's her name? I've forgotten."

"Katie. Her name is Katie."

"You look organised, Bobby."

"You've got to be organised in life if you don't want problems. My father taught me to think ahead. To always make a reconnaissance. Part of his military training. Poor Dad. He's so bored with nothing to do. One minute he was in command of a brigade, everyone at his beck and call.

Everyone waiting for his decisions. Now nothing. No one takes any notice of him. Just another old fart with a piddling pension, of no use to anyone. If they can't get something out of you they leave you alone. With power or money you're always in demand. It's a lesson I won't forget. You have to be someone or have something or people ignore you. Retired brigadiers from the days of empire are a bit of a joke these days. A mild embarrassment. Says he enjoyed his life. I hope so... I don't want to get old. The girls are married with lives of their own. And there's Mum and Dad stuck in a ghastly suburban home they were lucky to buy with Mum's family money. Grandfather was in textiles. Still alive. Made a fortune during the war making uniforms for the army. When Dad retired my grandfather gave them the money to buy the house in Epsom. Doesn't seem fair. Dad got close to the top of his profession and ended up with bugger all himself, no bloody use to anyone... How many sausages, Vince?"

"How many you got?"

"How many you want?

"There's something about food cooked over a campfire. Tastes much better."

"Old Koos Hendrik said it's the woodsmoke. I think it's primal. In our blood. Part of our ancestry from all those years living close to the land without all the modern conveniences. Modern life is so sterile. So plastic. I'd go nuts if I had to live my life in that suburban house in Epsom, cheek by jowl with my neighbours all looking at me over a fence, everyone knowing your business. This is how we were meant to live, doing everything ourselves... You got any tomatoes in those boxes from Bergit?... Good. Give me three. You want four eggs? I had four eggs."

"When do you start the seed beds?"

"Next month. Preparing the beds. Burning off. I'll send soil samples to the research station so I know what additives I'll need to add to the nitrogen fertiliser. This may be rural living but you still need science to tell you what to do. Suppose I shouldn't complain about modern life. Maybe I'm trying to convince myself this is the ideal way to live. Who knows? It's sure a long, long way from anywhere. Good to see you, Vince. You can make your own toast with that toasting fork."

Having put the food from the frying pan onto Vince's breakfast plate,

Bobby settled back into his canvas chair. Vince was right. A man needed company. Better still, a man needed a wife.

After Vince had eaten his breakfast they walked down the slope to the river to look for signs of the kill. It was a slow, lazy Sunday with neither of them having much to do. Vince found the signs of the struggle a hundred yards from Bobby's tent.

"The cat spoor is too small for a leopard. Over here you can see the scuffle. Where the buck tried to get away. My guess is a lynx. What the Afrikaners call a rooikat and others a caracal. You can see where the cat dragged the small buck, probably a duiker, through the long grass. A mother with kittens or she'd have eaten at the kill."

"Where'd you learn all that?"

"I spend hours in the bush. In the end your eyes are drawn to anything unusual, anything out of place. The faintest spoor sticks out. I take a shotgun with me. Bring back a guinea fowl. I only shoot what I'm going to eat."

"Poor little buck."

"It's the food chain, Bobby. The hunt for survival. We're all products of the hunt for survival or we wouldn't be here. Our ancestors wouldn't have survived so we could live on. We're just animals in the food chain. Be careful."

"I sleep with a gun next to my bed. Close the flap to the tent at night when I sleep. The slightest sound of danger brings me awake. I'm always reminded by the painting of Carmen, Jeremy's first wife, in the lounge at World's View. Got drunk, drove into the bush at night and ran out of petrol. They think a pride of lions attacked her when she was trying to walk down the bush road looking for help the next morning. I never forget I live in Africa. Carmen forgot. Got herself killed. Those poor boys. Randall was only two years old when she died. Phillip four. Never to know their mother except from that Livy Johnson painting in the lounge. I thought Jeremy would take it down when he married Bergit. But he didn't. Said it wouldn't be fair to the boys. Phillip must be turning eleven. Life can be cruel, sudden, violent. Like last night."

"Life goes on."

"Yes, I suppose it does. Provided some of us survive, that's all it is about. We all think the world revolves around ourselves. But it doesn't. Each of us are just one small member of a great big herd of people we grandly call the human race. You know, they say man came out of Africa. I like it. Why I feel so comfortable in the bush."

"You want to drive down to the club for a beer?"

"I've got beers in the fridge. Bit early to start."

"Never too early to start drinking. Too much of the old philosophy makes me thirsty."

"I'm sorry. You're right. Drunk we talk crap for hours and never remember a word of it. It was that kill last night. Gets you to thinking, Vince."

"Sometimes it's better not to think too much. Like what's going to happen in this country. We all thought international economic sanctions would be a ten-day wonder. Didn't work that way. The rest of the world wants us whites out of Africa. To say nothing of the local blacks. I live from day to day. Why I don't want my own farm. If I'm kicked out of Rhodesia I'll drift somewhere else... You really got some beers?"

"Come on. There's a spare case of Castles we can put in the fridge. I know you, Vince. Once you start, be prepared. First job, fill up the fridge."

"They call it the slippery slope. What the hell? You only live once. Those small buck eat well. Split them open and put them on the *braai* so the fat drips into a basting dish and baste them with the fat mixed with red wine and fresh herbs. What you got for lunch?"

"You've just eaten breakfast!"

"A man gets hungry living in the country. Does that shower system of yours really work?"

"Like a charm. You remember those Sunday lunches in England when we were growing up, Vince?"

"Best part of growing up. Church for the eleven o'clock service and back for the family lunch. The whole family. That's all changed now, my brother says. Everything is fast food. Everyone's in a hurry."

"If we don't drink too many beers we can make a salad, put some chops and steaks on the fire and talk about the good old days."

"Ah, the semi-detached in Wimbledon. Shared a bedroom with Francis. Tea in bed on a Sunday morning before church. Mother brought in the tea to get us up. Always let it go cold. 'Drink your tea, Vince.' Why is it so much better when you look back?... Just look at that eagle riding the thermals. He's so high in the sky I can't make out who he is... Ah, now I can. The triple call. That's a fish eagle. We live in a beautiful place. That must be the most evocative sound on earth. They fly up on the thermals just for pleasure. Circle each other. There are four of them, two smaller than the others. Ma and Pa and the kids. I'd love to have wings."

"One day you can buy yourself an aeroplane."

"Not the same. Just look at them. Going higher and higher, calling out to each other with pleasure. Wouldn't you like to be there, Bobby?"

"Yes, I would. Only snag, they don't serve cold Castles up in the sky. How does that one feel?"

"Just perfect. I'll help you pack the warm ones into the fridge. Don't you want to play your gramophone? Make it a party. I always remember the sound of those records when we were both working for Jeremy. In the middle of the bush in the still of the night. What was that one you always played again and again? Something about taking a photograph."

"Tommy Steele's 'Flash Bang Wallop' from *Half a Sixpence*."

"That's the one... Cheers, old boy."

"I've got the LP of *Hello, Dolly!*."

"Play it. Maybe those fish eagles will enjoy a good English musical."

"It's American. Jerry Herman. Recorded in London."

"Then it's a West End musical."

Vince had stretched out his legs from his canvas chair in the shade of the tree, the bottle of ice-cold beer in his hand. Bobby smiled at him as they drank the cold beer straight from the bottles. They were comfortable with each other. Old friends. Bobby looked up but couldn't see the eagles.

"They're above that patch of cloud."

3

On Thursday morning Bobby's alarm clock went off an hour before sunrise getting him out of bed. It was the day he hated, having to drive into Salisbury, the capital of Rhodesia, on a dirt road. He had a shopping list as long as his arm. There was so much needed to turn virgin bush into a viable farm. Every day for the last two months he had added to the list.

The cold shower in the first blush of dawn brought him fully awake. For breakfast he ate a tin of baked beans with a spoon straight from the tin. Sekuru arrived for instructions.

"Get those tap roots out, Sekuru, or they bugger up the plough. You can start cutting cords of wood. Next week we'll start loading the cut wood onto the tractor-trailer and take it to where the builders have started digging foundations for the barns. The length of wood I measured for you will fit into the fires at the base of the barns. I'm going into town. If I'm lucky I'll get through the shopping today. If not you'll be in charge again tomorrow. If I don't get back, tell Welcome to sleep in the camp. I don't want a pack of baboons ripping my tent apart."

One day, Bobby was going to learn Shona so he was certain what he said got through. Fanagalo was too limited. Too easily misunderstood. Sekuru went off as Welcome came down the path. They stopped and spoke, both looking back at him. Bobby hoped his instructions in Fanagalo had been sufficiently specific.

"Just never stops," Bobby said to himself as he walked from his closed tent to the truck.

He put the Winchester and an overnight bag in the front of the truck next to him. The engine fired first time. With a swift look of pleasure at what he was leaving behind, Bobby drove out of camp down the new road he had cut from the bush to the main road that went left to Mount Darwin and right to the small village of Centenary. It was dirt road and corrugations all the way to Concession where ten miles of strip road would take him to the tarred road at Mazoe with its small hotel.

By four o'clock in the afternoon, Bobby knew he was not going to finish the shopping. He had spent from nine o'clock in the morning in the industrial site going from one factory and workshop to another. Bobby liked seeing what equipment he bought and would never have used the telephone, even if he had one. Most of the purchases would be sent to the railways which sent them up to Centenary by the Road Motor Service. The railway line from Salisbury only went as far as Concession. By five o'clock the businesses were closing. Tired, impatient and irritated, Bobby drove into the centre of Salisbury and parked outside the front entrance of Meikles Hotel. The old Zulu doorman greeted him, dressed in traditional wild animal skins for the tourists. Bobby took his gun and the overnight bag into the hotel lobby.

"Bess, look after these for me while I park the truck in the garage. Anyone in the bar I know? I need a room for the night. Still haven't finished the shopping."

"Old Koos Hendriks has been in the men's bar since lunchtime entertaining the customers."

"Wonderful. Your cheapest room at the back. I'll eat in the bar. All I've eaten today was a tin of baked beans."

"How's the new farm?"

"Hard work."

"I'll lock the gun in the safe. Is it loaded?"

"No, it's not loaded. Didn't want to leave it on the farm. The shells are in the glove compartment of the truck. Have you any idea why they still call it the glove compartment? No one wears gloves to drive a car anymore."

The receptionist who did the hotel bookings had her back to him as she took away the gun without a reply. There was a lock-up garage at the back of the hotel where his truck and the smaller purchases would be safe.

In the men's bar Koos Hendriks, the old prospector, was surrounded by people buying him drinks. The old man was on a roll telling one of his stories. Bobby waited for the punchline and the guffaw of laughter. The bar was full. Koos hadn't seen him.

Walking back through the lobby of the hotel, Bobby made his way to the ladies' bar. If he was lucky there were young girls with their escorts. The bar was empty. He sat on a barstool up at the bar. There was nothing to do until eight o'clock in the morning when the shops and small businesses opened for trade. He ordered a beer and sat quietly drinking.

"What are you doing on your own, Bobby?"

"You were surrounded by people, Koos. Bess said you've been in the bar since lunchtime."

"You know me, man. Never turn down a free drink. Where are the ladies?"

"There aren't any girls in Salisbury. Have you found anything of value?"

"Nothing but my own company until I came into town. I brought in some rock samples for analysis in the laboratory. One day I'll get lucky."

"What do you live on, Koos?"

"A retainer, very small, from Anglo-US. Friend of mine works for them. Pays for provisions and keeps the old Kombi running."

"What were you looking for this time? You'll want a drink. Mr Barman, give Mr Hendriks whatever he wants. Every morning under the shower I think of you, Koos."

"Chrome. Chrome and nickel in the Great Dyke. What's new with you?"

"I've asked a girl to marry me. I'm on the new farm. Shopping list as long as your arm. Waiting for her letter from England. You ever been married, Koos?"

"Oh, yes. I was married. A long time ago. When I was a geologist and not an itinerant prospector."

"You've got a degree!"

"BSc in geology from the University of Cape Town."

"Where's your wife?"

"She's dead... I'll have a beer. Been drinking beer all afternoon. The trick is never to change your drink."

"Do you want to tell me?"

"Not really. Too painful. Why I've been running away all these years. We're all running away from something, Bobby... What's her name?"

"Katie. Her name is Katie."

"From England straight into the bush."

"Something like that."

"She'll have to be a brave girl."

"I hope so. I've got my own farm. Now I want my own family."

"Oh, the optimism of youth. Here's to your happiness. I wish you luck. You want to hear a story?"

"Of course I do. There's a price to pay for everything... I'm sorry. Have I said something wrong?"

The old man had put both arms on the bar and buried his head in his arms. He was sobbing."

"I'm drunk and now I'm crying. I'll be all right in a moment."

"You take your time. If you ever want to tell me I'm here to listen. It's better sometimes to talk rather than bottle it all up."

"I've been bottling it up for twenty years."

Bobby put his hand on the old man's shoulder, leaving it there for a brief moment. The barman had gone down to the other end of the bar. A farmer and his wife came in, looked at Koos with his head in his arms, and sat down opposite the barman. Drunks, asleep at bars, were not uncommon. Bobby sat waiting, drinking his beer. When Koos looked up he was smiling. Only the moist eyes said he had been crying.

"I'd better tell you that story... There was a man, an old man that kept a dog. The dog's name was Rabbit. The dog was a mix of every known breed in Rhodesia with a long face, wet eyes and ears that stood up just like the ears of a rabbit..."

Bobby let the old man talk, thinking whatever had upset him was forgotten by telling one of his stories. The barman had moved back up the bar to listen. The couple at the end of the bar had stopped talking as they picked up on the story. Koos Hendriks, master storyteller, was in full flight, the telling of the story as enthralling as the story itself. When Koos finished, the memory of his moment of pain had gone. Everyone was enjoying themselves.

"Can I buy you a drink?" said the man as he moved up the bar. "Mabel. Come on. Don't often hear a story that good."

"I don't mind if I do. You have a lovely wife. This is my young friend Bobby. Bobby is twenty-four. The exact same age my son would have been had he lived."

"You never mentioned a son, Koos."

"I never talk of Jack. Ella had named him Jack before he was born. She wanted a boy so much. Took five years with a broken heart before she died. Jack lived three days in the hospital after he was born. Ella nearly died giving birth. Looking back it would have been better for Ella. We had tried for seven years after we married to have a child. Of all things Ella wanted most in the world it was to have a child of her own. She would have been a wonderful mother. Smothered in love. We tried afterwards but she never fell pregnant. There was something wrong with her heart we found out in that hospital. Nature wouldn't let her fall pregnant with a fluttering heart. I always like to think she died of a broken heart losing Jack. I gave up my job and went into the bush where I've been ever since. Broke both our hearts, I suppose. But that's not the story anyone wants to hear... Now, let me tell you about the man with one leg. Piet had a parrot. A very old parrot. The parrot had belonged to his grandfather, a sea captain. Whenever his friends met Piet they never asked him how he was. The first thing they asked was, 'How's the parrot?'"

By the time Koos finished his second story the bar had filled up, everyone listening. Piet's wife hated the parrot. The parrot hated Piet's wife. During the telling, Koos had drunk his beer, pausing to drink at the crucial points in the story. Bobby could see the old man was drunker than usual. Outside the window it was dark, the light going from twilight to dark in half an hour. Koos managed to get off the barstool and stand on his feet.

"Give me a hand to the Kombi, Bobby. Goodnight, everyone. Splendid afternoon. Thank you all for the drink."

Bobby had the old man firmly by the arm as they walked out of the hotel. Behind them the bar returned to normal conversation, people turning back to themselves, the entertainment over.

In the street, under a tree next to Cecil Square, they found the old Kombi.

"Are you going to eat any food, Koos?"

"I never eat on a full stomach. Help me up into the back. Just look at it. The pleasures of home. A bed, a cooker and a portable loo. What else could an old man want? Goodnight, Bobby. Go back and enjoy your evening... Katie. I hope you'll be happy with Katie. Katie with the light brown hair, or so the song goes. Or was it Jeannie? Does she have light brown hair, Bobby?"

"Yes, she does. Sleep well, Koos. Hope the samples come out well."

When Bobby quietly pushed the handle to close the sliding door to the Kombi he could hear the old man snoring inside. The dead son explained a lot. Why the old man had taken so much interest in him, he and the son the same age.

Back in the ladies' bar, Bobby found an empty stool and sat there thinking. There was always so much more to people than he expected. The farmer and his wife had gone. Bobby, surrounded by people, was on his own. More lonely than he was in his camp on the farm. The barman had put a new cold beer in front of him. He was tired. On the farm he would have gone into his tent, closed the flap and got into his camp bed. Slowly, feeling melancholy, Bobby drank his beer.

In the morning, when he walked to his truck, the old Kombi with Koos Hendriks had gone. Birds were singing in the tall trees that filled the square.

By lunchtime, Bobby had finished his shopping, the back of the truck full of his purchases. Glad to get out of town, Bobby drove on his way back to the farm.

Almost at the end of the bone-rattling journey, he stopped the truck at the Dax turnoff to look for his mail bag and his hoped-for letter from Katie. Sometimes the bags of mail stayed by the side of the road for days, waiting for the farmers. No one ever touched them, other people's letters being of no value to anyone. The leather pouches, tossed on the ground by the driver of the RMS truck, were tough. There were three bags still on the side of the road. With his heart beating, Bobby stepped out of his truck to check the tags on the bags. There was one for Private Bag 9. All the post office gave was the farmer's number. Bobby picked up his mail, hoping to find his future inside. He had never before had a letter from Katie. Most of the letters, bills, had Rhodesian stamps. One, a small white envelope with his name, was in small handwriting addressed to Robert Preston Esquire, Private Bag 9, Centenary, Rhodesia. The stamp showed the face of Queen Elizabeth, no mention of country. Bobby's hands were shaking from a mixture of fear and excitement. On the back of the envelope was Katie's name and address as the sender. Katie had written to him. Not sure if a reply was good or bad, Bobby ripped open the envelope, his future in his hand; the bush, the truck, the world around him of solitude no longer part of him. Then he whooped, yelling her name at the sky. She was going to marry him. Katie was going to be his wife.

Bobby ran back to the truck leaving the open mail bag with the bills on the side of the road. Halfway home he remembered. The idea was for the farmers to return the small bags to the post office when they went into town. It was a long letter from Katie. The first line, 'Of course I will marry you', had sent him into euphoria.

When he reached the farm with the rest of the letter unread, Welcome was waiting for him. It was too late to check the two days' work of the gang. The sun was setting, splashing the sky with colour. The cooking fire was set, the camp tidy. There was peace all round him, the birds beginning to sing, telling each other where they were roosting for the night. The river below the camp was quiet, not an animal to be seen.

"You can go back to your hut when you've emptied the truck of food. Put the meat in the fridge. The big box of meat, give to Sekuru to distribute to the gang."

Bobby sat in his canvas chair. There were seven pages of letter. Bobby began to read, the doves calling, night beginning to fall, Katie's letter taking him into another world.

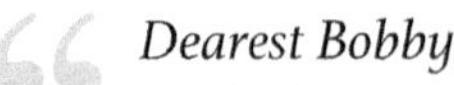

Dearest Bobby,

What a wonderful letter. What a wonderful surprise. Of course I will marry you. I knew the first moment I saw you it was love at first sight. I'm so excited I've been making little mistakes at work. Of course I correct them. All the girls in the comptometer-typing pool are envious. That Katie has found the love of her life. That I'm going to be Mrs Robert Preston and live on an African farm. It makes our lives here seem so drab. All that space, all that sunshine. You know, in the winter, I go to work in the dark and come home in the dark. On alternate Saturdays we have to work in the mornings and all for four pounds eleven shillings a week and my little room in Notting Hill Gate costs two pounds fifteen shillings a week. Don't worry about living in a tent. We'll be married and loving each other. My friend Linda can't believe I'll be living on four thousand acres. So much land is beyond anyone here's comprehension. When we are ready, with lots of children, we can build a big house. Linda, she's my best friend, we went to school together, wants to come too. She's tired of drab old England. All the men here want to do is sleep with you. That's Linda talking of course. My friend Linda is a little bit naughty. We are oh so different. Could you find a nice man for Linda who will make her his wife? The boat trip sounds wonderful. It's all so romantic. A marriage proposal, a trip on a boat, living in Africa among all those wonderful birds and animals. You will protect me, won't you Bobby? I'm a bit frightened of big wild animals. Do you have lions and tigers on the farm? Oh, I just can't wait.

Today, poor Poppy Snodgrass has her twenty-third birthday. Poppy and I are the same age. We've all bought her a cake, the girls in the pool. She's so fat and wears glasses and has never been on a date. Ever since your letter she's been watching me sadly, knowing she'll never have what I'm going to have with my wonderful Robert Preston. Now let me tell you about the girls I've been working with these last few years.

Bobby put down the letter, not wanting to read it too fast. When he looked up, the family of warthog were drinking down by the river. The sky was blood red, the mosquitoes beginning to bite. Bobby lit the fire that Welcome had laid, changing the position of his chair to be downwind, the smoke keeping him free from the biting mosquitoes. The light was beginning to go, so Bobby lit the hurricane lamp that he hung on the stand he had made from a tree they had cut when they were clearing the lands. The light from the lamp was just enough to read the rest of Katie's letter. She was coming. That was all that mattered. He was no longer going to live on his own.

"Children. Goodness. I never thought of all those children."

Looking around in the last glimmer of daylight, the cicadas screeching from the surrounding long grass, the frogs calling to their mates down by the river, Bobby tried to imagine the future with a wife and children, the children impossible to see in his mind. Even Katie was difficult to see. He didn't really know his Katie. Was he in love? He had no idea. But did it matter? Of course it didn't matter. He was going to have a wife. A wife and children. A family. A wonderful farm, a wonderful wife and a wonderful family. Katie was right. Everything was going to be wonderful.

PART II

JUNE TO SEPTEMBER 1967 – "INTO THE UNKNOWN"

1

When Katie Frost looked up from her work in the typing pool the girl from reception was standing in front of her desk.

"What's the matter, Rosie?"

"An old man is at reception asking to see you. He's quite a giggle. Very military. Moustache, straight back, tweed suit."

"I don't know any old gentleman."

"He knows you. Very specific. 'Miss Katie Frost. I wish to see a Miss Katie Frost. I believe Katie is short for Katherine.' What he said. Looked straight at me. Have you done something wrong, Katie?"

"I'd better come and see what it's all about. What's the time, Rosie?"

"Almost knocking off time. Friday night. My boyfriend's taking me to the flicks... I'll tell 'im you're coming. Wouldn't keep the old bugger waiting." Rosie was having a high old time at Katie's expense. "Not often I come in the typing pool. Heard you and Linda were leaving the firm."

Outside in reception the man had his back to the reception desk. When he turned round to see Katie standing close to him he smiled.

"Are you Miss Katie Frost?"

"I am."

"My name is Roland Preston. My son Robert asked me to give you some money. Just before the British government cut off financial ties with Rhodesia my son sent me his last bonus from Jeremy Crookshank. The money is under my signature. The bank's in Rhodesia. Can't transfer money to London without a lot of questions. You'll find what you require in this envelope. Well, I'll be away. If all goes well my wife and I will see you in Rhodesia at the wedding. Welcome to the family, Miss Frost."

"Thank you, Colonel," Katie blurted out.

"Brigadier, actually. Doesn't make any difference anymore. I hope you and my son will be happy together. Not sure about the situation in Rhodesia. You young people have to make your own decisions. No one ever quite knows what will transpire in the future."

"Thank you."

"My pleasure. Be careful with all that money. What do you do here, Miss Frost?"

"I operate a comptometer."

"What's a comptometer?"

"A large adding machine."

"So you're an accountant!"

"Not exactly." Katie was smiling her best smile.

"By ship, I believe?"

"*Pendennis Castle*. Sails for Cape Town on the twenty-second."

"Have a pleasant voyage."

Katie's future father-in-law did an about turn and marched out of reception.

"Stop giggling, Rosie. He looked a very nice man. Bobby said his father had been in the army. People like that won the war."

"Straight out of the movies... How much money you got?"

"Enough for the boat fare, I hope."

"I'm off. Have a nice weekend."

With a real purpose in her life, Katie walked back to her desk, finished what she was doing and packed up for the weekend. The envelope, on the desk, had not been opened.

"You ready to go, Katie? It's not raining outside. You working tomorrow?"

"My Saturday morning off."

"What's in that envelope you keep looking at?"

"Money, Linda. Bobby's father just brought it."

"Did he now? How much?"

"Don't know."

Hands shaky, Katie tore open the envelope which she found stuffed with five pound notes. Slowly, carefully, with the help of Linda, Katie counted her money.

"Five hundred quid! Not even a letter. Oh, you and I are going to have to do a rethink, Miss Katie Frost. Quick run to Cape Town doesn't make sense anymore. Not with all that money at our disposal. You have got to build your memories. Did you know we can get a ten pound European rail ticket if we go by Lloyd Triestino from Trieste? Stop off where we like in Europe on the way. Valid three months. You and I, Katie Frost, are going to do the Grand Tour. Paris, Switzerland, Rome and all points in between. Then through the Med and the Suez Canal and down the east coast of Africa to Beira where we'll catch the train and go inland to Salisbury. It's an opportunity. You want memories for all those years stuck on a farm in the middle of nowhere. You can buy some nice clothes. Got to look good when you get there. Don't want to disappoint him. Never seen so much bloody cash. Better ask Roger to lock it in the company safe. He'll give you a receipt. Don't want someone ruining our holiday. Chance of a lifetime."

"Is it more expensive going that way round? How'd you find all this out?"

"You only booked on Union-Castle. Didn't give a deposit. Far more exotic on an Italian boat."

"Won't Bobby mind?"

"Why should he? Tomorrow morning, you and I are going into that travel agent I went to in Regent Street and book the trip of our lives. You're a lucky girl. Your man has money."

"It's about more than money."

"Of course it is, Katie. Now let's find Roger, deposit the money and you and I go celebrate."

"How long are we going to be in Europe?"

"As long as it takes. I'll have a bit of money. Leave pay and my last month's pay cheque."

"What are you going to live on before you get a job in Salisbury?"

"Let the gods decide. We're young. Good looking. Got a piss-pot full of money. We're going to enjoy ourselves before it's too late."

"Oh, it's good to be young."

"Don't you tell me. And best of all, we chose the perfect time to be young. The world swings. It's all flower power and free love."

"You won't tell Bobby what we get up to!"

"Don't be daft. Does he know you're not a virgin?"

"Subject never came up. We just kissed. What I leave behind must stay behind. I'm going to be a married woman. A mother."

"First you have to get yourself pregnant, darling. My advice, stay on the pill a few months after you get to Rhodesia. Even after you marry. Make sure the life of a farmer's wife is what you want. We're the first generation of liberated women. Don't you forget it. We now have minds of our own. No longer barefoot in the kitchen and pregnant."

"So you think it may not work?"

"Who knows, Katie? People's needs change. You know how it is. You see a man you fancy and get him in the sack and find out he's one of those 'wham, bam, thank you ma'am' types. No bloody good to man or beast. And people change. That's the worst of it. Get bored with each other. You get yourself pregnant when you're absolutely certain you want to live with Bobby on an African farm for the rest of your life. Meantime, we're going to have a ball. If you'll excuse the pun."

"Linda, you're terrible. You know, behind your back some of the girls in the typing pool say you're growing mushrooms on your bed sheets?"

"They're just jealous. Who cares, I'm on the pill. There's no risk to being promiscuous. You know they're calling it the swinging sixties? Get it out of the system. Before we get too old and can't pull the men... You know how we'll go? We'll take the train at night. Sleep on the trains. Save the hotel bills. Stretch that five hundred quid of yours as far as it goes. Men can buy us the drinks and food. It's party time for Linda and Katie."

"What if Bobby were to find out?"

"How could he? He's seven thousand miles away. Tell him you're doing the art galleries of Europe as part of your education. That will impress him."

"I know nothing about art."

"Florence. We'll stop off in Florence. I think that's the place for the Italian art. Pick up some brochures. Come on, Katie. This is our chance of a lifetime. What the eye doesn't see the heart won't grieve about."

"But it's his money."

"If he's the nice man you hope he is he'll be happy for you.

Memories. You'll want all those memories when you're a married woman and can't get up to mischief."

"You're incorrigible."

"But it's nice."

Later, Katie, both apprehensive and excited, put on a smile as the two girls, arm in arm, left the office, the five hundred pounds in the safe, their journey to Africa begun.

THE SS *AFRICA* left Trieste two months later, many of the great cities of Europe a blur in Katie's mind. There had been too much to see. Too much to comprehend. To Linda's surprise, neither of them had got up to any mischief, the sleeping on trains at night and sightseeing during the day not leading them once astray. Katie was glad. It was Bobby's money. Hopefully, she was going to be his wife. At Linda's insistence they had booked single berths on the ship. She could relax, what Linda got up to at night was none of her business. With the slow journey across Europe, England had receded as both of them grew used to the unfamiliar.

The following day they sailed down the Adriatic Sea into the Mediterranean, stopping at Brindisi, then on across to Africa. As the ship approached the new coast Katie had her first scent of the dark continent. They got off the ship at Port Said and took the train to Cairo while the SS *Africa* slowly traversed the Suez Canal. The Egyptian Museum, the Sphinx and the Pyramids all crowded her mind as they boarded the ship once again at the Port of Suez on the Red Sea. Aden, Mogadishu, Mombasa, Zanzibar followed. Then Beira in Mozambique where the girls disembarked, brief friends left behind on board the ship. For a day the train slowly made its way through the African bush, climbing up into the highveld and crossing the border into Rhodesia. In the afternoon, as the steam engine pulled the long line of carriages into Salisbury Station, Katie had never been so happy, both of them leaning out of the carriage window.

"Where is he, Katie?"

"Over there. The tall, slim man wearing a hat."

Katie waved frantically as their train moved slowly along the platform.

"He's good looking. Money and good looks!... He's seen you."

"This is it, Linda. I've finally arrived."

"Who's the man with him?"

"I have no idea."

"Katie! You made it." Bobby, walking along as the train ground to a halt, was trying to hold Katie's hand through the carriage window. The train stopped. Katie and Linda stepped down onto the platform.

"Have a good trip? We're all going to be staying in Meikles and drive back to the farm on Monday. Do you want to stay in Salisbury or come back with us? I mean it must be all a bit overwhelming. Yes, you'd better stay in town. You look wonderful, Katie."

"The trunks are in the goods van at the back of the train. You look so suntanned. You were much paler in England."

"Yes. Suppose I was."

"Let's decide where we go at the end of the weekend. How's the farm? Still in a tent?"

"Afraid so. Look, do you still want to marry me? I mean, we'll have a house next year."

"Of course I do, Bobby."

"Can't really kiss too much in public. Yes, well. Here you are. Wonderful. Everything is wonderful. Let's find the trunks. The truck's outside. Plenty of room for the trunks. Come and meet Linda, Vince. This is my old friend Vince Ranger. Manager of World's View. Not far from Hopewell. This is all so wonderful."

As Katie followed down the platform she had forgotten how young he looked. Both of them were boys. Excited boys in their hats and khaki clothes. For all intents and purposes she and Bobby were strangers. It was hot, the sun beating down on her head as they reached the guard's van stopped at the end of the platform. Katie had never seen so many black people. Deep inside she felt fear and apprehension, everything was strange, unfamiliar, all so far from home. Linda had taken up with the man Bobby had introduced as Vince. For Linda it was still a game. They waited, not sure what to say, waiting for the luggage to be unloaded. A black man with a big smile and a four-wheel trolley had attached himself to them.

"Did you have lunch on the train, Katie?"

"There they are. Cabin trunks. That one and that one."

Bobby spoke to the black man in a foreign language. With the help of a second black man the trunks were loaded onto the trolley. They all walked back down the platform, the trolley and the two blacks following, Bobby carrying the overnight cases Linda had handed out of the railway carriage. All round Katie were people off the train. She waved at a familiar face from the boat. She wanted to hold Bobby's hand but wasn't sure. Linda, relaxed with Vince, looked far more comfortable. A whistle blew, followed by the train moving backwards away from the platform. There was only one platform at Salisbury Station. Outside the station building, Bobby walked across to a truck. The black men unloaded the trunks onto the back of the vehicle.

"Vince has his own farm truck. Linda can drive with Vince or we can all squeeze in the front."

With Bobby leading, they drove out of the railway station, Linda in the cab of the second truck with Vince, both of them looking happy. Bobby had placed his left free hand on the seat of the car. Katie took his hand quietly, neither of them sure.

"Better use both hands to drive," said Bobby, withdrawing his hand.

There were cars, buses and trucks up and down the road, people moving up and down the pavements, most of them blacks.

"This is Pioneer Street. Named after the pioneers who came up on the column. Rhodes didn't go with them though some say he did. 1890, I think… I'm so nervous, Katie."

"So am I."

"I can get you both a flat in town until we get to know each other better. You can visit the farm. Yes, that will be better… Dad said in his letter he liked you, Katie."

There was a warm smell in the air that was unfamiliar. Everything looked different. The trees they passed were bursting with pale blue flowers without any leaves. Away from the station the buildings were newer, some of them two storeys high. There were shops. Street vendors on the pavements. They drove to the back of a building that seemed to cover a square. On one side was a park full of trees. Inside the small park, Katie could see the water of a fountain catching the light of the sun. When they parked, two black men in hotel uniform lifted the trunks from the back of the truck.

"Meikles Hotel. They'll store the trunks until you need them. We'd better go and have a drink. Your rooms are booked. The chaps will put your suitcases in the rooms. If they muddle the cases you'll have to swap them."

"It's so hot."

"Next month is October. Some call it suicide month. Then the rains break and it becomes cooler... They seem to have hit it off. We walk round the building under the jacaranda trees to the hotel entrance. We're going to be having the reception in the hotel. The cathedral is just up the road."

"When do you want us to get married?"

"When you're sure, Katie. You must be sure. See what you're getting. Want to live in Africa. I didn't like my first year. Suppose I was homesick."

"Let's have a drink."

"Did you have lunch?"

"On the train."

"We'll dine in the hotel. Very colonial, I'm afraid. They have fans in the ceiling going round and round. Doesn't make a lot of difference at this time of year. The food is good."

"Do they have dancing?"

"Not in Meikles Hotel, I'm afraid."

With Linda and Vince following behind in animated conversation, they arrived at the front entrance of the hotel. A black man with a big protruding belly, with what looked like to Katie long cat's tails hanging from his waist, an animal skin thrown over his shoulder, a spear in his right hand, was standing at the entrance.

"Afternoon, Mason." Bobby put a coin in the man's outstretched hand. The biggest black man Katie had ever seen opened the door to the hotel. They all went inside. Above the foyer, fans like paddles were turning round and round, moving the humid air. Katie stared up at them.

"Punkahs. This building went up fifty years ago. There's talk of knocking it down and building a new hotel with air conditioning. We're still a bit behind the times, I'm afraid. You'll have to sign the register. Both of you."

"Do they want our passports?"

"Goodness, no. I vouched for you... What did you think of Mason? All for the tourists. We call him a Zulu but he's a Matabele. His ancestors came up from Zululand in the days of Shaka. Most of the Matabele live around Bulawayo nearer the South African border. The tourists love him in all his paraphernalia."

"Has he got anything under those skins? Where did the coin go?"

"Why don't you ask him?"

"I'd be too frightened."

"That's a genuine lion skin over his shoulder. The long tails round his belly are from different wild animals. Some of them are pretty mangy by now."

Katie and Linda signed the register, people coming and going. Katie waved at the same people she had seen at the railway station.

"Let's go and find a table in the lounge. The dining room is through from the lounge."

"Are you sure our cases and trunks will be all right?"

"Of course I am. This is Rhodesia. Nothing ever gets stolen in Rhodesia. Never heard of. Well, what do you think of your new country?"

"It's hot." They both laughed nervously.

"You'll get used to it... What are you going to drink?"

"Something cold. Something very, very cold... Is his name really Mason?"

"Probably not. Their African names are difficult for us Europeans to remember. They take European names to make it easy for us."

"Do they like changing their names?"

"Seem to. Most of them have taken Christian names. They're all having to learn English these days to get a job in town. Some say it's part of progress. Who knows?... You'd better have a beer. In Rhodesia we either drink Castle lager or Lion lager. Rather appropriate... Here we are. What are you going to have, Linda?"

"Why is everyone looking at us?"

"We don't see too many good-looking young girls dressed so well, Linda. Are the women looking?"

"Just the men."

"Sorry about that. A lot of the chaps are single farmers in town to do the shopping."

"A Lion lager, please. When in Rome."

"Did you visit Rome?"

"It was incredible. All those old ruins."

"That ten pound railway ticket was such a good idea. I'm still getting your postcards, Katie. One day when I've developed the farm, we'll do Europe together. So, tell us all about your trip... Thank you. You can bring us four Lion lagers... Preston. Put it on my bill, waiter."

"Yes, boss."

Katie watched the waiter walk away.

"Why does he call you boss?"

"It's how they call us. Some of the whites call them 'boy'. I think it's rude. A man has his pride. He's a man, not a boy. One day it will all change. Africa has a long way to go... Well, you and old Vince seem to have hit it off, Linda. So you worked with Katie. Went to school together. You'll miss each other when you go back to England."

"Maybe I won't. Who knows? You never know which way the cookie is going to crumble."

"Katie's very brave coming all the way to Africa."

Before the drinks came, three people came across to talk to Bobby and Vince. Others had waved from where they were sitting at their tables. All three were men, checked out carefully by Linda, Katie not sure if the young men had come across to see Bobby and Vince or Linda and herself. Each time Bobby had stood up while he introduced the girls. Katie watched Linda look at the men. Her friend was all smiles, in her perfect element. Never in England had either of them received so much attention.

"Do you know any of the auditors in Salisbury, Bobby? I need a job. This is just my kind of place."

"Most of the big British firms have offices in Salisbury. I enquired for you both. In case Katie wants to work a little before we get married. The chap I spoke to will give you a job. Mitchell and Cox. They're going to do my accounts. Any kind of skill is in short supply in Rhodesia, especially in something like accounting. I asked about salary. You'll be able to afford your own flats. Live well. Tax is low. I'm sure you've both brought references. Oh if you want to stay, Linda, you won't be short of a job. Chances are you'll be able to start work on Monday morning."

"I've spent all my money. And some of yours, Bobby. Well, Katie's."

"You've paid me back already by bringing Katie... Are those bottles of beer cold enough or aren't they? You've got to pour slowly. How does that look Katie?... And one for Linda poured masterfully by Vince... Cheers, both of you. Welcome to Rhodesia. The most beautiful country on earth."

For a moment they all looked at each other. Another young man came across to say hello. This time Bobby did not stand up when he made the introductions. Linda was looking round the big room at the people taking tea and drinking at the tables. She was enjoying herself and leaned forward so the young man could get a good look down the front of her dress.

"You did start taking your anti-malarial pills three weeks ago as I wrote you, Katie? All newcomers to the country have to take them if they're going into the bush. The old hands build up some kind of immunity. Or so they think."

"We'd better go and check out our rooms. Make sure about the suitcases. Linda and I will want to change out of our travelling clothes. Have a bath. The chemist in London didn't know what to give us."

"That's happened before. I have two packets in my room. You can start taking them right now."

"You don't have to come up. Stay and have another beer with Vince. We've got the room keys."

"I'll get the pills. You're my responsibility now. Vince, order a couple more beers. Be right down."

Upstairs Katie found the right cases in the right rooms. Her room overlooked what Bobby had called Cecil Square. The sun was down, no longer shining on the water in the fountain. With the glass of water Bobby had poured for her she took one of the pills. The window was open. From the square she could hear the doves and pigeons calling to each other. There was a sweet smell of flowers drifting up into her room through the window. The bed was turned down, on the pillow one small chocolate. Katie ate the chocolate. It was delicious. She ran the bath and began to take off her clothes. She was excited, everything was going so well.

2

Half an hour later in the corridor Katie knocked on the door next to her room. When Linda came out she was dressed for the kill.

"So which one is it going to be tonight, Linda?"

"The night's but a pup. Go with the flow. Never seen so much talent. Did you see them looking down the front of my dress?"

"You were leaning forward. One poor sod had an instant erection."

"You were looking!"

"He was wearing shorts. Why are their shorts so short in Rhodesia?"

"I like it. Come on. I'm ready. Let the night begin."

"How many men did you sleep with on the boat?"

"Don't ask questions... Why is it when a girl enjoys herself she's a slut? When a man does it he's considered quite the lad. Anyway, who cares? I like to enjoy myself. My greatest pleasures are lying in bed with a man on top of me. There are so many of them in this town. All of them horny. Can't we persuade Bobby to take us out dancing? It's Friday night. Party time."

"Are you going to get a job?"

"Straight away. Are you?"

"First I want to see his farm. Get the feel of it."

"Sleep with him."

"Not until the day we're married. I want to start this one properly. He's such a gentleman. Did you see the way he stood up? They don't do that in the Pig and Whistle. Can you imagine Dave or Eric standing up to introduce us when someone came to our table?... Are you wearing a bra?"

"Don't be daft. This must be the only two-storey hotel I've ever been in. It's so colonial. Like those places in India you see in the flicks. Men. Never seen so many men."

"What do you think of Vince?"

"I like him. But then I like all of them."

"He doesn't have his own farm."

"Who cares? I'm not the one wanting to get married and settle down. I've got years ahead of me before I want to settle down and breed kids. Let's have some fun, Katie. Did you take your pill? Don't want to get sick. This place looks far too good... I remember once getting the flu and for a whole week I didn't want to have sex. Thought there was something seriously wrong with me. I don't want to get old. Can you imagine the time when men don't look at you? Mum was good looking according to Dad and now look at her. She's put on so much weight."

"Maybe she's happy. Perfectly content."

"You think so? She's sweet. Mind you, Dad isn't a picture of male virility. His paunch isn't much smaller than that Zulu's at the front entrance. You think he knows how to throw a spear? They frighten me. So different. Why are we always frightened of people who are different?"

"Underneath the skin I'm sure they love, dream and hope the same as us."

"I'm going to have some fun. Make enough money to sail back to England the other way round Africa. Are you sure you want to spend the rest of your life in Africa? We can have all the fun we want and go back together. If the salaries are so good we can share a flat, save our money and pay back Bobby his five hundred pounds. I know how you feel about taking money from a man. You know what they call a girl who takes money from a man? A whore. Doesn't make sense though. A man takes you out and he pays the dinner bill. What's the difference?"

"The difference is right now I want to marry him. If the political situation gets worse we can always go back to England."

"I never read the newspapers or turn on the news. Politics bore me."

"We didn't have men offering to marry us in England. They didn't have the money."

"He won't have money in England."

"We'll cross that bridge when we get to it."

"We're such good friends and just so different."

"You'll feel the same when you meet the right man."

"You don't even know him, Katie."

"My aunt met a man one week and married him the next. Went to live in Sarawak."

"Where's Sarawak?"

"In Borneo."

"What happened to them?"

"He was killed by the Japs in Malaya during the war. I have a cousin ten years older than me."

"What happened to them?"

"Aunty Freda married again after the war."

"She must have had something... Where are they, Katie? Weren't they at that table over there? Wouldn't that be fun? Being dumped in the middle of darkest Africa without any money."

"Here they come... Hello, Bobby. Linda thought you made a run for it."

Bobby smiled and took her by the arm, Vince and Linda following behind.

"Let's go straight through to the dining room. You must be hungry. I am. So is Vince. We can get a bottle of South African wine at the table. With sanctions we don't get French wine anymore. Doesn't make any difference. The South African wines are just as good."

"Is there a nightclub in this town?"

"Within walking distance, Linda. Bretts. Live band. They say if the piano player went to America he'd become famous. Vince and I were talking about it. The food is the best in town. Afterwards we'll take you girls to Bretts."

"Now you're talking."

The dining room of the hotel was much the same as the lounge except the tables were higher for eating. The windows ran from the ceiling to the floor. The punkahs were going round and round above the diners. Everyone at the tables was white, just like the people in the lounge. Bobby and Vince had changed out of their shorts. Both of them wore jackets and ties.

"You look so handsome in a suit."

"Have to wear them in the evenings in the dining room. That's the rules. Bit archaic if you ask me. In this heat who needs a jacket and tie? You look so nice in that dress."

Bobby pulled back her chair as Katie went to sit down. Opposite, Vince did the same for Linda. The chair was gently pushed in as she sat. The gallantry made Katie feel like a princess. The headwaiter, a white man, opened her linen serviette and placed it on her lap. Menus were put in front of them. At the far end of the room a woman was playing a grand piano. The music, Katie recognised, was Gershwin. From one of the American's shows. The pianist played softly, letting the music mingle with the sound of conversation, the chink of cutlery on plates, a brief burst of subdued, well-mannered laughter. Looking through the sash windows into a courtyard she could see lights shining up into small trees growing in wooden tubs. The curtains on the other side of the dining room were drawn. Long, heavy curtains.

"Try the rack of lamb, Katie. We always go for meat in Rhodesia. Too far from the sea for fish. So, what do you think of a typical colonial dining room? Looking around you'd never think the empire was over. Went so quickly after the war. The Americans want our markets, according to Callum McFay. I worked for Callum as his manager before I went onto Hopewell Estate. Politics is all about money, was what he said. The Americans didn't like all that colonial preference when it came to trade. I let the politicians get on with the politics. Far bigger things to worry about building a farm. Will it rain? Will it rain too much? What to spray on the tobacco to keep down the parasites. Anyway, after Smith declared UDI we're on our own. We said we were independent. The British said we're not. Who knows what will happen? No point in worrying. Just get on with life... So what will it be?"

"Rack of lamb sounds good. Do they serve it with mint sauce?"

"Of course."

"How silly of me. Let's all have the rack of lamb."

"Got that, Felix? And a bottle of Nederburg Cabernet Sauvignon."

"To start with, sir? The soup is quite excellent."

"Not for me. I'm hungry. Bring on the lamb and the roast potatoes."

"Certainly. The ladies?... Very well."

A black waiter wearing a red sash across his uniform replaced the head waiter. The wine arrived. The cork was popped. Bobby did the wine tasting and smiled. The glasses were half filled with red wine by the waiter. They all said 'cheers'. The piano changed to a different tune. The punkahs went round. It was all like a dream for Katie. The perfect dream. She let them talk, listening to each of them in turn. When the racks of lamb were put in front of them, on what looked to Katie more like serving dishes than dinner plates they were so big, the racks, with small white paper collars tied to the highest protruding bone of the rib, filled the plates. The waiter offered her dishes of four different vegetables, spooning them onto her plate. They all tucked in, the conversation flagging as they ate, all of them hungry. Katie smiled to herself: for once, her friend Linda was interested in something other than men.

The pianist finished playing to move among the seated guests, briefly stopping at some of the tables. She was a middle-aged woman in a long black dress, red hair down to her shoulders. As she passed, Katie noticed the woman wasn't wearing a wedding ring. She sat down where another woman, on her own, was eating her dinner. The pianist covered the other woman's hand on the table. They smiled at each other. Katie couldn't fully understand what was going on.

By the time Katie finished her food the piano was playing again. The solitary woman at the table had gone. The new music was sad but beautiful. A second bottle of red wine was brought to the table and opened.

"Coffee, Katie?"

"Black... That was so good. Just a little wine for me. Who was that woman alone at the table?"

"Lynette's girlfriend."

"What kind of girlfriend?"

"They don't talk about it. Does it matter?"

"They looked so happy together."

"The other woman plays the harp. Sometimes they play together. They were both in the London Symphony Orchestra for twenty years."

After coffee, Bobby signed the bill adding his room number. The wine was finished, mostly by Bobby and Vince.

"Do you mind walking to Bretts, Katie? Seems silly to bring the trucks round to the front when Bretts is down the road opposite the hotel. It's a lovely evening. No chance of rain in September."

"Are there street lights?"

"Of course. From the lady's light classical music to jazz. Quite a change. The first time we danced was at that bottle party in London where we met. You remember? Come on. Before Vince orders another bottle of wine. Do you like dancing, Linda?"

"It's my passion. I wanted to be a dancer. Not a comptometer. Can we go just like this?"

They walked out of the dining room, Bobby again pulling back her chair, and through the lounge still full of people into the hotel foyer. The big Zulu was still at the door. Vince gave him a coin which disappeared under the cat tails strung round his belly. There was little traffic on the road as they crossed the street. At a men's clothing store they turned into a passageway with shop windows full of light on either side. At the end of the passage they walked down a flight of stairs into a basement. Katie had heard the music out on the street. Downstairs the place was packed with young people, so different from the Meikles dining room. A bar was full of cigarette smoke and the noise of people. On the other side of the basement nightclub, over a half wall, were tables where young people were sitting and drinking, some eating food. A six-piece band was playing. In front of the band dais was a small dance floor full of people doing the jive. Katie's foot began to tap.

"We can drink at the bar and try and get a table. I know the new owner. The previous owner named the place after his son Brett who was killed in a hunting accident. The boy was ten years old. The name, Bretts, has stayed... Tony. Can you find a table? This is Katie I was talking about."

"How's the new farm?"

"Still living in a tent. Tony Bird, please meet Katie Frost and her best friend Linda Gaskell. Just arrived from England."

"Have a drink at the bar and I'll call you when there's a table. Enjoy yourselves, ladies. How are you, Vince?"

They were left standing at the bar, Bobby ordering drinks from the barman over the head of the customers. The place was swinging, the noise level in the bar just good enough to talk. The best-looking man in the room detached himself from his friends, all of them men, and came across. The barman was handing Bobby the drinks over the other customers' heads. Katie had asked for a lemonade, Linda a gin and tonic.

"Hello, Vince. Hello, Bobby. How's the farm?"

"Slow and frustrating. One job at a time... Katie and Linda, this is Constable Donald Henderson, BSAP."

"Do they call you Don or Donny? I'm Linda, Katie's friend."

"Donald, I'm afraid. At school there were three of us called Henderson, one of them younger than me. Boarding school in Surrey. The eldest was Henderson Major, the youngest Henderson Minor. I was plain Henderson. Plain Donald Henderson. After that I never abbreviated my name. Would you care to dance, Linda?"

"We're having a drink and waiting for a table. What does BSAP stand for?"

"British South Africa Police. Nothing to do with South Africa. The country was started by a company before it became a self-governing colony. A bit like India. The first colonisation in India was done by the East India Company. Afterwards the king of England became King-Emperor. Emperor of India. Here it was Cecil Rhodes and his British South Africa Company under royal charter from Queen Victoria. The first police force was the British South African Police. In 1923 it came under the Rhodesian government."

Katie watched Linda, eyes big and welcoming, hang on his every word, a trick Linda had perfected. The young man was stunning to look at, and Linda was visibly licking her lips. He was tall, blue-eyed, broad shoulders, a husky voice that came right up from the area around his genitals.

"So what do you do?"

"Ride a horse in the outback most of the time. In places that are difficult for even a Land Rover."

"How did you meet Bobby and Vince?"

"When they were both working for Jeremy Crookshank on World's View."

"Join us at the table, Donald."

"You don't mind, Bobby?"

"Of course not. More the merrier."

"Maybe later."

Donald walked back to his friends. The owner of the club signalled them from the other side of the low wall that separated the bar from the dancing. There was a glass partition from the top of the wall to the ceiling keeping some of the noise from the band and allowing conversation. A black waiter carried their drinks on a tray as they walked from the bar. The table was small, in a corner. Vince took Linda onto the small dance floor before they sat down.

"You want to dance, Katie?"

"Let's sit... Good. Now we're alone." Leaning forward, Katie kissed him on the mouth.

"That was much better than dancing, Katie. Fact is, I'm not much good at the jive. Just look at Vince and Linda."

"Will Donald come and join us?"

"Probably. Or they'll meet later if she wants to. Salisbury is a small town. So, what do you think?"

"I love it. I loved dinner. Love Rhodesia. Love this club. We'll dance when they play a slow number... She's a bit of a flirt, I'm afraid."

"I did notice. Anyway, Vince doesn't have a monopoly... That's Henny on the piano. Writes some of his own music. Eddie on trumpet. Eddie was a mercenary in Katanga under Major Mike Hoare. A few white mercenaries managed to split the copper-rich province of Katanga from the rest of the Congo for Moise Tshombe when the Belgians gave up their colony and the communists took over. Some say the Americans were behind it. The rest of the Congo stayed under Russian influence. You never really know what's going on in Africa now the colonial powers have pulled out. Capitalism against communism. Russian imperialism against American imperialism. They denounce colonialism and start all over again. A lot of young chaps joined the mercenaries to make money. You don't get rich playing a trumpet."

"Is it safe in Rhodesia?"

"Yes. So long as we're in control. You need an incorruptible military and civil service to run a country properly. Honest people. Anyway, no more of politics. Tell me all about your trip. Can you hear me or is the band too loud?"

"Understood the bit about the trumpet. Rest was a bit over my head... Just look at Linda. She can really dance. Here comes Donald Henderson."

"The others are dancing, Donald. You want a drink?" Bobby raised his right hand. In a moment the waiter who carried their drinks from the bar was standing in front of their table.

"Cold Castle, boy," said Donald.

The waiter went off to get the drink.

"He's a man, not a boy, Donald."

"You know what I mean, Bobby."

"I just hope he does. A man needs his pride as well as a job."

"You're right. Force of habit. Too often we don't think of other people's feelings... She can dance, your friend, Katie. Just look at her. So when did you arrive?"

"I can't hear you."

Katie watched Vince keep Linda on the dance floor for as long as possible before they came back to their table. Immediately, Donald asked Linda to dance. The three friends Donald had been with were standing looking through the window from the bar room. They were all smiling. Katie thought it must be some kind of bet. When their dance was finished and the band had stopped playing, Katie signalled to Linda they should go to the loo. Katie had seen the ladies sign halfway up the flight of stairs down into the basement. Excited from all the dancing, Linda followed her across the room. The ladies, when they found it, was the least occupied room in the club.

"He's so gorgeous, Katie. I just want to get my hands on him."

"Vince is nice. He and Bobby have been friends for years."

"Not Vince, silly. Donald. The policeman."

"I don't like him."

"You're not going to get him. Anyway, you have Bobby."

"There's something about him I don't like. We were a foursome. He shouldn't have butted in."

"All's fair in love and war. I like this Rhodesia. It's full of good-looking men. I'm going to have the time of my life. He's so tall. Did you see those shoulders? His body's so strong. You don't see men like that in the Pig and Whistle. Do you want to go to the loo or was this an excuse to talk to me? Have fun, Katie. We're young. There's plenty of time when we're old to behave ourselves."

"It was a bet. By his friends. To get you to dance."

"I don't even have a phone number I can slip him."

"You'll find a way. Tonight's the four of us. Two best friends with two best friends."

"You go on back to the table. Fact is, I do need the loo. Too much wine and gin and tonic."

When Katie got back to the table Donald had gone. He and his friends were in the bar drinking. The band, all except the piano player, were leaving the dais. Waiters were moving around serving the food and drinks. The man Bobby had introduced as Tony Bird was standing next to the doorway into the bar keeping an eye on his customers. Bobby had seen the direction she was looking.

"He's good at making money is Tony."

With the rest of the band on a break, the piano player played alone, softly, as if to himself, the music more classical. No one in the room took any notice. When Katie looked back through the glass partition, Donald and his friends had gone from sight. Two couples got up and danced to the music. Taking Bobby's hand, Katie led him onto the dance floor. They swayed to the strange music.

"What's the matter, Bobby?"

"That music reminds me of Mahler's tenth symphony. A half-jazz, half-classical version. I have a wind-up gramophone in my tent which I play in the evening before I go to sleep. A few LPs of London musicals and a few symphonies. The music reminds me of where I came from... It's so wonderful to hold you in my arms."

They swayed together, oblivious of other people, Katie's head on his shoulder. For Katie it was more than sexual attraction, it was peace, her soul and being at rest. Neither of them spoke until the music finished. When it did, they were standing next to the piano.

"Strangely reminded me of Gustav Mahler, Henny."

"Apart from me I'll bet you're the only one here who would know. Becker, on a theme by – Mahler. Just playing to myself. Remembering how I started playing the piano as a classical pianist. Enjoy your evening. Here comes Eddie and the boys. Back to the rock and roll."

When they returned to the hotel it was one o'clock in the morning. The boys saw the girls to their rooms and the evening was over. Alone in the quiet of the night, Katie sat on the edge of the bed. She was tired, happy with her day. Happy with Bobby. The windows, covered in fine mosquito gauze, were open, the sweet scent of flowers from Cecil

Square drifting up into her room. Next door, Linda's room was quiet, no sound of Vince. When Katie got into bed she fell into a deep, peaceful sleep.

WHEN SHE WOKE sunlight was streaming in through the window. There was noise from the street, the usual sounds of people. The day had begun. Katie bathed, dressed in shorts and a loose blouse and went down to look for breakfast. Bobby was sitting at the breakfast table with Vince. There was no sign of Linda.

"Morning, all. I knocked on Linda's door. There was no answer. I ate all that lamb last night and I'm hungry again. What's a full English breakfast, Bobby? Sleep well? What a beautiful morning. What's on the agenda?"

"Finding you both a flat. Driving round Salisbury. The lion park. A swim in the municipal pool. Whatever you want."

"After we find a flat, can't we drive up to the farm? Linda is very independent. She can call a taxi to take her to your auditors. I want to see the farm. Where I'm going to live."

"Then on Monday we'll drive back into town and you can both go for a job interview. Vince will be happy to look after Linda, won't you, Vince?"

"Isn't it far?"

"You'll see the countryside. Animals in the wild and not in a lion park. So, what are you having for breakfast?"

"What I want first is a cup of tea."

When Linda joined them she was all smiles. Five minutes later Donald Henderson sat down alone at a table to eat his breakfast, Linda trying to look as innocent as the day she was born. Apart from Katie, no one else at the table seemed to notice anything was wrong.

When Katie looked up from eating her English breakfast the policeman had finished his food and left the dining room, the same room where they had eaten the saddle of lamb the night before. The trees in their tubs in the courtyard looked different in sunlight. They were fruit trees bearing little red oranges.

"We'd better pack, Linda. If we find a small flat we can move in straight away. I'm sure it will be cheaper for Bobby than us staying in the hotel. Come on. We'll be down in the foyer with our bags in fifteen minutes."

Upstairs, Katie followed Linda into her room.

"How did you do it, Linda?"

"Men are so easy to seduce. When you returned from the loo, Donald was in the bar with his friends. I gave him my room number in the hotel. He stayed all night. His friends had driven the only car back to the Salisbury police barracks. He's walking back now."

"Won't the hotel charge Bobby for an extra person?"

"Why he stayed for breakfast. Said he'd pay back Bobby if the hotel charged Bobby's account. It wasn't worth it. He's a lousy lover. Why is it so often the best looking men are so selfish in bed? He was off in a flash and then went to sleep. Tried it again this morning but it wasn't much better. All that suntanned hulk of a man and a failure. Poor chap's got a half-sized ding. So, you're going up to the farm. Does this mean we won't be sharing a flat?"

"I don't know. We'll look for a one-bedroomed flat. If I stay in Salisbury while I'm making certain Bobby wants to marry me for all the right reasons I'll sleep in the lounge so you and your men friends can have the bedroom. If we leave the hotel rooms by ten o'clock Bobby won't be charged another day."

By lunchtime they had taken a flat halfway up Second Street from Meikles Hotel. It was on the road to Bobby's farm. With Linda and Vince going off for a swim in the public swimming pool, Bobby and Katie began her first drive into the bush.

"Did they charge you for Donald Henderson?"

"Yes they did. Bed and breakfast. All one price."

"Will he pay you back?"

"Probably not. Constables in the BSAP don't get much when it comes to money. They live well in the police barracks but receive little pay. Bit like being in the army. Dad said he was always short of money as a subaltern. Still is, I suppose. No one ever made money in a government job."

"Do you mind?"

"He was discreet. Vince may have seen him at breakfast without jumping to conclusions. People come into breakfast who don't stay the night in the hotel. Especially the farmers who drive into town early, eat breakfast and then do the shopping. During selling season, if you have tobacco on auction, the floors give you a free breakfast for having to leave the farm so early... Isn't the countryside beautiful? Once we get off the tarred road we have five miles of strip road and then dirt for the rest of the journey. Then you'll really feel you're in Africa with miles and miles of bush on either side of us."

"What about the farms?"

"There are some cultivated lands you can see from the road. Not many. Will that flat really be big enough for both of you? Poor old Vince. She'll hurt him, won't she?"

"Probably. Linda doesn't want to be serious with anyone. She likes men. The more the merrier. One day, I hope, she'll fall in love, settle down and have a family."

"Will she change?"

"Some of them do. You can call it sowing your wild oats. Fathers encourage men to sow their oats but never want their daughters to be promiscuous. Doesn't make any sense. Takes two to tango. In the end, the promiscuity of men and women has to be exactly the same. These days, with the pill, the girls don't get pregnant. She won't be seeing Donald again. Apparently he's a lousy lover. That's Linda's problem. Why she's insatiable. She's never found a man yet that can satisfy her let alone hold her interest... Look over there. Cows. Do you mind having to drive all the way back to town on Monday?"

"I'll come in every weekend until we're married."

With both windows down it was still hot in the cab. The tar road finished soon after they passed a small hotel. Two strips of tar, big enough for the wheels of the car, took them into the African bush.

"What happens if someone is coming the other way?"

"We both get one wheel off the strips so we can pass each other. It's a bit of a bump getting down off the strip. Trick is to wait until the last moment so as not to blow too much dust for the other fellow. You get used to it. When we reach the dirt road and the corrugations we won't want to talk. The whole truck shakes. You'll get used to it."

Putting her trust in Bobby, Katie looked out of the window. When the strip road finished the truck dropped from the end of the tar onto the dirt, jolting Katie half out of the seat.

"Sorry. You'll get used to it."

For three hours, driving fast, with a hundred yard tail of dust behind them, they drove through the bush. Not once did Katie see a wild animal.

There was a wooden sign where they turned off the road saying Hopewell Estate. Katie was not sure whether she was relieved or frightened her long journey from England had finally come to an end.

"Over there you can see where the gang have made the seed beds. Those are tobacco barns going up. That long building above ground will be the grading shed. The one next to it is the tractor shed. It's Saturday but the tractor works every day with two drivers taking turns. We've got to get the lands finished by the middle of next month so when the rains come we can plant our tobacco seedlings from those seed beds. The tent camp's a bit further down. So what do you think, Katie? Is this your kind of place?"

"I'm not sure. It's so far from anywhere. I've seen two farmhouses with what must be tobacco barns and a few thatched huts since we passed that hotel and got on the strips. It's all so wild. So uninhabited."

"It's a bit different from London. You'll get used to it. There it is. Over there. Down by the river."

"What, Bobby?"

"The tent. Your new home. Our home to be."

"Oh, my goodness. You live here!"

"For the time being."

"I suppose we bathe in the river?"

"There are crocodiles in the river. We have showers. A hot shower every morning out in the open under that big tree. I hoist a bucket of water up by a pulley system. Friend of mine taught me the trick. You'll love it."

"People can see."

"There aren't any people, Katie. The labourers have their own huts further downriver. The cook doesn't come up until after I've showered in the morning."

"Why are you hooting the horn?"

"To call Welcome. Don't you want dinner? That's my fridge under the tree. Works from that big cylinder of gas. Want a cold beer?"

"You've got to be kidding."

"Matter of fact, I'm not... Afraid we'll have to both sleep in the same tent. Only way to keep the mosquitoes away at night. I've put in an extra camp bed for you. So, what do you think? Aren't the big trees by the river beautiful? Their roots go down under the river which makes the trees grow tall. In the evening, the wild animals come down to drink. Over there is where I cook round the fire. We've got some kudu venison to go on the *braai*. In Africa, a barbecue is called a *braai*. It's Afrikaans. The language of the Boers. We'll leave everything in the truck for Welcome. We'll sit on those camp chairs under the trees and have a nice cold beer. Don't look so amazed, Katie. You'll get used to it. We all did. In time you'll never want to live any other way. Just imagine a lovely thatched roofed cottage instead of my tent. And a swimming pool. Even a tennis court. Did you know we have a cricket field up the top of the Centenary block? The Centenary West club. Closer, we have our own club with a big clubhouse, swimming pool and tennis courts. The Centenary East club. All this since the Centenary block was opened fourteen years ago on the Centenary of the birth of Cecil Rhodes. Do you play tennis?"

"A little."

"I'm not much good. It's more social. We'll go up to our club tomorrow. Introduce you to my friends."

"It's all so peaceful."

"All you can hear are the doves and the pigeons. The pigeons make a different call to the pigeons in England. Sit you down in that canvas chair in the shade and I'll get us a couple of beers out of the fridge."

"You really think I'll get used to it?"

"Of course you will. We British have been getting used to new places for three hundred years. I'll bet America and Australia felt just as strange to the first British settlers."

"There's a black man walking towards us along the river."

"That's Welcome. The cook and bottle washer. He looks after my tent camp. You'll like Welcome. Always helpful. How does that one feel? Cold enough? The condensation positively streams down the sides of a cold bottle of beer. I keep the glasses in the fridge next to the beers. Let me pour yours... So, here we are. Cheers, Katie... You can bring the stuff out of the truck, Welcome. Then make the fire. Kudu chops tonight. This is the future Mrs Preston. Say hello to Welcome, Katie. He only understands when I speak Fanagalo."

"So he doesn't speak English?"

"Couple of words. Sekuru the foreman speaks a little more. Sekuru was with me on World's View when I worked for Jeremy Crookshank. Welcome will make a nice big mixed salad to go with the venison. We'll bake some potatoes in the coals."

"What are those animals on the other side of the river?"

"A family of warthog. Wild pigs. They come down every morning to the river to drink."

"They look too adorable for words!... This beer tastes so good."

"Thought you'd like it. My first one always goes down without touching sides... Just look at that sunset. In a few minutes the whole horizon will be red."

The fire blazed as the sun set and the light began to fade. Katie watched Welcome build a second fire close to the first one. The light wind was blowing a trail of smoke in their direction. The pigs on the other side of the small river took no notice. Other, unfamiliar sounds were coming out of the darkening bush. Far away, Katie could hear drums being played, a rhythmic beat that went on and on. Bobby brought her a second beer from the fridge with a cold glass and poured the beer into it. Drums began beating much closer to their camp from a little way downriver. Bobby didn't seem to notice. Katie assumed the drums were coming from the place where Bobby's labourers lived. The sound was more comforting than threatening. While he was up, Bobby pulled the cork from a bottle of red wine. Welcome had placed a camp table next to their canvas chairs where Bobby put the open bottle with two big wine glasses. The sunset reflected in the glasses mingling with the light of the flickering fire. The second fire had been lit by Welcome blowing more smoke in her direction. Katie got up to move her chair.

"You'll want to stay with the woodsmoke, Katie. Once the sun goes down the mosquitoes come out in earnest. Spray yourself with that can of spray Welcome put on the table... The light goes quickly in Africa. Why we have two fires. One to let die down to hot coals for the *braai* and the other to keep off the mosquitoes. The chaps in the compound are having their Saturday night party. I give them one of those barrels of white beer made from maize and sorghum that were in the back of the truck. They play the drums all night. When you hear the drums you know all is well with the gang. They have to relax just as we do. Worked hard all week stumping out trees and making bricks. I like to hear them enjoying themselves... Welcome will put the meat on the fire and go back to the compound. He puts the beer barrel in a wheelbarrow and pushes it down the path along the river to where they built their huts. Pole and dagga huts with thatched roofs. They're waiting for him. Why they started playing the drums. When the light finally goes our world will shrink to the two of us in the firelight. When we eat I'll light the kerosene lamp."

Alone, with the drums beating, Welcome having gone off in the dark pushing his wheelbarrow with the beer, they were silent.

"I'm not frightened anymore."

Bobby had got up to turn the meat on the fire. As he turned back to her the firelight caught the side of his face. He was smiling. Far away, the last glimmer of light painted a faint white light, tinged with red at its heart, on the horizon. There were sounds of animals coming from the bush. All of them unfamiliar. Then the light went completely. They were alone, in mind, body and spirit.

When Bobby came back to his chair he handed Katie a glass of wine, which had been in the fridge, the first time Katie had tasted cold red wine. It was delicious, sending a warm glow through her body. Bobby was still standing, watching her taste the wine. Then he leaned down and kissed her gently on the lips.

"You don't have to be afraid of me, Katie. You're my guest on the farm. Royal game. Untouchable until the day we're married. I'm a bit old-fashioned, unlike Donald and your friend Linda... How's the wine?"

"Everything is lovely. Not one bite from a mosquito. And I'm used to the smoke from the fire. Those chops smell good. I'm so lucky. So lucky we met in London."

"Thank you, Katie. Getting to know each other properly is so important. What we have said we're going to do in letters is a commitment for life. I want you to be certain. There will never be a divorce once we're married. You do understand. Everything in the future won't be perfect. That's life. The nature of things. The way life works out with all its ups and downs. The good and the bad."

"I feel safe with you."

"You'll be safe with me for the rest of your life. You have my solemn promise. As to what happens in the world around us, there are no promises. Rhodesia? I don't know. In 1938 Chamberlain said there was going to be 'peace for our time' when he came back to England from talks with Hitler in Munich. A year later we were at war. There are always wars and rumours of war. Some happen, most of them don't. We have to hope. Why I called this farm Hopewell Estate. Together, as husband and wife, we will take the rough with the smooth. From outside and inside our marriage. Living on my own here has given me time to think. To try and work out how life goes around. So much of suburban life in England was trivial. Or competitive. Trying to get ahead. Trying to have those extra material things of life most of which we find out don't make us any happier. I want us to have a good marriage. I want that more than the success of this farm and all its vulnerability to politics... Let's sit up at the table and eat our supper. The spuds are ready. So are the chops. Sorry to become serious. You don't have to make up your mind to marry me in one big rush... African drums. Aren't they something?"

The table and chairs were close to the fire that Bobby kept fed from a pile of wood stacked by Welcome. They sat down to supper. Bobby poured a second glass of the wine. Outside of the firelight the night was black. No sign of a moon. High up in the sky Katie looked up at the layers of stars, some of the bigger stars twinkling. The night sky was so beautiful. Bobby put two chops on her plate and passed her the salad bowl. He dug out the potatoes, wrapped in tinfoil, from the embers of the fire that had cooked the chops. There were still chops left on the grill over the fire that had died down to a dull red glow.

"I stick butter in my baked potatoes. This is the first time I have properly entertained on this farm. Vince comes over and we drink, which is different. Maybe it isn't... How's the food? Welcome does a lovely salad dressing with lots of fresh herbs. Enough light from the lamp? Nothing worse than not being able to see what you're eating."

By the time they had finished their food and the bottle of wine the moon had risen. A big, full moon, orange and clear in the dark of the sky. All round, some near, some far, Katie could hear the sounds of animals and birds.

"Are those owls?"

"Spotted eagle owls. Husband and wife. They call to each other. I love the sound. When one calls, the other bird always answers."

"You love Africa."

"Yes, Katie, I do. It gets to you in the end. Nature at its best... Are you tired? On the farm we go to bed early and get up early. The rhythm of

Africa. All they had was firelight and the moon after sunset. You want to go to bed? We can take the lamp. Or you can undress in the dark. Welcome put your case in the tent."

"Do I put on pyjamas?"

"Bit hot in Africa for pyjamas. I sleep in my underpants."

"Thank you for such a lovely evening. That spray works. Not one mosquito bite."

"Let's go to bed. I sleep like a log. You'll have to tell me if I snore. I've never before slept in the same room as a girl."

"Maybe I snore."

"We'll find out."

In the tent, Bobby closed the flaps. On either side were big windows covered in a fine meshed netting. Over each of the camp beds, from the centre pole that ran the length of the big tent, hung mosquito nets, the two camp beds head to toe in a line under the pole.

"Are you ready for lights out, Katie?"

Instantly they were plunged into darkness. Outside the fire had gone down. The moon, hidden behind the tall riverine trees, did not throw moonlight into the tent. Katie took off her shorts and her top, felt behind and released her bra. She could hear Bobby under his mosquito net getting into his bed.

"You have to feel for the net. In case you're worried about wild animals, I sleep with a loaded rifle beside my bed. Goodnight, Katie."

"Goodnight, Bobby. Sweet dreams."

Slowly, carefully, wearing nothing but her panties, Katie felt her way into bed. On her back in the darkness she lay awake. Bobby was quickly asleep. She had heard the change in rhythm of his breathing. In the middle of nowhere, with a man with a gun two feet from the bottom of her bed, a man she barely knew, seven thousand miles from home, Katie felt the tiredness of a full day come over her and bring her into sleep.

3

Waking with a fright, Katie knew there was something right outside the tent. A pale moon was playing colourless light in through a window of the tent. She listened, fear gripping her whole body. Whatever it was pushed at the side of the tent. It was big. She could hear the soft rhythm of Bobby's undisturbed sleep. Katie tried to scream but nothing came out. She was shaking with fear, her windpipe choked by her fright. She could hear the animal three feet from her bed. She made a noise, a squeak. Bobby did not wake. The owls had stopped hooting. There was no sound of the drums. Just the grunts with a thin layer of canvas between Katie's naked body and the animal outside. Flaying at the mosquito net, she pulled herself off the camp bed. On hands and knees she crawled to the side of Bobby's bed. Pushing at the mosquito net, ethereal in the moonlight, she gave him a shake.

"What! What's the matter?... Katie! What are you doing?"

"There's something big just outside the tent."

"Oh, that. Probably a hyena. They scavenge round the camp at night. The bones from the *braai*. We're all right inside the tent. Sleeping outside, people have been known to have problems. Why if you sleep outside you keep a big fire burning."

"Can I get into your bed? I'm so frightened. I couldn't shout... I don't have any clothes on."

"Nor do I. Can you feel your way in? Here you go. My poor Katie. This must be all so strange to you."

Under the net, Katie lay down next to Bobby on the small bed. She put her arms round him and began to sob. The animal, whatever it was, was still outside. She was shaking as Bobby put his arms around her. Katie pulled into him, thrusting her naked body against his, in a primal urge to procreate before it was too late.

"Make love to me, Bobby. I'm so frightened. Are we going to die?"

"Don't be silly."

"Please make love to me. I can feel you, Bobby. Yes. Now. That's it!"

With her whole mind and being concentrated on making love, she lost her fear. When it was over her body was no longer shaking. They were both breathing heavily, wrapped in each other's arms. Then she laughed. And laughed. She couldn't stop laughing.

"What's the matter now, Katie?"

"That's one thing off my list to worry about. Whether we'd be any good together in bed."

They were both laughing, rolling around in the small camp bed.

Later, slowly, carefully, they again made love. Katie no longer with a care in the world.

In the first light of morning they woke. They were still holding each other. Again they made love. Katie was smiling. It was the right time of her monthly cycle.

Bobby got up first, opening the flap of the tent. Birds were singing to Katie, so many of them. A bird that Bobby had said was a Cape turtle dove seemed to be calling 'how's Katie, how's Katie'. And Katie was fine. There was no sign of Welcome, the dawn still breaking. It was cool so early in the morning. Bobby had put on his underpants. She watched him pick up a bucket and walk away. He was whistling. Katie got up, put on her shorts and a top and went outside. It was a beautiful morning. Down by the river, Bobby was filling his bucket with water from it. Walking back she could see all he had on was his underpants and his shoes. He filled another bucket, attached to a hose, with the water.

"In twenty minutes out in the sun, the water will be warm. Then I haul the bucket up into the tree. *Voilà*. We have the perfect shower bath."

Bobby began putting wood on last night's fire, poking the embers.

White smoke drifted straight up into the sky. The dry wood burst into flames.

"Sunday. Told Welcome not to come. Bacon and eggs. You'll find living in the countryside makes you enjoy every one of your meals. Did you sleep well?"

"In the end."

"So did I. Instead of going to the club I thought we could drive through to the top of the Centenary block and show you the Zambezi escarpment. Maybe a call at the Centenary West club. There's a cricket match on today. My old boss Jeremy Crookshank is a keen cricketer. We have reciprocal membership between the two clubs, the Centenary East and Centenary West. What a lovely day. I've never felt better in my life. The kettle only takes a minute to boil in the heat of those flames. Tea first, then a shower, then I'll cook you breakfast."

"Can't I cook?"

"Not yet. You're still a guest. You can cook when you're Mrs Preston."

"Are we going into town tomorrow? It doesn't seem to matter now."

"I'll be working in the lands all day if we stay."

"I'll enjoy waiting for you... Where are you going to build our house?"

"On the exact spot where we first made love. I think it's appropriate don't you? Later, when we build our big house, we'll build on the same spot. Or next to the cottage. Yes, next to the cottage so we can sneak into it every now and again."

"How many kids do you want?"

"Four. Two boys and two girls. Boy, girl, boy, girl. Eighteen months apart."

"You've got it all worked out... I didn't tell you. I'm not on the pill."

"There you are, you see. You knew what I wanted... See what I mean? The kettle's boiled. Tea for two and a tent. What else can a person want?"

"Aren't you going to put on some clothes?"

"Well, I thought, after tea, before the water gets hot in the bucket, we'd have some time to spare. Then we can shower together and both get dressed."

"That bird is saying 'how's Katie, how's Katie'!"

"No it is not. It's singing 'how's Katie, how's Bobby'. Tea with milk and two sugars? I remember these things. Come and sit under the trees. What a lovely morning."

By the time they showered the water was hot, the sun's rays burning Katie's pure white skin when she stepped from the shade of the trees. Her dove was still calling. They didn't use towels to dry themselves, just stood in the sun. They dressed outside the tent, watching each other. Bobby found a frying pan and put it on the grill over the hot fire. Soon Katie could smell the frying bacon. Bobby seemed to be enjoying himself doing the cooking.

"You can make yourself useful with that toasting fork. I've cut the bread."

"Yes, master."

"Oh, I'm going to have a wonderful marriage. Pass me that packet of pork sausages. Colcom. Our Cold Storage Commission. Best sausages in the world. We'll have a look in the club and then drive up to the escarpment. Best you see some people to get back your equilibrium."

"My equilibrium is just right."

"Then pass the sausages. How many do you want?"

"One's enough."

"You can toast the bread on the fire just next to my frying pan. I'm making coffee to go with breakfast."

"Is it always so peaceful on Hopewell Estate?"

"Always. From the day I found the place. This is going to be our home forever, I hope... Don't put the bread too close to the fire."

"Yes, master. If I do it wrong you can spank my bottom."

"You kinky little girl."

"Was it really a hyena?"

"All last night's bones from the *braai* are gone. The jaws of a hyena are so strong they can bite off your leg when they're hungry enough."

"Don't you worry?"

"Nature looks after itself. If we don't disturb them, they won't disturb us. They've got used to my camp. Used to me. I never worry. Just keep a gun close in case. Living among wild animals is a real life. Not fake. It's how it should be. But like men there is always a bad one out there, somewhere."

The sausages went into the pan and sizzled. Bobby had put the bacon onto a plate and placed it next to the heat from the fire. Katie could smell the coffee. With the toast piled up next to the cooked bacon, tomatoes in the pan, the coffee ready in the percolator, she laid the table under the tree for breakfast.

"You look after yourself, Bobby."

"Only way to go... How does that lot look? Can you think of a better way to live?"

"You don't always need other people."

"That's how I feel. We'll skip the club and drive straight to the top of the block and the Zambezi escarpment."

Katie's morning went by in a dream. A breeze had come up, making the heat of the day more pleasant. She was shown round the visible progress on the farm, none of it meaning much to her. Growing up in the suburbs she had never been taught to grow anything. With a picnic basket in the back of the truck they drove off the farm. Half an hour later, at the end of the dirt road that had started outside Salisbury, Bobby stopped the truck.

"You can get down into the Zambezi Valley but it's a difficult winding road. Going down there we have a rule, to always take two vehicles in case one of us breaks down. You have to think when living in the wilds of Africa. Isn't the view from here down into the valley spectacular? In that heat haze two thousand feet below you can just make out the waters of the Zambezi River meandering across the plane in the far distance. Here, have a look through my binoculars. Where you're looking at the water is Mozambique."

"Does anyone live in the valley?"

"A few villages. They live off the game and fish from the river. It's so hot down there in the summer it's suffocating. Next month a white man would be best to keep out of the valley. Mile after mile of largely uninhabited bush. That's real wild country as far as you can see in any direction... Let's have our picnic. You'll want some tea. We English always need our tea."

"I can see something through the binoculars in the bushes. There's a splash of colour and what looks like a cross. Yes, it's a wooden cross with a jar or something full of cut flowers. What on earth are they doing there?"

"You weren't meant to see them, Katie. It's the grave of Jeremy

Crookshank's first wife. Her boys come out here with their father to put flowers on her grave."

"Why's she buried there?"

"She was attacked by lions. Most of her body was eaten. She was an alcoholic and had driven into the bush along the road we have just taken. Ran out of petrol and tried to walk back. Poor old Jeremy. He married again, as much to give his boys a mother though he's happy with his second wife. Whatever we do we must never forget we're living in Africa... You want a hard-boiled egg? There's salt in that twist of greaseproof paper. A friend of mine once said an egg without salt was like a woman without a climax. Wouldn't have told you that yesterday."

"How old are the boys?"

"Phillip must be eleven by now. Randall nine."

"How awful to lose their mother in such a terrible way."

"Yes, it was. If we go to the club you'll meet them today. They always watch their father play cricket. Jeremy is quite a good batsman. Says cricket always reminds him of where he comes from. Of England."

"Does that small river over there just run out over the cliff?"

"Like a bridal veil. By the time the water hits the top of the trees way down in the valley, it's mist."

"Have you been down there?"

"Not yet."

"Do those trees have a name?"

"Msasa trees. They're called msasa trees... Tea?"

"Thank you, Bobby... I can't believe this is all happening to me."

"It's what life should be all about. Seeing new things. New experiences."

Before they left to drive to the Centenary West club and the cricket, Bobby again scanned the valley through the binoculars, standing for a long moment looking at the same spot.

"That's odd. I thought there was something there earlier. At first I thought it was a bush fire but it's just in the one spot some ten miles this side of the Zambezi River, ten miles into the valley from the bottom of the escarpment. It must be a campfire though I can't make out a vehicle. The fire's among a clump of trees on a small feeder river that flows on into the Zambezi."

"Can you see any people?"

"I thought I saw movement among the trees but it could be animals. How odd. If I had to guess I'd say someone has made a camp in among the trees."

"Who could be down there?"

"I have no idea."

Down below in the overwhelming heat of the Zambezi Valley, oblivious of a man at the top of the escarpment watching their camp through high-powered binoculars, Canaan Moyo picked up his backpack to continue the journey. In the pack, compliments of the Russian government, were six, ten-pound land mines. All three of them in the cadre had similar packs on their backs. Slowly, painfully, they made their way forward towards the bottom of the escarpment where they could see a small river flowing over the top into the void, making a wide spray of water touched by the rays of the sun. They had caught and killed a porcupine, made a fire and cooked the meat over the fire. Their stomachs full for the first time in days, they plodded forward, none of them looking forward to the terrible climb up the side of the escarpment.

Canaan, the leader, took his binoculars from the brown leather case and searched the distant path up the escarpment, the sixty pounds on his back feeling more like a ton.

"There's someone up there, Jacob," he said in Shona. "He's standing next to where the river starts its fall into the valley."

"They've come to meet us. To help carry the mines."

"I don't think so. He's a white man. What's he doing up there?"

"You think someone has warned them we are bringing in munitions? You think we've got a traitor in the movement?"

"There's a woman with him. Must be one of their farmers."

"Can you see a vehicle?"

"Not on the lip of the escarpment. When we get up into the highveld we'll only move at night. You can hear better at night. Let's keep moving."

By the time Canaan, Jacob and Joshua reached the bottom of the escarpment, the light spray of river water welcome on their faces, Bobby was driving into the Centenary West club up the avenue of trees with the cricket field on their left and the clubhouse up in front of them. Katie, mildly interested, was watching the cricket. A tall man in whites was running up to bowl; the ball was hit hard back over his head. From the clubhouse came the polite sound of clapping. A fielder picked up the ball from the boundary in front of the sight screen and threw it back in the direction of the bowler.

"Do you understand cricket, Bobby?"

"Played it at school. We had to. That was Jeremy Crookshank hitting the four. So what do you think of the club?"

"A small island."

"Yes, I suppose it is. There's Phillip and Randall. Don't mention you saw the flowers on their mother's grave."

"Don't they want to talk about her?"

"I don't know. That's Bergit with them. Jeremy's second wife."

"That's a German name. Is she German?"

"Named after a German. Something to do with the war and Harry Brigandshaw. His father was one of the first whites to settle in Rhodesia at the end of the last century. Harry Brigandshaw was a friend of Jeremy's father."

"Everything is so new to me. It's going to take a long time to fit in."

"Let's start by introducing you to some people. We'll go into the bar."

"He's hit another four."

"I told you Jeremy was good."

"Do the kids play?"

"Phillip's going to be a star. Come and meet them... Hello, Bergit. This is my fiancée, Katie Frost. Just arrived from England. How many has he got, Phillip?"

"Twenty-one. Did you see those two fours?"

"Phillip, Randall, meet Aunty Katie."

"Hello."

"We're going into the bar. See you all later. How's the crop on World's View, Bergit?"

"Seedbeds are looking good. Your new farm?"

"Still living in a tent."

"Jeremy said the first five years was work, work, work."

"Yes, I suppose it is."

Katie smiled at the two boys sitting on the grass under a big umbrella with their stepmother. She wanted to give them a hug. With Bobby holding her hand they walked into the clubhouse and through to a room with a long bar away from windows that looked onto a veranda and through to the cricket. At the bar were three men, drinks in their hands, backs to the bar, watching the cricket.

"Must be visitors from the other side," whispered Bobby in her ear. "Never seen them before."

"You said you knew everyone in the club."

"I'm inclined to exaggerate."

"Aren't we all?"

"What are you going to drink?"

"Gin and tonic."

"That's my girl... Noah, make mine a cold Castle."

"Coming up, Mr Preston."

"You chaps ever go down into the valley?"

"Not me, Mr Preston."

"There was woodsmoke from a fire halfway between the Zambezi River and the bottom of the escarpment just now, I could see it through my binoculars. Do you know anyone who lives down there?"

"You want a slice of lemon in your drink, madam?"

"Thank you."

Katie watched Noah turn his back on them. By the look in his eyes at the mention of woodsmoke in the valley, something was wrong. When he turned back the look in his eyes had gone.

"Probably a bush fire, Mr Preston. Is that one cold enough?"

Katie watched Bobby touch his hand on the bottle of beer.

"Perfect. Noah speaks impeccable English. Went to a Catholic mission school, didn't you, Noah? He's well educated."

"Lots of ice, madam?"

"It wasn't a bush fire, Noah. Just a single line of smoke rising up into the sky."

Again the barman looked up sharply before moving away to the back of the bar where he sat on a barstool.

"Cheers, Katie."

"Cheers, Bobby. What a lovely clubhouse. What a lovely day... What's the matter with the barman?"

"Why? What's the matter with him?"

"He doesn't want to talk about what you saw in the valley."

"He's always like that. Serves the drinks and moves away. Some of the members don't like a barman listening to their conversation."

"In England they say the barman is their best friend."

"Yes, well this isn't England. In Rhodesia the blacks keep to themselves. So do we."

"Then you'll never get to know each other. What a shame."

The three men at the bar were joined by two men. The two men looked at Noah on his stool at the other end of the bar before speaking. The men left the bar without ordering a drink or acknowledging Bobby's greeting. Outside they stood under a tree, the five of them deep in conversation. Then they left, getting into a police Land Rover that Katie had seen drive up with the two men.

"Did you know those two, Bobby?"

"Clay Barry, member-in-charge for Centenary. Station commander of local police. The other chap is Fred Rankin, his second-in-command. I wondered why Fred wasn't playing cricket. Fred asked me the other day to join the police reserve. Said I'd think about it. After Smith declared our independence unilateral, people are jittery."

"Are you going to join?"

"Probably. See what the other chaps do."

"Why didn't he want to talk to you today?"

"Must have been police business. If I had a second guess I'd say those three chaps were policemen. If they had been supporters of the visiting side they'd have been on the grass under umbrellas. I don't like policemen as a rule. They never tell you what they're really up to."

"But you'll be a policeman if you join the reserve."

"Yes, I suppose I will."

"Something is happening with the cricket. Everyone is clapping and they're coming off the field."

"Seems Centenary have won the match. Now the bar will fill up. Just you watch."

"I'll never remember everyone's names."

"You'll get to know all of them by name in the end. Takes time. When we are married you'll have all the time in the world... You think Linda will be all right on her own if you don't go in tomorrow? Vince will have to be back on World's View tonight."

"Linda will be fine with so many good-looking men around. But you're right. I should be with her in the flat until she settles in with a job."

"We'll drive back tomorrow. Let's go back to the farm before we get into a drinking session. I'd think less of you if you didn't think of your friend. What's upset you, Katie?"

"I'm not sure. Can't we talk in the truck?"

With her empty glass left on the bar, Katie followed Bobby out of the clubhouse. Bobby opened her door and she got in the truck. When he got in the other side he did not start the engine.

"What is it, Katie?"

"It was Noah. When you mentioned the woodsmoke in the valley he had a frightened look in his eyes. I was watching him while you two were talking. He knows something."

"Whatever could he know, Katie?"

"Who it was you saw through your binoculars."

"We can drive into Salisbury tonight if you want to."

"Maybe we should. Do you mind?"

"Of course not... You do still want to marry me?"

"Of course I do. It's Linda. If Vince is driving back tonight, Linda will be all alone in a strange country. I was being selfish."

"So was I. Back to camp, pack your bag and we'll hit the road... So who on earth could have that been in the valley without a vehicle?"

Katie's feeling of disquiet would not go away. She was good at reading people's faces. Often the look on the face was more explicit than words. The man's eyes had gone from alarm to fright to fear all in the space of a second. Only when he turned back had the eyes lost their hidden expression. Noah had immediately looked from Bobby to the three men sitting with their backs to the bar to see if they had heard. Then he had moved to his barstool. When the local policemen came into the bar he again looked rattled. Bobby, concentrating on her, had seen none of the barman's body language. She put her hand on Bobby's knee, not wanting to think she was running away. What with the hyena in the night and Noah in the bar with so many policemen, her nerves were on edge. Africa was so different to England, so intimidating. Most of the way they drove in silence, Bobby concentrating on the pitfalls in the bad road. In parts, drift sand had built up, making the truck more difficult to control.

Getting back on the strip road and then back on the tar was a relief for both of them.

"You won't mind if I turn the truck round and drive back to the farm tonight? There's so much work to be done. If I don't keep an eye on everything, things go wrong. Sekuru, my foreman, is good at doing what he's told but he can't think for himself. When something does go wrong he just waits for me and the job stands idle. Understandable, I suppose. It isn't his farm. Same with the tractor driver. He can't hear a problem with the tractor before it breaks down so he can bring it back for me to fix. Jeremy said it was the same with all employees. They never think. Jeremy was an officer in the Royal Navy just after the war. Said the men were just the same. Waited for an officer to tell them what to do. It can be frustrating. We want to plant out in the land with the first rains. Sometimes work, if you want to succeed, has to come before everything. I'll drive in after work on Saturday."

"It'll be dark when you drive back."

"Just have to keep an eye open for wild animals on the road. I want to do it all for you, Katie. You and our kids. You need money in this world just to get by, let alone educate the kids. So succeeding with the farm is all that much more important now you're here."

"You won't fall asleep at the wheel?"

"Of course I won't."

"Does the truck ever break down? We haven't seen another vehicle since we left the club."

"I have a tool kit in the back. Two spare tyres. Spare battery. The trick is to listen for knocks and keep her well serviced. You have to think all the time. Think ahead of the problem. If I get tired on the way back I'll get off the road and have a nap. You'd be amazed at what a ten-minute nap can do for your concentration."

SALISBURY ON A SUNDAY afternoon was quiet. Outside the block of flats in Second Street they parked the truck.

"Isn't that Vince's truck?"

"Do you have your key?"

"You never know with Linda."

Katie let herself in. The two-roomed flat was quiet.

"Linda? It's me. Are you there?"

Vince Ranger opened the bedroom door looking guilty. He was wearing his pants, his shirt unbuttoned.

"Taking a nap before driving back to World's View."

"Centenary won the cricket. Your boss hit the winning shot. Well, I'll be off. Get a head start on you, Vince, so my dust doesn't blow in your face."

Linda came to the bedroom door looking dishevelled. Her hair was all mushed up. Bobby put Katie's bag down on the floor and turned to leave. They were all feeling awkward for different reasons.

"Didn't expect you so soon."

"Got to get jobs, Linda. Remember? Friends stick together."

Katie saw Bobby back to the truck, watched him turn the vehicle round and drive back up the road. For a long moment she stood in the street watching the tail lights of the truck disappear. Then she went back to the flat she was to share with Linda.

"You don't have to go because of me, Vince."

"Yes, well, it's getting late. Up with the sun tomorrow morning."

"Drive carefully. That road is terrible."

"Don't have to tell me. And you never get used to it."

Alone together for the first time since arriving at the train station, they looked at each other. Linda, still half dressed, had not seen Vince to his truck.

"You want a drink, Katie? Vince took me shopping. Helped me stock up the flat. Tomorrow we go and find a job. Don't look at me like that. The man had spent a fortune on booze, food and two nice pairs of sheets. What else could I do? He's nice. Might even see him again. I'm going to open a bottle of white wine. We put the wine in the fridge. What's the matter? You look agitated."

"His place is so wild. I'm not sure I can spend the rest of my life living in the African bush. There are so many undercurrents. I'm from the suburbs. The unknown frightens me. Bobby is better than I imagined but it's the way he lives. It's fun for a holiday, sleeping in a tent. There was a hyena right outside the tent. Weird smoke rising up from nowhere. All those strange sounds. I don't think I could get used to it."

"Then we'll have some fun. Vince says the auditors will pay us ninety pounds a month. This place is fifteen pounds a month fully furnished.

We can save enough by next July to go back in style. Do the trip all over again."

"If I go back I owe Bobby five hundred pounds. Anyway, I'm probably pregnant. The hyena frightened me so much I got out of my bed and crawled into his. Only after we made love did I stop shaking. And it's the middle of the month."

"You're not on the pill!"

"We are going to get married. That's how it was going to be."

"Not everyone gets pregnant by having sex in the middle of the month. If you want to pay him back I'll chip in half. You're young. Have fun. There are always more fish in the sea. From what I've heard from Vince and some of his friends, Rhodesia as they know it won't last. Why Vince hasn't bought his own farm and saddled himself with a mortgage. Vince says if he had any other skills but tobacco farming he'd go back to England. Instead of telling me how wonderful it was in Rhodesia he wanted to know all about what it's now like in England. What he could do for a job. There are a quarter of a million whites in this country and two million blacks. The whites will be submerged without help from England. Vince says a lot of whites are leaving. Going to Australia. Canada. Even back to England. The old colonial lifestyle can't last."

"Can all that money we save up be got out of Rhodesia?"

"Then we just have fun, pay back Bobby and buy ourselves a plane ticket back to England. But there are always ways of getting money out of a country. We should know, working all those figures in accounting."

"Do you understand all the figures?"

"Not always. Have a glass of wine... So? How was he?"

"He was wonderful."

THE NEXT DAY, while Katie and Linda were being interviewed by the office manager of Mitchell and Cox and being offered jobs to start immediately at ninety pounds a month, Inspector Fred Rankin was driving round Hopewell Estate in a police Land Rover looking for Bobby Preston.

"You come to help us do the stumping? Or recruit me for the police reserve?"

"Good morning to you, Bobby. Come and walk with me... You said something yesterday in the club to Noah that interests us. The three men sitting with you at the bar were from intelligence in Salisbury. You were overheard talking about a campfire you saw in the valley. How much did you see?"

"Just a single line of smoke rising out of the valley. I was up on the escarpment with a pair of binoculars."

"We've sent a patrol to look for them. Our intelligence says Mugabe and his friends are infiltrating the country with well-trained terrorists in preparation for a war."

"Oh, my God! That's far worse than sanctions. You think there could be a war in the Centenary?"

"Why we want you to join the reserve. We want you farmers to train to be anti-terrorist units. You know the bush. Why that fire looked so odd to you. Just taking precautions. Nothing to panic about... You mind driving with me up to the escarpment to show me what you saw? Where's your fiancée?"

"Drove her back to Salisbury last night."

"So that was why I couldn't find you. We won't be more than a couple of hours. Can you spare the time?"

"Of course I can. So there's more going on than we know about?"

"There always is. A policeman's job is never done. So they said at police college."

"You want to fill me in a bit?"

"Not really. Just want you to pinpoint where the smoke was coming from so we can have a look. Tell the patrol in the valley where to go."

"I'll never be able to pick out the same clump of trees without the smoke rising."

"Do your best. It'll help us narrow down the area so we can look for tracks. I have radio contact with the chaps on patrol in the valley."

"What will you do if you find them?"

"Shoot them most probably. What else do you do to people who are trying to kill you?"

"If I'd known this I would never have bought Hopewell Estate."

"We'll win, Bobby. When it's all over you'll have a thriving tobacco estate and all of us in the police will be envious. Many of the farmers in the Centenary came out after the war from England. There was preference given to people who had been in the military during the war when they handed out Crown Land farms."

"Sounds like the Rhodesian government was creating a buffer zone. There's always a reason for getting anything that looks cheap. But it isn't, of course. Even without the risk of being attacked. The land cost me seven and sixpence an acre. Only half arable. And it costs ten pounds an acre to take out the trees and make the land usable for crops. It would have been cheaper to buy an existing farm in America. Why is life always such a fight?"

"The nature of life. The nature of man. Get in the other side. On the way, I'll teach you how to use the police radio."

WHILE BOBBY PRESTON was being driven by Fred Rankin off Hopewell Estate, the two-way radio crackling as Fred tried to make contact with the patrol in the Zambezi Valley, Canaan Moyo was leading his men into the Chiweshe Reserve. In the light of the full moon they had climbed up the escarpment and walked at sunrise through Centenary to the reserve where they were met by friends who relieved them of their burden. The land mines, flat, round and smooth, joined the rest of the munitions that had been carried out of Zambia, through Mozambique and up into the highveld of Rhodesia. Canaan, Joshua and Jacob were greeted as heroes by the people. All three of them felt good, excited, free from the weight of the packs.

"What are you going to do with the mines?" he asked the man in Shona who had relieved him of the contents in his backpack.

"When the time is right. When we begin the second Chimurenga, the war of liberation to free our people from oppression, we will dig holes at night in their roads and bury your mines so when the farmer drives into town in his fancy car he will blow himself to pieces. You want to come and have some food? You'll all need a rest before you start your walk back to Zambia. We need enough equipment to arm two thousand fighters before we launch the first attack."

"When will that be?"

"Probably years. AK-47 assault rifles and landmines don't deteriorate. It's a long process, building up enough equipment. It's the only way to bring it in... We brewed beer on Saturday. Did you have any problems?"

"Only the journey and the weight of the mines."

"Well done, Canaan. The people will be grateful to you. To you, Joshua and Jacob. Come and meet some of the girls. All the girls love a young hero."

"What is your position in the party?"

"I'm the comrade in charge of party affairs in the Chiweshe Reserve."

"Are you more important than the chief?"

"Let's say we share some of the responsibilities. But we all answer to Comrade Mugabe and the Zimbabwe African National Union."

Feeling excited, they followed the man through the huts to a tall tree under which people gathered, cooking pots over the fires, young girls smiling. No longer tired, smiling, the three young friends walked forward.

PART III

JUNE 1968 – "IN THE DARK OF THE NIGHT"

1

Nine months had flashed by, and Katie was neither married nor pregnant. At the end of June she and Linda set sail from Beira on the *Windsor Castle* headed back to England. They were going the other way, round the Cape of Good Hope, stopping at all the ports on the journey. To conserve their money they shared an inner cabin with two other girls in the tourist section of the ship. Bobby had refused his five hundred pounds. Linda, always practical, had changed her money into dollars and sterling note by note through the months: any tourist or immigrant she came across was asked to exchange the notes left in their wallets for Rhodesian currency. Exchange control, strict like petrol rationing in sanctioned Rhodesia, was smoothly navigated.

"Don't look so sad, Katie. You got to be practical in this life. Love is temporary. Money a lot more permanent. He's got no future in Rhodesia. I know it, you know it and so does he. What's the point of a nice little cottage in the middle of nowhere if some black man in the future wants you out of it? It was all great fun, lots of fun, lots of nice young men, but we're twenty-four and have to be practical."

"I wish I had got pregnant."

"But you didn't thank goodness. Back in England no one has to know what we've been up to. We need husbands with prospects. You know, they say sexual attraction is largely over after a couple of years of a relationship. When that happens you want to be with a man of substance. All we've got to offer is our bodies. Neither of us has any real money. Your mother's family may have a bit but that won't help you find a husband, someone to look after you and your children for the rest of your very long life. By twenty-five, that animal power of attraction we have at the moment will begin to fade. We'll be tarting ourselves up with fancy clothes and a whole lot more make-up. I will look back on my nine months in Rhodesia as a good time in my life. But it wouldn't have lasted. You need a solid roof over your head. Not a roof threatened by someone else's politics. I got it out of some of the men in the end. Amazing what they'll talk about in bed. Four of them said there was going to be a terrorist war directed at the farmers. Two were in the Rhodesian army, two in the police. It's going to explode. We're nicely out of it with both of us carrying back five hundred pounds in sterling and US dollars."

"Poor Bobby. He did so love me."

"They all say that when they want something. Look, if he really loves you he'll follow you back to England."

"What would he do? We talked about it."

"He's living with his head in the sand like the rest of them. By the time we're old and grey there won't be white people living in Africa. And that includes South Africa. Oh, there'll be white expatriates providing the skills to run the country but there won't be many white Rhodesians. It won't even be called Rhodesia. Once you find another man in England with solid prospects Bobby will just become a memory. A pleasant memory. But a memory just the same. When the shit really hits the fan we'll be safely married in England and watch it all on television from the safety of our living room. You've got to be practical, Katie. You've got to think of yourself. And your kids when you have them. Now, did you take your pill? All we need at this stage in our lives is an unwanted pregnancy. We'll enjoy this voyage round the Cape, find ourselves a nice little flat in London, and both set about finding a man to look after us. Use what we've got while we've still got it."

"Is life really so mercenary?"

"I'm afraid it is. Now, let's you and I go up on deck and find ourselves a bar and a nice man or two to buy us a drink. I like the other two girls sharing the cabin. They're a lot older and not a chance of competition."

"Oh, Linda. You always think of yourself."

"Well, no one else does. They all tell you they do but they don't. You should think more of yourself, Katie."

"I miss him. I even miss the farm. Once you get used to living in the bush it isn't so frightening."

"You know, there was a whole month I didn't buy myself any food."

"Yes, the men were generous. They all wanted us to stay."

"Of course they did. They had to stay. Most of them don't have a way out. They have a saying for what we're doing going back to England. They call it taking the gap."

"You're as hard as nails."

"Don't be nasty to your best friend... Now, there are lots of nice men on board. I had a good look while we were boarding. And please, Katie. Stop thinking of Bobby."

"He's all on his own... Could you really marry a man you didn't love?"

"If he had enough money. Love's just a word. With a whole lot of different meanings. Mostly, when someone says they love you, they want something for themselves. Mostly they want something material. Or they feel insecure in themselves and want someone to love them. To make them feel happy. To make them feel good. It's all about the other person, never about you."

"Haven't you ever been in love, Linda?"

"I've been in lust a few times but never what people like to call 'in love'."

"Don't you love your parents?"

"I respect them. I'm eternally grateful to them for growing up in a secure and happy home. I will do anything for them. But I wouldn't call it this word 'love' people bandy about so glibly. Are we ever 'in love' with our parents? I hope not. Words, Katie. I'm no different to anyone else except I don't kid myself. Come on. Let's go see what we can find. There won't be any men with money in the third class section of the boat but we'll find ourselves some fun. Get you away from mooning over Robert Preston. Do I look all right?"

"Poor Bobby. I wonder what he's doing?"

"It doesn't matter anymore."

"No. I suppose it doesn't. I just feel so sad. I was the one that did all the taking."

"You gave him your body. Wasn't that enough? In my mother's

generation a man had to marry you before he got you into bed. My goodness. Thank heaven I was born in an age where girls have the pill and can have some fun before settling down."

"Maybe you won't settle down and have a family."

"Oh, I will if he's stinking rich."

"Young men are rarely rich."

"Then I'll find an older man. There's another saying, 'It's better to be an old man's darling than a young man's slave'. I suppose it will be up in the lifeboat if the man I fancy doesn't have a cabin to himself. When we look back on our lives in old age we want to have a smile on our face. Rhodesia had its wonderful moments but I can't wait to hit the London clubs. And there is something else we are going to do, Katie Frost, when we get back to England. You and I are going to school to learn the next stage forward from comptometer operating. We're going to learn all about computer programming and get ourselves better-paying jobs. Computers are the future of accounting. Everything will be automatic. Enter the figures once and the machine does the rest right through to producing the company's balance sheet. Women are going to be more independent of men in the future world. We both got top marks for mathematics at school. That way if I don't find a nice rich man to look after me I'll be able to look after myself. A small flat in Shepherd's Bush, nicely on the Central line to the West End of London, and our money from Rhodesia will last us a year before we need a job. If the year isn't enough we'll go to night school until we both get our diplomas in computer programming."

"Whatever would I have done without you, Linda?"

"Sometimes I have to wonder."

Happily, together, they left their inside cabin to find the action.

WHILE KATIE and Linda were settling in up at the bar overlooking the third class swimming pool, checking out the talent, Canaan Moyo, with Jacob and Joshua, was being paddled across the Zambezi River in three *mokoris*, their equipment in the bottom of the dugout canoes. The late rains in Angola had swollen the river, pushing them downstream as they fought to cross over from Mozambique into Rhodesia. The air was pleasantly cool so early in the morning, Canaan enjoying sitting still in the back of the boat. The river was beautiful. Islands thick with trees in the stream. Flotsam rushing down with the river flow. Birds calling from the trees. Animals on both banks of the great wide river.

"You're going to make it today or tomorrow," he said in Shona to the old man working the boat with his paddle to use the powerful flow of the water to get them across to the Rhodesian side of the river.

He smiled at the man, happy to be alive. It was a perfect winter's day, white patches of cloud high in the powder-blue sky. The old man he had hired, instead of hijacking his boat, smiled back at him. They were winning hearts and minds in the Zambezi Valley by paying the fishermen to take them across the river. On the bottom of the dugout, in front of his feet, lay the AK-47 rifle and his backpack full of automatic rifle ammunition. Even his feet and back were no longer hurting. Close by, Jacob and Joshua, their boats one on either side of him, waved from their comfortable seats. They were also grinning, happy for the transport after their slog through the Mozambique bush after the ZANU truck dropped them at the Zambian border to continue their journey on foot.

"Once we get out of the main stream which is pushing us downriver it will be easy. Is it important where I land you?"

"As long as it is on the other side it doesn't matter. The more varied our journeys out of the valley, the better for security. The Rhodesian army patrol the valley in Land Rovers. We can hear them coming a mile away. Would you like a cigarette?"

"You'll have to light it. Need both hands on the paddle. How many times you done the trip?"

"This is our fourth trip in almost a year."

"Are you going to start a war?"

"Eventually. Don't you want to be free of white men running your country?"

"I just fish and paddle this canoe."

Canaan lit a cigarette, half got up and leaned over, being careful not to tip the balance of the boat, and handed the man his cigarette.

"Don't fall in the water, young man. Crocodiles and hippos. My cousin's canoe was bitten in half by a hippo."

"Why did it attack your cousin?"

"The canoe got between the mother and its calf. You got to be careful. Got to know what you're doing. Thanks for the cigarette. When

I can afford to buy tobacco from the trader on the big boat I buy it loose and roll my own cigarettes in newspaper. The trader buys my dried fish."

"Lots of fish in the river?"

"Plenty. Find a calm spot away from the flow and drop in a line with lots of baited hooks, mopane worms are the best. We've tried netting the fish but it's not so good. My family live off the fish."

"How do you get back upstream?"

"Paddle. It's hard work. Everything is hard work."

"It'll be better after the revolution."

"Nothing ever changes in the Zambezi Valley."

"You'll see."

"You're young. Idealistic. I was like you long ago. All I wanted then was my own canoe and a wife to tend my vegetable garden next to the river, preferably two. How old are you, if I may ask?"

"I'm twenty-one. The leader. Joshua over there is nineteen. Jacob twenty. We're already veterans of the struggle... How many wives have you got?"

"Three. They fight with each other all the time. So do all the children. My best times are alone on the boat far away from all of them... This cigarette tastes nice. They say Rhodesian tobacco is the best in the world."

"Soon it will be Zimbabwean tobacco."

"How can the name of tobacco change?"

"When the name of the country changes, old man. When we win the second Chimurenga and throw the white men out of our country. Or kill them."

"Be careful they don't kill you... You see what I mean. We've lost the pull from the flow of the river. We'll be across in no time."

"There's no hurry. I'm enjoying the rest. We're going to camp on the bank of the river, do some fishing, and rest up for the day. After walking through the bush all day that backpack weighs a ton. So does the rifle."

"Where do you get it all from?"

"The Russians. They give it to us."

"Why do they give it to you?"

"To help our revolution."

"But why?"

"I don't know. I suppose they have some reason. It doesn't matter so long as we get the guns to win our freedom."

"A white man buys my fish. What will happen to him?"

"One of your brothers will buy your fish."

"I tried that once. He never paid me. Took the fish and said he was coming back with the money. Never saw him again. He was my third wife's cousin. Didn't speak to her for a week."

"You got your money from me before we got on the boats."

"Yes, I did. Thank you. I'm glad you didn't take my boat like someone did to my brother-in-law when all this started."

"Do the police or army ever ask if you bring us across?"

"No one has asked me about anything except my fish."

"Best you don't talk about us to your wives. Anyone telling the police we are crossing will be hunted down and killed. And that's a warning."

"Why would I say anything? I get money... Can you give me one of your packets of cigarettes?"

"When all three canoes are safely landed I'll give you a packet. What's your name?"

"My Shona name or my English name?"

"What are you known by?"

"I like to be known as James. Innocent, the name my mother gave me, sounds silly when you're sixty years old and know what I do."

"Are you really that old?... Just remember, James. Don't tell anyone what you've done today. And tell your sons in the other two canoes to keep their mouths shut. This is war. War is dangerous... Doesn't that fish eagle look so beautiful?"

"All I ever want is to be left in peace. The older you get the more important it becomes. Peace and quiet. You'll find out one day. I hope so... Can you see any crocodiles on the bank of the river? My old eyes aren't as good as they used to be. At this time of the day when the sun isn't too hot they bask on the bank. They're cold-blooded. The sun warms them up. If they see another animal like you or me they slide into the water. Always got to watch out when you're in the water."

"Can't see anything."

"Then jump in the water and grab the front of the canoe."

With the front of the three canoes stuck in the mud under the riverbank the three men unloaded their equipment. Canaan gave the old man a packet of twenty First Lord cigarettes and waved him goodbye. The three friends stood on the high bank of the river and watched the canoes paddle back up the river close to the bank where the water flowed gently. When the canoes were out of sight behind the trees Canaan made camp.

"You think it's all right to rest up?" asked Jacob.

"We'll hear them. The white man never walks. I'm going fishing. Joshua, you're the best climber. Shin up that mopane tree and look for some worms among the leaves. The fisherman said mopane worms are the best bait."

"Can I fish?"

"We're all going to fish, Joshua. How are your feet?"

"They're terrible."

The hand lines, unlike the fisherman's, only had one hook. In the survival kit with the fishing lines were wires made into nooses for snaring small animals. With the sound of a gunshot travelling so far in the bush, none of the guns were loaded in case one of them became over-excited and shot at a buck. A fish eagle, sitting high up in the tree looking for its own food, took no notice of Canaan. The riverine trees rose a hundred feet above the river, their roots in the water. Everything was peaceful. Joshua, as excited as a small boy, came back with a handful of the furry mopane worms that fed off the leaves of the mopane trees. They baited their hooks, looked again for any signs of lurking crocodiles, and threw their lines far out into the river. Where they sat was a small bay, thick with weeds, close to the shore. The tall trees gave them shade. Canaan pulled his bush hat over his face and closed his eyes. There was birdsong all round him, high up from the trees. Gently, full of content, Canaan dropped off to sleep and the world of dreams that made him happy. For an hour, the lines in the water producing nothing, he moved in and out of a drowsy sleep, satisfied with his day of peace, his back no longer aching from the weight of his pack. Instead of holding the line in his hand he had taken off his boots, removed his socks, and looped the line round his big toe. Once, the fish eagle woke him, swooping down on the surface of the river, its claws lowered and trawling the water for fish. Like the three men, the bird found nothing, circled the river, and flew back to its perch. Canaan was fast asleep when a fish took his bait, the nylon line running out and scorching his big toe. Awake, concentrating and hungry, Canaan played his fish, making sure whatever it was had swallowed the hook. The fish was heavy, pulling hard in the water. Canaan pulled it in hand over fist, yard by yard, Jacob and Joshua watching. When Canaan brought his fish into the reeds they could see what he had caught.

"Get in the water, both of you, and grab the bastard with your hands."

"I'm frightened of crocodiles."

"Get in the bloody water, Joshua."

"What is it?"

"It's a vundu. All of thirty pounds by the look of him. Give us enough food until we get to Chiweshi."

Laughing, Canaan holding the fish on the line, Jacob and Joshua ran into the water with sticks in their hands and grabbed at the fish.

"Get it by the gills. Hit it with the bloody sticks, you idiots... That's better. Now pull it out of the water... Just look at him. That's some fish. Take it up to the top of the bank. We'll start a fire. What a day. Rest and food. What more can a man want?"

"A nice young girl."

"You'll have to wait for that till we get to Chiweshe. We'll skewer the fish and cook it whole over the fire. What we don't eat we'll carry on top of the ammunition in the packs. That fish has made my trip."

Canaan gutted the big fish, went back to the river and washed it in the water, the fish eagle watching him. Joshua and Jacob were collecting dry wood from under the trees. When Canaan came up the bank he could smell woodsmoke from the new fire. Jacob had cut and trimmed a long, thin bow with his hunting knife. Other pieces of wood had been fashioned into cradles on either side of the fire. The smoke had driven the fish eagle from its perch and it flew high up into the powder-blue sky catching a lift from the thermals, higher and higher, the great wings spread, Canaan watching him rise.

"When he's high and comfortable he'll call to his mate... There he goes. What an evocative sound. The cry of the fish eagle is the most beautiful sound I ever heard. It calls to your soul."

"You want to skewer the fish or shall I do it, Canaan?"

"You know how to cook a fish?"

Two big logs, that had fallen with age from the boughs of the trees, were placed around the fire. The three men sat down, cigarettes lit, a pan of river water over the fire, the ground coffee ready to throw in the boiling water, the fish beginning to slowly cook high up over the fire. Canaan looked up. The fish eagle, easy on the thermals, was still calling for its mate. He took a drag of his cigarette down deep into his lungs. In the shade of the trees the flowing river looked even more beautiful. Then he saw him. On an island some hundred yards away in the stream. The crocodile, big eyes on the middle of its head, was watching him, the evil of the crocodile contrasting with the eagle's love of flying high in the sky. The crocodile's mouth was half open, showing the size of its teeth.

"Why did you join the liberation army, Canaan?"

"Why did you, Joshua?"

"Couldn't get a job. I'd done some schooling. The farm my dad worked at had a farm school. Learnt to read and write. There was a football team. The farmer had made a pitch between the huts and the classrooms of the school. Having learnt a little, I didn't want to spend the rest of my life reaping the white man's tobacco, living in the compound. When a recruiter for ZANLA came by he offered me a job in the army. Said one day I'd own a piece of the boss's farm."

"Do you know how to farm?"

"As long as you have a tractor to plough the soil it's easy. Why did you join, Canaan?"

"I believe in our liberation. That no man should be owned by a foreigner. Those farms are no different to American slavery. Sure, you get paid but how much? You get given basic food stuffs. The Americans in the South did the same for the slaves. You worked all day and lived in a compound... I want to be somebody."

"What are you going to do when we win?"

"Get a better education... You'd better turn the fish... And you, Jacob?"

"Any job would have done. I like being with people. This is all right. Today is good... Why does that crocodile keep watching me?"

"He's hungry. Like us."

"Are we going to win the war?"

"Of course we are. There's only a few whites left in Africa."

"What about the Boers?"

"They'll be swamped like the rest of them. Most of the whites have left Kenya. They're all getting out of Zambia. We saw what happened once Kaunda nationalised the copper mines. That was a clever move. All those mines they built up over the years now belong to the people. How it should be. The means of production, according to the Russians, should be in the hands of the people. Not the capitalists."

"How do you know all this?"

"They sent me to Russia on a course."

"All these months together and I didn't know."

"There are lots of things you don't know about other people. The Russians want the whole world to be communist."

"Why?"

"It's the better way to live, I suppose... Keep turning that fish."

"Can I have another of your cigarettes?... What did they teach you on the course?"

"To be a good communist."

"What's a good communist?"

"Doing what you're told, I suppose. It was cold in Russia. I've never been so cold in my life. The snow was six feet deep in the drifts. You ever seen snow, Joshua?"

"In pictures. I prefer being warm. I hope they don't send me to Russia."

"I'd been to secondary school."

"Can I have a cigarette?"

"Not now. I've one pack left. Gave one to the fisherman."

"Why'd you do that? They were our cigarettes."

"They told us to make friends with the locals."

"Doesn't mean you have to pass out our cigarettes... The water's boiling. Give me the coffee. Can we really stay here for the rest of the day?"

"That's the idea. On the seventh day 'thou shalt rest'. That also applies to soldiers."

BY THE NEXT morning when they continued their journey they had eaten all of the fish. In the night, a wire set up in the long grass on a path made by wild animals had hooked a warthog. Canaan, too content with his day, had listened to the animal dying. The small, half-grown pig had taken most of the night to die. Now gutted, hung by its four legs, it was to be carried in turn by the three of them. The long walk to the Zambezi escarpment began. Away from the river the trees were scattered and small. The grass, dry and brown, came up to their waists. They were all happy and smiling, the rifles and packs of ammunition not yet a burden. There was no sign of the fish eagle.

At noon, when the sun was right overhead, the elephant came from nowhere. They were passing through mopane trees, the three men's heads down, and had not seen the great animal. To their right, on the other side of the trumpeting elephant, its trunk high over its head, its tusks at the ready as it charged Joshua, was an elephant calf half hidden in the long grass. The elephant picked up Joshua with its trunk and threw him with a violent jerk back over its head. The AK-47 rifle flew off into the bush as Joshua hit the ground like a broken doll. Terrified, Canaan and Jacob dropped their rifles and ran away. Canaan ran for a mopane tree and shinned up the trunk. When he looked back the female elephant, her calf at her feet, was walking away. He could not see what had happened to Joshua. Jacob was still running back towards the river. His heart beating, his stomach sick, Canaan climbed down the tree.

When he found Joshua his friend looked dead, his body twisted by the whip force of the elephant's trunk. The head of his friend was facing the ground along with his bottom, everything out of line, the pack of ammunition ripped from his pack. Canaan began to cry. Then he got up and walked slowly back to the river to look for Jacob. He had picked up Joshua's rifle and the pack of ammunition, whose strap was broken. The carcase of the warthog had been thrown to the ground.

"He's dead, Jacob."

"Of course he's dead. He was dead before he hit the ground. That elephant flipped him with all its strength."

"You're going the wrong way. We're not going back to Zambia."

"Do we have to go on?"

"Of course we do. One of us will carry his gun, the other his pack."

"Are we going to bury him?"

"Best we leave him to the wild animals. We don't have spades. How can we dig him a grave? In the dry season the ground is as hard as nails."

"How did it happen?"

"He got between a mother and her calf."

"We're both going to die."

"We're not going to die, Jacob. It's just got a bit harder. Nothing worth doing in life is ever easy."

"I want to sit down."

"Get up! Now. Here, take Joshua's pack."

"He was only nineteen years old."

"We'd better find the warthog. We can carry it on a pole hung between us. Don't argue with me. I also lost a friend."

"Did you see he was really dead?"

"He was twisted right round, his bum on the ground along with his face, half his guts spilled out."

The two men began to walk away from the river, the tears making furrows in the dust down Jacob's black face. Neither of them spoke. At the body, Jacob knelt down and felt Joshua's neck. Canaan picked up the carcase of the warthog and pushed a stick through the sinews at the back of its legs, the back and forefeet crossed over. With the extra weight straining their backs they walked on, plodding, one foot in front of the other. When the sun went down they stopped in a clump of mopane trees, both of them exhausted. Canaan made the fire and skinned the warthog. Jacob looked terrible. Through the trees a stream on its way to the big river gave them water to drink. The light went quickly, the fire still burning, the pig cooking, both men flat on their backs round the fire. Canaan, too tired to care, had broken the rule of not making a fire at night. They ate well, feeling better. When the fire burned down to a red glow they both fell asleep, the half-eaten carcase of the warthog still on the improvised spit over the dead embers. Canaan slept right through the night and was woken by birdsong in the morning. During the night, wild animals had gone off with the carcase. Jacob was still asleep.

"Some bugger ate our breakfast during the night. Come on. Up you get."

"I can't face that climb up the escarpment."

"Of course you can. You're tough, Jacob. One of the toughest men I've known."

"Am I really?... Didn't hear a thing during the night."

"Neither did I."

"What food have we left?"

"With all that fish and pig inside us we can get to the Chiweshe reserve and Comrade Tangwena and all those lovely young girls without eating... Best foot forward, Jacob my friend."

"We three were together so long."

Canaan looked back over his shoulder, back towards the Zambezi River. The vultures were circling. Going round and round, getting lower and lower.

Before the sun was high they reached the path that wound up the escarpment to the highveld and the white man's farming block the settlers had called Centenary. There were tracks of a vehicle on the path, light dust on the tyre tracks from the wind that was blowing the mist from the falling stream over to their left, the stream two thousand feet above them dropping into the void.

"Yesterday. Or the day before. We missed them. If that elephant hadn't attacked Joshua we might have walked right into them."

Looking back, there was no sign of the circling birds. The vultures had landed to tear the flesh from Canaan's friend. He walked on, knowing that if he stopped he wouldn't make the climb. Head down, his turn to carry two rifles, he forced himself up the winding slope, the sound of Jacob's boots on the hard ground behind him, one foot placed painfully in front of the other, his mind thankfully numb.

His mind in neutral, Jacob was first to hear the truck. It was down behind them, far off in the valley. Looking back through his binoculars, Canaan could see the dust trail behind the vehicle coming their way. The vehicle was travelling fast along the one road that led through the Zambezi Valley to the track they were climbing, the only way up out of the valley. Wearily, Canaan led Jacob off the road to an outcrop of rocks. There were small trees growing out of the crevices in the rocks. Looking back down the rocky path, blasted years before by a road builder who had wound the easiest path up the face of the escarpment, Canaan could see no spoor left by their boots. By the time the police Land Rover ground its way past where they were hiding among the rocks, both men's hearts beating, they were well off the track. They could hear the white men in the truck talking in English. One of the policemen laughed. They lay where they were for an hour after the truck had gone past. There was still enough daylight to reach the top. Picking up their burdens they plodded on, following the fresh spoor of the white man's truck to the top of the road. At the top the small river fell into the vacuum over the escarpment. Scooping water into the palms of their hands, they drank. They smiled at each other when they sat back. Far away behind the Zambezi River the sun was setting, the sky blood-red, the soft belly of the few fluffy clouds turning pink. Birds were singing. A breeze brushed them from the highveld. A buck barked from down in the valley. Within minutes they were both fast asleep.

In the morning when they woke they were hungry. Canaan went to the stream and pulled out a handful of small snails. Jacob came to help. With the cooking pan Canaan carried tied to his pack now full of snails and covered in water, they made a fire. The water had gouged a dip in the bedrock of the small river, the surface of the rock smoothed out over the ages. With the pot of snails on the fire, both men took off their clothes and got into the river. Lying down on their backs facing each other with their heads out of the water at either end of the dip, they were immersed up to their bellies. The water flowed over and round their bodies. For another fifty yards the river flowed on before falling over the cliff into the emptiness. They lay paddling their hands in a state of exquisite pleasure, the dirt and the horror of the previous day washing away. Above them the early morning sun dappled the rocks through the leaves of the msasa trees, the red-brown leaves rich above them. The water, clean, sweet and cool, flowed and flowed over their naked bodies. It was paradise on earth.

After half an hour in the water, a lizard came out of a crevice to look at them, flicking its tongue. Further upstream the frogs were croaking. Remembering the snails, lost in his reverie, Canaan climbed out of the water. The pot of snails had stopped bubbling, the fire underneath having burned down. With a quick movement Canaan flicked a snail out of the pot with his fingers onto the rocks where they had built the fire in a crevice. He was still naked, his body cool, the breeze drying the water on his skin. Picking up a small rock he cracked open the snail and pulled out the cooked flesh, held up his head and popped the food into his mouth.

"What's it taste like, Canaan?"

"Needs just a touch of salt... You getting out of the water?"

"In a moment."

In all this pain they were alive. Swimming in the river. Eating snails.

"You think they'll come back again?"

"Not likely... We'll walk at night until we hand in the guns and ammunition."

"This water has brought me alive. Yesterday, I wanted to run away. I can't stop thinking of Joshua."

"That's the luck of the draw. The chance of life."

"He'll be a hero of the struggle."

"Will he? When this is all over no one else will remember him."

"Of course they will. They told us heroes are always remembered."

"Out of the water, Jacob, and come and eat your snails... I can still smell the oil from that police Land Rover. It makes me nervous. Why can't people stay in their own countries? Why did they have to come here?"

"You ever think who they are?"

"They're greedy bastards who stole our land and we're going to take it back again."

"I can stay all day lying in this water. Why don't you bring me some of those snails? Better still, bring the pot and get back in the water... And bring the salt... You're wrong, you know. Joshua will still be a hero long after we are old men. Long after we are dead. His life will have been worth something."

"I hope so. He was a good man. He was a friend."

"Am I a friend, Canaan?"

"Of course you are... Here. Have a snail. I was reading somewhere in school that in France snails are a highly prized delicacy."

"Where's France?"

"Somewhere in Europe... You know they had a war with each other in Europe not so long ago. My teacher told me. My secondary school teacher was a Catholic missionary."

"Where was he from?"

"He was from England."

"So if he hadn't come out from England you wouldn't have got educated?"

"I suppose so. Never thought of it that way."

"Would you kill him?"

"Of course not... What do you think?"

"They're delicious. Pass the salt. With this twig I can hoick them out without breaking the shells. You know what I hated most growing up in the compound? When we walked to another farm or went to Bob Hallyday's store, it was the dust from the white man's car. We choked in his dust, his life so damned easy, our lives so difficult."

"What did you buy?"

"Sweets. A small packet of red suckers. What a luxury."

"Were you ever hungry?"

"I don't think so. Some of the kids went hungry. They had big pot bellies. Once a month the gang was paid by the boss. A ticket system. Thirty days' work on the ticket and you got paid. My dad gave the money to my mother. She bought food from the store. She said it was better in the old days when the boss handed out rations. Maize meal. Sugar. Dried beans. Salt. Tea. Once a week they got a ration of boys' meat as they called it. All of us blacks were boys, however old we were. The meat was the cut of the cow the white man didn't like to eat. A lot of fat and bones. Mum said when she cooked it slowly over the fire in the big round cooking pot with the cast iron lid it was delicious. She threw in vegetables she grew next to the river. The vegetables were easy to grow close to the water. Mum watered them from a bucket. The farmer gave her fertiliser for the vegetables. I suppose it wasn't so bad. It was just that dust all over me I hated. The white man's arrogance. Bet they didn't even notice us on the side of the road."

"Growing up on a farm sounds good. Better than the Harare black location. I was just lucky getting to the Catholic mission school. My father had become a Catholic when he married my mother. My mother had grown up on the mission... You want some more snails?"

"Pass the pot. Can we stay all day in the water?"

"I don't see why not. I've hidden the guns and ammunition. If they were to find us we'd just be a couple of blacks having a swim."

"Wouldn't they ask how we got here?"

"You're right. If we hear a truck we'll make another run for it. Tell me more about how you grew up, Jacob. I like listening to other people's stories... Just look at that cloud. One white cloud in the blue of the sky. Not even moving. You wonder how it got there."

"What did your father do?"

"He drove a delivery motorcycle for a company in Salisbury. Delivering their mail to the different insurance companies. They called him Speedy. A motorbike with a big metal box on the back. Mother worked as a maid for a family in the Avenues. There were buses from the township. Took her three hours every day to get to work and back. With two salaries we did all right. Still are, I suppose."

"Do they know you joined the struggle?"

"Better they don't."

"Have you been home?"

"Not for a while."

"Neither have I."

"Where was the farm?"

"Macheke. Near Marandellas. The owner's daughter became a communist and went to live in England. Can you believe it? She's part of the struggle. Don't remember her. She was gone when I was very young."

"What was the area like?"

"Much the same as we'll walk through tonight. Four thousand-acre farms with tobacco barns and sheds. Some of the whites built fancy houses. Not all of them. They all had swimming pools."

"Were they as nice as this?"

"Never got into one. Two of my friends did. Their mother was nanny to the white kids on the next farm. They all swam together until my friends grew up. Then the friendships broke up... Why are we a different colour?"

"Must be the sun. There's no sun in England. They burn in the sun. We don't. Over the centuries we got black and they got white. My teacher said we all come from the same origin. That we all came out of Africa. Don't believe him. We're so different. Why we want it all back for ourselves."

Like the cloud in the sky the day stood motionless. When the sun dipped they put on their clothes, their feet hurting again inside their boots. They began to walk, trying not to think, one foot placed in front of the other. Later, far away, they could hear the noise of a white man's generator. As they walked up the slope of the road they could see the lights of the farm. They could hear music.

"It's a gramophone. Sound travels so far in the still of the night. I recognise the music. My old teacher played it in his room. Father Gregory. It's Beethoven. One of Beethoven's symphonies."

"What's a symphony?... Can we stop and listen to the music?"

"Must keep on. Have to be in the reserve and off the white man's land before the sun gets up. Some of the farmers drive at first light into town to do their shopping."

"What's a symphony?"

"That sound far over there."

"How do they make it?"

"I have no idea."

"There aren't any drums. No one is singing. Are you sure that is music, Canaan?"

"Listen. Just listen. I came to like Father Gregory's music. He played the piano."

"You learnt so much on that mission. Wish I'd been to secondary school. There's so much I don't know."

They plodded on, the pain from the weight of the rifles and ammunition increasing, the snails long eaten, the bush quiet but for the music growing nearer as they walked. The generator and lights had gone out but the music was still playing.

"The music is a lot closer than where we saw the lights."

"It's still some way away. It's strangely so beautiful. Like all the birds singing the same song with different voices. The small birds. The big birds. I was listening to them lying in the water."

"I hear the birds calling from your symphony, Canaan... Can we stop for a while?"

"Once you stop I'll never get you going again. We can't be on their road in daylight. If we can hear that music so plainly they must be all around us. The stars give so little light down on the ground."

"They're so heavenly. The stars, I mean. Where do they come from? Why do they shine in the night but we can't see them in the day? So many of them. Some are brighter than others. Why, Canaan?"

"I didn't learn everything from Father Gregory."

"Did he have a wife?"

"They don't have wives in the mission."

"Then how do they have children?"

"They're God's children."

"If they're God's children how were they born?"

"Stop asking questions. I don't know."

"Maybe he was too old to have a wife."

"He never had a wife. None of them did. And the nuns never had husbands."

"Oh, I get it. One big happy family... Did the nuns have kids?"

"No, Jacob."

"The music has stopped. I liked that music. It was beautiful. Maybe whoever was playing it has gone to bed... You want to swap Joshua's pack for his rifle? I can't believe he's dead... Oh, good, the music has started again. He hasn't gone to bed. If I only think of the music my back and feet don't hurt so much. I can't see any light. Not even the light of a fire... How long will it be before the sun comes up?"

"Four or five hours. I've lost track of time, Jacob."

"What's the point of life if you don't have children? Who's going to look after you when you get old? When I've got my money from the liberation army I'm going to find myself some land, get myself three wives and have twenty children. Then I'll be rich. I'll be richer than all of them. And the wives will do all the work. Can you imagine it? A thatched hut next to a river. A cooking pot over a fire, the pot tended by wife number one, the food just as I like it. Sitting under the shade of the thatched overhang of my hut. Wife number two bringing me a bowl of home-brewed beer. The fields of maize in the distance nicely tended, not a weed in the lands. A few cows tended by one of my kids. Wife number three, the really young one, smiling at me from the door of her hut. Lots of kids running around. Now that's paradise. What I'm going to have, Canaan, when we win our war of liberation. I want to live the old way. In comfort. None of this township living for me. I want to hear the birds in the morning. Listen to my symphony... What a shame. The music has stopped again. He must be over there somewhere. In the dell. There's probably a river down there in the dell."

"He's playing records. Probably turning over the record... There he goes. I was right. He just turned over the record."

"How nice of him... What do you want to do, Canaan, when all this is over?"

"I want to be a politician. Join the party. The money and the power, which both go together according to Father Gregory, are all in the Zimbabwe African National Union and people like Sithole, Mugabe and Josiah Makoni. I want to be in the party where everything will be controlled, the people, the economy, the money."

"You don't think Nkomo of the Zimbabwe African Peoples Union will be our leader?"

"He's a Matabele. A Zulu. We're both Shona. Sithole and Mugabe are Shona. We Shona never again want to be ruled by the Matabele."

"But they are fighting with us against the whites."

"When we win the struggle we'll kill any Zulus who don't want to be ruled by the Shona."

"I don't understand it."

"You don't have to, Jacob. Just do your job and imagine that pretty hut on the banks of your river. You'll have what you want. So will I. I'll have the patronage of the party. A nice house in the suburbs of Salisbury. A swimming pool. Television. A nice new car. A wife dressed to kill. Trips overseas. The whole world at my feet. I'll have everything money can buy."

"Why's he playing music in the dead of the night?"

"Maybe he's lonely. Far from home. Doesn't have a wife. Quite a few of their men don't have wives. There's a shortage of their women in Rhodesia."

"Maybe they'll want some of ours."

"Don't be silly. They never do that. They think they're far too superior to take one of our girls as a wife. That's the trouble with the white settlers. They keep to themselves. Think they're above everybody. Father Gregory said everyone looks the same under a bus."

"You never hear of a Shona marrying a Matabele. Or a Bemba. We all keep to ourselves. No, my three wives will all be Shona."

Two owls began calling to each other, calling and answering, their calls echoing through the sound of the plaintive music. Canaan heard a scuffle in the bush. With his mind falling back into neutral he plodded on down the white man's road. The music finally stopped. One foot in front of the other. Plodding on in the dark of the night. One thought in his mind. Repeating itself. Time after time. Making him go on. Making the pain in his feet, the pain in his back, the hunger in his belly all worthwhile. One day, he repeated and repeated to himself, he was going to be rich.

They reached the Chiweshe reserve in the first blush of morning, the landscape changing the moment they crossed from the white man's farming block of Centenary into the tribal trust land of the native reserve. On one side of the fence erected by the white farmer the land was lush with grass. The other side, where too many goats had grazed the earth, was barren, even the roots of the grass ripped out by the grazing goats. In the reserve anyone who could afford it could have his cows and goats and graze them wherever he wanted.

"Just look at it. All that land of the white bloody farmer with plenty of grazing and our side not a blade of grass. Once we win the war that fence and all the other fences come down. All they farm is a few patches of tobacco. From here, apart from the fence, you can't see a sign of them. Our struggle is going to be worth it. Joshua won't have died for nothing. These people in the reserve will have plenty of grazing for their animals."

"My feet are bleeding."

"So are mine, Jacob. Come on. Let's give the guns and ammunition to Comrade Tangwena to hide and then we can both relax."

"I just want to sit down. To stop moving. I'm hungry, Canaan. All my strength has gone."

The birds began singing in unison, greeting the day. The sun rose up behind the distant range of mountains, turning it purple. People came out into the fields, all of them women and children, all of the women with babies strapped by lengths of dirty cloth to their backs. All the young children had extended bellies, the product of malnutrition. The one nearest to Canaan was picking his nose, flies in the corners of his big brown eyes. Canaan smiled at him. The boy, three or four years old by the look of him, smiled shyly back. All the women were carrying hoes. They looked as tired as Canaan felt and the day had only just started. The women tried not to look at the two men walking past their fields with guns, as if they hadn't seen them. The fields were fenced with thorn bushes to keep out the roaming cattle and goats. Canaan, looking over the short shrubs, could see nothing growing in the fields.

"They must be preparing the lands for the rainy season," he said to Jacob.

Neither of them called to the women. Later, if anyone asked, they were ghosts. Tangwena, when they found him, was sitting outside his hut eating his breakfast, a young girl tending his needs.

"What happened to Joshua, Canaan? Did you come under attack?" The man looked frightened.

"An elephant down in the valley. We got between the mother and her calf."

"Thank goodness."

"The elephant picked him up by the trunk. By the time Joshua hit the ground his body was twisted right around, his stomach split open. We had to leave him for the vultures."

"But you brought his gun and his pack. Good man. Let's get that stuff out of the way. The police check up on us without any warning. Inspector Barry. I hate the arrogant bastard. He's the member-in-charge for Centenary. When he visits he always looks as if there's a bad smell right under his nose. All his life in Africa and he still won't speak Shona. First he tries English and if that doesn't work he speaks Fanagalo, the arrogant bastards. How they talk to the cook boy in pidgin."

"Can I have some food?"

"When we've hidden the military equipment, Jacob."

"Where do you hide it?"

"That's none of your business."

"My feet are bleeding."

"Then wash them in the river... Grace, go and tell my sons to come here."

"Can I put these packs here on the ground?"

"Of course you can. They're not your responsibility anymore, Jacob. So, did you have a good trip?"

Grace smiled at Canaan. A shy, hooded smile, her big brown eyes making the weight of the guns go away. She was young, smooth-skinned and exquisitely beautiful. Canaan watched her go off to find Tangwena's sons, once looking back at him over her shoulder. For a moment, Canaan had wanted to throttle Tangwena for so flippantly ignoring the death of Joshua.

The AK-47 rifles, one from each shoulder, were quickly taken away when Grace came back with two young men, neither of them greeting Jacob or Canaan. Once the guns and backpacks full of ammunition were taken Canaan and Jacob were no longer important. Tangwena, a cynical smile on his face, was looking at Canaan. He still hadn't got up from the ground where he was eating his breakfast seated on an old dusty cushion.

"Follow Grace, Canaan. She'll look after you."

"Don't we get any thanks?"

"Grace and her friends will thank you. The struggle's as difficult for all of us. I have to put up with Inspector Barry. And yes, I am sorry about Joshua. In wars there are always casualties. Well done, Canaan. We'll drink some beer together before you start the walk back to Zambia. Run along. She's waiting for you. Now let me get back to my breakfast."

Wondering whether Tangwena gave a shit about anyone other than himself, Canaan followed Grace who was walking lithely towards the rest of the rondavel huts in the small village, her firm, round bottom moving seductively against the soft material of her dress.

2

While Canaan was walking away from Comrade Tangwena to begin his life-changing love affair with Grace, Bobby Preston, unaware that the music from his gramophone had been heard in the night, tired from so little sleep, was going through the motions, preparing himself for another day of loneliness. By now she would be on the boat sailing away from him, taking with her every one of his dreams. Apathetic, sad with melancholy, he walked to the site of his house, the open foundations no longer of interest.

"What's the bloody point, old boy?" he asked himself. "To hell with it... Welcome! I'm going into town."

"When you coming back, boss?"

"When I feel like it. Nothing much to do on the farm at this time of the year. I was going to build the house. I'll call you in the compound when I get back. Sekuru and the gang are stumping. He knows what to do."

"You want breakfast?"

"Not today."

PASSING his four new tobacco curing barns without bothering to look at them, Bobby drove down the driveway of Hopewell Estate, the new jacaranda saplings he had planted at the end of the rains on either side, and turned onto the road that would take him into Salisbury, his overnight bag packed next to him, the sun in his face, the purple mountains behind the Chiweshe reserve rising in the distance. She had gone, never to come back again. Driving fast, Bobby looked neither to left or right of him, his mind far away, the trail of dust streaming out behind, the corrugations in the road rattling the truck, shaking his body, his hands firm on the wheel.

"Now what the hell do I do for the rest of my life? No wife. No kids. Just a bloody big farm in the middle of nowhere... She wouldn't look at me with no money or prospects in England. Anyway, she was probably right. This whole country is going to blow up one of these days. Even if I wanted, I couldn't get the money from last year's crop out of the country. Exchange control is as tight as a fish's arse. The economy with sanctions is going down the drain and no one wants to buy a tobacco farm. She was right to bugger off but it still doesn't help me. Anyway, no one knows what's really going to happen in life... And stop talking to yourself... Shit! Who let that bloody cow on the road? Just missed the bastard. At this rate if I don't hit a cow, I'll be at Meikles for opening time. There are always a few lonely buggers looking for a drinking companion. Better get used to it. So far as women are concerned, Bobby Preston, you are going to spend the rest of your life on your own. So goodbye, Katie. Hello the bottle, your new best friend. You're twenty-five years old and your life has just finished. Nothing matters anymore. You, the farm or what happens to Rhodesia. She said she loved you and buggered off. So what's the bloody point, you silly old shit? And stop talking to yourself if you don't want to end up in the loony bin."

Raging at himself as much as Katie, Bobby hurtled on down the road, the idea of temporary friends in a pub ever more appealing. He had filled up the truck with petrol from the tank on the farm and had money from the safe in his pocket. If the gang didn't stump out all the roots of the trees the plough would get broken and he just didn't care.

When Bobby reached Meikles Hotel and booked into a room it was half past ten in the morning. The lounge of the old hotel was half full of people drinking their morning tea. Bobby looked around to see if he knew anyone, couldn't see a soul, and walked back past reception to the bar that only served men. The black barman was cleaning the top of the bar, polishing the old, booze-soaked wood with a cloth, the wood of the bar top black from age.

"Good morning. Make mine a cold Castle. What's your name? Aren't you new?"

"Julius, boss."

"Hello, Julius. Does the bar fill up?"

The young man gave him a nervous smile, not sure what to say, bent down under the bar and came up with a frosty bottle of Castle lager, removed the cap and placed the bottle next to a glass in front of Bobby on the bar. Bobby poured some of the beer into his glass and left the rest to stay cold in the bottle. Starting so early on an empty stomach, Bobby sipped at the icy cold beer, thought to himself 'what the hell', finished what was in the glass, emptied the rest of the bottle and drank down his beer. Only then did he light his first cigarette. The new barman had gone to the end of the bar, next to the metal wash basin where he was polishing glasses before putting them back on the shelf. Bobby asked for another beer and was given it, Julius marking the price of the beer on a tab.

"Have you seen old Koos Hendriks in the bar lately? He's a prospector."

"No, boss. Don't know him."

"Where did you learn your English?"

"Mission school."

"They say that's the best place to learn."

Again the man went to the end of the bar to polish glasses, leaving Bobby at the bar on his own.

"You got the place to yourself, young man. Always prefer the men's bar. Women make me behave myself. My name is Colonel Sanderson. Retired. Pension goes further in Rhodesia. The weather's better. Spent most of my years in India."

When Bobby turned round an elderly man was standing next to him.

"Bobby Preston... My father was in the army."

"Was he a commissioned officer?"

"Oh, yes. Retired a brigadier."

"Has he got any money?"

"My mother has a little."

"Lucky chap. Retiring from the British Army on the pay of a half colonel doesn't give a chap much to live on. I have a room in a boarding house in the Avenues. Can walk to the bar. Bit early, I suppose. Not much else to do... So what do you do, young man?... Julius, be a good fellow and give me a double whisky. Usual brand... Hasn't been working here long but Julius has a good memory for what a chap drinks... Have you got a job, Preston? Thought of getting myself a job but no one wants to employ an old codger. Lucky I never married. Only have to look after myself."

"I'm a tobacco farmer."

"You're someone's assistant?"

"No. I have my own farm."

"Goodness. So why are you here?"

"My fiancée left me to go back to England. Says Rhodesia is going to collapse now Smith and the government are arguing with England."

"Had the same thing about your age. Her name was Barbara. Had come out to India with the 'fishing fleet', looking for a husband. Found me and then didn't like Colonial India. Said she felt sorry for the Indians. Never heard a word from her ever again. Cheers, old boy. How many you had?"

"This is my second."

"To better days."

"To better days... You never heard from her again?"

"Not a word... When did she go?"

"Katie left from Beira on the *Windsor Castle* yesterday. Why I drove into town. To drown my sorrows... Can I buy you another whisky?"

"I don't mind if I do. I miss the old life in India. Why I came to Rhodesia. The last colony, long may it last. Good old Smithy."

"You think he did the right thing declaring UDI?"

"Probably not. Give us a few more good years. All you can hope for at my time of life... What was her name again?"

"Her name was Katie."

"Then we'll drink to Katie and Barbara. There was one good thing that came out of Barbara going home. She was twenty-three. I can still see her as clearly as when she came off the boat. Young. Beautiful. Happy... She'll never grow old for me."

"How old is she now?"

"Sixty, I suppose. If she's still alive... To Katie and Barbara. Oh,

Freddie. There you are. This young man has bought me a drink. What did you say your name was?"

"Bobby Preston."

"Well, there you are, Freddie. Bobby and I have something in common. We've both been jilted in our lives. Freddie here is my regular drinking companion. We both have just enough pension money to drink. Why we drink in the men's bar which is cheap, don't we, Freddie? And you know what they say about drinking companions, young man? The worst drinking companion is one with a memory. When we get tight we forget what we said... Julius... Bring Colonel Makepeace his usual. Freddie and I were in India together. Has a brother who farms in Macheke. How we got to this country. Until all this latest nonsense, no one in England knew much about Rhodesia."

"Why don't you live on the farm?"

"Can't be a burden on others, young man. Anyway, living on a farm would be boring. Don't meet new people. Cheers, young man. To Katie and Barbara. Long may they live in our memories. Young, beautiful and happy."

Leaving the two men to reminisce, Bobby kept out of the conversation, each of them ordering drinks for each other, Bobby now forgotten. Julius sat on a stool next to the wash basin, getting up when he was called to replenish their drinks. The black man had a faraway look. The two old men, happy to be with each other, were enjoying themselves, so much of their lives lived in common. The bar filled up nearer lunchtime leaving Bobby, surrounded by people, even more on his own.

"Nice meeting you, Colonel Sanderson. I'll be off."

"Jolly good show."

From the men's bar Bobby walked to the ladies' bar where the drinks were more expensive. He still wasn't hungry. He found a stool right in the corner and waited to order his drink. He was still sober. Horribly sober, thinking of Katie on board the ship. By now, surrounded by men, Katie would have forgotten him.

"What you want, boss?"

"Make mine a brandy. Double. Ice. I'll add the water."

All round him, at the bar, at the small tables, people looked happy. There was a general hum of light conversation. People came and went. A group at the table in front of Bobby were laughing, enjoying each other's company, three men and two girls not much older than Bobby. All the men's attention was directed at the girls. Bobby ate a bowl of salted peanuts, not thinking of anything. The barman filled up the bowl of peanuts. A group Bobby recognised from the Centenary West club came into the room looking for a table. Mrs Wells, who Bobby had last seen making a play for Hammond Taylor, waved at him. Stanley Wells, her much older husband, did not look at Bobby. Idly, Bobby wondered if Hammond was having an affair with Elizabeth Wells. Glad it wasn't his problem, he turned back to his drink. The sudden hand on his shoulder made him look round expecting to see Mr or Mrs Wells.

"Oh, it's you."

Standing behind Bobby, smiling at him, was Vince Ranger.

"That's a nice way to greet a friend. Saw your truck in the parking lot. Got some time off from Jeremy Crookshank. Not much happens on an established farm at this time of year. Isn't that Elizabeth Wells over there?"

"How are you, Vince?"

"More important, how are you? They sailed yesterday."

"Why I came into town. Came in for a bender."

"How's the bending going?"

"Not so good. Started drinking at eleven in the men's bar. Now I'm on the brandy. Still sober as a judge."

"I get drunk when I'm happy. Much better. We're putting in two hundred acres of Virginia this year. Fifty acres of Burley. Three hundred acres of maize. Jeremy says he needs the money to educate his children. His boys have grown up so fast. That Linda Gaskell was something. Trouble was she flitted from man to man. Oh, well. It was fun whilst it lasted. What would a girl who looked like that want with a farm manager anyway? Katie was different... I'm sorry, Bobby. Are you having lunch?"

"Have a peanut. The thought of sitting in the dining room all on my own was too appalling. Everything in Salisbury reminds me of Katie."

"So she's definitely not coming back to Rhodesia?"

"Not a chance... I hate politics. It's difficult enough building up a farm that works without having to worry about the government... Do you think anyone has a future?"

"Why I live in the present. Live for the day, Bobby. Take what you get.

Enjoy it while you've got it. Which includes Rhodesia and the likes of Linda Gaskell. So often people work hard for a future and the future never comes. Are you buying me a drink?"

"Sorry. You're right. I'm in the chair. Have a peanut. One of my neighbours is going to grow chillies. Has a contract to supply a firm in Durban. One way round British sanctions... You think there'll be a happy end to all this nonsense?"

"You've drunk yourself morbid."

"Probably. We should pack up, I suppose, and go back to England."

"If I have to go back to a suburban, trivial life in England I'd rather shoot myself. What are you drinking?"

"Brandy, ice and water. South African brandy. Not so expensive and scarce as Scotch... You want a beer after that road?... Mr Barman. Double brandy and a Castle. Good to see you, Vince. This is a bit of luck. If I don't fall off the barstool first we can go out on the town."

"Well, there's this bar or Bretts. Take your pick. Why I love Salisbury. Not too many decisions... Do you miss her?"

"Terribly."

"Poor old Bobby. You'll get over her."

"Will I? Old chap I met in the men's bar still remembers the girl who jilted him forty years ago. Her name was Barbara."

"Cheers, Bobby. To better times. You sure you don't want lunch?"

"Have a peanut."

"Are you staying in the hotel?"

"Booked in when I arrived. Have to change later or go back to the men's bar. No shorts in the ladies' bar after six. Got to wear a tie. Are you staying the night?"

"I am now. Came in to do the shopping but there's nothing I need to do on World's View. Get a bit bored, frankly. We can both go on a bender."

"Drink up. I'm way ahead of you. You never know when the booze is going to catch up. Hammond Taylor can be sober as a judge one minute and pissed as a newt the next. Why do people think newts get pissed? They say he's having an affair with Elizabeth over there. I don't like Hammond. Doesn't pay his bar bill. Always bumming drinks.... Have a peanut... What I don't understand in the police reserve is why they train us on bolt-action .303 rifles left over from the First World War... It's only rumours, of course. Stanley, poor old bugger, can't do anything about it. Three kids and a wife half his age. Rumour says Hammond isn't the only one... I mean, what can we do against a modern machine gun? If they come against us poor farmers they'll have Russian AK-47 automatic rifles. They say the bloody things can sit in water a year and still fire perfectly. Only rumours."

"Elizabeth Wells and Hammond or the AK-47 rifle, Bobby?"

"I'm rambling, old boy. Must be pissed. Have a peanut."

"What we'll do is go and have some lunch in the dining room. They don't mind shorts at lunchtime. I'll book into a room."

"You think so? You're right. If I'm drinking out the day I'd better eat. Buy me another drink first. I mean, what does he do? If he kicks her out for adultery he either has to bring up those three kids on his own or lose them entirely. She's got him over a barrel. That's the trouble marrying such a young girl when you're old."

"The farmers' wives get bored. They either drink on their own like Jeremy Crookshank's first wife or have affairs with the young assistants. You end up with a drunk or a wife you can't trust. We're better off single."

"We loved each other."

"Mr Barman? A double brandy and a cold Castle... What's the barman's name?"

"I have no idea."

"Linda said they all look the same."

"Not to me. They're as different as we are. A lot of us whites just don't look at them. Don't look at them square in the face. Am I drunk, Vince?"

"You're not sober."

"A lunch, a nap and then we'll hit Bretts for sundowners."

"Now you're talking. Good to see you, Bobby."

"Good to see you, Vince."

"She's smiling at you, you know."

"Who is?"

"Elizabeth Wells. She must know Katie has gone home."

"Don't talk rubbish. She's old enough to be my mother."

"She's thirty-eight. You know what they say. Any port in a storm."

"Stanley would kill me."

"He hasn't shot Hammond Taylor. And that little affair's been going on for a year."

"I don't like older women."

"Drink her pretty, Bobby. Cheers. Have a peanut."

"If they hit my farm it doesn't matter anymore. Katie's gone. All the way back to England... You think there will be a war? How do you fight them? We'll be sitting ducks in our houses at night. Maybe Katie going was best. She was right. Africa for the white man is changing. And not for the best."

"You are morbid. Drink it down. Lunch and a nap."

"I hate interrupted drinking. I'll wake with a hangover. Better to keep going, Vince. You'll look after your old friend... Mr Barman. Can you fill up this bowl of peanuts?... And you're right. She is smiling at me. For an older woman she isn't that bad looking... You think they'll meet men on the boat? Shipboard romances. Even the thought gnaws at my stomach. What makes us love another person so much? It's not fair."

"You'll get over Katie."

"No I won't... Why do people want to kill each other? Why do we have to argue with each other? Why can't we all get along? Black, white and khaki. If it wasn't for all this political nonsense in Rhodesia Katie wouldn't have gone home. We'd have been married. Have our own three kids. Be happy. The perfect life. Why does it always have to go sour? Why can't Elizabeth over there be happy? She's got a husband. Got her children. Nice big farm. What's she want with me or Hammond? Don't understand people anymore. They're always fighting. So, Vince Ranger, what are you going to do with the rest of your life?"

"Get through it, I hope. Bit at a time. Please don't go philosophical on me, Bobby."

"Wasn't being philosophical as you call it. I was just asking a question. What are you going to do with the rest of your life?"

"I have absolutely no idea."

"At least you're honest. I'm going to become a drunk. Cheers, old boy."

"They're going. Must be going into lunch. Is the hotel full?"

"Plenty of empty rooms. Not so many tourists from Europe and America. The safari companies are moaning. Sanctions are biting in more ways than one. You just can't win. On one side our own people won't do business with us and on the other the communist Russians and Chinese are training an army of terrorists to kill us. But what do you do?

Can't run away. This is where I made my home. For better or worse... You think it'll get like the Mau Mau in Kenya? That wasn't so good for the English. In the end they gave up. Handed over to Kenyatta. Took the easy way out. Do you think it's over for us whites in Africa? Who's going to run the place if they kick us out? The place will disintegrate. All the lights will go out."

"They didn't have electricity before we got here."

"I suppose so. The life of an African must have been all right before we got here. There were so few people. Plenty of grazing land. You just moved on with the cattle to fresh grazing. A lazy, happy life in the sun."

"The tribes still fought with each other. When the Zulus came up from Natal they treated the local Shona much like slaves. Attacking the Shona villages, stealing their grain and cattle and raping their women. Rape and pillage. Been going on since man came down from the trees. Survival of the fittest. Darwin's theory of evolution. The Matabele, as the Zulus called themselves, would have absorbed the Shona if we hadn't come along and stopped the fighting. Now I'm philosophising, Bobby. They killed the men and old women and took the kids and young women back to Matabeleland. Went on in Europe for centuries before we became civilised. If we ever did. Putting on clothes doesn't necessarily make a person civilised. Underneath the surface we're all a bunch of savages. My father said we're all a product of rape and pillage. We're the survivors. Somewhere back in our ancestry one of our ancestors raped another one of our ancestors without which you and I wouldn't have life. In our very being is the rapist and the victim. And it never stops and never will. Religion tried to make us behave ourselves but that didn't work. Oh, the politicians give lip service to what's right and wrong. Mostly they fudge it. Do what suits them. The same old rape and pillage with a different face... Have a peanut. No, I have a better idea. They can bring us a sandwich to the bar."

"That's a good one... So we're all a bunch of thugs."

"Not everyone. Or the human race wouldn't have survived."

"Is it going to survive?"

"For as long as we need it, I hope. Wouldn't mind a trip on a boat myself."

"Please don't remind me. I hoped she would get pregnant. Must have been on the pill."

"Didn't you discuss it?"

"Said she wasn't on the pill when I asked after the first time. She was frightened, poor girl. Frightened of a hyena outside the tent. The first time we made love it was more by accident... Mr Barman? Can you order us a plate of sandwiches? Thank you. And the same again."

"Put more water in your brandy, Bobby. You won't bend so quickly... You think there'll be any girls in Bretts?"

"With sanctions the young English girls don't come out anymore. They go to South Africa. They say Johannesburg is the place to be. Lots of money. Lots of girls. The price of gold is sky high. Without South Africa, Rhodesia wouldn't survive. At least we have one friend. Two, really. South Africa and Portugal. Until the Portuguese lose Angola and Mozambique. There are wars going on all over Africa. What are we doing here, Vince?"

"Getting drunk, old boy. Remember?"

"To Katie and Barbara."

"Who the hell's Barbara?"

"The girl that jilted the colonel years ago."

"He must have got married afterwards."

"No, he didn't. Stayed faithful to Barbara all his life. I'm going to stay faithful to Katie for the rest of my life."

"Now I know you're drunk."

"I'm not kidding. To Katie and Barbara. Cheers, old boy. Good to see you."

AT FIVE O'CLOCK they walked to the first of the avenues that crossed Second Street to the passageway between the shop fronts that led them down the stairs to the basement that was Bretts. Vince had made Bobby drink two cups of black coffee with his sandwiches. The nightclub was empty, the cocktail bar with its tables and chairs beginning to fill up with people leaving their offices. There was no sign of Tony Bird the owner, Vince happy to seat Bobby up at the bar without any questions, Bobby showing early signs he was bending. There were two girls on their own in the corner of the bar, one of them smiling at the beaming Bobby, the alcohol having overcome his sadness at losing Katie. Vince shook his head at the girl only making it worse, the young girl's attention now became fully focused on Bobby. Vince was still sober, well behind Bobby in his drinking. The girl was neither pretty nor ugly to Vince, somewhere in between, and her smile showing two buck teeth which spoiled her face.

Vince sat Bobby down on the barstool in the corner, with his back to the wall, at the other end of the bar. From his position at the angle of the bar, Vince could see through the glass partition into the empty nightclub just as Constable Donald Henderson had looked through at Linda Gaskell before ending up with her in Meikles Hotel. Making Vince realise Linda was out from England to enjoy herself with as many men as possible. It gave the phrase 'making hay while the sun shone' in sunny Rhodesia, a whole new connotation. After more double brandies, Bobby was beginning to find things more difficult to pronounce, his tongue not quite getting round his words without ever so slightly slurring. To half-sober Vince his friend was hilarious with his fingers naughtily waving from the bar top to the girl with the buck teeth. Two hours later, Bobby fell off his barstool trying to get up to go to the loo, his foot caught by the heel of his shoe on the metal ring at the bottom of the barstool. On the floor, looking up, Bobby was laughing, making no effort to get to his feet. The girl with the buck teeth, who by then had herself done some drinking, saw it all happen and laughed. When Bobby stayed down behind the corner of the bar she came round. She was still laughing. So was Bobby.

"Are you all right? Can I help you? What happened?"

"I fell off the barstool," said Bobby, slowly and thickly pronouncing his words. "Would you be kind enough to help me up? I'm a little tight. Then my friend Vince here will take me back to my hotel. My name is Bobby Preston."

"He's been drinking since eleven o'clock," said Vince as they lifted Bobby back up onto his barstool. "Poor chap's in a state. His fiancée jilted him and went back to England, not wanting to live in Rhodesia."

"What do you do, Bobby? Do you work?"

"I own Hopewell Estate though there isn't much hope. I was going to build a fine little cottage. I live in a tent."

"I'm Vince Ranger," Vince said to the girl. "We're staying in Meikles just up the road."

"Wendy Cox. You'd better get him home. I'll help if you want. One on either side will make it easier. My brother does this every now and again. Put Mickey to bed more than once. We'd better get Bobby out of the bar before Tony comes on duty. Might not let him back again. Eleven o'clock! That's eight hours of drinking."

"Have a peanut, Wendy," said Bobby, grinning. "You're both most kind."

"How did he get in, in shorts?... Put your hand on my shoulder. Come on. Let's go. Where's Hopewell Estate?"

"Far away in the country. We were going to have three children."

"My goodness. She's silly to have lost you."

"I'm rather drunk, I'm afraid. But tomorrow I'll be sober. Will you have dinner with me in Meikles? I'll wait for you downstairs at seven o'clock. Don't want to go back to the farm."

"So the farm belongs to you?"

"All four thousand acres. Come along, Vince. Thank you Wendy. I'm quite capable of walking. The heel of my shoe caught in the bottom of the barstool. Can happen to anyone. I've done enough drinking for one day. Never really helps. Come on. Here comes Tony. Let's get out of here. Don't want to compound my problems."

"What was her name?"

"Her name was Katie. Katie Frost."

One foot in front of the other, Bobby walked back to the hotel.

"Why do we drink, Vince?"

"I have no idea."

"Are you really going to give that girl dinner?"

"Any port in a storm. Said so yourself. Anyway, it's not meant to be the looks that count, she was kind. Came to help me. I'll have the hangover of all hangovers tomorrow but who the hell cares? My life is over. What you going to do on your own, Vince?

"Have some dinner I suppose. On the farm in my cottage I never get lonely. Only among people do I feel on my own."

"You'll have to count me out tonight. Food would make me throw up. You think she still thinks of me? You're a good friend. Thanks, Vince. Sorry to be such a pain in the arse."

"What friends are for. Here we are. Good evening, Bafana," Vince said to the Zulu doorman in all the regalia of his traditional skins.

"I'll be all right now," said Bobby to Vince. "Walk and the cooler air has sobered me up."

"Sleep well."

"I'll sleep well to start with. Then I'll wake up and think of Katie the rest of the night. There's nothing more pathetic than a man feeling sorry for himself. What we have now is the real world. With all its warts. That fantasy of living happily ever after doesn't exist anymore. It doesn't for me. All my dreams are gone on a boat. Hope she'll be happy. When we're old and grey we'll both look back and wonder what it would have been like. Married to each other. Bringing up our children. Avoiding the pitfalls of life, most of them made by ourselves. Wars come and go. So do people. Only ourselves stay behind to look at it all... Goodnight, Vince."

"Goodnight, Bobby. Don't let the bed bugs bite."

"I'll try not to."

Vince watched Bobby collect his room keys from reception and walk away up the stairs. Feeling lonely, Vince walked across the dining room.

"Table for one," he said to the man standing next to the desk with menus tucked under his arm.

"Are you staying in the hotel, sir?"

"Yes, I am. Room forty-three."

"Follow me, sir."

The headwaiter seated Vince and gave him one of the menus.

"Something to drink, sir?"

"No thank you. It's food and a good night's sleep."

"Very well, sir."

The other girl at the bar hadn't been so bad looking. Tomorrow, if the girl with the buck teeth pitched up, he'd suggest they go fetch her friend. Make it a foursome. Have some fun. Despite Bobby's feelings of hopelessness, life went on.

PART IV

DECEMBER 1972 – "WITH YOUR BACK TO AN ANT HILL"

1

When Vince Ranger drove up to the house four years after Bobby Preston fell off his barstool Hopewell Estate was flourishing, a prize worth having. Every cent of profit had been ploughed back into the land. All the arable land had been stumped out and contoured ready for the five-year cycles of crop planting: one year tobacco, one year maize to use up the surplus fertiliser left over from the tobacco, and three years fallow planted with grass to protect the topsoil from the erosion of wind and rain. The new house looked out across the farm to the Chiweshe tribal trust lands and the distant range of purple-coloured mountains. The river that had flowed in front of Bobby's first encampment had been dammed, the water of the dam spreading back to give Bobby water to irrigate in droughts with miles of pipes to the lands and a pump station where once Bobby had drawn his buckets of water when he had lived in the tent. Mango trees, drip irrigated at their roots, ran over forty acres. Forty tobacco curing barns, grading sheds, a long sorting shed for the mangos with a cold room attached, workshops, sheds for six Nuffield tractors spread close to the house. In the compound, one hundred families, the men working the estate, lived in houses with running water from the dam. Next to the houses, along the river above the dam wall, was a football field and a primary school. Electricity pylons had brought power onto the farm from the Electricity

Supply Commission making the farm work better than Bobby had ever hoped or imagined.

"Why the glum face, Vince? It's Christmas. You want some breakfast? Hell, it's hot. Have you started reaping on World's View?... Well say something, Vince. Don't just stand there."

"Where's Wendy?"

"She's taken the twins to see Alice Swart. Their kids are the same age take a year or two. You want a cup of tea? You know it's always a pleasure to see you, Vince. Sit down. I just got up. Sunday, my one day of rest. There's nothing better than lying back in bed on Sundays and have Welcome bring me in a pot of tea to drink lying in bed looking out through the French windows."

"They attacked George Stacy last night. He'd gone outside with a shotgun to see why his dogs were barking. They shot him six times with automatic rifles. The war's started, Bobby. The terrorist war Inspector Clay Barry has been warning us about for years."

"Is the reserve being called up? George Stacy!"

"There were three other attacks last night across the Centenary. They struck soon after dusk and got out of the area before the police could do anything about it. They're well armed and well trained. Four farm attacks in one night and not a sign of them this morning. Just tracks leading back into the bush. No, the reserve has not been called up. They want us to stay on our own properties. From now on we don't move without a loaded gun close at hand."

"I'll send Wendy and the kids to stay with her parents. What the hell do we do, Vince?"

"High steel electric fences round the perimeter of the gardens. Floodlights into the bush. Clear the land on the other side of the fence. They're putting together police anti-terrorist units made up from us farmers to patrol at night. Set ambushes on the roads. Our informers have been warning us of this for years."

"Has anyone ever won a war against terrorists?"

"Malaya. We defeated the communists in Malaya... Thank you, Welcome. I'll pour my own tea."

They waited for Welcome to leave the breakfast room, both of them silent.

"Did he hear what I said?"

"Probably. They hear everything. His English has improved considerably since he looked after me in a tent... Poor old George. The only family he had was in England. Hadn't been back for twenty-five years... The man was a legend. Do you remember that story he told of an old lion killing his cattle? Laid a trap for it with wires and string attached to a twelve bore shotgun. Baited the trap with a dead carcase. Lion shot itself right through the back of its head. George told the story to anyone new who came to the Centenary West club. He had Wendy listening open-mouthed to the story. I don't think he ever married... Why'd anyone want to kill an old man like George?"

"To terrorise us. They think we'll run for it. Pack up and go back to England."

"Maybe we should. So Katie was right. Bugger. I was just getting on top of it. What's Jeremy doing with Bergit and the children?"

"Sending them for a visit to her parents in England until he's protected the farmhouse and seen how bad it is."

"And Christmas tomorrow."

"Just Bergit and her kids. Randall and Phillip won't go. Phillip is sixteen. Randall turned fifteen ten days ago. When I left both boys were talking about joining the Rhodesian army. To hell with their schooling but of course they're too young. What a bloody world. Just when you get organised in life it all blows up in your face."

"Are they going to attack again tonight?"

"Who knows? Jeremy and the boys are going to sleep in the office next to the barns. Slip out when the cook goes back to the compound. We can't trust anyone. I don't know what I'm going to do."

"Poor Wendy. What the hell did I get her into?"

"She wanted to get married. Nothing's ever smooth in life."

"Why didn't the police phone me?"

"On a party line? Any of the staff could be listening. They're going to give us police radios. An Agric-Alert system. So the lines can't be cut by the terrs."

"So we are at war with the likes of Josiah Makoni and Livingstone Sithole. Who's the brains behind all this?"

"The communist Russians and Chinese. They want to control the supply of Africa's raw materials. We're just an extension of the cold war."

"Have there been any attacks elsewhere in the country?"

"Not yet."

"So what are you going to do, Vince? You're footloose and fancy-free. You don't own a farm."

"I don't know at the moment. My first feeling was fear and panic. I wanted to run away. Driving over here in the cold light of day I'm not so sure. Rhodesia is now my country. Where all of my friends are. I'm thirty years old. Bit late to start a new career. Anyway, what the hell would I do in England? All that cold and fog. No money. No friends. I'd be positively miserable. No, I made my bed and I'll lie in it. If they kill me I'm dead and nothing will matter anymore. Here comes Wendy. Do you want me to tell her?"

"No. I'll do it. She can take the car to the family farm outside Salisbury. Her mother will love having the kids."

Vince got up when Wendy walked into the breakfast room as Bobby went back to eating his breakfast, both of them trying to look normal. The nanny had taken charge of the two children out on the lawn by the swimming pool. The children were playing with the dogs, their voices trilling, the dogs chasing each other round the flowerbeds.

"So you've heard. Alice told me of the attacks when I arrived with the kids. Poor old George Stacy."

"You're going to take the twins to your mother, Wendy. It's not safe."

"And you?"

"I'm staying on the farm."

"Then so am I... How are you, Vince?"

"Jeremy is sending Craig and Myra to England."

"I'm not running away. I can use a gun as well as you."

"We're going to sleep in the office tonight. I'd be much happier if you went."

"The army are sending troops up from Salisbury. Alice says the terrs want us to panic. No, I'm staying put."

After crossing to the sideboard, Wendy rang the small silver handbell for Welcome, then walked over to the window to look out at her children. She was silently crying, tears trickling down the sides of her face. Bobby got up and went to his wife and put his arms right round her shoulders. Welcome came in and waited, not sure what to do. Bobby turned back to look at him.

"Do they know in the compound, Welcome? Boss Stacy was killed last night in a terrorist attack. You can put the cup on the table before you drop it."

The man's hands were shaking, rattling the teacup in the saucer he had brought from the kitchen. He put down the cup and left the room, not saying a word.

"Oh, he knew," said Vince. "They all know. Knew before we did. The bush telegraph in Africa is better than any telephone system. The police say our labour has been intimidated. They'll be as frightened as us. Caught between us and the terrorists."

"Wendy, I want you to go."

"We're married, Bobby. I've loved you since you fell off that bloody barstool."

"What about the kids?"

"All right. Tomorrow I'll drive the kids to my mother and then come back again. She'll love having them for Christmas. They can all stay in the flat in Salisbury if the farm isn't safe. We'll get used to it. Part of human nature. You think you won't be able to cope but you do. My great-grandfather came up from South Africa on the pioneer column with F C Selous and Sebastian Brigandshaw and I'm not leaving anytime soon. We've built this country from scratch. Made it what it is. Just look at this farm. When I first came up you were living in a bloody tent. Now look at it. There was nothing in Rhodesia before the white man arrived other than tribes making war with each other. We stopped them killing each other. Doubled their life expectancy. They should be grateful, not resentful of our success."

"It's the Russians," said Vince.

"Then we are going to fight the Russians like the Americans in Vietnam if we want to continue living in a prosperous country. I'm not going anywhere. I wasn't born in England. Neither were my children. Now, who wants another cup of tea? Those tears just now were for George Stacy. Not for me. During the Matabele and Shona uprisings in the last century the English and Afrikaners didn't run away. And we're not going to run away now. Our farms are worth fighting for. When great-grandfather got here there were less than half a million blacks in this country. Peasant farmers and hunters. One step forward from hunters and gatherers. We brought our skills that will one day bring everyone into a modern lifestyle. If they chase us out they'll go back to where they were before, living from hand to mouth with a life expectancy of thirty. They need us as much as we need them. But bringing them all up to our standards is going to take time. And after last night's attacks it's going to take a bloody sight longer. So, both of you. You want tea?"

Bobby looked from his children on the lawn to his wife standing poised over the tea tray. Even if he did think of Katie Frost more often than he should do, he was happy with his wife.

"Thanks, Wendy," he said, smiling. "I'd love another cup of tea with my toast and marmalade. So you'll take the kids tomorrow?"

"Said I would."

"We'll sleep tonight in the office. All of us. Go down after Welcome goes back to the compound."

"Good idea. One of us will sleep. The other will stand guard. If we're attacked we get away into the bush. My grandfather taught me and my brothers how to survive alone in the bush. I'm as African as they are. I'm not running away with my tail between my legs. I love this place. I love Africa. I love you and the kids. What we have here is worth fighting for. Literally."

"Where are you going?"

"To get the guns out of the gun cabinet."

With his world turned upside down, Bobby sat down at the table to eat the rest of his breakfast. He was thinking of Katie. Whether she would have coped. Having himself only been in the country twelve years, he didn't have his wife's passion.

"I'd better go," said Vince. "Look after yourselves. What a bloody world. The moment you got something worth having they all want it. For a while, Bobby, I was a bit jealous of you. This farm. Wendy. The kids. Now I'm not so sure. There doesn't seem much point sticking my neck out. Dad had a saying, 'They can take away your money but they can't take away your brains'. Hope I've still got some brains left. Can a quarter of a million whites really hold back the tide of history? We're a bit like King Canute ordering the tide to go out. What did Harold Macmillan call it when as British prime minister he addressed the South African parliament in Cape Town? 'The winds of change!' Last night was a cold blast of wind. The first of many. I'm not going to sleep a wink tonight. Neither are any of us. Suddenly everything is fragile, the permanence gone. Maybe we should all go back to England and start our lives over again."

"I'm not going," said Wendy, walking back through the door and handing Bobby a bolt-action .303 rifle. "And it's loaded."

"Right," said Bobby. "You want a late breakfast?"

"Had breakfast with Alice. Now there's a tough lady. She's Afrikaans. Says if we hold the line in Rhodesia, South Africa will survive as we know it. She says the South African government will back us up to the hilt. Send troops if necessary. Don't look so grim. Life goes on."

"Not for George Stacy, Wendy."

"That's why we don't run away. Did you bring a gun, Vince?"

"No, I did not."

"Why the hell not? When those kids out there grow up we will say it was worth it. We'll take your old camping mattresses down to the office... They're three years old, just look at them. Swim as well as they walk. We're survivors, Bobby. Put that old smile back on your face. If we can't sleep tonight we'll drink ourselves a bottle of brandy... Can you hear that thumping sound getting closer? Helicopters. The army is arriving and I don't have to drive down to Mum's. You see? It's all about being organised. Tell you what, let's have a drink to celebrate."

"It's half past eleven!"

"And it's Sunday, Christmas Eve. Stay and join us, Vince. Nothing more we can do."

Smiling at his wife, Bobby got up from his chair and gave her a hug before turning back to Vince.

"It's never as bad as it seems, Vince. Wendy's right. It's Christmas Eve. We'll open the bar a bit early. Whatever would I do without you, Wendy? Did you put one up the spout?"

"Five in the magazine, one up the spout. Grandfather could shoot the eye out of a buck at five hundred yards with one of these Lee-Enfields. Come on, lover. Let's you and me and Vince go get a drink in the lounge... Welcome! Bring some ice. Three cold beers. We'll have our very own wake for George Stacy, God bless his soul. You can put Beethoven on the gramophone, Bobby. Play some music. We're not going to let them grind us down... Just look at the dogs out on the lawn. Those dogs are quite mad. If I was one of those terrs I'd be running right back to Zambia. The Rhodesian Army fought the communist guerrillas in

Malaya with the British. We've all that experience of fighting a terrorist war. Hugh Quinton on North Ridge Estate fought the Japs in Burma with General Wingate. And they chased the Japanese through the jungle down the Malayan peninsula without the help of the Americans. When the history of Rhodesia is written it will either say we British stayed and beat the communists or it will say the country disintegrated. Which isn't going to happen. The terrorists have no place to hide from those helicopters."

"Unless they bury their guns," said Vince, "and disappear into the local populace. Jeremy Crookshank and I never go into the labourers' compound unless we're invited. You don't walk into a man's home without an invitation. They could be hiding the terrs in our compounds right now, willingly or unwillingly. They won't have any compunction about killing one of their own. They're fanatics. Brainwashed by their political masters. Young chaps looking for a job and then they can't get out. The politicians in Moscow or the terrorist camps in Zambia won't care. The likes of Makoni, Sithole and Mugabe want power. Their own lives are not on the line. Any black selling them out will be taken out. They'll just disappear. Our workers are between a rock and a hard place. Revolutionaries are ruthless, which is how they win. In our compound there are relatives of our employees we know nothing about. And over there, Bobby," said Vince, pointing. "What's going on in the Chiweshe reserve? Is Chief Chiweshe on our side or on the side of the terrs? If he's clever, which I'm told he is, he'll be siding with the terrs and siding with the police, depending on who's confronting him. What else can he do? He doesn't have an army. And his salary is paid by the Rhodesian government. Wouldn't like his job right now. Terrorist wars can go on for decades until one side or the other grows tired. We British in Rhodesia have somewhere to go. The blacks don't. And if we go back to England, what happens to one of them who supported us? The likely result of all this is we'll both destroy Rhodesia. Turn it into a wasteland with starving women and children. You've only got to look at what's happening in Vietnam. The Americans are pulling out leaving the South to the mercy of the communists. When the communist North finally take over the South, anyone who sided with the Americans will be dead meat. Oh, no. What happened last night in the Centenary isn't going to go away with the arrival of the helicopters, Wendy. It's not that easy. And it won't be easy for the blacks to run this country without our skills. Modern countries need modern skills."

"What else can we do?"

"Have a drink. Where's Welcome with the ice and the beers?"

"You watch," went on Vince. "The Americans will get what they're calling their military advisors out of South Vietnam before the North Vietnamese overwhelm the South. But the poor sods who are left behind will have to face the music. No, I wouldn't like to be Chief Chiweshe right now. Or your Sekuru in your compound, Bobby. Or Welcome for that matter."

"So what the hell are we going to do?"

"Have a drink, Bobby. Have a drink."

"We'd better shut up before Welcome arrives with the beers and the ice."

"We'll see," said Wendy. "Two can play tough arse. Inspector Clay Barry, the esteemed member-in-charge of our local police, knows a lot more about what's going on than he's telling us."

"That's what worries me," said Vince. "If I knew what he knew I'd be shitting in my pants instead of waiting for Welcome."

"I'd better go and find Welcome," said Bobby. "He can't be enjoying this any more than we are. Why the hell can't people get on with each other? Why do they always have to fight? Not just people but families. You just have to look at Elizabeth and Stanley Wells. Mostly, I feel sorry for their kids. So, he's much older than her. Back then she agreed to marry him. Bear his kids."

"If they are his kids, Bobby," said Vince. "Why I'm still a bachelor. No offence, Wendy."

"I'll go get Welcome."

When Bobby came back from the kitchen carrying a tray with the beers and the bucket of ice he was worried.

"Welcome's not in the house. He's never gone off like that before. Not even when I lived in the tent."

"Betty is still outside with the twins."

"He never leaves during the day without asking me."

"Unless you want to chase off down to the compound, there's not much you can do about it, darling. When one thing goes so wrong we become paranoid. Think problems into everything. And Elizabeth Wells isn't the only one of the farmers' wives who isn't faithful from what I hear from Alice. Elizabeth just flaunts it. Doesn't care. Knows poor old Stanley is too old to do anything about it... Cheers. Happy Christmas. To poor old George Stacy. May he be telling his stories in heaven."

"Better bring the kids in," said Bobby.

"I can watch them just as well from here. Happy Christmas."

"Happy Christmas," said Bobby and Vince together, neither of them convincing.

Drinking beers made Bobby more apprehensive. The compound was silent. No drums. No sounds of the people. The dogs on the lawn had settled down, his children playing quietly. Everything around Bobby felt different. The calling dove from the msasa tree by the pool was failing to comfort him as it usually did. There were black rain clouds behind the distant range of purple mountains, a sight that yesterday would have brought him joy. There had been no rain for a week and the tobacco in the lands needed it to give the plants weight, the bottom leaves almost ready for reaping. A gentle wind was blowing the scent of flowers in through the lounge window, a sickly smell that had once smelt perfect. Bobby looked at his gun against the back of the couch. A gun that shouldn't have been there. A loaded gun inside the house. Wendy's gun was propped against the sill of the window. Bobby had never understood why the police had issued him with two of the rifles. Now he understood why. Vince looked just as agitated, glancing from gun to gun. Looking out of the window. Moving his feet. Fidgeting. 'Where the hell is Welcome?' kept running through his head, the call of the dove now sounding like 'Where's Welcome? Where's Welcome?' Bobby wanted to scream.

One of the Alsatian dogs, Whiskey, had gone to the edge of the lawn and was sniffing at the tall elephant grass that ran on down to the dam. The dog was standing poised, looking out. Then she trotted back to the pool. Far away, Bobby thought he heard a rumble of thunder from the distant clouds. It was getting hotter, if that was possible, a prelude to rain. Bobby looked at his wife, her small buck teeth his favourite part of her elfin face, her eyes no longer sparkling despite the smile that showed on her face. They were all terribly worried. None of them wanted to say it. Once again, like the time he fell off the barstool, his life had changed. Now all the comfort was gone. All the hope for their future evaporated. It was difficult enough to grow a good crop every year to pay for all the development without having to leave his family and go out on patrol at night. Trying to kill someone he didn't even know. Yes, the wives and children would go to one house, the house protected by the police. But that wouldn't help. And who was the enemy? What did he look like? Was it Welcome or Sekuru? Or Chirow, the headman in the tribal trust land close to Jeremy Crookshank's World View? Last night their whole world had been changed, never to be the same again. They were at war, like in England during the Blitz, his father away fighting, his mother living in an air-raid shelter while some German pilot she would never know was dropping bombs on her from the sky. And now the thumping sound of a helicopter right over his house, the dogs on the lawn not sure, Betty looking up at the sky, his children stopping their playing. They were at war. Like his parents and grandparents. Another war so far from England. It all made Bobby sick in his stomach as the helicopter passed over his roof, the dove flown away, the dogs now barking, the tops of the msasa trees brushed flat by the rotors of the helicopter coming into land.

"He's landing on the lawn," said Vince.

The door to the side of the helicopter slid open. A man, holding onto something inside with his back to Bobby, got his foot on the landing bar of the helicopter and stepped back onto the well-cut grass. The scream of the engine began to fade, the rotors slowly rotating. The man turned round, looked at the house and waved.

"It's Inspector Rankin. I'll be buggered." Now Vince was beaming.

By the time Fred Rankin reached the steps that led up to the veranda to the right of the lounge, the helicopter was silent, its rotors stopped.

"We're checking on everyone, Bobby. Are you all right? Poor old George Stacy got killed last night. He'd got up and gone outside to see why the dogs were barking. It must have been quick. So you are all right. Good morning, Wendy. Bit early for a beer."

"It's Christmas Eve."

"Of course."

"You want a beer, Fred?"

"Not today, Bobby. It's all a bit of a bugger. Under control, of course. The army have sent us three platoons of the Rhodesian Light Infantry. We all feel better now the RLI has come to our help. One of their helicopters." Fred Rankin turned his head to look at the helicopter on the lawn.

"Four attacks," said Vince.

"So you heard. Morning, Vince. Everything all right on World's View?"

"Jeremy's sending Bergit and the children to her parents in England. Until it all settles down."

"No real need. Now they know we're waiting for them they won't come back. By the time it was light this morning they were out of the Centenary."

"Are you sure?"

"Mostly."

"Couldn't they be in the TTL or the compounds?"

"Who really knows in a terrorist war?... Oh good. You've got the guns out. What we're recommending to everyone. Be alert. Stay on your guard. That sort of thing."

"The compound is quiet."

"All the compounds are quiet. Well, if you're safe I'll report back to Clay. A merry Christmas to all of you. Sorry to land on the lawn. Only patch we could see without trees. Lucky you only left the trees on half of your lawn. It's going to rain tonight. How's the crop, Bobby?"

"Start reaping after Christmas."

"Good for you... Alouette helicopters, French-built. The army got them before sanctions. Your twins look well, Wendy. You all have a nice Christmas. Are you coming to watch the cricket on Boxing Day at Centenary West? I'll be playing. Nothing has really changed. Those beers look nice and cold. Have one for me."

Fred walked back to the helicopter, still trying to give them the impression everything was under control. The engine restarted, scaring the dogs and the children. Betty's mouth was wide open. The rotors whirred, sending a ripple across the pool, splashing water up onto the tiles that ran round the edge. The three of them clustered on the top of the steps of the open veranda watching the strange machine lift up off their lawn. All three still had their beers in their hands, none of them drinking.

"It's so ugly," said Wendy. "Is that a machine gun pointing out the door?"

"Heavy calibre," said Vince. "Well, I'd better be going. Jeremy will be wondering what has happened to me."

"You could phone."

"Yes, I could phone. Could have phoned earlier this morning I suppose. Yes, I'll be on my way. See you at the cricket if you're coming."

From the door of the helicopter, standing next to the machine gun on its mounting, Fred Rankin was waving at the children as he flew overhead. The twins waved back, shouting with excitement. Betty looked terrified. Bobby walked Vince to his truck while Wendy crossed the lawn to the over-excited children.

"Thanks for coming, Vince. A phone call would have been a lot more frightening for Wendy."

"My pleasure. What old friends are for. Next time I'll remember to take a gun."

Alone, vulnerable, frightened, Bobby walked back to his home. There was still no sign of Welcome. At the small cocktail cabinet in the lounge he poured himself a large brandy and dropped in some of the ice he had fetched from the kitchen. Down at the pool, Wendy was talking to Betty. Bobby watched them through the open window as he drank, his hand shaking, the ice rattling against the side of the crystal glass. Betty walked away across the lawn, leaving the twins with Wendy. Far away now, Bobby could still hear the thump of the helicopter. His whole mind had gone from peace to turmoil in the space of half a morning.

"The twins want lunch. Betty has gone back to the compound to look after her children. The poor girl is terrified out of her wits."

"Did she say anything?"

"I asked her if they had known in the compound. Just looked at me, her eyes pleading. Oh, they knew. Know more than we do. Welcome's probably done the same. Gone back to his hut to comfort his wife. Their lives are upside down as much as ours. Thank God the children are too young to understand. Keep an eye on the twins. I want to make up our beds on the floor of the office now no one is around. Then I'll make them lunch."

"You're being very brave."

"What else can I do? Throw a fit? Start screaming? Blaming you or anyone else that comes to mind? We're not the only ones in this boat."

"We could pack up and go to England. When my mother hears of the attack on the BBC news she'll be hysterical. We could stay with them in Epsom until I find some kind of a job. You can type, Wendy. You could get a job in London as a typist. We'd survive. The kids would be safe."

"Give me a sip of your drink... That's better. Don't panic, lover. It's a one-off attack. By now, with the army and police chasing them, the terrs will be a spent force. They want to scare us as much as kill us. Make us panic. Make us run back to England. That's how successful wars of terror are meant to work. On your minds. Keeping you awake at night. Igniting the worst in our imaginations. Fear is built into us. So is running from danger. Primal. Man's first instincts of survival. If man had run away from danger instead of facing it we wouldn't have survived. The species would have been destroyed. And don't forget, those people who attacked the farms last night are just as frightened. You only had to see the fear in Betty's eyes. We stay, take precautions, and ride out the storm. Give me another sip of that drink."

When Wendy handed back his glass all that was left was the ice. Bobby poured himself another, forcing his hands not to shake. He had never felt more vulnerable. More out of control. His gun next to the sofa made it worse.

"What's the matter with Mummy?"

"She's making you both a surprise for tonight. We're all going to have a sleep-out."

"What's a sleep-out?"

"It's like camping."

"That sounds nice. Can we go back and play with the dogs on the lawn?"

"Of course you can."

"I'm hungry."

"After Mummy has prepared the sleep-out she'll make you lunch."

"I want orange juice."

"You'll have to wait a little, Stephanie. Mummy has to crush the oranges now Betty has gone back to the compound."

"Where's Welcome?"

"He's also gone back to the compound. Don't get the dogs too excited so they knock you over."

"I don't mind. Susy is my favourite dog."

"No she's not."

"Off you go, Deborah. Don't contradict your sister. If Steph says she likes Susy best, that's how it is. Just mind you know Daddy is watching you."

The gun under the window sill had gone with Wendy. When the engine of the car in the garage started it made Bobby jump. Sensibly, Wendy was going to drive down to the barns and his office next to the workshop where he paid out the wages and did his accounts. From the house, it was five hundred yards to the barns. The car drove off down the driveway between the fledgling jacaranda trees. Through the small back window on the other side of the lounge, Bobby could just see his wife's car, a second-hand Ford Zephyr she used to visit her friends. They could still all get in the front of the truck for long trips to Salisbury but that would change with the kids getting bigger. Buying a new car with all the sanctions on Rhodesia was difficult. He had put their name down for a French Peugeot a year ago and still had a year to wait.

By the time Bobby had finished his third brandy, Wendy was back with the children's lunch, a smile on her face. Bobby's hand had stopped shaking.

"They want some fresh orange juice."

"I know... Sekuru was in the tractor shed with the tractor driver. I don't know his name. There are six tractor drivers. I get them muddled up."

"Did he know what's happened to Welcome?"

"Hasn't seen Welcome since Welcome left the compound to come up to the house this morning."

"How was Sekuru?"

"Didn't mention the attacks. There's something wrong with a bolt on the tractor that attaches to the trailer. They were trying to fix it."

"Three of the tractors work on a Sunday. I'd better go and see."

"Take the gun."

"Better not. Don't want to frighten them. Did he mention the helicopter?"

"Not a word."

"He must have seen you take the stuff into the office."

"They couldn't see from the tractor shed."

"So nothing's changed for them?"

"Didn't seem so. Normal Sunday."

"Maybe tonight we should stay in our beds."

"Let's wait and see what it feels like."

"If Sekuru or the tractor driver look through the office window they'll see the beds on the floor."

"I suppose so. You think some of them in the compound will side with the terrorists?"

"I don't know, Wendy. After last night I don't know anymore... The girls are playing with the dogs. I'll go check the tractor."

"Are you all right, lover?"

"Not really. Wars are a bit out of my territory. More my Dad's line of work. Now I know what he must have felt like in Burma. In the jungle. Not sure if the Japs were round the next tree, the tension never leaving. We're so isolated on the farm. Surrounded by people we know so little about. I've never had a heart-to-heart talk with any of them. Not even Sekuru. There's always a mile of distance between the boss and the labour force. If you get too familiar you lose your authority. Dad said it was the same with the men in the army. The officers lived separate lives, their only contact with the men to command and lead. Class, rank, and here it's race on top of both of them."

"Are you taking your Sunday afternoon nap?"

"Maybe we should drive to the Centenary East Club and get the feeling of what's happening to us. Talking to the other farmers may make me feel less on my own."

"Kids!" shouted Wendy through the lounge window. "Come and get your lunch."

"I want orange juice."

"When you've finished your lunch Daddy is taking us to the club."

"Oh, goodie."

"You can have your orange juice at the club."

While the children were eating, Bobby walked down to the sheds. Wendy would take half an hour to get herself and the children ready. On his way past the office he looked through the window with its steel burglar bars. It was difficult to tell what was on the floor in front of the safe. To the labourers, the sleeping bags could have looked like sacking. There was always something being delivered to the office by the RMS bringing stores up from Salisbury to the farm.

"What's wrong, Sekuru?" Bobby asked in Fanagalo as he walked into the long tractor shed, open in the front.

"It's the hydraulic lift. Don't go up and down properly."

"Can we fix it?"

"Have to get the mechanic out from Salisbury."

"Jackson. Take one of the other tractors. What's your job today?"

"Grading the road on the bottom lands next to the river. When I hear noise when I pull the grader I come back and tell Bossboy."

"Well done. You'll get your bonus for bringing it in before it broke."

If his drivers heard a knock and brought in the tractor they received a bonus on top of their wages, the system cutting Bobby's repair bill in half, the drivers happy with the bargain. Bobby wanted to bring up the subject of Welcome but left it alone. Now, even more, he had to look in control.

"Thanks for coming up, Sekuru. See you tomorrow when the sun comes up."

They had known each other for years, ever since Bobby had been manager of World's View, and Sekuru had been Jeremy Crookshank's assistant-bossboy. Their eyes did not meet. Hydraulics were tricky, best left to a qualified motor mechanic even if it would cost a fortune bringing the man out from town. In the office was a list of jobs to be done on the farm when Ricky Anderson paid one of his visits, Bobby storing them up. There was often one or more tractors in for repairs. Still avoiding the main issue, Bobby left the shed.

2

When they drove to the club there were still three hours of daylight, enough to hear from the others what was happening in the rest of the block. Trucks and cars were parked in the driveway, many more than would have been usual on a Sunday afternoon when nothing particular was happening at the club.

"Why are you and Mummy carrying guns?"

"There's a shooting match today, Debbie."

"What's a shooting match?"

"It's like a game."

"Oh, goodie. I like games. When are we getting our orange juice?"

"Just now, darling," said Wendy, taking Stephanie with her free hand leaving Deborah for Bobby.

It was ten minutes to the east club from the farm, an hour to the west club. No one was playing tennis. Bobby could hear the high-pitched voices of children playing by the pool.

"Can we go and swim, Daddy?"

"Don't you want your orange juice?"

The bar and the lounge area that ran out from the bar were full of people. Against the wall were a row of guns where before had been tennis rackets and carrier bags. At a table sat Alice Swart with her husband Blackie and their two-year-old girl and three-year-old boy.

Stephanie and Deborah ran over to the children and climbed up onto chairs. Alice waved at Wendy. Blackie looked as grim as everyone else at the surrounding tables. The still-single Hammond Taylor was up at the bar, his mistress, Elizabeth Wells, sitting at one of the tables with her husband. There was no sign of their children. Wendy had sat down to talk with Alice and Blackie Swart. Bobby walked up to the bar.

"What's happening, Hammond?"

"Much the same as usual."

"Where are the kids?"

"Down at the pool... She's pregnant again."

"That should be fun. Did Fred Rankin pay you a visit?"

"He dropped in this morning." Hammond was trying to make a joke, trying to smile. "It's all under control. Poor old George Stacy. The funeral is going to be in the Salisbury Cathedral where you got married. He left a will saying he wanted to be cremated, his ashes scattered on the water of his dam at his farm. There were six bullets in him... You bring your gun? They're going to replace the old Lee-Enfields with Belgium FN automatic rifles. It's a far better gun than the Russian AK-47, so they say. I'm going to buy an automatic shotgun when I go into Salisbury, if I can find one. More effective at night. Fred says the danger time is dusk so the terrs can bugger off into the bush and have the night to get away."

"Have they caught any of them?"

"Not a sign of them. A few footprints around the houses they attacked. Military boots. The bastards are organised."

"They should be. The Russians trained them, by reports."

"Some say it's the Chinese... You want a drink?"

"Is it yours? Her baby?"

"Probably. Does it matter? What'll you have?"

"A Castle... We're going to sleep in the office tonight."

"What for?"

"If they attack, won't they attack the house?"

"Your dogs will wake you. Haven't you got your Alsatians? Morris, give us two cold Castles... Everyone seems to be here."

"Looks like it."

"Have you had lunch?"

"Had a late breakfast. Sort of tradition on Sundays. Like to lie in with a pot of tea."

"You want a glass?"

"I'll drink it out of the bottle. Wendy's with Alice and Blackie Swart. Our kids are friends with their kids. How's the crop?"

"Looks all right in the lands. The secret is in the curing."

"It's going to rain tonight. Building up behind the mountains."

"We could do with the rain. Cheers, old boy."

"Cheers. Poor old George. Bit of a bugger."

"Yes, it was. If I hear you under attack I'll come over. I'd hear gunfire from my house at night."

"I'll do the same."

"Thanks, old boy. At times like these I'm glad I don't have a wife and children."

"Isn't she a bit old to have another kid?"

"She's forty-two. She'd stopped taking the pill thinking she wouldn't fall pregnant again."

"Silly girl. What are you going to do?"

"Convince myself it's Stanley's. He won't say anything."

"Were you the only one?"

"I don't know. Women like that only tell you what they want you to hear. Or what they think you want to hear. Usually the truth isn't an option."

"And if he grows up the spitting image of you?"

"Let's hope it's a girl."

"Does Stanley know?"

"Not yet."

"Poor bugger. What's Clay Barry over there doing at the east club? He's normally at the west."

"Rallying the troops, Bobby. Rallying the troops. What people fear most is the uncertainty of not knowing if there is going to be an attack. Sends my imagination into overdrive. Living on my own, I think more than most people. No one to talk to about a problem. No one to share your tension."

"You want to spend nights with us? You'll be more than welcome. Drive over before it's dark. One more mouth at dinner won't make any difference. I think I'm going to be drinking too much to calm my nerves. Drink's a way of running away from a problem. Running away from oneself. Which is bloody stupid. No one has ever run away from himself."

"Would you mind?"

"Not at all."

"Better not tell Wendy what I said about Elizabeth."

"Probably not. With three of us in the house with guns we'll all be better off. We won't have to sleep in the office. The dogs hear far more than we do. I know their barks. They make a different sound when something is wrong. That kind of barking always wakes me up. There was a porcupine in the long bushgrass next to the lawn the other night. Bloody dogs barked at it all night. Went outside with a torch to find out what was going on. The porcupine had its quills stuck out to keep off the dogs."

"Clay says it's best to push the beds under the window sill at night for better protection."

"I'll remember... I've got some Scotch whisky."

"Scotch whisky! That's a treasure. Shows you what the world has come to when your own kith and kin won't sell you their whisky. How much you got?"

"Just the one bottle."

"After George's funeral in Salisbury they're having a wake in the west club."

"He'd have liked that. You'd better pack a suitcase. You mind if I go and talk to Clay? See you later. You want to go home first?"

"Not really."

Their eyes met and looked away, uncertainty in both of them. Wendy was still sitting at the table with Alice Swart and the children.

"What's going on, Clay?" The member-in-charge of the Centenary police was surrounded by farmers. Bobby noticed Clay wasn't drinking alcohol. "Thanks for sending Fred in the helicopter this morning. Anything new? Hammond's coming over to Hopewell Estate tonight to stay the night."

"Everything all right then?"

"One strange thing. My cook, Welcome, has disappeared. Never before left the house when he was on duty. When I called for him he'd gone. Probably went back to the compound to check on his family. My nerves are on edge... What's the matter, Clay?"

"Oh, nothing. I was thinking. What time did your cook boy leave the house?"

"After he made my late breakfast. I lie in bed on Sundays drinking tea. You know how it is. Why do you want to know?"

"No particular reason."

"Nice seeing you, Clay."

"You look after yourself."

Bobby walked back to join Hammond Taylor.

"Why would the police be interested in when my cook left my house?"

"He's a policeman, Bobby. How did that come up?"

"I said Welcome had gone AWOL and he all tensed up. You want another beer? It's my round."

"Why not? Relax, Bobby. You're starting to read too much into things. Why don't you visit your compound when you get back? Most likely Welcome will be back in the kitchen getting your supper ready when you get back to the farm."

"Stanley's looking at you."

"I know he is."

"You think he knows?"

"She'll have to tell him sometime. He hates me."

"So would I if you were poking my wife."

"I would never do that to you, Bobby."

"Don't worry. Wendy thinks you're very nice but not in the slightest bit sexually attractive. If I thought otherwise you think I'd let you sleep in my house?"

"You're kidding me."

"Of course I am."

"You ever think of Katie?"

"Of course I don't. I'm a married man with two children."

Having lied to Hammond about thinking of Katie, Bobby tried to order another round. Katie would often jump into his mind. From nowhere, there she was. Morris was down the bar taking an order from Koos Hendriks the storyteller. Trying not to let Katie invade his mind, he looked at the bottles on the shelf. He could see himself as a reflection in the mirror behind the shelves of bottles. In his mind, Katie was looking at him sadly, the same look on her face she had given him when they discussed the future of Rhodesia, the same words she had said five years ago coming from her lips: 'We can want something to work so much, Bobby, that it blinds us to the reality. We don't all get what we want. Mostly we have to take what comes along. Rhodesia just isn't going to work. I know it and so do you. Give up the impossible dream, Bobby, and come back to England. We'll still have a life. We'll still have a future. Who knows what will come along? You're young, fit and have a good brain. Don't waste the best years of your life on a country that in the end is going to fall apart. Find at the end when you're too old to do anything about it that you have nothing. If you lose your farm in five, ten or twenty years' time, not only will you lose your business, you'll lose your home. A few more good years in Africa are just not worth it. Face reality, Bobby. Colonialism is a thing of the past. The world has moved on. We must move on too. We can both make a living in England. A two-income family. Yes, it probably will be a semi-detached with a mortgage somewhere surrounded by neighbours. But we will survive. You won't have four thousand acres but you will have stability. England's been around for thousands of years. Rhodesia for less than a hundred. There are so many benefits in England as well as the disadvantages.' Katie's words ran on and on through his mind, the present for Bobby no longer existing.

"Are you all right, boss? What you want? Beer or a brandy?"

"Two more Castles, Morris. Sorry, I was miles away."

When Morris put the opened beers on the bar counter Bobby turned to Hammond.

"Let's go join Wendy and the Swarts. Tell her you're going to be staying the nights with us until we find out what's really happening."

"You're as white as a sheet."

"Sorry. I was thinking. Sometimes the past comes back to haunt you."

"Did you see a ghost?"

"Not a ghost exactly… Is Stanley still staring at you?"

"They've left."

"So they have. I'm not thinking straight today. What a balls-up."

WHEN THEY GOT BACK to Hopewell Estate half an hour before sunset there was still no sign of Welcome in the kitchen, which was separate from the rest of the locked-up house. Hammond had gone back to his farm to pack an overnight bag. The four dogs that roamed the garden were pleased to see them, and began running around with the kids.

"Where can he be? I'm taking the motorbike down to the compound. Hammond will be over soon. You want Betty to come up and put the kids to bed?"

"It's Sunday. I'll do it. Don't be long."

Bobby drove the bike to the first house occupied by the schoolteacher. Bobby had built the teacher a brick house with a tin roof. Sekuru and four of the senior workers also had brick houses with tin roofs. The rest of the gang lived in pole and dagga huts built by themselves, the same mud and thatched huts their ancestors had lived in for centuries.

"Raymond, sorry to worry you on a Sunday. Can you go and look for Welcome for me?"

The two always spoke in English to help Raymond improve his second language. Still sitting on the bike with the engine running, Bobby waited. When Raymond came back the teacher looked puzzled.

"His wife think him up at the house."

"He left the house hours ago. Where can he have gone?"

"He's not here, boss. Must have gone to one of the other farm compounds. Or into the Chiweshe reserve. Welcome has friends and family in the reserve."

"Thank you, Raymond. How are the kids doing?"

"Those books you brought us. We're building a little library. Kids very excited."

"I'm glad."

Back at the house, Hammond's truck was in the driveway, Hammond sitting alone in the lounge.

"Wendy's making food for the kids in the kitchen. You find Welcome?"

"Not a sign of him. Not been back to the compound since he left to come up to the house this morning."

"You got some of that Scotch you were boasting about?"

"You drink too much, Hammond."

"Especially when it's Scotch."

"I'll get some ice from the freezer in the kitchen. Did Wendy show you a bedroom? Where's your gun? You did bring a gun."

"Left in the bedroom with my bag."

"Better get it. From dusk onwards we carry loaded guns. Something's gone wrong with Welcome. Never in all the years he has worked for me has he done this before. If he wants to go he asks me first."

"He'll turn up. We're all on edge. All of us. Blacks and whites. The sun from here looks so beautiful now it's going down. The whole sky is painted red. I'll get my gun. You get the ice."

By the time Wendy had fed the children it was almost dark. Bobby's nerves were at breaking point, he was so on edge. Hammond had barely touched his Scotch. The kids sat on the sofa in the lounge surrounded by the four dogs, Bobby watching the dogs for signs that anything was out of the ordinary. All three loaded guns were close at hand. Outside the cicadas were screeching, the croaking of the frogs adding their calls to the night. Far away an owl called, which Bobby thought unusual. Mostly the owls called to each other later in the night. Bobby was not sure whether to turn on the lights. Make them a target. Show the terrorists where to come. All of them had gone silent, including the children. Bobby had no idea what to do for the best. Should the kids be put down in their own beds or stay up in the lounge? When the dark came should they all go quietly down to the office and cower on the floor? Or should the lights go up and tell anyone watching that life hadn't changed? Except for the guns. With the lights on, should he regularly show himself with a gun out on the veranda? Listen for danger nearer to the night? Or would he be making himself a target? Inviting an attack?

"I'm going to put the dogs outside."

No one said anything, all of them tense.

"I'm going to put the kids to bed," said Wendy suddenly getting up.

"Are you sure?"

"No I'm bloody well not. Hammond, either drink that Scotch or throw it out the bloody window."

"Sorry, Wendy. You going to turn the lights on, Bobby?"

"Think I should?"

"This is all new to me. Apart from the crickets and the frogs it's too darn quiet for my liking. How far's your compound?"

"About a mile."

"Can't hear a bloody thing. Not a drum. Not a shout. Not a bloody thing. What the hell?"

Hammond threw down his drink and offered Bobby his empty glass. Bobby got up and turned on the light. Wendy took the children off to bed. Bobby poured Hammond his second drink and handed him the glass, the ice clinking against the side of the glass, the new light reflecting the cut-glass crystal as he passed it across.

"It's Welcome. If Welcome was here serving us supper I'd feel less insecure. Where the hell can he be?"

"Cheers, Bobby."

"I'm not going to sleep a wink."

"Neither am I. Tomorrow we were meant to start reaping on Cotswold Grange."

"It's like being on the front line in a war."

"Yes, I suppose it is. The dogs will give us warning."

"You think so?"

"Have a drink, Bobby. So where do we sleep tonight?"

"Let's stay up until midnight and make our decision."

"From what I heard in the club, the terrs attack in the beginning of the night to give themselves time to escape in the dark. How far away from here is the Chiweshe reserve?"

"The village is about ten miles as the crow flies. You think they're in the TTL?"

"I have no idea. Neither does the army or the police. How did we all get into this shit? No, that's stupid. We all knew it was coming. Just wouldn't admit it. Even to ourselves."

"It's probably not as bad as you think."

"Probably not."

Wendy came back, her mouth slightly open, her two small front teeth protruding.

"The girls are asleep."

"They have no idea what's going on, thank God. We're staying up until midnight."

"I'll never sleep. I've put the kids' mattresses in the bathroom where there aren't any outside windows."

"Didn't they complain?"

"Too tired from all that running around with the Swart kids in the club. You want to put on the radio? Hear the news?"

"I'd feel better in the quiet listening to the dogs and the crickets. Any change outside and I'll turn out the lights. If they're trying to intimidate us to run away, or make us sit cowering in the dark, we will have them winning the war."

"You think it's a war?"

"What the hell else is it? Have a drink, Wendy. Sit down. What's for supper?"

"Cold lamb and salads. I made a lettuce, tomato and cucumber salad with a French dressing. Potato salad and mayonnaise."

"Sounds good to me, Wendy," said Hammond, getting up to look out at the dark. "Thanks for having me."

"You're welcome."

The last word put Bobby straight back on edge. He got up and looked out the window in the direction of the Chiweshe reserve. Outside was pitch dark. The dogs were quiet. Bobby couldn't even see their shapes on the lawn. Later, with pale light from the stars, the dogs would be visible. For all these years the African bush at night had been comforting for Bobby. A place familiar. Now everything about it was menacing.

"Let's sit at the table," said Wendy. "You won't be able to see anything. Come and sit down, both of you. Bobby, you can carve the shoulder of lamb. You like mint sauce, Hammond?"

"Can't eat lamb without mint sauce can we? Wouldn't be British... How far can they shoot from?"

"Hammond, shut up."

"Sorry, Wendy. Bit on edge. Good idea putting the kids to bed in the bathroom. How about us tonight sleeping in the corridor? No windows."

"That's a good one, Hammond. Probably better than the office. Yes, I'll move three single mattresses into the corridor... Listen to that. Whose ring is it?"

"Elizabeth and Stanley Wells," said Hammond without thinking. "One short and two long. I wonder who's calling them?"

"You can always pick up our phone and listen," said Wendy, making a smile. "You can all help yourselves to salad and potatoes."

"They're not picking up. Must be still at the club."

"Hadn't they left before us?"

All three sitting at the dining room table in the alcove off the lounge listened for the party line to stop ringing, all of them looking at the phone on its small shelf attached to the wall at the end of the room. When it finally stopped ringing Bobby picked up the carving knife and began carving the lamb.

"Hand me your plate, Wendy. How many slices?"

"Three please."

When the dogs began barking outside, Bobby dropped the carving knife on the oval serving dish with a clatter. All of them froze at the table. Wendy got up and went back into the lounge, coming back with her gun. The dogs kept on barking.

"Turn out the lights," said Wendy.

"It's a normal bark. They've found something to play with. Come and sit down and eat your supper. There goes the phone again. Whose ring is that? Who's three long rings?"

"There are over forty on the party line. Can't remember all of them."

"Pass your plate, Hammond. Whoever it is has picked up. At least the terrorists haven't cut the telephone lines. That's a good sign isn't it?... How many slices?"

"Make it two. I'm not very hungry."

Wendy had propped her rifle against the wall behind her chair. She was helping herself to the potato salad. Before she took from the bowl of green salad she mixed in the dressing from the white boat with its hooked silver spoon, mixing the lettuce, tomatoes and cucumber with the oil and vinegar dressing.

"Lots of garlic in the dressing," said Wendy. "So we're all going to be head-to-toe in the corridor... The dogs have stopped barking. At least this alcove is away from the windows. Enjoy the food."

"Elizabeth is pregnant."

"Oh, my God! Whose is it?"

"Probably mine. Elizabeth says she's lucky if Stanley makes love once a month."

"Oh, my God!" said Wendy again.

"Stop giggling, darling."

"But how awful. Once a month! That's terrible. You want a glass of wine, Hammond? There's an open bottle of red on the sideboard. Local Rhodesian plonk but it's vaguely drinkable... Has she told Stanley?"

"Not yet."

"How old is she?"

"Forty-two."

"My goodness. She'll be sixty-four when the kid turns twenty-one. Stanley will be in his rocking chair."

Bobby got up and fetched the bottle of wine, picking three wine glasses from the sideboard cabinet.

"May we never run out of alcohol," he said, putting the bottle and glasses down on the table.

"I'll second that, old boy. Thanks for having me."

"You're welcome."

"Where the hell is he?" Bobby said vehemently.

They sat in silence, neither Wendy nor Hammond moving in their chairs as Bobby walked round filling up their glasses.

"There will be a perfectly logical explanation," said Wendy. "There always is. We could always turn out the lights and light some candles. Celebrate poor old Elizabeth getting herself pregnant."

"Sarcasm is the lowest form of wit. Someone said that."

"Probably Oscar Wilde."

"Wasn't he a queer?"

"Still had children," said Bobby. "Saw one of his plays in London. *Importance of Being Earnest*. The man was a great playwright whatever his sexual predilection. Darling, pass the salad."

"Do you ever think of Katie, Bobby?"

"What a terrible question."

"Do you?"

"Does it matter?"

"Not anymore."

"Do you think of your old boyfriends, Wendy?"

"Not anymore... Cheers. To getting through the night."

"To getting through life," said Hammond. "I wonder what he will look like? You think a child would want to come into this world if he knew what it was all about?"

"To George Stacy," said Bobby, lifting his glass. "May he rest in peace."

"You think he's looking down on us?"

"I hope so. If there isn't a God, if there isn't a heaven, none of what we go through would have been worth living. What would the point be? The point of life? You know George threw a wake for that old lion that he killed on his farm in a gun trap. The lion had been killing his cows. Hope they're both together in peace. Or do animals go to heaven? I'm not sure."

"What's the matter with you, Bobby?" asked Wendy. "It's the here and now that counts. Who the hell really knows what happens to us afterwards?"

"Don't you believe in God, Wendy?"

"Of course I do. I don't want to get morbid, Bobby. Those dogs are barking again. This time I'm going outside to have a look. Cheers to George Stacy. And you're right. May he rest in peace. May we all one day rest in peace. Just not tonight or tomorrow."

"She's one tough girl," whispered Hammond to Bobby as Wendy picked up her gun and walked out through the lounge. They both listened to the fly screen door to the veranda being shut before going back to eating their supper. The dogs had again stopped barking.

"All four of them right now will be wagging their tails," said Bobby.

"Why did she bring up Katie?"

"Women have long memories when it comes to their man's other women. You want some more lamb? See your appetite came back."

"One slice."

"How long can we go on night after night living like this?"

"Dad said fighting the Japs in the jungles of Burma and Malaya, he got used to it. Resigned to it. Resigned to dying and killing. He was a professional soldier. The family had been in the army for five generations. I broke the tradition. He was thirty-nine years in the army. Retired as a brigadier general. Bugger-all pension. Mum's parents were in trade. Textiles. They have the money... What's she doing out there?"

"Standing in the dark. After your eyes get used to it you can see quite well by the light of the stars. There's no moon for a couple of days. Why they chose to attack last night I suppose."

"Do you think of Katie?"

"Please, Hammond. I married Wendy. Can you imagine Katie standing outside in the night with a .303 rifle in her hand? And believe me, Wendy knows how to use it. The first of the Coxes came up on the pioneer column."

"How soon after meeting Wendy did you marry her?"

"A couple of months. Fell off a barstool in Bretts. She helped me up off the floor."

"Love at first sight."

"Not exactly," said Bobby very quietly. "Katie had just gone back to England."

"That was some wedding in Salisbury Cathedral. Vince Ranger best man. A real party of a reception at Meikles afterwards. Half of Centenary block came to your wedding. Anyway, it all worked out well. Two lovely kids. A practical wife. You're happy aren't you?"

"More than happy, Hammond. She's a wonderful woman."

"Who is?" asked Wendy, coming back into the house."

"You, darling."

"There was a bullfrog in the rose garden puffing up its chest."

"Could you see that well?"

"After a while. It's all very quiet. Not a sound coming from our compound. The worst time for an attack is over, hopefully."

"You want some more lamb?"

"Just a slice. Where are the cats?"

"Haven't seen either of them since we got back from the club. Must be out hunting. Bruce is the best ratter I ever had. We had rats in the bulk shed the year before last. Left Bruce in the shed at night for a week. Never saw a rat again. Or a carcase. That cat eats what he kills."

"Why'd you call him Bruce?"

"Because apart from killing rats and mice, he's stupid. When he falls off the window sill he falls off. Right onto the floor. A solid thunk. Our Bruce doesn't land on his feet."

"What's Bruce got to do with being stupid?"

"Bruce and Sheila. It's Australian. You never heard a Bruce and Sheila joke?

"Tell me one."

"They're all a bit crude. Really crude. You want some more of this wine? Tastes like vinegar but who cares?... Where you going this time, Wendy? I'm not going to tell him why Sheila threatened to jump off the Sydney Harbour Bridge."

"I'm going to look at the twins."

"Why did Sheila want to jump off the bridge?" asked Hammond as Wendy left the room taking her gun.

"She was pregnant by Bruce. Quite appropriate under your circumstances, Hammond. When she threatened to jump off the bridge if Bruce wouldn't marry her, Bruce told her she was not only a good screw but a good sport. Sounds better told with an Australian accent. Sorry, Hammond. I'm gabbling."

"I know how you feel... You think Elizabeth should jump off the Sydney Harbour Bridge?"

"Of course not. Just something to say. Something else to think about other than what's lurking outside."

"They're miles away."

"That's what I've been trying to convince myself."

They sat in silence drinking the wine until Wendy came back through the door that led into the corridor with its bedrooms on either side.

"Sound asleep. Both of them."

"Sit down and finish your food."

"I've had enough. We'll leave the things on the table until morning. Let's go back and sit in the lounge."

"We were just talking about your wedding," said Hammond.

"You should get yourself married, Hammond. Before it's too late."

"No one will marry me. We don't get young girls out from England anymore. Everything has changed in Rhodesia."

"You want to sit near a window?" said Bobby. "Let's stay where we are. I'll open another bottle of plonk. But first I'm going to move those three mattresses into the corridor. You want to help, Hammond?"

"How many mattresses you got?"

"The ones in the store are camping mattresses. We'll take the three from the guest bedrooms. It's so bloody hot and oppressive, we won't need sheets or blankets."

"We can do that when we all want to sleep. Open the wine."

Wendy was sitting bolt upright looking at the wall that made the dining room area into an alcove. Where they sat at the table no one outside the house could see them. The bottle of plonk, a new effort to overcome sanctions and the lack of foreign exchange by a farmer in Rusape, had a screw top. Bobby sniffed at the wine in the bottle.

"You've got to be drunk to drink this stuff. Takes generations to know how to make good wine."

Bobby filled up all three glasses before sitting down. The violent crack of thunder frightened all of them, Wendy knocking over the glass she had been gripping by its stem. Red wine spilled out in a long balloon over the white tablecloth.

"There wasn't any lightning. Here comes the rain." Bobby's hand when he went to take up the bottle to refill his wife's glass was shaking, his nerves shot to ribbons by the sudden crack of thunder. Wendy was crying, making no sound. Hammond sat frozen in his chair. Bobby stood up holding the bottle, waiting to hear cries from his children through the open door to the corridor. Silence had come back into the house. They could hear the rain coming outside and then it hit the roof, a pounding noise so loud on the tin roof above them that it drowned out everything else.

"I'll go," said Bobby. He had refilled Wendy's wine having righted the glass.

The corridor was even more stifling than the dining alcove. The light was on in the corridor, the door to the outside locked at the end. The door to the bathroom was ajar. Bobby listened outside for any sound from the twins. Then he smiled. All was quiet. When he looked in he saw Wendy had put a mattress in the bath. With their heads at either end of the bath, Stephanie and Deborah lay toe to toe, both of them sound asleep. After smiling down at his children Bobby silently left, closing the bathroom door behind him but leaving it ajar. They were so adorable when they were asleep, the perfect time to enjoy them. The drumming of the rain on the roof stopped abruptly, a brief cloudburst that passed right over the house. Bobby walked back down the corridor.

"Short and sharp," he said sitting down at the table. "Where were we? Africa has that habit. One minute peace and quiet and then all hell lets loose. That one crept up on us... The girls are sleeping like angels. Good idea putting the mattress in the bath. Turns the bath into a cot. You did leave the plug out?"

"Of course I did," snapped Wendy.

"Trying to make a joke."

"Not at the expense of my children."

"They're also my children."

"Are we going to sit here all night fighting?"

"That drop of rain will be wonderful for the crop," said Bobby, trying to change the subject and lighten the tension.

"Hope I got some on Cotswold," said Hammond. "Sometimes you can be at a land of tobacco with it raining next to the land but not a drop is falling on the tobacco. Rain. Africa's final curse and blessing. Every year since I got my own farm I look up at the sky every day during the growing season. Rain's our biggest problem. Bigger than terrorists. Well, maybe not bigger. You were right to build a dam, Bobby. Don't have a river to dam running through my place. Two years ago we got too much rain. The lands of tobacco were waterlogged. Couldn't get in to reap. Lost ten per cent of my crop while it ripened and rotted in the lands. That was half of my profit."

"You remember that plague of caterpillars?"

"Who doesn't? They loved the DDT we sprayed on them. Bobby, why the hell did we both go farming?"

"We wanted to be lords of the manor. An old throwback to our British ancestry. Wasn't one of your ancestors a duke?"

"He was an earl. John Taylor, the last Earl of Stratton. That's in the Cotswolds. Fell out with Henry VIII and had his head cut off. We've been out of the limelight ever since. The hereditary title was lost with his head."

"The name Taylor suggests working class, Hammond."

"Does, doesn't it? He came up through the army I think. Don't know much about him. Most of what we know is family folklore. Passed down the generations. There's not much known about him in written history. The Tudors were a long time ago."

"So you named your farm after him?"

"Sort of. We all want to think we're better than we are. That somewhere in our background we amounted to something. All a lot of crap, really. Sorry, Wendy. Shouldn't swear in front of a lady."

"A cobbler turned Earl of Stratton. How fascinating. Sorry, Hammond. Just a joke."

"The barons were warlords in those days. Securing the king's dominions. They were probably thugs, Magna Carta or no Magna Carta that had started all the talk about democracy. Politicians give power so many different words to justify the means to their ends."

"How many earls of Stratton were there?"

"Seven of them."

"Quite a pedigree. Pity the last one had his head chopped off."

"Everything comes and goes, Bobby."

"Suppose it does. Suppose it does... We're a long way from Stratton."

"About seven thousand miles... It was why I wanted my own farm. Owning land must be in my blood."

"It's in all of us. Including the terrorists who attacked us last night. They say we stole their land. Maybe we did."

"They weren't doing much with it before we came along."

"Not a bloody thing. Bush. Miles and miles of bushveld teeming with game. Then we made the mistake of turning it into productive farmland. Made it worth something. Now they want it back again."

"Won't do them any good if they don't know how to farm it. Today's farming is big business. No more throwing seed on the ground and hoping it will grow. Or running cattle wild in the bush. To make money nowadays you've got to be scientific. Expensive equipment. And capital. Lots of capital. Not to say the infrastructure we've built in Salisbury to service the farms. Roads, power lines, telephones. The whole modern world. It's not the land that's worth anything. It's what you do with it. The crops you produce. Land left fallow is worthless. The Centenary was only opened up to farming twenty years ago. Now look at it. The country's most flourishing tobacco-growing area though they'll argue that point in Karoi and Sinoia. We made it what it is. Not them. And that's got bugger all to do with racism. It was our knowledge and expertise, not the colour of our skin. Now we're running around with guns trying to protect what we made of it. Not to say anything of all the jobs we created and all the food we produce. Oh yes. Now they want it. Now it's worth something. If they do get rid of us British they'll have thrown the baby out with the bathwater. Makes me a bit pissed off to add to all my other worries tonight. Why the hell did we bother, I ask myself. Better to have lived like Mum and Dad in a semi-detached in Wimbledon, dreaming of some long-lost relation who had his head chopped off."

"We're not going to lose our farms," said Wendy.

"After last night, I'm not so sure."

"You want some more wine, Hammond? We'll get through this. Wendy's right. We've all got to think positive. Stick together."

"All that stiff upper lip crap. I'm not so sure. Life sucks. You think you're doing something with your life and then this happens. I can't even go to sleep in peace in my own bloody home."

"Electrified security fences will help."

"Aren't we delaying the inevitable? Maybe this wine isn't so bad after all. What I wouldn't do for a nice bottle of South African Nederburg."

"Don't even mention it."

"Maybe if I get myself drunk I'll get some sleep. How much plonk have you got, Bobby?"

"A whole case of it."

"If they attack from outside we wouldn't be able to see them to shoot back anyway."

"We need electrified fences with spotlights flooding light into the surrounding bush."

"Couldn't they cut the power lines?"

"Not without electrocuting themselves. Have some more wine."

"You are most kind. Must have been a bit like this in London during the Blitz. And they got through it. Most of them. Your salad dressing, Wendy, was perfect. So here's another toast. 'To bed, to sleep, perchance to dream.' Hamlet. Shakespeare."

The sound of gunfire ripped the night to shreds.

Bobby froze, not knowing what to do as primal fear gripped his intestines. Both Wendy and Hammond looked terrified. "Where is it?" said Bobby when it stopped. "Nothing's hit the house. Someone's shooting up the compound. Or the sheds. They can't see us, thank God."

The dogs hadn't barked, everything was now silent outside. They waited, upright in their chairs.

"Where are you going, Wendy?"

"To get the girls. We'll go out the back door by the kitchen. Hide in the bush."

"You taking your gun?"

"I've only got one pair of hands. Both of you. Down the corridor. In the bush in the dark they won't find us. Leave the lights on."

Outside behind the house the grass was wet. Bobby carried Stephanie. Wendy carried Deborah. Hammond carried the guns. The second burst of automatic gunfire erupted as they reached the long grass, Bobby and Hammond following Wendy, the children half asleep.

They followed Wendy into the bush away from the dam and the buildings. Wendy stopped next to an ant hill. They waited, listening. Back at the house the dogs were barking. The night sky had cleared, the stars appearing giving them a glimmer of light. They were wet through from brushing the wet grass. Wendy sat down with her back to the tall, spiral-shaped ant hill, the child asleep in her arms. Bobby sat next to her. Stephanie had gone back to sleep. His heart was pounding, the first fearful terror receding. Hammond got down next to him and gave them their guns. The wet grass made them cold, all except the children who, held in Bobby and Wendy's arms, had not brushed the grass. Bobby put his arm round Wendy. She was shivering. Uncontrollably shivering. Above him, the second and third layers of stars had appeared in the heavens. Bobby could see the Southern Cross pointing towards the south. A bushbuck barked from behind them. Far away, thunder rolled. They huddled for warmth and human comfort, all of them waiting. It was just past one o'clock by Bobby's luminous wrist watch when a hyena howled not far behind them, the sound reminiscent of somebody laughing. Strangely it was comforting, a normal sound. At half past one Bobby got up, walked a few yards away and had himself a pee, Stephanie left on the ground still asleep. Hammond was asleep on his back, a soft whistling coming from his open mouth.

"Must you do it so close?" asked Wendy when he sat back down.

"In the house, with the first shots, I pissed in my pants. Right down inside my legs. You all right?"

"We're all right, lover."

"They must have hit the office. Someone was watching you when you took down the camping mattresses. When they couldn't see us in the house with the lights on they must have thought we had gone to sleep in my office. Can we go back into the house?"

"We'll wait for sunrise. Thank God the dogs didn't hear us and follow."

"Yes, that was luck. Sometimes you need some luck. Put your head on my shoulder."

With the children on their laps, their backs to the ant hill, they fell asleep, Bobby holding her hand, the call of the birds waking them hidden in the long elephant grass when the sun rose in the morning.

Hammond had already got up and walked away into the trees behind the ant hill to relieve himself.

"Can you see anything?" asked Bobby. "I thought we were much further from the house."

"Everything looks so bloody normal."

"You want some breakfast? Let's go back to the house. Welcome should be up there by now."

"Your kids can really sleep."

"Come on, sleepy heads. Happy Christmas. We're going back to the house."

"Why are we here?"

"Don't ask so many questions. Aren't you hungry?"

"I'm starving," said each of the girls.

In the light of morning Bobby saw they were five hundred yards from the back of the house. With the kids running ahead, they walked to the house. The dogs found them outside the kitchen with the cats, Bruce and Jemima, rubbing up against the backs of their legs. There was no one in the outside kitchen. No one in the house. The *simby*, an old plough disc hit with a metal bolt, rang out, calling the labourers to work. From the compound, they heard the tractor start up.

"This just isn't right," said Bobby. "Where the hell is Welcome? I'm taking the motorbike down to the sheds. See you tonight, Hammond, if you want to come back again."

The tractor with the trailer had brought the labourers up to the sheds. Bobby got off the bike and walked to his office. The window glass behind the burglar bars had been shattered. Bobby unlocked the door. Pieces of cloth from the bedding on the floor were strewn all over the desk and the safe. Bobby felt sick and closed the door. When he came out Sekuru was watching.

"Someone was trying to kill me last night," said Bobby in Fanagalo.

"I'm sorry, boss."

"I think we all will be, Sekuru. Everything all right in the compound? There's still no sign of Welcome up at the house."

"His wife and kids still haven't seen him."

Not sure whether Sekuru was friend or foe, Bobby got back on the bike and kick-started the motor. Only Sekuru and Jackson had been at the sheds when Wendy visited the office. He and Sekuru, first at World's

View when they worked for Jeremy Crookshank, had known each other a long time. Now the trust was gone.

"Why they think you in office?" asked Sekuru.

"Do you know why, Sekuru?"

"No, boss. Why you want to go the office in the night?"

Back at the house Bobby picked up the phone from its shelf in the dining alcove to call the police. The line was dead. Bobby gripped the phone, his intestines lurching.

"What's the matter?"

"The line's been cut. Get the kids."

"Where are we going?"

"To the Centenary police station. We've got an informer in the compound."

At the police station half an hour later, closer to the Centenary West club, they were kept waiting. Everyone was running around in the charge office not taking any notice of them. They had left the children in the car with the nanny.

Half an hour later Clay Barry came out of his closed office. The man looked ten years older.

"Sorry to keep you, Bobby. There were two more attacks last night."

"They hit my office."

"Shit! Why the office? Come in. Fred's with me. This just gets worse. Why didn't you phone me? I'd have sent someone."

"They cut the phone line. There's an informer in my compound. Someone saw Wendy taking bedding to the office."

"Has Welcome come back?"

"No. Why do you ask?" said Bobby, following the policeman into his office where Clay closed the door.

"He's an informer, Bobby. He's been keeping an eye on the Chiweshe reserve for us for a couple of years. We pay him for information. Somewhere in that Tribal Trust Land they've been stashing munitions brought in from Zambia."

"Well he's gone. He must be the informer who tried to get us killed last night."

"Or they took him. Your office can be seen from the bush. More likely they were watching your house and sheds from the surrounding hills through binoculars. They're well trained. Good equipment. Know what they're doing by the look of it. We shot dead three of them last night trying to get back into the Chiweshe reserve. The three of them walked into our police ambush."

"Who were they?"

"We don't know yet. I was hoping Welcome would tell me. Maybe that's why they abducted him, to shut his mouth."

"It just gets worse."

"Yes it does. I'll send Fred here to Hopewell to make a report. Put up a security fence as soon as you can. You might have to wait a bit. There's only one firm in Salisbury with the right equipment. Otherwise, you and the family all right?"

"Spent the night next to an ant hill, along with Hammond. What's going to happen, Clay?"

"Time will tell. It always does. See you at the cricket on Boxing Day. Not much of a Christmas for any of us this year. The farm still working?"

"Start reaping after Christmas."

"That's the stuff. If Welcome comes back let me know."

"But you don't think he will?"

"Probably not. I never believe in coincidences."

"Did he just do it for money?"

"Never asked him... Fred, you see Bobby and Wendy to their truck."

"Brought the car, what with the nanny and the kids."

"See him to the car."

Clay Barry briefly got up and put out his hand. The handshake was firm and strong. Feeling worse than when he came in, Bobby left the member-in-charge's office. Fred Rankin put a hand on his shoulder. At the car the twins were throwing a tantrum.

"So?" said Wendy.

"We're pretty much on our own."

"See you later, Bobby."

"I hope so, Fred. You opening the batting?"

"Second wicket down. That's if the chaps from Macheke want to come up to the Centenary. The captain called and said they would. Bit of a show of solidarity. We'll see what happens come Sunday."

"Aren't you coming to the farm?"

"This afternoon. I'll bring one of my constables. Write a full report."

"Are you all right, Fred?"

"Haven't slept a wink since the first attack."

"Sorry to be difficult."

"Don't you worry. You were the one who got attacked... My word, those kids grow up quickly. It's all about the kids, really. Poor little buggers."

"Get some sleep before the cricket."

"I'll do my best. All you can do."

"Were you in the ambush?"

"I led the ambush. Never killed another man before. Made me feel terrible. The kid I shot looked not much older than my kid. Fifteen, going on sixteen. Now the poor sod's dead. At fifteen, would he have known what he was doing?"

"Give my love to Joyce. How are the kids?"

"Mine are fine. Yes, mine are fine. You look after yourselves."

PART V

JANUARY TO MAY 1973 – "EVERYONE HAS A PRICE"

1

Thirteen days after Christmas, Katie Frost woke to the morning of her twenty-ninth birthday with a smile on her face until she realised what date it was. The dream had been perfect. A warm African sun, no sign of other people, animals in the endless bush and Bobby Preston next to her. The reality as she got up and looked out the window of her newly purchased flat in Shepherd's Bush was oh so different. Outside it was wet, windy and grey. She was alone. She had no children. All she ever did in her life was about money, her money as a computer programmer and the money of her clients she so diligently sorted and placed. Sadly, feeling old, Katie made herself a cup of tea in the smart new kitchen, all chrome and plastic and shining surfaces. She wasn't even hungry for her breakfast, had no wish to lie in bed, no real wish to do anything exciting. Her life fundamentally was boring. In the week she worked on other people's money setting up their accounting programmes. At night she came home in the dark to the sterile sanctity of her new home, thanks to her bank manager granting her a mortgage. She and her friends went clubbing. They went dining. They even went to a classical concert every now and again to imagine they were getting some culture. But all of it, year after year, from the time of working for her programmer's qualification to her fancy job with IBM, to the huge increase in her salary, was boring compared to the time she had spent with Bobby in Rhodesia. When the phone rang in the lounge she was still standing at the window feeling sorry for herself, coupled with guilt at having so much with so little appreciation. Someone had said that when you get bored with London you were bored with life. With a deep sigh of discontent Katie put the mug of tea on the small table under the window and walked to the phone that stood next to her comfortable chair looking at the television.

"Hello, Katie Frost speaking." Even on a Sunday it was likely to be business. Some programme broken down. Some terrible emergency.

"Happy birthday, darling."

"Linda! Where are you? Where the hell have you been?"

"In America. Andy wanted to tour America."

"Have you got a job?"

"Whatever for? Andy's so rich."

"Are you going to marry him?"

"Don't be silly. I may be an unemployed computer programmer with a fancy diploma but I can always get a job. I can enjoy men and what they give me without having to look to them for a future. How are you, darling?"

"Feeling old. Nearly thirty. Feels like the end of my life. No kids, no husband, not even a boyfriend."

"Don't you have a lover?"

"Lovers when I want them, Linda. It's all so pointless. Temporary satisfaction that isn't real satisfaction at all. I woke up this morning dreaming of Bobby. Should never have left Rhodesia, even with all its problems. What's life without a real lover? Someone you really love."

"Love is temporary. Life is temporary. You go through it enjoying yourself. Milking the old cow for what it's worth. Live for today, darling. To hell with tomorrow. Tomorrow may never come. What are you doing for your birthday?"

"Nothing planned. Absolutely nothing."

"Then you're coming to dinner with us at the Dorchester. Andy has a friend. An American friend. You'll like him."

"How old is he?"

"Fortyish. Maybe fifty. Stinking rich. Quite a charmer. He'll blow away your blues."

"Where are you now?"

"At the Dorchester. Tuesday we go to Paris."

"They always said you'd grow mushrooms on your bedsheets." Katie was laughing, suddenly excited.

"That sounds like the old Katie. You need to get out more often. All work and no play makes Katie a dull girl. You got to enjoy yourself. Do a little living. Seven-thirty. You can afford a taxi?"

"I do have money."

"See you later, alligator."

"In a while, crocodile. Hey it's good to hear from you, Linda. It's been too long."

With a little purpose back in her day, Katie made breakfast, taking her bacon and eggs to the table in the little alcove in her lounge. Outside the window it wasn't so grey. A pigeon on the wet slate rooftop was cooing, the sound just reaching Katie through her double-glazed window. At one o'clock, to give herself something to do, she turned on the news and sat down on the couch. Outside the rain had turned to sleet. She was late, the news a few minutes into the broadcast, Katie not giving the television her full attention. Comfortable with a book on her lap in the warmth of the central heating, Katie looked at the picture on the screen, a picture joltingly familiar. Katie sat up in the chair, the book falling onto the carpet at her feet.

Last night a white farmer was killed in the Rhodesian insurgency behind where I am standing. The office of the Zimbabwe African National Union in Lusaka has claimed responsibility. These are the first pictures we are able to bring you of the Centenary, a farming block in the northeast of the country. We are told by the Rhodesian authorities the first such deadly attack on a white farmer occurred a few days before Christmas. ZANU claim they have begun a war of liberation, a Chimurenga in the native vernacular. We do not know the name of the dead farmer but we are told he was British. This is Ben Carron reporting for the BBC from close to the northeast border of Rhodesia.

The news moved on. The story changed. For Katie, the colonial bungalow on its hill surrounded by bush was so familiar she wanted to vomit, the question screaming through her mind: was it Bobby's house or wasn't it? Feeling impotent, Katie turned off the television, the thought that she'd been right to leave bringing little consolation.

"My poor Bobby. My poor Bobby. You should have got out when I asked you to. Nothing's worth dying for."

When the phone rang calling Katie to a client she agreed to help her supervisor sort out the crashed programme immediately. Three hours later, with the problem solved and the client's mainframe computer up and running, Katie went home for a bath and to watch the six o'clock news.

By the time she had bathed, changed and found a taxi she was going to be late but none of it mattered. The dead farmer was not Bobby Preston, the name on the news not one Katie had immediately recognised. Relieved, happy and excited as the cab drove down Park Lane into the circular drive of the entrance to the Dorchester Hotel, Katie overtipped the cab driver and ran into the foyer. In the hotel restaurant she found Linda and two elderly men seated at one of the tables.

"What's got you so flushed, darling?"

"It wasn't Bobby."

"What wasn't Bobby?"

"It's on the news. A farmer killed in the Centenary."

They all looked at her with blank expressions.

"This is Andy and Finn. Finn's from Kansas City, Missouri. You're late, darling. It's eight o'clock."

"Got called out to a client. Hello, Andy. Hello, Finn. Sorry I'm late."

The man called Finn was looking at her, smiling, appraising. He got up and helped Katie into the fourth chair at the table.

"One war finishes, another one starts," he said. "So much for calling it a cold war. The Russians like other people to fight their wars. You got friends in Rhodesia, Katie?"

"Linda and I lived in Rhodesia for almost a year. Over five years ago."

"Lucky you got out in time... You want a drink?... My son was killed in Vietnam. There are no nice wars for anyone."

"I'm so sorry."

"So am I. Every day of my life. He was the only child I ever had. It's like you've died yourself. Your future gone... You have any children, Katie?"

"Not yet."

"Have some. They're the only reason for living your life. So what will it be?"

"A glass of that red wine."

The table lapsed into silence.

"Did you love him?" asked Finn.

"Who are you talking about?"

"The man you are worrying about in Rhodesia. I also saw the news. White farmer by the name of Stanley Wells. Was it him?"

"No, thank God... Stanley Wells? Was that the name? I think Bobby may have mentioned him in passing."

"Have the fish. There's one thing about eating fish in England. It's fresh. You're always close to the sea... Are you going to marry him?"

"He's married with two children... How are you, Linda? You look well. The trip to America must have been good."

"New York. It's amazing. Takes your breath away. Finn is Andy's business associate in America."

"What about Kansas City?"

"If you want to make real money in finance you move to New York. Been in the Big Apple these last twenty years. I was raised in the Midwest. Irish stock. Cheers, as you say in England. To Katie. I'm glad you made it... What do you do, Katie?"

"I'm a computer programmer for IBM. The reason I'm late is because I was called out to a client."

"Now that's a good American company. You should come to New York. Let me show you around. I'm sure IBM would give you a job. Get you a green card with those qualifications... Working on a Sunday. I'm impressed. We believe in hard work in America. You'd be a great success in the States."

The small talk continued for most of the evening, Finn doing his best to chat her up, Katie thinking of Bobby. Finn was nice, comfortable, no sign of a threat. Andy, the less talkative of the men, had most of his attention centred on Linda's bosom, her evening dress low cut and revealing. Were it not for the BBC news, Katie would have enjoyed her evening.

"What d'you want to do, Katie? We can go on to the Mayfair. Cabaret. Dancing. That sort of thing. London's nightlife goes into the small hours of the morning."

"I have to work tomorrow."

"You worked on a Sunday. Relax a little. Take your mind off Stanley Wells. Did he have a wife and children?"

"I'm not sure. I think so. Can't put a face to the name. There were two sport clubs in the Centenary. I was always the visitor. Everyone else knew each other. You get introduced to so many people at once you can't put names to the faces until you've met them a few times. Thank you both for supper."

"Come on. Be a devil. I'm sure Linda's game for a party. Anyway, as I'm Andy's American business associate I'm sure he can charge tonight against the tax man. Only foreign business clients are tax deductible. Or we can go on to Annabel's. Take your mind off your friend. Have you ever been to America?"

"The furthest I went was to Rhodesia. On a boat. There and back. I've circumnavigated Africa but never been to America... Don't you have a wife in New York?"

"But not in London. You coming with us?"

"Why not? If the tax man is paying, why not?"

"You're my kind of girl, Katie. My kind of girl."

It was always the same for Katie. The men with money were married, just looking for a night out and sex. The eligible men her own age took out the nineteen-year-olds, not interested in a girl of nearly thirty. Glad Linda hadn't brought up her birthday, she went along. The doorman had found them a taxi. None of it really mattered. Wondering what his wife would do if Katie went to New York, she sat down next to Finn in the back of the taxi. If nothing else, it was nice being wanted. The poor wife. Lost her son. Her man philandering... As they drove out of the hotel driveway into Park Lane Katie found herself holding his hand, no longer caring. There was a price for everything. The booze had dulled her wits, the images of Bobby terrified in his house in Rhodesia slowly fading from her mind. Would she have been able to cope? She doubted it. Being seduced by an old married man in the back of a taxi, Linda smiling encouragement, was probably better than lying in bed on Hopewell Estate not knowing what was coming at her through the window. There was always a price to pay. Finn was pleasant, gentle, so did it matter what she did? Ships in the night trying to find more from life than the boring. He'd forget her. She'd forget him. At twenty-nine she was going to be a spinster without any children... Having rationalised, Katie felt better. When they got out of the cab at the Mayfair she was ready for a party. With a few more drinks her inhibitions would likely fly out the window.

"We'll have some champagne," said Andy. "You girls like champagne? Now this is what I call a real night out on the tiles... Keep the change, driver... This is living."

"Do you have to book, Andy?" asked Katie.

"I already did," he said with a smile. "This afternoon. You got to have influence to get into the Mayfair. Come on, folks. Let the party begin."

Katie slept with Finn Cousins in his room at the Dorchester, too drunk to care what she was doing. At six in the morning, feeling not a little like a high-class whore, she took a taxi back to her flat, the hangover just beginning. In the IBM office her supervisor said she looked terrible.

"Go home, Katie. Get back into bed. You worked yesterday. Better a clear mind tomorrow than mucking it up today. Wasn't yesterday your birthday? I'll tell the boss you called in sick. What happened?"

"A rich American took me to the Mayfair."

"Is he married?"

"Of course he is. Wants me to go to America. Would IBM give me a transfer to New York?"

"Probably. The world is short of programmers. You want me to ask them?"

"Let's wait and see. I'm not as bad as I look. Drank three pints of water when I got home. Better than any aspirin. Coffee. I need coffee."

"Can you think straight?"

"I had some bad news yesterday before I went out. You remember me talking about Bobby Preston? A farm close to his was attacked the other night. One of the farmers killed."

"Wasn't it on the news? I remember hearing something. You never listen properly when it isn't your problem."

"Better I work than worry. Thanks, Glynnis. You always look after me when I need you."

"What are supervisors for?"

When Finn phoned at eleven o'clock Katie was feeling better.

"You want some lunch, Katie? I'm not far from the City."

"Don't you work on your trips?"

"It's more maintaining trust with Andy than going into detail. When we do trades we get down to detail. How are you feeling?"

"I've felt a lot better. But no lunch, thank you."

"Dinner?"

"Not tonight. When are you going home?"

"Tomorrow… Can I have your phone number at home?"

"Why not? Oh, you don't have to worry. I'm on the pill. Have a good flight, Finn. Nice meeting you. Have a good life."

"It was more than a one-night stand."

"Was it? It was my birthday yesterday. I understand. The world has changed. Women are liberated. We're now the same as the men. We go to work, get a good job, make our own futures. Not like the old days. In the old days a girl had no option. She used her youth and good looks to nail a husband. Any husband. Marriage and children was her only chance. We're liberated. There were no obligations for either of us last night."

"Would you come to America?"

"For you or for me? Maybe. You've got to go forward, Finn. I own my flat. That won't go away. Chances are any rent I get will pay the mortgage. I'm footloose and fancy-free. Why not? Be hearing from you, Finn. Don't hurt your wife. She got hurt badly once."

"She hates me. Ever since Lance was killed she's hated me. Blames me for not getting our boy out of the draft. It's not easy living with a woman who hates you, Katie. With all the people around me, with all my money, I get lonely. Last night was special to me. Maybe not to you. You'll be hearing from me."

"Thanks for the call."

"My pleasure, Katie. You take care of yourself. We could do a tour of America. Just the two of us. You did say he was married?"

"Soon after I left Rhodesia. Just shows. Have a nice day."

It was nice of him to phone. Made her feel less like a whore. A girl she knew, Angela Tate, was a high-class whore. Worked at a place in Hay Street called Le Rififi. Very expensive whore. Had a flat behind the Dorchester fully paid for. A degree in history from Oxford. Was writing a historical novel. Katie and Linda had known her at school. Angela had spoken the truth when Katie had questioned her profession.

"What's the difference, Katie? When the boyfriends take you out, who pays the bill? You don't. Sometimes they have to take you out half a dozen times before they get you into bed. Or take you to some place that is really fancy. I only go with the ones I like. Officially I'm a hostess. Men from out of town. Out of the country. Le Rififi is as much a business venue as the smart London clubs. The world of finance bring their clients to us to entertain them. I'm part of the service. I get a thousand pounds which has nothing to do with Le Rififi. You get a couple of free dinners. What's the difference? We're all whores. You know the most expensive whore in America? It's called an ex-wife. Some women make it a profession. I'm a working girl. I work for my money. When I've got enough I'm getting a nice place in the country where there aren't too many people and write myself some books. You'd be surprised how many plot lines I pick up in the club. Men tell me things they'd never tell a friend. I'm just a machine to them. A listening machine. A machine to slake their sexual frustrations. The only difference between you and me, my Katie, is that I get to keep some of the money. So that I can do something with my life. Something important. One day I'm going to explain what life is really all about for people like you and Linda to read and understand. Not all the bullshit. All the 'be nice'. I am what I am and proud of it. You got to have money, Katie. Lots of it. Then you don't have to be polite to people who behind all the smiles and good manners don't care a shit about you or me. All they care about is themselves. We both got good educations. I just used mine a little differently. To work at the club with its kind of clientele you've got to have a degree. They don't want to think of us as whores so we ask them to give us a present. While in the club we talk to them intelligently. Are you any happier than me? Is Linda? I don't think so. But there's one big difference. You'll work your fingers to the bone for some big corporation while I get rich. And yes, I know what I'm doing with my money. An offshore bank account for instance. I buy shares in corporations that work hard to make you bigger profits and push up the share price. There's another saying in life I heard from one of my clients: 'The most difficult thing in life is to hold onto your money once you have made it.' You think of that, Katie, after one of your boyfriends dumps you having had what he wanted. You end up with bugger-all. Sometimes soured by the ending, not even a happy memory. I never remember their names. I just remember their money.

Nicely tucked away in a Global Equity Fund. You think when I'm Lady Muck, the well-known novelist in the comfort of my paid-for country estate, anyone will care how I made my start in life? They'll be too busy being nice to a rich and famous lady. Remember that when you visit an old classmate when I'm rich and forty. It's always the money, Katie. Always the money. If you got it no one gives a shit how you made it. It's one big wicked world of take, take, take."

Smiling at her recollection of the conversation she had had in a rented flat with Angela before she obtained her programmer's qualifications, Katie tried to concentrate on the figures in front of her.

"You're right, Glynnis. I'm going to do more harm than good."

"Go home. And happy birthday for yesterday. I hope last night was worth the hangover."

"So do I. It's one of those creeping hangovers. It's getting worse. Fusing my mind."

"Don't do it again when you have to work in the morning."

"I won't. I promise I won't."

"What was his name?"

"Finn Cousins."

"The financier? I've heard of him. Made his fortune in hostile takeovers of public companies. He's American. I'm impressed. Sounds worth the late night if he follows up on you. There are three ways of making a fortune: you make it, inherit it, or marry it."

"See you tomorrow."

"Bright-eyed and bushy-tailed... Finn Cousins. I'll be blowed."

Unhappy, hungover and sad, Katie went home on the Tube, the Underground railway out of rush hour providing her with an unaccustomed seat. So he was rich. Stinking rich. Did it make any difference? All she could think of was Bobby. At least that had been love and not money. In her mind's eye she could still see the tent. Hear the hyena brush on the outside of the canvas. It made her smile. The man opposite in the half-empty carriage smiled back at her. She wanted to shout, 'not you, idiot'. But the game never stopped. The game of men and women. And he wasn't that bad looking. When he got up and sat next to her, Katie waited for the train to stop at the next station. Then she got out. The doors slid shut. The young man had turned to look at her through the window. Katie gave him the smallest of smiles. Ships, passing in the day. When the next train pulled into the station Katie got in and went on her way. And you'll never know what would have happened, she said to herself. Was that man the next love of her life? Who was he? Where had he come from? Where was he going?... At Shepherd's Bush Station Katie got out. Above ground it was raining. Katie walked home. Her flat was cold, uninviting. She had turned off the central heating during the day to save money. Katie took off her clothes and got into bed. Tried to sleep. Tossed and turned, her mouth dry from all the wine and champagne. And when she slept she was back in Rhodesia. Back in the tent. When she woke, Katie was full of fear and premonition. Night-long drinking was never worth it. She was going to feel sick for the rest of the day.

"You're a fool, Katie Frost. You should have stayed with him in Rhodesia. The good and the bad. Now all you've got is the mother and father of a hangover. And bugger-all else. You lost your chance when you had one."

Feeling hungry, Katie raided her fridge. Hangovers made her hungry. She ate up Saturday's leftovers from the takeaway. What had she eaten at the Dorchester? She couldn't so much as remember. What a waste. What a waste of a life... At six she turned on the television. There was nothing about Rhodesia. The news had passed on, and Katie wasn't interested in British politics. With the warmth from the central heating, she fell asleep in the chair. When she woke, the TV was still on. Leaning forward, Katie pressed the off button and went to bed. Through the night she slept, not a dream in her mind. She got up, bathed, dressed and went to work, fighting her way down into the Underground. All to pay off a mortgage. Never to properly live. Her day had begun. The mundane ordinary life of an office worker cooped up with her work.

WHEN FINN COUSINS phoned her at the flat on Thursday it relieved her monotony.

"Didn't expect to hear from you, Mr Cousins."

"What's this 'Mr Cousins'?"

"My supervisor told me who you are."

"Did it make any difference, Katie?"

"Should it? Where are you?"

"In my flat in New York."

"And where's your wife?"

"She's gone out. Had another of our rows. We've lived with each other for twenty-three years and all we do is fight."

"Does she want a divorce?"

"She doesn't know what she wants. Except the return of her son."

"Don't you feel sorry for her?"

"Of course I do. The boy was her life. I was always the provider... You want to come over, Katie? Give me something to smile about. I'm all right buried in my work. It's when I get home to Blanche."

"So that's her name. I can't just go off, Finn. I have a job and responsibilities. I couldn't work on Monday with a hangover. Glynnis gave me the day off. Can't muck her around again. Aren't there any nice girls in New York?"

"You're different, Katie."

"Because I'm English?"

"Because you're Katie."

"You're an old flatterer."

"I had a word with the head of personnel at IBM. He looked at your CV. He'll give you a job in America. Anytime you choose."

"You Americans don't muck around."

"We try not to. My idea is a cruise before you start the new job. A cruise around America. It's a big country. You'll like it. Go down to South America. The Caribbean. The world, Katie. I can show you the world."

"All from a one-night stand. Frankly, Finn, I don't believe in fairy stories. I'm safe in England. Job, home and a future pension. I threw away my life five years ago for what I've got today."

"I won't take no for an answer. I'm lonely."

"A man like you? I don't believe it."

"I want you, Katie."

"Maybe. For a while. Then I'll be just another consumer item that's thrown away, no longer of use."

"Just try it. What can you lose? Think about it. If you threw away one opportunity, why throw away another?... The front door is opening. Got to go. Call you again."

Feeling more like a whore than ever, Katie looked at the silent phone. Angela was right. What the hell was the difference?

Not sure what a man like Finn Cousins saw in her, she went about her daily routine. Only then did she phone Linda.

"You're out of your mind, Katie. When opportunities like that come along you take them with both hands."

"I'd be no different to Angela."

"Who the hell cares? You took five hundred quid off Bobby to go to Africa and he wouldn't take it back."

"We loved each other. We were going to get married."

"One boat trip is much the same as the other when it's paid for by somebody else. Go and enjoy yourself. Store up some memories for your old age when the men won't so much as look at you. You're nearly thirty. Your pull on men won't last much longer. Take what you can get while you can."

"Is it all about take?"

"Mostly. A girl's got to be realistic. We've got something they want. And he's got the money. Pots of it. You do know who he is?"

"Glynnis told me."

"The man's worth bloody millions. Who knows? Play your cards right and he'll get rid of his wife and marry you, Katie. You'll live in the lap of luxury for the rest of your life."

"But will I be happy?"

"That's up to you."

"Anyway, after I brushed him off he won't call again."

"Don't be too sure. Playing hard to get is a girl's trump card. Especially with a man like that who expects to get what he wants."

"Money isn't everything."

"Only people with a good job and a flat of their own say things like that. You can never have too much money. Cushions all the bumps and jolts of life. He'll call. Mark my word. When he does, don't be a bloody fool."

"How are you getting along with Andy?"

"He dumped me. You can't win them all."

"What are you going to do?"

"Find another man. The excitement is in the chase. Once you get into bed the excitement wears off. Wore off for Andy. Wore off for me. Why so many so-called relationships end up on the rocks. Stuck with one man? I don't think so. Where's the excitement? There's a new one in the offing.

Loves classical music. There's a symphony concert at the Albert Hall on Saturday. Want to come along? I can phone up Hubert and suggest we make up a party."

"You phone up men you want to go out with?"

"Of course I do. Can't sit around waiting. A foursome. Don't you like music?"

"You hate classical music."

"He doesn't have to know that. We're not getting married. By the time I've had enough of the music I'll have had enough of him. I'll see if he's got a friend. Tell him we love classical music... Are you doing anything on Saturday?"

"Probably watching television."

"How boring. You need some excitement in your life."

"Where's it all going?"

"Life never goes anywhere, Katie, other than to where you are at the moment. It's day to day. Andy was fun while it lasted. Took me to America. Suited him, suited me. Now we move on. Nothing lasts. You got to enjoy yourself while you can."

"Oh, Linda. What am I going to do with you?"

"It's not that I'm worried about. It's you. He'll ring again. They all do. Until they've got what they wanted. Satisfied themselves. It's all a bit selfish I'm afraid."

"Are you ever satisfied?"

"Of course I am. A good solid multiple climax and I'm satisfied. Why I have to change my men. The same old bang gets boring."

KATIE HAD SEEN the old man with the military moustache looking at her during the interval. He had looked somehow familiar, but she had been unable to place him. The look he had given her while they were stretching their legs in the foyer was more inquisitive than sexual. At first she thought he was looking at Hubert or one of the people behind her. When she looked over her shoulder and back at the old man the audience were moving back into the main auditorium of the Royal Albert Hall. They had all paid for their own concert tickets, Hubert and his friend not having much money according to Linda. Linda looked bored, with Hubert and the music, sitting still and attentive while sixty people fiddled and trumpeted was not her strong suit. Surprisingly for Katie the music had transported her into another more beautiful world, soothing her nerves, making her happy. The first half of the London Symphony Orchestra concert had been Brahms's First Symphony. Katie, as she filed back into the big hall, was looking forward to hearing the second half, the Brahms Third Symphony. For the first time in her life classical music had properly caught her attention, the music played by Bobby on his wind-up gramophone in the tent had been only background to their lovemaking; she hadn't listened. When the concert finished they moved out into the aisle, Linda suggesting they find a nearby pub and have themselves a drink. With the preliminaries over, Linda was back at her old business of holding a man's hand. From bored she had turned vivacious.

"Excuse me. Aren't you Miss Katie Frost? Brigadier Preston. We met in your employer's office some years ago. Did you enjoy the concert? You were then my son's fiancée. Bobby always liked classical music. The London shows and classical music. I hope I'm not interrupting."

"Are you on your own, Brigadier Preston?"

"Good. You remember me. Yes, I'm afraid I am. My wife died two years ago. The girls are off married with their own lives to worry about. The small house in Epsom has become so lonely I brought myself up to town to go to a concert. Brahms is so beautiful. My wife loved Brahms. Listening to the music in the Hall brought me closer to her. So nice to see you again. Sorry to butt in."

"They want to find a pub close at hand before it closes. Why don't you join us? I saw the terrorist attacks in Rhodesia reported on the BBC news. How is Bobby?"

"Scared out of his wits I should think. Went through the Burma campaign myself. Know how it feels hunting and being hunted in the jungle. Would you really not mind me joining you?"

"This is my friend Linda... Came out on the boat with me to Rhodesia... Hubert and Georgy. We all went Dutch for the concert."

"Hello. Such lovely music. My name is Roland. My son and grandchildren live in Rhodesia so I don't see enough of young people. Would you really not mind my tagging along? Did you meet my son, Linda?"

"Many times. Please come with us. There's an hour before closing time."

"Let me buy you all a drink. There's a little pub round the corner I know from my days at Sandhurst. Forty-eight hour pass. That sort of thing. I'm sure it will still be full of young people. The Mitre. Fond memories. Don't need a taxi."

"That's a bit of luck," said Hubert.

"Glad to be of help."

"Are you still in the army, sir?"

"Long retired. Call me Roland. The world's changed a bit since I last visited the Mitre with my friends. We used to have an empire in those days. But enough of old man's talk. Come along. I'll show you the way. Brahms's number three. The most beautiful symphony ever written."

Roland Preston bought the first round, the round that was also the last. Hubert and Georgy didn't seem to have any money.

"Nice meeting you, Mr Preston. Thanks for the drink." Hubert, having nursed his drink for as long as possible, got up quickly followed by Georgy who had not said a word. Every now and again Georgy had given Katie a look. Katie, not interested, had ignored him.

"Lovely evening," said Katie. "We must do it again."

"Oh definitely," said Linda, sarcastically.

When the party broke up outside the Mitre, Roland Preston had been the only one to buy a round of drinks. Linda went off with Hubert, Georgy on his own.

"Can I buy you supper, Katie?" For a moment they stood looking at each other awkwardly.

"Do you miss him?" asked the old man in the silence.

"Is he happy?"

"I think so. Until the attacks. You can't live in a war zone and still be happy."

"Don't you have to catch the train back to Epsom?"

"I'm staying at my club in Piccadilly. 126 Piccadilly to be exact. Cavalry Club. Been a member since I left Sandhurst and joined the regiment. Makes it easier. My wife's father left her some money in a trust for the children. They get it when I die. Helen insisted I get the interest during my lifetime. One day Bobby is going to be rather rich. Ironic, really. I've told him on the phone to come home. He won't listen to me. Says Africa is in his blood. His wife's pioneer stock. Wendy has never been to England. Must have something to do with it. They'll never win, of course. Too few of them. Bobby and his friends when they went out in 1961 were the last of the Colonials I suppose. Bit silly now, looking back. We often can't see what's staring us in the face. My fault. I should have stopped him. He was eighteen. Never thought he would stay. I wanted him to go to Sandhurst."

"What would he do back in England?"

"I have no idea. He'd have to start all over again."

"So you don't think they can win a war against terrorists?"

"Not a chance. Those chaps are funded by the Russians and Chinese... Rhodesia is the last of the old colonial lifestyle. It was a good life. It's difficult to go backwards. And you, Katie, how's your life been these last five years?"

"He married so quickly after I left."

"Rebound. Pride. Filling a void. Take your pick."

"Would you mind if I went home? Talking about Bobby makes me upset."

"No. Of course. You go home, Katie. Lovely to see you. Can I mention I've seen you to Bobby?"

"Doesn't that depend on his wife?"

"Yes, I suppose it does. Better not then. Where are you living?"

"I bought myself a flat in Shepherd's Bush. Bobby wouldn't take back the five hundred pounds of his money you handed me in the offices of Sedgewick and Biggs. I used it to go to college when I got back to England. I'm now a computer programmer with IBM. Pays the mortgage. Better pay than working a comptometer."

"Wonderful. You did something constructive with the money. Most young girls would have spent it on clothes... All rather sad, really. The end of the biggest empire the world has ever known. Now we're all going to be little provincials on our little island surrounded by the sea. No great ambitions. No great futures. An ordinary people living ordinary lives. In thirty years' time they'll all have forgotten the empire. We'll be like Switzerland. London a financial centre. Making money on paper. Never seeing it. It'll just be about money... Computer programmer? I'm impressed... One day you have a four-thousand acre African farm. The next you have nothing. That farm's not worth their lives. Look, I'm talking too much. Happens when you live alone."

"Won't the South Africans help?"

"Probably. For a while. They're going to be next. The world's changed. I just watch. What else can I do? What else can any of us do? There's your Tube station. I'm going to walk a little further. Not much to do at my age. You have a long life, Katie. Why didn't you get married?"

"When you lose the right one it becomes a whole lot more difficult."

"So you loved my son?"

"Very much. I still do... Goodnight, Brigadier Preston."

Katie walked towards the Underground roundel staring at her from the tops of the steps. She was sad. Felt guilty at not wanting to have supper with a lonely old man. At the top of the steps she looked back. The old man was still looking at her. Pulling her overcoat closer Katie began to walk back.

"What the hell, Brigadier Preston. You probably want to talk about Bobby as much as I do. It's Saturday night. With luck they won't call me out tomorrow."

The old man brightened up, his shoulders straightening.

"There's an Indian restaurant a block away. Do you mind walking?"

"I enjoy the exercise. Don't get enough of it sitting in an office."

"They keep open after the concerts. Their main trade, I suppose. They don't have a wine licence but Deepak looks after me. He's from the Punjab. Came to England when India broke up. Most of the Hindus were in India. Most of the Muslims in Pakistan. Religion split the country. They had more problems in 1947 than during the Raj when the British and Indian armies kept the lid on things. The officers in the Indian Army were mostly British. At the height of the British Raj there were only twenty thousand English, Scots, Welsh and Irish running India. We trained up the Indians under us to run the place. They've got our language, our laws and all the railways we left them. It'll be interesting to see what they do with it... Here we are. It's warm inside. There's a lovely smell of the orient. Brings back fond memories... I'm so pleased you turned back. Who were those two men at the concert?"

"Never met them before. Linda fancies Hubert."

"So I didn't interrupt anything?"

"Not at all."

Inside the restaurant most of the tables were occupied. An old Indian smiled at the old man, and came towards them wringing his hands. Katie wasn't sure if seeing the old soldier was pleasure or business. The old man whispered something in the Indian's ear.

"Of course, Brigadier. Of course. Always happy to oblige."

"Katie here was Bobby's fiancée a few years ago."

"Welcome to my restaurant, Miss Katie. My name is Deepak. Please come this way."

The wine came first with two small long-stemmed glasses. The old world charm of the brigadier-general was pleasant, a complete contrast to Hubert and Georgy. She was hungry. The man called Deepak had taken her coat, seating her at the small round table with its white tablecloth almost down to the floor. Roland Preston gave Deepak his hat, coat and cane. They sat opposite each other. The tables around them were full. Under the low ceiling, the smell of spices thick in the air, everyone was talking, leaning at each other across their small tables. There was no music. Just the quiet hum of comfortable conversation.

"You've known him a long time?" Katie was looking at the old Indian hanging their coats on a rack at the back of the restaurant.

"A very long time, as a matter of fact. My first tour of India with the regiment. I was in my twenties. Deepak was a young waiter in the officers' mess. We rather liked each other. He showed me around the Punjab when I took my leave and stayed in India instead of taking the boat back like the rest of them. I didn't have the private income of most of my fellow officers. Had to live off my pay. I never forgot that three-month trip. You enjoy travel more when you're young. We kept in touch over the years. When India got its independence he wrote to me. He is a Hindu. His wife is a Muslim. There were problems. I helped get him into England in 1949 to avoid the Muslim-Hindu problems that came with independence."

"I thought he was smiling at you for your business."

"No. As young men we were friends. Still are. Four of his children and seven of his grandchildren are now in England. In thirty years' time Deepak's family will be as English as we are... Here comes the food. Hope you like what I ordered. The Indians can cook, Katie. Far better than the English. When the English make a curry they put in far too much curry powder. It's the spices that make the food so interesting. You like my friend's restaurant?"

"It's perfect."

"Did you hear that, Deepak? Katie says it's perfect."

With a mix of silver dishes in front of them the old man began serving the food.

"Are you hungry?... Good. Let me fill your plate. Not too much rice. Not too much fresh fruit on the curry... Cheers, Katie. Do you like the wine?"

"It's perfect. Just a pity Bobby is not with us. Have you seen your granddaughters?"

"Once. When I went out after Helen died. Wendy had stayed on the farm when Bobby flew over for the funeral. The children had only just been born. Wendy's mother went up to the farm and stayed with them while Bobby was away."

"What's Wendy like?"

"A good wife and mother. What else can I say?"

"That you hate her."

They laughed, Katie a little nervously, not wishing to offend the mother of the old man's grandchildren. Katie picked up her fork and mixed the food on her plate. Then she ate.

"What's the food like to you, Katie?"

"Delicious."

"I haven't enjoyed myself so much for a very long time. Life is full of coincidences. Luck, I suppose, meeting you at the concert. So, what are you going to do with your life?"

"I was twenty-nine the other day. When a girl is close to thirty and she still isn't married she's inclined to think she's on the shelf. I like my job. Makes me think. Every programme I create is different. I'll get used to the new flat in the end. I have friends. England I love. Sometimes I get bored but don't we all? Maybe some lovely man like Bobby will come along and I'll marry and have children. I hope so."

"You were right about Rhodesia."

"But that doesn't help. Being right makes it worse. I just hope nothing happens to him... You think he's in any real danger?"

"They were attacked just before Christmas. Wendy and Bobby ran out into the bush with the twins. Stayed the night with their backs to an ant hill. They were lucky. For some reason the terrorists thought Bobby and the family were sleeping in his office down by the tobacco barns. They shot the store up, giving Bobby time to get out of the house. No one was hurt on the farm. It's war, Katie. What some call an insurgency. The blacks want their land back."

"Then we should give it to them."

"People don't like giving away their property. What they worked for. In the time of your grandchildren when no one remembers the empire they'll look back on the Rhodesians and wonder why they were so stupid. Ask why they didn't get out. They were going to lose everything anyway... Now they look at it differently. Many of those on the farms and in the Rhodesian government think they can win. Think the old colonial life will never come to an end. Fact is, they've got their heads buried in the sand."

"But they were attacked!" Katie, white as a sheet, was staring at him. "How can that not have changed their minds?"

"Yes, Katie. Don't worry yourself. You did your best. Bobby wanted to stay. Now it's too late."

"It's never too late."

"Some say it is. I've done my best to persuade him. So did you. Have some more wine. Sitting here worrying won't help the situation."

"Why did he do it in the first place? Why did he go to Rhodesia?"

"People like Bobby were trained for it. The only training they ever got. The good old English public school system. Wellington College. Where I went, and my father before me. We were trained to run an empire. When Bobby got to Africa at the end of 1961 there wasn't much left. India had gone. Most of Asia. Africa was going fast. All that was left was the self-governing colony of Southern Rhodesia. South Africa was run by the Afrikaners. Not a welcome place for the English. I wanted him to go into the British Army but that was shrinking fast once National Service came to an end. Bobby liked the idea of running a tobacco estate so he went to Rhodesia. He was eighteen. Young. Full of hope. We didn't have the money to send him to university. If he'd stayed in England Bobby would have ended up as a clerk. In a bank or an insurance company. Wellington hadn't given him that idea for his future. So he left. Three years later Smith declares Rhodesia independent from Britain. Now they've got a war on their hands. You see, Wellington gave him too many big ideas, stuck in the old time warp. But it was over. The empire was over. He'd got the wrong education."

"So what does he do now?"

"Face up to it. We all have to face up to life in the end. Even an old retired brigadier general. Once I had real authority. A place in society. Now I have nothing but a thousand pound a year pension and nobody gives a damn what I did. And why should they? Without my father-in-law's income from the trust I wouldn't be able to buy you dinner. Each year they let me draw one per cent of the capital. And I reached close to the top of my profession. Like me, Bobby's got to face up to it. Come home. Start from scratch. He's still got his brain. That much governments and wars can't take away from you unless they kill you. My son is too young to die. He's got a life ahead of him. And so have his children. Some might call it running away. Some might call it using his brains. He's got to come back to England before it's too late."

"Why didn't he join his grandfather's business?"

"A Lancashire textile mill? He wasn't trained for it. Or, more correctly, Wellington College had put loftier ideas in his head. In retrospect I should have let him go through the government education system of the new welfare state. Be more equipped for the new Britain."

"But he would have had money if he'd joined his mother's family business."

"Money isn't everything, Katie. It's the lifestyle some of us want. The lifestyle of a British Army officer at the time of empire. Or a tobacco farmer on his own estate in Africa. Stupidly we looked down our noses at running a textile mill. It was called being in trade. After coming from five generations of army officers and being sent to Wellington, it wasn't for Bobby. Now money is all that counts in this world. Not breeding. Not your family. Not your place in society. It's just money. If you want any respect all you need is money. Always was that way, I suppose. We were stupid. So for the Prestons it's over. Many would say it's about time. They're probably right. But how much fun you get out of life running a textile mill with all that money I'm not so sure about. The breed that made an empire is no longer required. We're dead. Never to rise again. It's over."

"You sound bitter."

"Not bitter. Just annoyed with myself for being such a damn fool. My father-in-law would have taken you to Simpson's in the Strand, not some backstreet Indian restaurant."

"But would the food have been so good? Or the company?"

"Thank you, Katie."

Katie was tired, mentally and physically. The old brigadier put her into a taxi and paid the driver the fare to Shepherd's Bush, like the epitome of an English gentleman. When she looked back through the rear window of the taxi she could see him leaning on his cane, staring forlornly after the taxi. He was standing under the light of a lamp post with the fog beginning to thicken. Then he turned and went back into the restaurant to be with his friend.

As the taxi drove on, the thought of Hopewell Estate being attacked raced through her head, the images of the African farm so different from the wet streets of a wintry London. She felt flat. The good in her world had drained out of her. Knowing she wouldn't be able to sleep, she found a half-empty bottle of white wine, took a glass from the same kitchen cupboard and went and sat in front of the blank television. All she could think of was Bobby. In the light of a small table lamp she slowly drank down the wine before taking herself off to bed, the wind and rain outside rattling the frames of the windows. She had drunk just the right amount of wine to send her to sleep. Thankfully, Katie drifted off into dreams.

2

At the end of March the manager called Katie into his office. There had been no more farm attacks in Rhodesia reported on television in what the Russians and many liberals in the West were calling a war of liberation. To Katie, either nothing had happened or the foreign media had been prevented from seeing what was happening. Every time Katie turned on the news she was thinking of Bobby. During the weeks after supper with his father there had been two telephone calls from America, both from Finn Cousins, one to her flat and one to her office. Both times Katie had been evasive.

"IBM are offering you a promotion if you go to America. New York," her manager said. "Came as a surprise to all of us. You're very privileged, Miss Frost. We of course send our monthly reports to the Americans. Each successful job has the name of our programmer at the bottom. The salary they are offering you is double what we're paying you in London. The tax is lower in the States, the cost of living in New York not much different to London. Congratulations, Miss Frost. I wish they'd offer me a job in New York. It's a chance in a lifetime. A big step up the corporate ladder."

"But I don't want to leave England."

"Well, you can refuse of course. But I wouldn't advise it. They are more progressive in the States than we are. The upliftment of women in the workplace is taken seriously. Part of the Civil Rights Movement. Equal rights for everybody. Women, people of colour, gays. That sort of thing. They want you to start at the end of the month."

"In four days' time!"

"Yes, Miss Frost. Congratulations."

"What will I be doing?"

"I have no idea. Your supervisor here has been informed. Hard work and dedication pays off. All those weekends. Jolly good show."

"How do I get there?"

"Oh, this is your ticket. You'll be met at Kennedy airport. We'll be sad to lose you. Good luck, Miss Frost."

"What do I do with my flat?"

"Oh, you'll sort it out. If it was me I'd be very excited."

"It's not IBM who want me."

"What do you mean?"

"It's a man called Finn Cousins."

"The financier? Do you know him?"

"We met briefly for dinner."

"They always say it's not what you know but who you know that counts. Please close the door when you go out." The man now looked miffed.

"Don't I need a visa to get into America?"

"It's all been taken care of. Take your passport to the American embassy and they will stamp it with a multiple entry visa. The instructions are all in that envelope with your ticket. You do have a valid passport?"

"Yes. From when I travelled to Rhodesia."

"Then have a pleasant trip."

Back at her desk, feeling as if the bottom had fallen out of her world, Katie looked in the envelope. Along with the ticket and the visa application form for her to sign was a cheque for three thousand pounds and a sealed envelope. In the envelope was a handwritten letter from Finn Cousins.

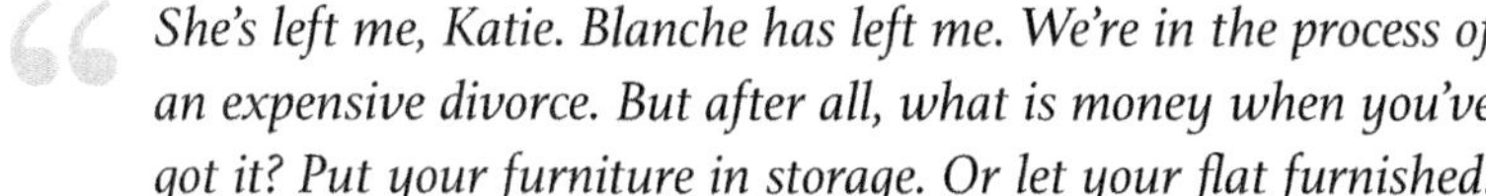

She's left me, Katie. Blanche has left me. We're in the process of an expensive divorce. But after all, what is money when you've got it? Put your furniture in storage. Or let your flat furnished.

I'll be at Kennedy when your plane lands. Oh, and this job with IBM is genuine. They did a careful study of your career and liked what they saw. In America, especially in corporate America, you don't get a job unless they think you can do it properly. No favours in that department. I've rented you a flat in Manhattan as you call them in England. In America we call them apartments. It'll be wonderful to see you again. Have a safe flight, my Katie

Katie putting down the letter, began to laugh, going from quiet to hilarious.

"What's the matter with you, Katie?"

"Glynnis, I've just been bought. Lock, stock and barrel. I'm going to America but I'm sure you know. Now I know why you haven't given me a new project these last ten days. You knew."

"There was a delay in your visa application. The Americans are quite stiff with their immigration laws. I gave you a top-flight reference."

"Thank you, Glynnis."

"It's my pleasure."

What made her pulse race was the thought of flying. Both trips to Africa had been by boat. In all her years Katie had never flown in an aeroplane. The first phone call she made was to her parents in Dorking. The second was to Linda. In her mind the new journey was on its way. The same excitement. The same fear. Everyone, even her mother, was happy for Katie. Linda was more specific.

"If you don't like it, darling, come home. Three thousand pounds is not a bad start. Angela would be proud of you."

"The cheque is from IBM."

"Then you earned it legitimately. Anyway, what's the difference? What's wrong with a little help from your friends? I'll miss you."

"If I can get you a job why don't you come over? I'll miss you too."

"Well, that's an idea. They're all rich in America."

"I'm flying first class."

"Gets better and better. And Katie, darling. Please don't forget who introduced you to Finn."

"Any word from Andy?"

"Not a dicky bird."

"Who's currently on the menu?"

"You know, Katie, sometimes I think you envy me."

"He's got me a flat in Manhattan. You can share it with me."

"Just like old times. Manhattan. I'm impressed. That's where the rich live, darling. The very rich. A bit like the West End of London only bigger. Very much bigger. You want me to come to Heathrow?"

"Would you? Never flown before, can you believe it? Not sure whether to be excited or scared out of my wits."

"You'll love flying. Especially first class. If you've got somewhere to stay maybe I'll come for a holiday. See what I can find. Think of a job afterwards."

"That's my girl. A lady of leisure. Where do you get the money, I'd like to know?"

"Andy was generous when he wanted me. The secret is to save it when they give you money to spend."

"What are we really, Linda?"

"Never think too much. Enjoy life while you can. In the flutter of an eye we'll be old and wrinkled. No one interested. Not even the time of day. And these days, getting married doesn't provide you with any security unless you screw the bastard when he divorces you. Divorce is too easy. Society accepts it. When couples find it isn't just what they wanted they split up. That was me and Andy. You and Bobby."

"Bobby was different. It had nothing to do with our relationship. It was the African politics."

"If you had loved each other so much that wouldn't have come into it. It's a short life. A girl has to look after herself. Nobody else does. They all say they'll look after you when it suits them. Even the politicians when they're looking for votes. When they want you. Build up some more capital. Don't sell your flat. Money is the only protection against the vagaries of life. Money. Lots and lots of lovely money. When do you fly out?"

"On Tuesday. Ten in the morning."

"I'll be at your flat at seven. Have breakfast. Take a taxi to the airport together."

"Thank you, Linda. I need the moral support."

"What are friends for?"

"Do you want to live in my Shepherd's Bush flat?"

"You need the rent. To pay the mortgage. I'm not much good at paying rent. See you on Tuesday morning."

The British Airways Boeing 707 took off from Heathrow Airport at exactly ten o'clock on the Tuesday morning, Katie headed for America. The take-off was so smooth she only realised they were airborne when she looked out of the window.

"It's my first flight in an aeroplane," she said to the woman next to her, an elderly woman who said nothing but just stared back at her. She was covered in jewellery, the diamond on her left hand uncomfortably big, the smell of expensive perfume overpowering. The woman literally stank of money while Katie, in her off-the-peg business suit, not a ring on her fingers, had just a touch of deodorant under her young armpits. They could not have been more different. The woman made Katie uncomfortable. Back through the curtain into the tourist class would have been Katie's preference for her first flight in an aeroplane. Among friends, people her own class, people she could have related to. In first class, in the front of the plane, they all looked the same to Katie. Snobs with their noses in the air. Not her kind of people. Disconcerted, Katie looked out of the window at her last glimpses of London. She was tired, having slept very little. At the airport Linda had cried as they parted, one friend going forward, the other staying behind.

Her world left behind, she kept staring out of the window. She was sad, lonely, afraid of where she was going. The plane climbed to its cruising height and flew on, the sound of the jet engines dulling her thoughts, making her drowsy. She put the seat back as far as possible and curled up her feet. When she woke a woman in a blue uniform was offering her lunch. The elderly women had shaken her awake.

"No thank you. I was enjoying my sleep. How long before we land in America?"

"Three hours and twenty minutes. Would you like something to drink?"

"I didn't sleep last night. My first flight. Please let me sleep."

Putting her head against the small pillow she had lodged against the portal of the window, she went back to her sleep. When she woke again the aircraft was losing height. The elderly woman had moved to another seat.

"Why did she move?"

"You kicked her in your sleep." The air hostess in the blue uniform was smiling. "Please fasten your seatbelt. We're about to land at Kennedy Airport. Welcome to America, Miss Frost."

In the airport building they stood waiting for their baggage next to the conveyor belt, the first-class luggage coming off first. Her fellow passenger was standing on the other side of the conveyor. Katie walked round.

"I'm so sorry. I must have kicked out in my sleep."

The luggage was appearing, and the woman pointed to hers which a man in airport uniform took from the conveyor belt. Then she glared at Katie and walked off without a word. Katie was left wondering if all that money was a joy or a burden.

Customs and immigration were quick. Her passport stamped, the glass door opened and Katie walked through, pushing her trolley, looking around. Then she saw him. Waved. He looked much older than she remembered from the Dorchester Hotel. His smile when he saw her lit up his whole face. The woman she had kicked in her sleep watched them meet. Watched Finn Cousins give her a kiss. She was now looking at Katie differently. Katie gave her a wave.

"Who was that, Katie?"

"A woman I kicked on the aeroplane. How are you, Finn?"

"How are you, Katie?"

"Better after some sleep."

He was relaxed, making Katie relaxed. Outside, a car the size of a bus was waiting. Again the woman with the rings and perfume was watching Katie, trying to catch her eye.

"Now she wants to talk to me… Where are we going, Finn?"

"To the docks. I promised you a cruise before you started work. I'm a man of my word."

"You planned it all."

"Most of it. It's just so good to see you again."

"I'd love to see where I'm going to work."

"First things first."

"She recognised you, Finn."

"Probably. In America financiers are photographed as much as football players in Britain. Goes with the job. We call it celebrity. At first it's exciting. Then it wears off. Tom, put Miss Frost's luggage in the trunk. Do you have a bathing costume?"

"Luckily yes. From my days in Rhodesia. Most of Bobby's friends had swimming pools on their farms. You'll call it a ranch, I suppose."

"Who's Bobby?"

"My fiancé. He married someone else when I refused to live in Rhodesia."

"Wise girl."

"I've never been in a car this big before."

"Welcome to America. You can make so much money in this country that money becomes irrelevant. First you buy everything you can possibly want. Big cars. Smart apartment. Place in Florida with a boat that rides the tide unused for most of the year. Then you start looking for good causes so you can give it away."

"Where are you at, Finn?"

"Giving it away. I sometimes think it's more difficult to give it away than make it. You have to turn philanthropy into a business or you throw good money down a rat hole. A bit like all that money for the poor that was given to African dictators when the colonial powers got out of their colonies. All ended up in numbered Swiss bank accounts."

"How old are you, Finn?"

"Do you really want to know? Does it matter?"

"I'm sorry. I told my parents I was going to a new job in America. If I'd told my father it was orchestrated after a one-night stand with a man much older than me it would have broken his heart."

"You're in good hands."

"I'm sure I am. IBM are one of the most reputable companies in the world. Why would they wish to tarnish their image? No, Finn. What we do is get our ducks in a row first. I start my new job on Monday as expected. Move into my flat today. And we go out a few times. See how it goes."

"I'm fifty, Katie. Does that make any difference?"

"Of course it doesn't. I'm twenty-nine. Not a teenager. As you get older the age gap is less important. Is the flat furnished? Have I to sign a lease?"

"I signed the lease. Put in the furniture."

"Then that's no good. You can't buy me, Finn. I can live on my salary. I've three thousand pounds from IBM to help me settle in."

"So what do you want now?"

"A nice little room in a boarding house. Not too expensive. Let me find my feet. Look around. Then I'll decide what to do. First I have to fit into my job. Make new friends... I just can't believe I'm in America. Oh, and Linda's coming over. She's broken up with your friend Andy. How does all that sound?"

"Not as I planned."

"No, I suppose it doesn't."

"Can I take you to dinner when we've found you a room?"

"I don't see why not. How's Blanche?"

"Being difficult."

"Yes, I can imagine."

"Don't you want to just have a look at the flat?"

"Not really. I might fall in love with it. Lose my independence. If I move into that flat right now, Finn, all I'd be is your mistress."

"Don't you want to be my mistress? Most girls would jump at it."

"The only people I ever wish to be beholden to are my parents, my husband and my children."

Finn leaned forward and slid back the partition that separated the passengers from the driver.

"Tom, do you know a rooming house that's not too expensive?"

"Coming up, boss. How much you want to spend?"

"How much you want to spend, Katie?"

"No more than one fifth of my salary. And seeing you arranged everything I expect you know how much I'm paid."

"Two hundred bucks a month, Tom."

Finn slid back the partition, cutting them off. He looked annoyed, no longer the suave man about town.

"There you are, Finn. That wasn't difficult. Now we're on equal terms. No one obliged to anyone."

Later, when the limousine drove over a long bridge, all Katie could see was skyscrapers.

"I'm going to enjoy the States."

"I hope so, Katie."

"Not quite Africa. But it'll do... That's a joke, Finn. Don't look so grim."

The glass partition slid open again, Finn leaning forward in his seat.

"My office first, Tom."

"As you wish, boss."

Ten minutes later the car stopped by the side of the road. Behind, a car hooted. Finn got out onto the kerb, the door still open.

"You look after yourself, Katie."

"I'll try."

The door shut and the car drove on into the traffic. With only a multiple entry visa IBM had given Katie a return ticket, valid for a year. Katie slid open the glass partition.

"Can you stop the car, Tom, and give me my luggage?"

"As you wish, miss."

With her case out on the kerb, Katie smiled at Tom.

"You going to be all right?" he asked.

"I hope so, Tom. Sometimes things turn out a little different to what we expected."

"You got money?"

"Traveller's cheques. A few dollars. Don't worry about me. I'll go straight to the IBM office. You could flag me down a cab... Has he really left his wife?"

"That side of his life is none of my business... Here you go. Just be careful."

"You always have to be careful. There's a good chance I'll soon be back on the aeroplane. Life is full of surprises."

"Here you are, miss". The driver had opened the door to a yellow taxi. "Do you know the address where you're going?" He was young, sad, almost apologetic.

"I wrote it down. What's the time in New York?"

"Twelve-thirty."

"Perfect. They'll all be in the office. Thanks for your help."

Twenty minutes later, Katie walked into the IBM office and up to reception.

"Hello. I'm Katie Frost. In London they said you had a job for me."

"We were expecting you on Monday." The girl was young, happy, smiling.

"I'm a little early. You know a cheap hotel? The arrangements I made in London didn't quite work out."

"I'll call your supervisor. Shouldn't be a problem. Take a seat. You can leave your suitcase behind reception. So, you worked for IBM in London?"

"That's how it was. Luckily, computer programming is the same the world over."

With her suitcase safely behind the long reception desk, Katie sat down and waited. There was a hum, a feeling of purpose. People came and went, the lift doors opening and closing. Katie got up and looked at the paintings on the walls. They were all originals, all of them modern, full of colour. None of them meant anything to Katie.

"They're insured for a fortune," said the girl from reception.

"Yes, I suppose they would be."

When Katie looked round a woman in her mid-thirties was standing next to her.

"Hello. I'm Celeste Fox, your supervisor. What happened to Mr Cousins? I was going to meet you at the airport. It's always uncertain arriving alone in a new country. Have you had lunch? It's lunchtime. You weren't expected in the office until Monday. Can you start work after lunch? They bring sandwiches and coffee to my office. I'm so pleased to see you. We're shorthanded. So, what happened to Mr Cousins?"

"I prefer to be independent."

"Good for you." She was smiling broadly at Katie. "That's the way I feel. One day men and women will be equal in the workplace."

"Have you met Mr Cousins?"

"Don't be silly. He's rich. Really rich. They live in another world. There's more to life than men. Where are you going to be staying?"

"That's why I came straight from the airport."

"I'll ask some of the girls. They'll know something. Where's your luggage?"

"One case. Behind the desk. Most of my stuff's still in London."

"Your first trip to America?"

"My first trip on an aeroplane."

"My goodness. Good old England. My mother came from England. Met my father a week after landing in the States."

"By boat or aeroplane?"

"Oh, she flew all right. In more ways than one. We're Catholic. I have six brothers and sisters. Mother never had a job in America other than looking after us kids... A quick lunch and down to work. It never stops. Keeps us busy. You won't have time to get bored."

"And somewhere to stay?"

"It's only you and a suitcase... After work we go out for a drink. Girls go out alone in New York. Someone will put you up. If they don't, I have a spare room. So you told Finn Cousins where to go? In our world of women's lib you'll be a heroine."

"Or a fool."

"Only time will tell. Never make it too easy for them."

"Are you married?"

"Once. Now I'm single. Much better. You're in control of your life."

Katie's panic subsided. She was no longer alone in a strange country. Following the woman, she walked into a long, wide room full of people in open cubicles, heads down working. Most of the workers were men. No one looked up. Everything was bigger than it had been in London. At a cubicle the same as the others, Celeste Fox sat down behind her desk. Katie sat on a stool to the side of the desk.

"Was it like this in London?"

"Similar. Just not so many people."

"You get into your work and forget where you are."

"I suppose so..."

An old man came round pushing a food trolley. It was lunchtime.

"We all work and eat at the same time. They pay well in America but you work harder. Longer hours. More pressure. You got to be young. Do you work out, Katie?"

"Never thought of it."

"Now, this is what I want you to do."

By seven o'clock that evening, Katie was among friends. The cocktail room was humming with people, most of them women from the surrounding offices. Three girls had offered Katie a place to stay. They were relaxed, informal away from the office. By eight o'clock the girls were headed home.

"You fixed up, Katie?"

"Thanks, Celeste. See you tomorrow. Michelle is going to take me to her place when we've collected my suitcase."

"Three drinks is my maximum. Should be yours. The brain dulls the next day from too much alcohol."

By nine o'clock, tired, happy and relieved, Katie closed the door to her new bedroom. She was quickly asleep in a comfortable bed. When she woke it was pitch dark. For a long moment, her heart racing, she had no idea where she was. Then she remembered Michelle and went back to sleep. In her sleep, the hyena was outside the tent, Katie screaming, no sign of Bobby.

Finn Cousins enjoyed a challenge. He had started out in life as a life insurance salesman for the Southland Life Insurance Company ending up as their top salesman and starting his own insurance agency, The Cousins Agency Inc out of Kansas City, Missouri. His pitch was simple: if you don't invest your twenty dollars in this policy, you would drink it away instead. Finn was a big drinker himself, right from the word go, a good friend to have fun with. Everyone liked Finn Cousins, which was what made him so successful. In those first years his permanent quest was to find himself new contacts, new people to whom he could sell a policy. There was only so much to be had from personal contacts which was when Finn had his own personal epiphany that was to make him rich. In America, the oil companies sold their product through small independent gas stations, the owners of which paid higher insurance premiums than the employees of the oil companies. Finn just went to the Southland Life Insurance Company and sold them the concept of a group rate for the gas station owners if Finn could persuade the oil companies to sponsor a pension plan. With an exclusive, signed agreement from Southland, Finn sold the concept to the Continental Oil Company with its seventeen thousand, mostly independent, gas stations, the owners and staff all prime prospects for pension insurance. The product worked better than Finn had dreamed, Conoco recommending the pension plan, cementing their relationship once more with their operators. After that it was Union 76 gas stations out of Chicago. Within two years, the Cousins Agency Inc had one or more licensed representatives selling life insurance in every state of the USA, the share in their commissions making Finn rich. It was the perfect win-win situation. The salesmen were given the names and addresses of a limitless number of contacts, the gas station owners got the best product, Conoco had looked after their dealers and Southland issued policies in bulk, saving the costs of individual administration. From there it was into the world of finance as Finn looked to invest his new wealth, leveraging his own money with loans from the banks at a ten to one ratio. By the time Finn turned forty he was rich beyond most people's wildest expectations. By the time he met Katie in the London Dorchester Hotel his capital wealth exceeded one hundred million dollars. Even divorcing Blanche would leave him rich. When Katie rejected his offer of making her his mistress it made him the more determined. In his entire life it was money. Money bought everything. Everyone had their price. Even Katie. Having got her into the States, all it needed was time. Why Katie attracted him so much he was not completely certain. She was young, she was different, and he liked her way of speaking. But most of all, if he was honest with himself, it was because she didn't want him, a challenge he couldn't resist.

It took Finn a week to find out from his contacts at IBM that Katie was sharing an apartment with Michelle O'Reilly. Changing the lease of the flat to an outright purchase, Finn bided his time. Once a week on a Friday he sent flowers for Katie to the offices of IBM. Big, vulgar displays of flowers with his name prominently pinned in the centre for her co-workers to see. At the end of April Finn sent Katie and her co-workers an invitation to a Friday night party. Katie's flat, now even more splendid with flowers and the food of the caterers, looked thoroughly exotic, the view of the lights of New York from the balcony quite breathtaking. Smugly, Finn waited for her.

Katie, bulldozed into going by her new friends at IBM, arrived at half past eight looking radiant.

"So, what's the occasion, Finn?"

"The introduction to your new apartment. In England I believe you call this a housewarming. Come in. Look around... So what do you think?"

"Rather splendid."

"Ladies and gentlemen, may I have a moment. This is a presentation to Miss Katie Frost. The keys to the apartment, Katie. This is all yours. Your new home."

"Are you out of your mind?"

"Probably... So... What you think?"

Before Katie could open her mouth everyone in the big room was clapping and shouting her name. The music came up. The party got started.

"So, what do I owe you for all this, Finn?"

"Nothing. Just your company. What you going to drink?"

"What the hell, Finn? Make it a gin and tonic."

3

While Katie was being seduced by the overwhelming power of money, Grace was giving birth to Canaan Moyo's son in the Mozambican capital of Lourenço Marques, the headquarters of Robert Mugabe's Zimbabwe African National Liberation Army that was waging a war against white rule in Rhodesia. When Canaan reached the room they lived in together the baby had been born, the small new life nestled in the arms of Grace, a gentle beautiful smile on her face. It was their first child making Canaan so happy he wanted to burst. Kissing Grace gently on the lips he looked at their child, not sure what to do. Should he kiss the little face, pick him up, leave him in the arms of his mother, or go to the window and shout at the rooftops where far away he would see the spire of the Catholic cathedral? Instead he stood staring, rooted to the spot, his mind racing in all directions. Josiah Makoni, the political commissar of ZANLA, had given him the message in the office Canaan visited with Jacob and the rest of the cadres who had finally returned from the first attack on Rhodesia. Canaan was in awe of Josiah, the most senior party member in the building, a man of great education with degrees from Fort Hare University in the Eastern Cape of South Africa and the London School of Economics in England.

"You're a father, Canaan. Congratulations. A message has just been delivered. You'd better go to your wife. Grace is her name, my memory tells me. Now run along. There is nothing more important to a man than having a son."

"A son!"

"Off you go. Your debriefing can wait till tomorrow. The Rhodesian army won't lose any sleep. You and your men did a good job. Now go and enjoy yourself with Grace. Oh, and here's a bottle of Portuguese wine. You two do drink? Now she's had the baby you must celebrate. A son and jobs well done by both of you. Grace here in Lourenço Marques and you in the Centenary... We've had a report they're fencing the farmhouses. Claymore mines at the top of the poles. We're going to equip you with RPG rockets to fire from a distance over the fences. They've put floodlights on the fences so when someone tries to cut the fence open they can pull the wires inside the house and set off the mines on top of the poles. Now they've made themselves a perfect target for rocket-propelled grenades. See the farmhouses from miles away. A grenade through the front window will blow the room inside to pieces."

"Thank you, comrade."

"Don't thank me. Thank Robert Mugabe and the party. Now run along. The note says the nurse delivered a perfect baby. It's all in Portuguese so you can't read it."

"A perfect baby?"

"All the right number of fingers and toes... Where was your wife from in Rhodesia?"

"The Chiweshe reserve. Right next door to the Centenary."

"Our ever-faithful Chief Chiweshe. Now there's a good man. He'll be loyal to Robert Mugabe to his dying day, according to our man on the spot, Comrade Tangwena... Do you have any wine glasses?"

"Mugs."

"That'll do. If you can't find a corkscrew push in the cork... Chiweshe and Centenary bring back memories. I grew up in the compound of a white farm in Mazoe a hundred miles down the road. Grace will know it. When she went into Salisbury she would have travelled through Mazoe."

"I know it. Orange trees. Lots and lots of orange trees."

"My father was the bossboy, as they rudely call it, of Elephant Walk. The white owner was my mentor. Sent me to school and university. Life has strange twists in it. I don't think Harry Brigandshaw would approve of how I used his expensive education. Anyway, all the money he spent on me will help free our people, Canaan. Go off and enjoy your family and that bottle of wine. Life can be short. Enjoy the moments while you can."

"When do I go back into Rhodesia?"

"Next week. Trained operatives like you and Jacob can't be left idle for long."

"Thank you, comrade."

"My pleasure."

"What happened to your mentor?"

"He went back to England. Where they're all going to go in the end. Harry knew the white man didn't have a future in Africa. Said as much. Strangely, at the end, when he was dying, he came back to die on Elephant Walk. His father had started the place. Sebastian Brigandshaw was one of the first whites in Mashonaland as they called it then. Before Rhodes called it Rhodesia. Not long ago the family disinterred his bones and shipped them back to be buried in the ancestral home of his maternal grandfather in England. I owe Harry a lot. Hope he rests in peace."

"So you liked him?"

"Very much. So did my father. They were friends as kids, Sebastian saved my father's ancestors from the Zulu Matabele. Life really is quirky. Now we're fighting side by side: the Zulu army of the Zimbabwe People's Revolutionary Army and the Shona army of ZANLA. Makes you wonder where it will all end. Of course the Zulus invaded from the south so the country is really ours. We'll see. At the moment we need them to get rid of the English. You see, the Russians support ZIPRA and the Chinese ZANLA and the war of liberation needs all the help it can get. But you're a fighter. Leave the politics to me and Comrade Mugabe. We've all come a long way. And we're going to win. All of us. The people are going to win and take back our land. Once long ago, in the kingdom of Monomotapa, we Shonas ruled the heart of Africa. Comrade Mugabe says we will do it again."

The whole discussion, in Shona, had lasted less than five minutes, Canaan leaving the ZANLA office clutching his bottle of red wine thinking of Grace, their baby, and where he could lay his hands on a corkscrew. Josiah Makoni had walked out smiling, enjoying the awe his presence had brought to the room. Feeling proud to be a soldier and the father of a son, Canaan had walked out into the sun down the steep incline of the road where he could see the Indian Ocean, the sea calm and flat and blue to the distant horizon. A little further, Canaan had turned towards the long block of flats built by the colonial Portuguese. The building looked shabby, with washing hanging from the balconies and uncollected refuse out in the street.

"What are you thinking, Canaan? You look far away. Don't you want to hold your son?"

"Of course I do. Josiah Makoni has given us a bottle of wine. Do we have a corkscrew?"

His wife's words had brought him back to the present, away from where he had been.

"How nice of him. Come and sit with me on the bed. We'll drink the wine with our supper. One of the girls down the corridor may have a corkscrew... What's he like?"

"Who?"

"Josiah Makoni. Wasn't he the top man in the party in England? He organised that rally in Trafalgar Square back in 1963 demanding 'one man one vote' for Rhodesia. Some say he's almost as powerful in the party as Robert Mugabe. You're honoured, Canaan."

"We're going back to Rhodesia next week."

"I can't stand it when you go away. Now we have the boy to think of. What will we call him?"

"Joshua. After my friend who was killed by the elephant."

"You will be careful?"

"They're giving us rocket-propelled grenades so we can attack the farmhouses from a good distance. We'll be much safer... Can't we open the wine? Celebrate. Take a walk down to the ocean with Joshua. You know, my friend was a hero of the revolution but no one even remembers Joshua's name."

"I've just had a baby, Canaan. Tomorrow or the next day we'll go down to the ocean. Here, hold him in your arms."

"He's so small. Won't I hurt him picking him up?"

"Don't be silly... There. How does that feel, Daddy?"

"I'm so happy."

"So am I. When the war is over and we have our own farm we'll visit my friends and family in Chiweshe and show them Joshua. My parents will be so happy. When will the war be over, Canaan? What did Josiah Makoni say?"

"He said we're going to win and make the Shona people powerful like in the old days... He's so small. I think he knows I'm his father the way he's looking at me. I'm scared of dropping him."

"Then give him back to me... You're right. Go and find a corkscrew and we'll celebrate the birth of our first son. Joshua and I will watch you drink the wine."

CANAAN'S DEBRIEFING took place the next day, Canaan and the rest of the cadre explaining in detail what had happened while they were attacking the white farmers in the Centenary. When Canaan asked if any ZANLA cadres had been killed the subject was quickly avoided.

"Oh, we've got them on the run, Canaan, don't you worry about it. Already most of the farmers are trying to sell their farms and go back to England. The joke is they won't be able to take out their money as Smith has stopped all money from leaving the country. They'll get Rhodesian money which out of the country is worthless. The Smith government will soon collapse and we'll march into the capital we are going to call Harare with our heads held high. Every one of you in this room will be a hero of the revolution."

"Were any of our comrades killed?"

"Let's say there were a few accidents. Didn't you once lose one of your team to an elephant? What was his name?... Now, where were we? Did you return every item of your equipment to Comrade Tangwena in Chiweshe? It's so important to return your guns and unspent ammunition."

"Haven't the Rhodesian police found any of the hidden guns?"

"Why should they?"

"We heard not everyone of our comrades support Comrade Mugabe. I heard Comrade Makoni's brother was a sergeant in the Rhodesian police. That his name was Goodson."

"If that were true, which it isn't, we'd have him killed as a sellout. All the people of Zimbabwe every single Shona, are loyal to Robert Mugabe."

"What about the Matabele? Aren't they loyal to Nkomo?"

"You ask too many unimportant questions. Now, let me tell you how much the party appreciates you. Your leave has been extended to the end of May. You, Comrade Moyo, will be taking your wife and son back to Rhodesia. You will travel to Beira and up to the Rhodesian border by bus. Any others with families will be doing the same. The Rhodesians will never suspect a man with his wife and young son of being a terrorist, according to Comrade Makoni. The perfect cover. You'll be itinerant farm workers going back to your kraals when you get over the Rhodesian border. There will be some distance to walk round the border post. Then you buy your bus tickets like the rest of them to Salisbury. From Salisbury to Chiweshe by another bus."

"So my son is a cover?"

"How can you put it like that? Your wife will be overjoyed to be given the bus fare to take her son back home and show him to her parents in Chiweshe. Your marching orders will be given to you at the end of next month. You'll have training from our Chinese friends in the use of self-propelled grenades. And the laying of mines... All of you. On your feet. It's time to sing the songs of liberation. The glorious songs of freedom."

Dutifully, everyone in the room stood up, swaying and dancing as they sang, Canaan caught up with the rest of them in the great words of patriotism. It was like a drug and just as powerful.

The next day, with Joshua strapped to his mother's back, Canaan and Grace walked down the long hill to the beach. Both of them had never been more happy. There was no wind, the sun was cool in the autumn, and the Indian Ocean was sparkling all the way out to the horizon. In Canaan's pocket were a few escudos he had been given at the end of the previous day's meeting. Grace had borrowed an old umbrella from one of the girls down the corridor of her block of flats. She had taken one of the blankets from the bed to spread on the sand. At the beach they laid out the blanket and put up the umbrella close to the gently lapping water. The boy was still asleep when Grace laid him on the blanket in the shade of the old umbrella. They could smell the salt from the sea. Near the water it was cool. Without bathing costumes, neither of them took off their clothes. The other people on the beach were in bathing costumes, the girls in bikinis. Most of the people were white, all of them talking Portuguese. No one took any notice of the young couple with the baby.

"There's a man over there selling LM prawns."

"What's an LM prawn, Canaan?"

"LM for Lourenço Marques. They say the LM prawns are the biggest and best in the world. And they're cheap. That's a fisherman over there selling his morning catch."

"Are they cooked?"

"When they're red it means they have put the prawns in boiling water."

"How do you know all these things?"

"They were talking about the cheap prawns at yesterday's debriefing. After we'd stopped singing songs."

"What songs?"

"Songs of the revolution. I got quite carried away... I'll get us a bag of prawns. You have to pull off the heads and tails with your fingers. We have a whole month of this. Isn't it wonderful? You think you will be able to walk round the border post in a month's time?"

"I'm so looking forward to seeing my mother. Are you going to visit your parents and show them your son?"

"Better not. I haven't been home since I joined the army and went into the bush. I think the Rhodesian police know Speedy's son is a terrorist."

"You're not a terrorist. You're a freedom fighter. Why do they call him Speedy?"

"He drives a motor scooter for an insurance broker in Salisbury at an office five miles from the Harare location where I grew up. Why they called him Speedy. No, I won't go back. Wouldn't be safe for my parents. There are informers in the location. They're paid by the Rhodesian police for information. When the war's won we'll show my parents Joshua."

"Go and get those prawns. I'm hungry. I need food to build up my milk for the baby."

"I'll get two bags."

"I love you, Canaan."

"I love you, Grace... You think I can swim in my shorts?"

"You can try."

"Then I'll look after the baby while you go for a swim in the sea."

"Aren't there sharks?"

"Not close to the shore."

"Get the prawns, Canaan."

"I'm going."

"I might put my toes in the water. Can you swim, Canaan?"

"No. I never learnt to swim. Unlike all those rich white children we didn't have a swimming pool in the Harare location. In the city, the municipal swimming pool was only for whites. When we get our own farm and we're rich we'll build ourselves a swimming pool. Teach ourselves to swim then teach the children. I've always liked the idea of a shady spot round a pool, a cold beer in my hand, a servant laying out the lunch."

"Are we going to have servants?"

"Of course we are. All rich people have servants to do the work. That's the whole point of being rich."

When Canaan came back with the prawns he sat back on the blanket. The baby was wide awake. Without thinking, Grace gave Joshua her breast, smiling down on her son as he sucked. The white couple sitting closest were looking amazed, pointing to Grace feeding her baby. Canaan caught the man's eye, the look most unfriendly. Then he and the girl with him looked away and went on with their business.

"If the Portuguese still ran this place they'd toss us off the beach. Wouldn't have allowed us on it in the first place... Open your mouth."

The prawn Canaan shucked disappeared into her mouth, Grace smiling as she slowly chewed, Joshua sucking her enlarged breast, both of them happily feeding. Grace's small pink tongue came out and licked her lips, the baby made contented sucking noises.

"You want another?"

"Please. That was just so good."

"How does it feel, feeding a baby?"

"Maternal. We are so part of each other. I'm going to love him to my dying day."

She had both her hands to the child as she fed him her breast. The couple had got up and moved further away. The prawns almost finished, Canaan ran down to the water in his shorts. Throwing caution to the wind, he was so happy, he splashed out into the sea, kicking up water as he ran, diving head-first into a small wave, the water not two feet deep. He splashed in the water for a while before going back to Grace.

"I've finished the last of the prawns."

"Didn't you save me one?"

"Not one. I have to feed for Joshua, don't forget."

"It's your turn to run into the sea. Give him to me. You'd better leave your shirt on. The water's warm. The most wonderful feeling. Look, he's gone back to sleep."

"We're lucky he isn't crying."

"Run, Grace. It's such fun."

Canaan watched her slowly walk to the edge of the water. The tide was going out leaving the sand wet. He could see her footprints in the sand from where he sat cradling his son. Then she walked in a few paces. A slow wave curled into the shore making her scream with excitement. She was wet to the knees. Then she sat down in the water splashing all round, Canaan smiling with happiness. When he looked at the couple who had moved away, they too were smiling. Canaan gave them a wave. The girl waved back. Grace came back to the blanket soaked to the skin, her black hair shining.

"That was so nice, Canaan."

"It was, wasn't it?... She waved at me."

"Who?"

"The girl who moved further away. It strangely made me happy. You want another bag of prawns?"

"You remember the day we first met at Chiweshe? You and Jacob had brought your guns and landmines for Comrade Tangwena. Just after Joshua was killed by an elephant. You looked so sad, I smiled at you. Now Joshua is alive again in our son. This time I'll go and buy the prawns. Do we have enough money?"

"They're very cheap... Of course I remember. And after, when I talked to you round the cooking fire, I was so hungry."

"Then you lay back under a tree and went to sleep. Five years ago... Can you give me some money? It's such a beautiful day. I've never had a more beautiful day than today."

"Not when we first made love?"

"That was beautiful but different. This is so soft. None of it physical."

"Except the prawns."

"Except the prawns and the sea. I wish moments like this could last forever. Stay exactly as I am. Just the three of us."

"And the prawns."

They laughed quietly to themselves. Grace bent and kissed him on the mouth before walking away to buy the prawns, the coins in her hand. To Canaan, she looked like a gazelle she walked so easily, barefoot in the sand.

THE NEXT DAY, while Canaan was being taught by a Chinese instructor how to fire a rocket-propelled grenade, Clay Barry, the member-in-charge of the Rhodesian police in Centenary, was addressing the farmers in the Centenary West club function room. His uniform was immaculate, his peaked hat lay on the table in front of him, its peak pointing directly at the farmers in their wooden seats set out in the room for the occasion.

"Any of you who haven't already joined the police reserve and received training, the forms are here on the table. From our intelligence the first wave of attackers have left the country to lick their wounds. But make no mistake, they'll be back again. The fences you have all put up round your farmhouses will give you some warning and protection but the fences are not going to stop the terrorists, only make their job more difficult. Shortly, I'm going to hand the floor to Hugh Quinton, who fought in the successful British counterinsurgency against the communists in Malaya. Some of you in this room were officers in the British armed services during the war against Japan and Germany. Some of you have seen combat. It's the experience we wish to turn against the terrorists. In Malaya, the British went out and hunted the communists in the jungle. We're going to do the same here. In sticks of five, made up of you farmers wearing police reserve uniform, we are going out at night into the surrounding bush to lay ambushes. Some of you are trained hunters. All of you are familiar with the bush. All of you are good shots with a rifle. Two of you present in this room shot for Rhodesia at Bisley in England at the Commonwealth competition, even if you didn't bring back the trophy. The terrorists are not going to know what hit them when they come back again. They've lost the element of surprise. Fortunately, their original plan went wrong and they attacked the farms spasmodically instead of all their men attacking us on the same night. According to their plan, which we only found out about afterwards, they were all going to attack at dusk on Christmas Day, when all of you had had your Christmas lunches and likely too much to drink. Well, they didn't and now we know what they're up to. When they come back we're going to ambush them before they reach our houses, as they enter the Centenary. It's war and they will be armed so we will fire on them immediately. Instead of you farmers being the hunted you are going to be the hunters. From our reports, the terrorists think you farmers, many middle-aged or older, are a soft target. No one told them that many of you who came out from England after the war with promises of Crown Land farms if you completed five years of training in farming, were British officers, military men with war experience. We're going to shoot the holy shit out of them when they come back again. In history, we British have been passive until someone riles us. Only then do we become aggressive. And with our Afrikaans friends from South Africa who also farm in the Centenary, we are going to become particularly aggressive. Now, let Hugh tell you more about how the war was won in Malaya."

Bobby Preston, listening to Clay Barry's bravado, looked around the room as Hugh Quinton got up to address them. Remembering his night with his back to the ant hill when he had little idea what was going on in the dark of the night, he hoped these were words with real meaning. It was easy to talk. Putting words into action was a lot more difficult. So, instead of hunting the occasional buck for the pot, he was going to hunt men, making him sick in his stomach, a mix of fear and revulsion. Katie had been right. He should have gone back to England with her before it was all too late. And there it was again: he could run or he could stay. Looking at the others, he wondered what they were thinking. What they were really going to do. Be brave and stay with it, or be sensible and run like hell the other way, the hill of war not worth the climb? He was too young when he came out to have been in the British Army. He was a farmer not a soldier, and he wanted to stay a farmer. And then there was Wendy and the twins. It was a mess. He was in a mess and not sure how to get out of it, in the throes of a classic dither. And dithering never helped anyone.

"That was a good talk, Bobby."

"What you say, Vince?"

"Clay. Makes me feel a lot better. Instead of being sitting ducks we're going to do something positive. It's the way to go. Hunt down the bastards who want to kill us. Clay's right. We've got the experience. What do the terrs know about fighting a real war? We'll get our revenge for George Stacy and Stanley Wells."

"When's Elizabeth Wells having the baby?"

"I'm not sure. Hammond's still not taking responsibility. He still thinks the father could have been Stanley."

"But isn't he helping?"

"You know Hammond. A bit of sex is one thing. Taking responsibility quite another."

"So he won't marry her?"

"Are you kidding? Mention marriage to Hammond Taylor and he'll run a quick mile... I didn't know Hugh Quinton fought in Malaya. I knew he was in the Indian Army and fought against the Japs in Burma. Didn't know about Malaya. That was after the war."

"There are a lot of things about people we don't know, Vince. We'd better shut up. Hugh Quinton is beginning to speak. Didn't he once tell Hammond to pay his bar bill or get out of the club?"

"I rather think he did. Maybe Elizabeth should tell him what to do. Give him an ultimatum."

His mind wandering, Bobby wasn't really concentrating. There were bits about cooking the rice in Malaya before it was delivered to the outlying villages; apparently cooked rice went off after a couple of days and was no good to the communists far from their bases. Hugh, looking older than Bobby remembered, stood behind the desk on the raised platform, Clay next to him in a chair looking up at him. The old man's military moustache was white. Bobby picked up Hugh had left the Indian Army after Indian independence in 1947 and transferred to the British Army fighting the communists in Malaya. Or were they communists, thought Bobby, or ordinary Malaysians fighting for their independence? There were always two sides to a story, two ways to look. The thought of having to kill someone was at the core of Bobby's revulsion. But he'd shoot if someone threatened his children. In the row in front, listening attentively, sat Jeremy Crookshank, his one-time boss who had taught him most of what he knew about growing tobacco. Next to Jeremy were the boys, the boys he had known as children soon after their mother had been killed by lions. Phillip, tall and good looking, was verging on manhood. When Bobby came out of his thoughts, Hugh Quinton had finished speaking.

"How old are the boys, Vince?"

"Phil's seventeen in September. Randall turned fifteen December last. Phillip's down for Rhodes in Grahamstown to study history."

"Will that do him much good?... How long have you been working for Jeremy?"

"He thinks so... Getting on for ten years."

"You never wanted a wife and your own farm? A wife and kids?"

"The right girl never came along. As a bachelor I'm fine as Jeremy's manager. Got a bit of money out of the country from my bonuses."

"How'd you get it out?"

"There are ways. There are always ways. In the end you have to look after yourself. I'm thinking of going back to England. Not much point in getting myself killed. There are more girls in England. I'll find something to do. And you, Bobby? Didn't you get some money out when it was possible to transfer money legally?"

"Wendy won't hear of it. Says she'd die in that miserable climate. I'll miss you, Vince. You've been a good friend over so many years. I've got a few thousand pounds in England but not enough to live on for long."

"That's the big problem. Losing my friends. I won't know anyone in England. All the people I grew up with in Surrey will have moved on. Got wives and children. Do you know what happened to Linda Gaskell? Katie's friend. She came out with Katie on the boat. Do you remember?"

"Of course I remember. No idea what happened to her."

"She was the sexiest girl I ever met... Ever heard from Katie?"

"Not a word," said Bobby sharply.

"Sorry. Did I touch a sore spot?"

"Should have listened to her... You coming to the bar? Seems the morale-building talk is over."

"What about Wendy and the twins?"

"That's my point. She doesn't want to live in England. Says she's an African. Her family have been here for generations. African like the rest of them."

"I'm sorry I brought up Katie."

"I love Wendy and the kids. I just don't like the mess we're all in. Sometimes in life you have to do what you don't want. I love Africa and my farm as much as Wendy. It's just I have the feeling we're farting against thunder. Let's get a drink. Wendy's on the veranda with the rest of the women."

"I'm surprised she wasn't in the pep talk."

"So am I. Women are so unpredictable."

"Don't know myself."

"So when are you leaving for England?"

"Don't know. Maybe the terrs won't come back again. Let's get that drink. Jeremy and the boys are going to play tennis before we all drive back in convoy before the light goes."

"So you've no idea what you'd do in England?"

"Not the slightest idea... Don't tell Clay Barry or Fred Rankin. They think I'm part of the team. Never been in uniform before. Have you, Bobby?"

"No, I haven't. I missed National Service in England."

"So did I."

Through the window of the function room Bobby waved at his wife who was sitting with Elizabeth Wells. They walked through the door into the long bar, past the rows of guns in the gun rack along the inside wall of the bar, most of the farmers following.

"You think Hammond Taylor will one day get his comeuppance?"

"Probably not. Takes two to tango. Especially when it comes to making children, Bobby."

"History. What a complete waste of time. European history, I suppose."

"He thinks he's going to inherit the farm. What he really wants to do is play cricket for Rhodes University. For Rhodesia. For South Africa, seeing Rhodesians can play for South Africa."

"We all have our dreams. Nice boys. Life shouldn't all be about a career and making money."

"You got to have money in this life. It's easy for Phillip not to worry about money when his father's so rich. Did you know Jeremy jointly owns a block of flats in Chelsea with his old girlfriend? Price of property in England is going through the roof. So it's the polite world of a Bachelor of Arts in History for Phillip. He doesn't have to make his own fortune like the rest of us. He and Randall are going to inherit one. Takes the edge off the need. The ambition. The drive."

"Is he any good at tennis?" asked Bobby.

"Brilliant."

"Then he should go for tennis. More money in tennis. Or, better still, take up golf."

"They're building a nine-hole golf course right here."

"Golf. Who'd have thought you could make a fortune out of hitting a little ball."

"Do you know how difficult it is?"

"I have no idea. Never played golf in my life. Could never afford the equipment, let alone afford joining one of those fancy clubs... What are you going to have?"

"An ice-cold Castle, Noah," Vince said, looking at the barman.

"How long has Noah been the club's barman?"

"As long as I can remember. Did you ever find out what happened to your cook? What was his name?" asked Vince.

"Welcome. No, not a word."

"Strange name."

"When he was born, his mother said he was welcome. Don't think she'd had a son by then. Clay thinks he was abducted by the terrorists."

"What's Noah looking at me for?"

"Better be careful," said Bobby. "Noah's all right. He's part of the club's furniture. Clay says my cook was a police informer. Why he was abducted... Thank you, Noah. Put them both on my tab."

"You don't think they'll try and hit the club?"

"Not with all those loaded guns behind us. Cheers, old boy."

"Cheers, old boy... This one is really cold. Just how I like it."

Noah had gone down the bar to serve the rest of the members coming out of the function room. There was no doubt in Bobby's mind that Noah had listened to him mentioning Welcome. The whole thing made him nervous. Since Christmas, everything in his life had been going wrong. At first Hammond Taylor had come across at night to sleep in the house, giving Bobby a better feeling of security. Since the security fences had been installed on both farms, Hammond had slept in his own bed, a loaded gun next to him. On Hopewell they had built the fence with enough distance from the house to prevent the terrorists lobbing a grenade close to the building. All round the high fence, that turned over at the top to make it more difficult for someone to climb over, were square floodlights on the lawn pointing away from the house at the fence, and Claymores on top of the poles with their wires running back into the house. One pull of the wire from the house and the pin came out, exploding the mines on top of the fence, showering deadly shrapnel all round. Unlike some of the others, Bobby only turned on the lights when he heard something out in the night, thinking he would blind any attacker and making a perfect target for the new FN rifles the police had given the PATUs, the police anti-terrorist units made up of the farmers that were going to patrol the bush at night, ambushing anyone they could find on the paths and roads into the Centenary. While Bobby was to be out on patrol, Wendy and the twins would go to another farm where the wives would have police protection. As best they could, they had turned each of the farmhouses into fortresses, the success of which only time would tell.

As Bobby was finishing his first beer, Hammond Taylor joined them at the bar. He looked tired like the rest of them.

"You look washed out, Hammond," said Bobby, making way for him.

"Not surprised. Haven't had a good night's sleep since before Christmas. Thought you might like to know Fred Rankin has put the three of us in the same PATU."

"Who are the other two?"

"Jeremy Crookshank and Bob Harrington."

"Aren't they a bit old?"

"Jeremy was a naval officer during the war. He'll be leading the patrol. Can't get away from your boss, Vince."

"You want a drink? Noah, give Mr Hammond a beer."

"Are you ready to drive home? The light will be gone in an hour. It's the uncertainty of not knowing that gets to me."

"Does to all of us. You can never relax."

"Well, we made our beds. Now we'll have to sleep in them. Nothing good ever lasts for long. Anyway, cheers. To happier times."

When they set off for home quite sober, Hammond Taylor was leading the way. In the convoys they took it in turn taking the lead, a rota system to even out the risk of the lead car taking a landmine. No one had seen a landmine on the roads but they were told to look out for any new scuffs in the dirt roads where a terrorist might have buried one. Wendy was driving the truck, Bobby in the passenger seat riding shotgun, his FN stuck out of the open window. All the cars in the small convoy had guns out of their windows ready to repel an attack. There had been no rain since the end of March so the road was dry and dusty and full of corrugations. The twins sat in the middle chattering away, unaware of their parents' tension. The sun was beginning to sink when Wendy turned off onto Hopewell, and they both watched their own road for any tell-tale signs of a planted landmine. They passed slowly through the avenue of jacaranda trees Bobby had planted when he opened up the farm, the leaves on the trees beginning to fall. At the locked gate Wendy stopped the truck and handed the keys to Bobby to open the gate. All the servants had gone back to their compound. Betty, the twins' nanny, no longer came to the club or stayed in the house after dusk. They were all under threat after Welcome's disappearance. On the other side of the tall barbed wire metal gate the four Alsatian dogs were barking with excitement. Far away the tops of the purple hills were still in sunlight. There was colour in the sky, the few fluffy white clouds tinged red underneath from the setting sun. Bobby opened the gate, gave Wendy back the keys and waited for her to drive inside. Again they passed the keys.

"There's got to be a better way," said Wendy.

"I don't want spare keys lying around. This way we know the only key to the front gate is on the car ring."

"Have it your own way. Just close the gate and give me the key."

"Are you all right?"

"No, I'm not. And neither was Elizabeth. Our nerves are all shot to ribbons."

"We could all go back to England."

"This is my country. Why should I run away? Close the gate, Bobby. The girls want feeding and putting to bed. Elizabeth turns on her floodlights at night."

"She's a brave woman staying on that farm without a man."

"She's getting ready to plant another crop. The kids are helping."

"What's she going to do with the new baby now she's running the farm?"

"The eldest girl will look after the baby. What's her name?"

"Caroline. She must be fifteen by now. What happens when the kids are at boarding school during the week?"

"She has a nanny."

"What a mess. Did she talk about Hammond?"

"What for? He's not going to do anything about it. I'm going to feed the kids, put them to bed and have a drink. A proper drink."

"We all drink too much. We'll turn ourselves into alcoholics."

"The only way I can relax. With a few stiff drinks inside me is the only way I can get some sleep."

"I'm the same. There you are," said Bobby, handing his wife the bunch of keys. "Now you can put the truck in the garage."

"Yes, my lord. Your wish is my command."

"Hurry up. I want us to both hear the six o'clock news."

"They never tell us anything we don't want to hear."

Half an hour later the light had gone leaving a faint red glow on the horizon behind the Tribal Trust Land on the other side of the dam. The crickets were screeching, their high-pitched chirps mingling with the croaking of the frogs. Bobby had left the dogs outside on the lawn. The dogs had taken to running round the perimeter of the fence, chasing each other and scoring a path. The twins had gone to bed without any fuss, the nanny having bathed them in the morning.

"I'm in the PATU with Vince, Hammond, Jeremy Crookshank and Bob Harrington. Jeremy's going to lead the stick. He was a naval officer during the war."

"And me?" Wendy looked frightened, her eyes widening.

"All the women and kids will sleep on one farm when we're out patrolling. They'll have police and army guarding the house."

"And how are you going to run the farm the next day without any sleep?"

"I have no idea... How does that one look? Cheers, darling. I'm sorry it came to this."

"It's not your fault."

"Vince is going back to England. Or so he says."

"Good luck to him. He's only himself to think of."

"What are we eating for supper?"

"Cold meats and salads. Godfrey has laid it out ready in the kitchen. He's just as good as Welcome."

"I miss Welcome. He was as much a friend as a servant. He looked after me when I lived alone in the tent."

"Maybe he ran off to join the terrs."

"I hope so."

"What on earth do you mean, Bobby?"

"If he joined the terrs he isn't dead. His kids will see him again when we all stop trying to kill each other. What's the bloody point? In the end we'll destroy all this. There'll be nothing left for anyone. I don't want to kill people."

"If those dogs bark the wrong way outside you'll have to. So will I. It's called survival. Most generations go through it."

"Just look at this century. First the Boer War and now we're fighting the blacks with the Afrikaners on our side. The First World War and then the second. Now there's a common market in Europe with the French, Germans and British all being friendly to each other. What was the point of all the destruction and killing? I'm so damn tired I can't think straight... When's the baby due?"

"The second week of July if all goes well."

"Poor old Stanley. You think it might be his?"

"Elizabeth won't say one way or the other. She's a brave girl."

"Some might say a fool. Getting herself knocked up. If she was going to have affairs she should have gone on the pill."

For a long while they sat in silence in the lounge sipping their drinks. Bobby had poured them both a brandy, filling the glass with ice.

"The dogs are barking!"

"Not an alarm bark. They must have found something in the flowerbeds. Probably a frog."

"Turn on the floodlights. Please, Bobby. My nerves are shot to ribbons."

"Calm yourself down... Now, you see. They've stopped barking. Just look at that cat. Bruce is about to do his trick and fall off the windowsill... There he goes. That cat is so predictable. Goes to sleep, falls off his perch and lands on his back on the carpet."

"I've finished my drink."

"So I see. You want another one? No whisky, I'm afraid. Only had South African brandy in the bottle store."

"Of course I want another drink. Use the same glass. The ice is soaked in brandy."

They laughed, trying to make themselves feel better and reduce the tension.

"It gets so dark when there isn't a moon. I used to love the dark of the night and all those crickets and frogs. Now it's menacing. Can I come and sit on your lap, Bobby?"

"Of course you can, darling. When I've poured us another stiff drink. What would we do without booze?"

"The trouble is, the next day too much drink the previous night makes me jaded. Put your head in the kids' bedroom. Make sure they're still asleep. At least they sleep through the night which is a mercy. While you're looking at the kids and pouring the drinks I'm going outside to listen. The mosquitoes aren't so bad at this time of year."

Bobby took the drinks out onto the lawn and handed one to Wendy. The kids had been fast asleep, the small night light showing their sleeping faces. Bobby looked up at the heavens and the millions of stars, some of them twinkling. Looking at the heavens made him feel so insignificant, putting all their troubles into perspective and making his own life seem unimportant, the whole issue of life a passing moment, the world they lived and fought in one grain of sand in the vastness of the universe. Standing there on the lawn, he wondered where he came from, where he was going, what the purpose of his one little life had been all about. Did he or anything else matter? The human species, like so many others, had come and would go. Someday another type of animal would look up at the stars. Or this earth he stood on so firmly, glass in hand, would be barren. He thought of dinosaurs over in the faraway mountains, the starlight dimly showing the mountain's contours, the dinosaurs long gone and mostly forgotten. And before that, who knew? Was there a God in heaven who had made him and everything else? As much as he wanted to believe, he wasn't sure. Was religion another man-made system to keep the worst habits of men under control? Or was religion another form of politics for the few to use to gain control and live a life of comfort and privilege? He wasn't sure. Nothing in his life had ever been sure... The dogs, happy with company, sat round them, all of them part of the night, part of the great void. There wasn't one alien sound to disturb the peace of the night, not a bark, not a sound of man, just the frogs and crickets. Gently, he took his wife's hand, pressing his fingers into the soft warm palm. For the moment he was content. They were alone, the rest of the madness beyond them. The brandy, bless it, had calmed his nerves, making him mellow, making him smile.

"Aren't you hungry, Bobby? Let's go and eat our supper. Isn't it all so perfect out here?"

"Why does man bugger everything up?"

"It's our nature. How we are made."

"Doesn't make sense... Come on. We'll open a bottle of wine. Enjoy ourselves. Live for the moment. Are you happy, Wendy?"

"At this moment, under the stars, my kids asleep inside, holding my husband's hand, I've never been happier, Bobby. Thank you. Thank you for everything."

About to say 'you're welcome', Bobby said nothing as they walked inside, the dogs following. The question of what had happened to Welcome again went through his mind.

"Dogs, you're staying outside."

Inside, Bruce was back on his windowsill, again fast asleep. Bobby was hungry as he sat at the dining table in the small alcove off the lounge away from the windows and the void outside. Wendy served the sliced meat onto a plate and passed him the bowls of salad.

"What about the wine? You haven't popped the cork?"

"How silly of me."

They laughed a little nervously, the tension coming back again, neither of them saying it but both of them thinking of what might be there outside, men with guns, men intent on killing them, men who wanted to take away what Bobby had built, his farm worth having where once the empty bush had lain of little interest to anyone. Standing up, the bottle held between his knees, Bobby popped the cork. Behind him, under the bracket that held the telephone, stood the Agric-Alert system that connected them to all the surrounding farms and the Centenary police station by wireless, no telephone lines for the terrorists to cut. Throughout the house it was silent. Bobby sat down and poured two glasses of South African wine, South Africa being one of the few countries in the world that had not applied economic sanctions against Rhodesia. Like the farm, Rhodesia was completely isolated from the rest of the world, a group of people, Bobby thought, trying to hold onto what was theirs, no longer important to Britain or anyone else. After the war, with Britain short of dollars and Rhodesia in the sterling block, it had been different. The British could buy their tobacco from Rhodesia in sterling instead of using their precious dollars to buy Virginian tobacco from America. There was always money in it somewhere, thought Bobby, as he lifted his glass and smiled at Wendy, the worry lines back on her face.

"You can sit on my lap after supper. Cheers, darling. To the African Prestons."

"To us, Bobby... Do you ever miss her?"

"Who?"

"The girl you were going to marry that went back to England?"

"Of course I don't," Bobby lied, looking away.

"What was her name? Weren't you engaged?"

"Katie Frost. Her name was Katie Frost."

"What happened?"

"Please, Wendy. Do you really want to know?... She didn't want to live in Rhodesia. Said we had no future... Maybe she was right."

"There are always problems to be overcome. If we ran away every time it got difficult we would never have anything. Once you start running, you're always running from something. What my mother says. You've lived in England. I've never even been there. Were it not for being married to an Englishman I wouldn't have right of residence anywhere other than Rhodesia... What's she doing now?"

"I have no idea."

"Did she marry?"

"We haven't kept in contact, Wendy. I met you the day she sailed for England."

"That you did, lover. That you did. If you hadn't fallen off that barstool in Bretts I wouldn't have got to know you."

They drank and ate in silence, Katie hanging between them, Bobby in a brown mood of thinking. Why did women dig up the past? What was Katie to Wendy? Was she jealous? Was Katie still some kind of threat? Other people, male or female, were always difficult for Bobby to fathom. To understand what was really in their heads. People said one thing and thought another...

They both froze on the same instant, waiting for the second gunshot. All the colour had left both their faces, replaced by fear. Bobby looked at his gun propped against the wall next to the Agric-Alert.

Outside, nothing happened. The Agric-Alert began to crackle, briefly, and then went silent. In an attack it would have spoken, the system always on, provided the car battery that powered it was properly charged.

"What the hell was that?" asked Wendy.

"A single rifle shot. Probably one of our neighbours shot at a wild animal. Pigs in the maize. Not all the maize has been reaped. Could be the black guards."

"They use shotguns. That was a rifle."

"Yes, it was... Have you finished eating? Let's go in the lounge and you can sit on my lap. Bring your glass. If anything is happening they'll warn us. The dogs took no notice."

"Why should they? The shot was from far away. I'm so jumpy. I can't relax. I don't want to go to bed as I won't be able to go to sleep. It's a nightmare, Bobby. All the time I think something is going to happen to us."

"We'll have to get used to it."

"I'll never get used to a constant threat."

"Why they call it terrorism. They're terrorising us. They want us in constant fear. They don't even have to be out there and we're terrified. The new form of warfare."

"Well it's bloody effective."

"Then let's get out."

"Then they win. We lose everything."

"Not everything, Wendy. We'd still have each other and the children."

"Where is Katie?"

"What's that got to do with it?"

"If you see her in England and she's not happily married I could lose you."

"Don't be so silly. We're married. We have the girls. Nothing like that could happen."

In the silence they took their loaded guns the few yards into the lounge and propped them at either end of the settee, Wendy sitting down and curling up her legs. Bobby went back for the wine glasses and the bottle.

"Do you want me to play the gramophone? Or I can turn on the radio?"

"Then we won't be able to hear anything happening outside. Wouldn't it be better to turn on the floodlights?"

"No, Wendy. I'll turn them on if we're attacked."

"You could talk to the police on the radio."

"And tell our neighbours we were spooked by a single gunshot? It'll make everyone more nervous."

"We're so isolated."

"That's tobacco farming. Goes with the territory… I'm going to introduce fresh water bass into the dam. Do some fish farming. Give the labourers another source of protein."

"You can put the gramophone on if you want to. Play something nice. Something classical to sooth my nerves."

"How about Brahms's Third Symphony? It's one of my favourites… With the fish in the dam we can teach them to fish. Once we teach Sekuru, he'll teach the rest of them. Give them something to do on Sundays. Can you imagine it? Fresh fish right out of the water for supper. Hammond says you put cow dung round the edge of the dam for the fingerlings to feed on before the fish get big. A big bass can go five pounds."

"Shouldn't you introduce the Zambezi bream? Local fish. Adapt better. They say the bream and tiger fish are a great sport now on Kariba."

"I was going to buy us a boat. Moor it at Caribbea Bay. Take the kids up for weekends. Now we have to drive up in convoy with army trucks at either end of the cars."

"We can still do it… Brahms will be lovely. That stupid cat's going to fall off again."

"You want to drink the wine or go back to brandy?"

"Give me a brandy. I want to sleep. Tonight I'm going to knock myself out. I always have weird dreams when I'm drunk but I never remember them."

"I never remember anything when I'm drunk… At least the dogs are quiet."

"Wake him up before he falls off the windowsill again. I'm surprised he doesn't hurt himself."

"The carpet softens his fall. Where's the other one?"

"Out catching mice, poor things."

"Yes, there's always someone further down the food chain. How it works. How life goes on."

"I thought we were meant to be civilised."

"Don't be stupid. We're just the animal at the top of the food chain that now feeds off each other in one form or another. War or trade. Much the same. Go hand in hand. Get the British out of the colonies so the Americans or Russians can walk in and take our markets. That's the trouble, Wendy. We British have lost our power. Lose your power and you lose your money. We had a good run for three hundred years. Now, I suppose, it's someone else's turn. The two world wars exhausted us."

Later, a little drunk, they went to bed, Wendy first checking the children. The last thing Bobby remembered was the cold feel of his gun and Wendy snoring next to him. When he woke the sun was streaming through the window, neither of them having remembered to draw the bedroom curtains. To Bobby, it felt like a parrot had nested in his mouth but at least he had slept. There was always a price to pay for everything. Up on one elbow, Bobby smiled at Wendy.

"We slept," she said, her face breaking into a gentle smile. "You want something for the hangover?"

"Nothing really helps. Got to go. There goes the *simby*. Be up for breakfast. Oh, and by the sound of it, here come the kids."

The noise of well-slept excited children spread through the house, the plough disc gong calling the gang to work still sounding from the compound. Outside, the noise set the dogs to barking, the fly screen door on the veranda banging shut as the twins ran out to see them.

Bobby got dressed in his shorts, put on his bush hat, picked up both guns and took them to the rack near the Agric-Alert where he locked them with a chain and padlock. With the bunch of car keys in his pocket he went to the gate in the security fence and unlocked it. Betty and Godfrey were waiting on the outside to be let into the property. The sun was bright in his eyes, coming through the trees from the barns. Bobby walked down to the sheds, the car keys still in his pocket. In the grading shed everything was normal. At the rows of tables, the graders on either side were looking at the leaves of cured tobacco one by one and placing them on different piles according to their qualities. Another grader collected the piles, ensuring the same grades of tobacco went into the bailing box together. Bobby went up to Sekuru who was supervising the shed and told him about the bass, the previous night with all its tension forgotten. Then he walked up and down the lines checking the work, moving the odd leaf from one pile to another. It was a day in the grading shed like any other. At eight o'clock, hungover and thirsty, Bobby walked back to the house for his breakfast, the gate in the security fence still wide open. High in the sky, towards the TTL and the Chiweshe reserve, a pair of fish eagles were climbing the thermals, calling to each other, to Bobby, the most evocative sound on earth. They were high up, their great wings spread, small in the powder blue of the sky, their sound of calling joy making Bobby smile up at them. At the house, Bobby drank two large mugs of tea before sitting down to his breakfast.

"How's your hangover, Wendy?"

"Terrible."

"So is mine."

"During the day everything seems so damned normal. It's only at night."

"They only attack at night. If they tried in the day they'd have little chance of escape. Anyway, that's what they tell us. What's for breakfast?"

"Bacon and eggs. What else? You've eaten bacon and eggs for breakfast ever since I met you."

"Sausages and tomatoes?"

"Of course."

"What would I do without you?... Where are the kids?"

"At the pool with Betty. It's so lovely for them to be so young and innocent. We forget what it was like. Sometimes, I wish I'd never grown up... How's the grading going?"

"It's good. The quality is good. Had to move a few leaves to stop the buyers on the floors tearing a ticket and trying to say the bale they bought is mixed tobacco to reduce the price. The success of tobacco farming is in the detail. Grade it right, you get a higher price. It's that ten per cent extra that makes us a profit... What are you up to today?"

"Elizabeth's coming round. With her kids at boarding school in the week she gets frightened and lonely without Stanley... When will the grading be finished?"

"End of next month when the auction floors open. I like selling early. When the buyers are hungry for good middle-leaf tobacco."

"Fred Rankin phoned. Wants you to report to the police station."

"What's he want?"

"Didn't say, really. Something about PATU."

"Did you ask him about the gunshot last night?"

"He said it wasn't the terrs."

"When's he want me?"

"This afternoon. Three o'clock."

"You want to come? Go to the club afterwards?"

"I'm never drinking again. Even if I don't sleep a wink."

"It's what they all say on a raging hangover... That looks good, Godfrey. I could eat a horse. I always get hungry on a hangover. You got to feed a hangover. The only way... The fish eagles were up high on the thermals. You know their wingspan is over six feet?"

"I heard them. The cry of the fish eagle is so beautiful."

As Bobby was walking back to the grading shed after his breakfast, Elizabeth Wells, a much older looking Elizabeth Wells, drove in through the gate.

"Wendy's inside. How are you, Elizabeth?"

"Oh, I'm fine Bobby."

Bobby walked on. At the sheds, one of the tractor drivers had returned from the lands. There was a knock in the engine, a nasty knock that sounded expensive.

"You'll get a bonus for this, Jackson. Take off the plough and use the spare tractor. It's repaired. Ricky Anderson did a good job."

Amused at how easily his mind changed languages, Bobby walked on to the grading shed with its powerful smell of nicotine pervading everywhere.

ALWAYS ON TIME, Bobby drove into the police parking lot at five minutes to three dressed in his police reserve uniform, long, khaki shorts, long socks and boots, peaked hat on his head, uncomfortable in uniform and the power that it gave him. The parking bays were mostly full, Bobby recognising some of the trucks.

"Your first training session, Bobby," said Fred Rankin as Bobby went through the door in the busy police station. A chap from the Selous Scouts has come out from Salisbury to explain what your night patrols will be doing. You'll be blacking your faces like the Scouts. Your training will be every afternoon for a week, I'm afraid. You got to know what you're doing to catch these bastards before they do any more damage."

"Am I meant to salute you, Fred?"

"Don't worry."

Inside the police station, Jeremy Crookshank, the leader of the stick and Bobby's old boss, was waiting. He looked serious.

"This is Captain Prendegast. He'll be lecturing us today. Tomorrow we go into the bush. How's the new crop coming along, Bobby?"

"Looks all right. Depends on the floor prices."

"It always does."

When the rest of the farmers, many with previous military experience, gathered in Clay Barry's office the lecture began. For the first time in his life, Bobby was being taught how to kill his fellow man. They were at war. An experience Bobby had always hoped would never be his.

Later, as the sun was setting, Bobby drove back through the security fence gate which he padlocked as the night of fear began all over again.

"Did you learn anything?" asked Wendy. "Elizabeth's gone home, poor dear. Don't know how she faces it on her own."

"The terrorists don't have any idea what's going to be waiting for them if they come back again. Those Selous Scouts know how to hunt at night. This time, without the element of surprise, the terrs won't know what hit them."

"You sound confident, lover."

"What else can you be?"

"You having a drink? The light goes so quickly. Godfrey's put a meat pie in the oven."

"Thought you were never drinking again?"

They both laughed as they walked into the lounge. Bobby pulled down the side of the cocktail cabinet. The glass top looked up at him as he pulled out the bottle of brandy. On top of the cabinet, Godfrey had placed a full bucket of ice. Carefully, smiling, Bobby poured out the drinks.

"You know the Selous Scouts are named after Frederick Courtney Selous, the most famous white hunter of all time," said Wendy. "The three most famous hunters back in the last century were Selous, William Hartley and Sebastian Brigandshaw. Brigandshaw was killed by the

Great Elephant he unsuccessfully had hunted most of his life. The tusks were so big the elephant walked with his head bowed."

"We have a connection to Brigandshaw. Jeremy Crookshank's father knew Brigandshaw's son Harry during the Second World war. It's a small world. We're all connected somehow. How does that one look?"

"Rhodesia must have been truly wonderful in those days sparsely populated. Teeming in animals. Paradise on earth. Why does everything have to change?"

Leaving his own drink on the cabinet, Bobby went to the gun rack next to the Agric-Alert and unlocked the guns, taking them out to the veranda where the sun was setting over the Chiweshe reserve, great fingers of red pointing up into the darkening sky. Low to the southeast a sickle moon was just visible. The bigger stars, the planets, could now be seen in the paling sky. Back at the drinks cabinet he picked up his glass as the twins rushed up to greet him, hugging him round the knees. Holding his glass in one hand, mussing their hair with the other, Bobby played the game of lugging the girls, each holding a leg as Bobby walked from the lounge.

"They're getting too heavy for this."

Behind him, the screen door banged shut. It was a beautiful evening. Quiet and peaceful. The dogs on the lawn were sitting quietly together, their heads up waiting with expectation.

"I do so love my home," he said, raising his glass to Wendy.

"So do I. We've got ten minutes before the mosquitoes start biting. Do you want some of this spray? I've sprayed the children."

Bobby took the can and sprayed himself. Then he sat on the wall looking over his garden to the enclosed swimming pool, the gate locked against his children now the nanny had gone back to the compound. As dusk settled, the crickets began in earnest, the frogs answering. The dogs got up from the lawn and walked up the steps to the veranda where they sat down below Bobby on the floor inside of the wall. Bobby felt behind the ears of Whiskey, the dog's big brown eyes loving him. Everything was perfect except for the guns and their look of menace. When the light went they took the guns into the lounge. Wendy took the kids off to put them to bed. When she came back she was carrying the big white pie dish, the food smell permeating the lounge. In the small alcove off the lounge they sat down to eat their dinner, both of them hungry. The

Agric-Alert was silent. From outside a pair of owls began to call each other, the sound familiar and comforting. Silently they ate their dinner.

At eight o'clock they went to bed, both of them sober. Gently, with the familiarity of long practise, Bobby made love to his wife. When he lay back in the bed, the owls were still calling each other. Then he fell into a dreamless sleep, Wendy, sound asleep, next to him.

PART VI

JULY TO DECEMBER 1976 – "THIRTY-SOMETHING"

1

For Linda Gaskell her three years in New York, soaked in money, had been the best years of her life, all the talk of losing it at thirty a whole lot of rubbish. At thirty-two she was on top of her world, with a constant stream of rich men, some of them young and some of them old, passing through the apartment she shared with Katie one block from Central Park, the flat given to Katie by a besotted Finn Cousins to persuade Katie to live as his mistress. The IBM office, where they both worked as programmers, was ten minutes away. In the fall, three years after getting a working permit to live in America, it was Linda's habit to walk from the office to their apartment, a good walk, she said, a gal needed to stay in the business. And they loved her, the American men; her accent, her mind, but mostly her body, a body she enjoyed using as much as the men. To Linda, life was physical; money and sex. What money couldn't buy didn't much interest Linda Gaskell. Money bought the clothes, the shoes and the make-up, the rich, enticing wafts of perfume. Money bought comfort. With money a gal could do what she liked. Most of her salary went into saving for the day, God perish the thought she would say to Katie, when the men stopped calling. Most of her clothes and accoutrements had been given to her by men. Everything Linda wanted from money came mostly free. Even her old schoolfriend turned high-class hooker, Angela Tate, would be proud of her. The woman Linda felt sorry for most was Blanche Cousins, still married to Finn and living in hell, not knowing where else to go; the poor woman was getting old and was no longer sexually interesting to men.

Once a week, on a Monday, Finn Cousins called at the apartment he paid for and gave to Katie for sex. Sometimes they went out but not often. With Finn in the apartment Linda made herself scarce. If a man hadn't booked her for a Monday night date she took out the diary in the office and worked the phones. On the rare, unforgivable occasion when she couldn't find a date, Linda dressed to the nines, went out by herself to Jimmy's, her favourite bar not five minutes away in a cab. Twice a week in the evening she stayed at home with Katie, eating and talking.

"You ever think of getting married, Linda?"

"You ever think of dumping Finn?"

"Oh, giving him a little comfort on Monday nights is a small thank-you for what he gave me. Have you any idea how much the apartment is worth? And I still have my flat in Shepherd's Bush. The agent put the rent up again this year. The rent's now more than the mortgage repayment."

"You ever think of Bobby Preston?"

"Only when I'm lonely. Which isn't often with you around, Linda. What you up to tonight? Which one's taking you out?"

"I'm a bit bored with all of them. Thought I'd take myself to Jimmy's. Do you want to come?"

"Do you ever pay for a drink in Jimmy's?"

"Not very often after the first one. It's Saturday night. Get yourself tarted up and we'll hit the town."

"How was your work today?"

"You know what. I like my job. Getting a programme to work gives me deep satisfaction. Macy's are changing their accounting system. I've been working on it with Michelle O'Reilly for a month. Finished today. The client was impressed. You and I have the best of both worlds. Jobs we enjoy and I have plenty of boyfriends. Whoever said money can't buy love was talking crap. Who needs love when you've got the money? People say they love you when they want something. Usually sex. Or when you want to dump them. At this stage in my life I have no desire to have the responsibility of children. Children are always wanting something. Who wants to be a housewife, barefoot and pregnant in the kitchen, slaving away for some man who more than likely is being unfaithful, screwing some other woman?"

"We'll be lonely when we're old."

"Let's cross that bridge when we get to it, Katie... So, go and get changed. It's girls' night out... You ever hope Finn will divorce Blanche?"

"I did at first. Not anymore. We're comfortable as we are. Suits both of us."

"You know what it is? You're still pining after Bobby Preston. You don't want a commitment. The way you have it with Finn is safe."

"You've got to be realistic. With all that money, once I make a commitment and marry him he'll do to me what he's doing to Blanche. A leopard never changes its spots. He can buy everything except my commitment so for now he isn't bored with me. And no, I'm not pining after Bobby. He's married with children. You can't hold onto the past. I miss Africa. All that wonderful space uncluttered by people... I'll go get changed."

"You should date other men."

"I'm tired when I get home from a hard day's work. How you work and play, I'll never understand."

"Four hours' sleep is more than enough. And I never drink excessively during the week when I have to work in the morning."

"Eight hours for me. If I don't get eight hours' trouble-free sleep my brain doesn't work properly."

Dressed and ready to go, Linda waited for Katie. Outside on the balcony she stood by the rail looking out at the lights of New York, a sight that never failed to give her a thrill. The floor of the balcony she stood on was tiled with polished marble. Turning her back to the view she looked back into the lounge through the window. The furniture was sparse and mind-bogglingly expensive, the minimal look designed exclusively for the rich. The walls were painted in pastels, and hung with original paintings. A small chandelier hung from the ceiling. Soft lighting gave the feeling of space. Everything was polished and screaming of money. The flat was serviced daily by a Filipino maid and downstairs was a liveried doorman, always subservient and polite. Not a sound penetrated the walls from the adjacent apartments, above, below or on the sides. To Linda it was the epitome of civilised living.

When Katie came back in a five thousand-dollar designer dress, compliments of Finn Cousins, Linda smiled at her friend.

"Did you ever imagine this in school, Katie? The three musketeers. You, me and Angela. This has to be the ultimate way to live. Have you any idea what the furniture and décor cost Finn Cousins?"

"Not a clue... How do I look?"

"Knockout... Better than living in a tent in the middle of Africa."

"But not so interesting. Here, life is artificial. Everything made by man. There it was real. Vibrant. Alive. The core of nature. God's true world as he made it in all its primal glory. Every sound the sound of nature... Come on. Let's you and I go to Jimmy's. No one wants a lecture on the pros and cons of modern living. Whatever it is, you got to be thankful for living."

"There's a new singer. He's basic and as you put it, very primal."

"Now I know why you want to go tonight. I'll call down for a cab."

"I loved Africa. All those well-tanned men. But give me New York any day. Stuck in the bush with one man to make love to me would drive me out of my mind."

"You and I are so different, Linda."

"Not really. We just see it differently. Makes it interesting. Why we're such good friends... If you married and divorced Finn you'd be stinking rich for the rest of your life."

"I don't love him. I'm not that much of a bitch."

"Think of all those toyboys afterwards. Young, healthy bodies for the rest of your natural life. Oh, the pulling power of money."

"You're always thinking of sex, Linda. Anyway, a man never marries his mistress. I like Finn. He's interesting to talk to. Always knows what he's talking about. The trouble is, I don't love him."

"You could get yourself pregnant. That would make him marry you. Poor man. Must have been terrible losing his son in Vietnam. Thank goodness for the Americans that's all over."

"Finn's fifty-three. He'd be seventy-four by the time the kid turned twenty-one. A child needs a father to bring him up, not a doddering old man. They'd have nothing in common. No, it's fine as it is. May last a couple more years. Then Finn will go back to being Blanche's husband. She deserves it. It was her son as well as his."

"Maybe tonight you'll meet another man... How did Bobby meet Wendy?"

"He fell off a barstool, according to Vince. I still get a Christmas card from Vince. Always mentions you, Linda."

"Why didn't you tell me?"

"Didn't think it important."

"Did Vince marry?"

"He didn't tell me. Wendy has twins. Both girls."

"We're well out of Rhodesia. You hear anything about what's going on? There's little in the American press about Rhodesia or on the television."

"There's a war on, according to Vince. He and Bobby are in the police reserve."

"All on a Christmas card?"

"He puts in a letter."

"Do you write back?"

"I send him a Christmas card. How he knows my address in America. Vince still works as a manager for Jeremy Crookshank. Every year in his letter he says he's going back to England. Makes me sad for them now we have all this."

"Does Bobby know he's in touch with you?"

"Probably not... The four of us had fun, Linda. Don't you remember? We were so young in those days. Not so hard. Not so bruised by the world. Come on. I've got to see this singer you fancy. Oh, and Vince knows you aren't married. It's always the same postscript at the end of his letter. 'P.S. Is Linda married?' It was all so long ago. Nine years. I was twenty-three when I got Bobby's letter asking me to marry him. I was so young and naïve. Innocent. Now I look at life so differently. No longer through rose-tinted glasses."

"We all grow up... So Vince asks if I'm married?"

"Every year. The same postscript."

"You know, he said he loved me. Didn't take him seriously. Fact is I giggled... Every year?"

"Every Christmas."

"The rest of them all just wanted to screw me. You should have told me."

"No, I shouldn't. Wouldn't have made any difference. Wouldn't have done you any good. You can't be living in Rhodesia any more than I can."

Feeling nostalgic she might have missed something, Linda looked back through the balcony window at the lights of New York.

"Do you think the tiles on the balcony floor are made from real marble?" she asked Katie.

"Probably not. A lot of it is faux in America. So long as it looks real it doesn't matter."

JIMMY'S WAS PLUSH, full of well-dressed expensive-looking people in their evening attire and jewellery. So much of Linda's life had started in cocktail bars and nightclubs. The eyes of half the men followed them up to the bar. The trick, Linda knew, was to dress to show off her boobs. Men liked half-exposed breasts, it was that simple. With all the designer dresses, expensive hairstyles and sparkling jewellery, it was always a flash of tit that really caught their eye.

"Joseph. How are you tonight? This is my flatmate, Katie. Or, as you put it here in America, we share an apartment. We'll both have Manhattans and some of those delicious snacks. Is Giorgio playing tonight? Of course he is. Why would you have so many girls on their own on a Saturday night?... Well, here you are, Katie. What do you think of it? Is this rich enough or isn't it? The place crawls with denizens of Wall Street. That's the way to get rich. Playing with other people's money. What's the matter?"

"Over there behind us. No, don't look round."

"Then why tell me? Who is it?"

"Finn. Finn with another girl."

"It's his wife."

"More like his daughter by the look of her. Can't be more than twenty-two. The bastard's cheating on me as well as his wife."

"You got to share the happiness, Katie."

"Stop giggling. What am I going to do?"

"Enjoy your cocktail. The flat is in your name? You have seen the title deed haven't you, Katie?"

"He just said he'd bought the place for me."

"Oh, dear. That's why he's such a successful investment banker. He only tells the customer what they need to hear. The rest they find out afterwards. When something goes wrong and the problem is theirs, the investment banker denies all responsibility."

"You think he'd kick us out of our own apartment?"

"If it isn't ours. That's the trouble with us gals. We get older. There is always a younger gal. We get older and less valuable while the men get richer and more desirable. Fact of life. Why you should get yourself pregnant and make him marry you, with or without a prenuptial contract, though preferably without. If you had his kid you'd have something he'd really want. You'd be secure for life. It's a minefield, Katie. A gal's got to look after herself. The proof, by the sound of it, is right behind us... Just look at him. Isn't he just beautiful?"

"You talking about Finn?"

"No, you idiot. Giorgio, up on the stand."

"What are we going to do, Linda?"

"Listen to the music. Not only does he look like the perfect predator, he sings like a perfect angel... Has Finn seen you?"

"Doesn't seem to have done."

"Then ignore him. Pretend he isn't there. Under the circumstances, neither of you want to see each other. Just don't look at him. Some say if you look at a person they subconsciously feel your presence. Like staring at a bloke's head. Works for me. A good stare at the back of a nice-looking man makes him turn round. Then I smile at him. Works like a charm. Drink your drink. Don't worry. It won't take us long to give Finnie boy something to think about other than his latest girlfriend."

"Maybe she's a hooker."

"We're all hookers, Katie. You and I sink our hooks in a different way. I just told you. Get yourself pregnant. Whatever would you do without me, Katie?"

"She's so young."

"Don't look at them. We were all that age once."

"I've been a fool."

"We've all done that one in our lives. You see, we fool each other. And sometimes we fool ourselves... Cheers, Katie. To happy times."

"What are you doing now?"

"Staring at the back of that man's head at the table in front of us. When he turned round just now he was absolutely gorgeous... Just look at this place. It's packed. I wonder what they have to pay Giorgio when he brings in a crowd like this every night he sings?... Did I ever tell you I wanted to be a dancer and not a stuffy old computer programmer?"

"Ever since you were twelve years old, Linda. Now what are you doing? Do you have to drop our flat keys on the floor?"

When Linda came up from picking the keys off the floor she was smiling, her timing perfect. As her stare brought the man round to look at her, she had bent down to flash him her boobs. The man turned back to talk to his friend and signalled to a passing waiter. The man and the waiter had a brief discussion. Linda kept smiling. Then the waiter came up to Linda and Katie at the bar.

"Excuse me, ma'am. The man at the table would like to buy you both a drink."

"How splendidly kind of him. Why don't you go back and tell him we'd be delighted? Maybe he'd like to join us."

The man, watching her from his seat at the small table, was smiling. Linda smiled back, lifting her glass. As expected, the man got up. The stare and the boob-flash having worked as usual, Linda waited as the man came over from his table.

"Would you like to join us? My name is Mark."

"Linda and Katie. I'm Linda."

Leaving the remnants of their Manhattans on the bar counter next to a ten dollar note, Linda got off her barstool. Life was really so simple. Put a line in the water, get a bite and pull in the fish.

"Are you two English?"

"How did you know? What a silly question. We both work for IBM as computer programmers."

"I'm impressed. Been in the States long?"

"A couple of years. So, Mark, what do you do for a living?"

"I sell investment funds. After the recession, the market is picking up nicely again. This is my friend Anton. Anton, meet Linda and Katie. They're from England. So, what d'you want to drink? Have you eaten? With Giorgio singing, it's quite the night for singles."

As Linda prepared to sit down at Mark and Anton's table she looked around, looking for Finn. Katie was right. The girl with Finn, the dirty old man, was barely out of her teens. Finn, as she expected, tried not to look at her, though he'd seen them join the boys, that much was certain.

Oh, the power of money, she thought, looking at the animated young girl sitting with Finn. That much never changed. Like the boob-flash when she bent down to pick up her keys. The mating dance in two of its primal manifestations. Money for the gal. The inherent need to procreate for the man. Life was so simple. She gave the room a big smile as Giorgio started his song, making the young girl with Finn look up at the singer. Finn was indulgent, confident, still quite in control. At fifty-three, he was a consummate professional when it came to the art of seducing young girls with his charm, sophistication and money. At the bar, Joseph picked up her ten dollar note and gave her a smile of appreciation. Five dollars for the two manhattans. Five dollars for Joseph. When she came back on her own she would always be welcome. How it all worked. The power of money.

"You want to dance, Linda?"

"Of course."

Anton asked Katie, the waiter took the drinks order and they all walked out to the small dance floor that was filling with people. Finn was leaning back, looking up at the singer, still not wishing to see them. Gently, slowly, Linda folded herself into the young man's arms and danced closer to Giorgio.

"You like the singer, Linda?"

"He's dreamy. This place is dreamy. America is dreamy."

"Are you going to join us for dinner?"

"I don't see why not. Do you? It's Saturday night. Party time. Life is for the living. Or as they say in the classics, let the good times roll."

It was Linda's world. A place of modern sophistication. She was at home. In her element. Everything familiar. Everything comfortable. A world she wouldn't change for anything. The lights dim, the song flowing through her soul, a man close to her body... Poor old Vince, she thought. Stuck out on his farm. He didn't know what he was missing. But it was nice to be still remembered. Vince was the only man who had said he loved her and might have meant it. She wondered how he was. What they were doing. A flash of Africa passing through her mind.

When the music stopped and Giorgio left the stand, they went back to the table. Katie was deep in conversation with Anton.

"You won't believe it, Linda. Anton has been to Africa. A three-week safari in Kenya."

"Did you shoot anything, Anton?" asked Linda.

"Only with a camera. How could anyone shoot for the sake of killing a wild animal? So, did you like the bush, Katie?"

"With a passion. The trouble was it isn't going to last. Rhodesia is not going to be the place to live for the whites much longer. Probably the same for South Africa."

"Most of the white settlers had left Kenya."

"Are you going back again, Anton?"

"Next year. You want to come?"

"You are joking?"

"Probably. Just the idea is so appealing. All that bush and wild animals. It's so strange. Most people want to live in the cities. We've all lost our roots... Do you know Finn Cousins, the financier, Katie? He was in our office on Wednesday. Talking to my boss."

"Why do you ask?"

"He's staring at you. Has been ever since we got excited talking about Africa."

"Yes, I know Finn," said Katie, her voice going flat.

"What's the problem?"

"He's with another girl. Linda and I live in an apartment off Central Park he bought for me. Finn arranged the job that allows me to stay and work in America. Why I'm here tonight, I suppose. Is he coming over?"

"Doesn't look like it."

"Best I don't let him see that I've seen him."

"Isn't he married? There was something in the papers about a kid being killed in Vietnam. Mark and I were lucky. We got exemption from the draft."

"Blanche. Her name is Blanche."

"There's always more to life than meets the eye."

"You can say that again."

"So what do you do for a living, Anton?" asked Linda to change the subject.

"Oh, I work in an office in Madison Avenue. I'm a commercial artist. One of the links in the chain that makes people buy things they don't really want in our wonderful consumer society. Of course, I wanted to be a painter and live in the south of France like Van Gogh and Gauguin. But you have to have money in the modern world so I sold my soul to the devil. It's not so bad. The pay is better than good. One day, I'll have saved up enough money to buy myself a place in the hills and paint, paint, paint."

"Won't you be lonely?"

"Not when I'm painting. You don't have time to think of yourself when you're living in that other world... You know, she's very pretty, the girl with Finn Cousins. Now there's a rich dude. How old is he?"

"He's fifty-three."

"My goodness. Oh, well. It all makes sense in the big city. Oh, I'm sorry, Katie. So you're his girlfriend?"

"They say that after two years of any relationship the spark goes out of it. We've been together three. Looks as if Finn has found a new spark."

"Does it worry you?"

"Why should it? I'm not married to the man."

Linda had listened quietly to Katie's revelation. Finn had got up with his date and was dancing the girl closer to their table. He was looking at Katie, a cynical smile on his face, his expression almost shouting 'now look what I've got'. Linda wondered how long the free rent was going to last.

Soon after, Finn left Jimmy's with his young girl. With Giorgio still singing they left the cocktail lounge to go in to dinner.

"Are you okay, Katie?" asked Linda.

"Of course I am. There never was any future with Finn. Not even from the start. Why I was hesitant about the apartment."

"Just hope it's in your name or we'll be out on the street. He was enjoying himself showing that girl."

"Nothing ever lasts, Linda. We've known that all our lives. However hard we try to find something that is permanent. A home. A job. A man. Even a country. Maybe kids would have been different. The one thing in life you can't change is your parents or your children. You think America will always be like this? Rich, prosperous, in control of everything? I doubt it. Like that girl with Finn there's always someone coming up to challenge you. Poor Blanche. Thank goodness he never paraded me in front of Blanche. Maybe this time he'll be forced to divorce her if he wants that girl. If she's clever. Probably better for Blanche."

"You think he'll come round on Monday?"

"We'll have to see. Thank goodness I never sold my flat in Shepherd's Bush. I'm sorry, Anton. This is all a bit boring. Let's forget the subject."

"They say he's worth a hundred million."

"Probably more. But when you've got enough does the rest matter?"

They sat down at a table, the waiter giving each of them a menu. On Linda's menu there were no prices. It was Saturday night in Manhattan. For the moment all four of them had what they wanted. Under the table, Linda put her hand on Mark's knee, leaned close to him and whispered right in his ear.

"I never fuck on the first date." She waited, pausing for a second, enjoying his shocked expression. "Can we pretend it's the second?" Then she sat back, looking at the smile on his face. "Just joking. Good old-fashioned British humour. My word, the menu looks good. I'll start with the salmon, thank you, Mark. So, what's a good tip on the stock market? I put all my surplus cash in the equity market. A gal's got to gamble if she wants to get rich."

Slowly, caressingly, she took her hand off his knee, leaving him speechless. It was a normal evening for Linda, with everything going to plan. The poor man was still not sure if she had been joking or was serious.

2

There was no sign of Finn Cousins at the apartment on Monday, not even a phone call. Katie stayed at home through the evening expecting him to come round as usual. Linda had gone out with Mark, ecstatic about the performance of her new lover. After Jimmy's, Katie had gone back to the apartment alone in a taxi. Mark had paid the restaurant bill with his credit card and gone off with Linda, who had turned up at the flat in time to change for work that morning. During Sunday, Katie had spent the day on her own, walking in the park, thinking, trying to find out from herself what she wanted to do. Finn with the girl was not part of her problem. So much of the truth during her three years in America had been pushed under the carpet, her life going on from day to day, her job, talking to Linda, Finn on a Monday, Bobby too often in her thoughts. What was money and security anyway if she wasn't happy deep down in herself? For all the plush living she was hollow, empty, unsatisfied, floating from day to day, never coming to terms with herself.

When the office manager called her into his office on the Wednesday morning, saying there was a problem with her American visa that allowed her to work, she was relieved.

"Does Linda Gaskell have the same problem?"

"I'm afraid so, Miss Frost."

"When does my work permit expire?"

"At the end of December. Green cards are not easy to get these days, I'm afraid. So many refugees from the aftermath of the war in Vietnam. I'd be most happy to recommend both of you to our London office. I hope you enjoyed your stay with us in America."

"And if I want to go home straight away?"

"That's up to you. Celeste Fox will rearrange her department's work schedule... Have a nice day. Now, please ask Miss Gaskell to come into my office."

"Was our work good enough?"

"By all reports, the work of both of you was excellent. Didn't you once work in our London office? I'm sure they'll be delighted to get you back with your new-found experience in America... You can leave the door open."

When Katie looked back from the doorway, the man was head down writing at his desk. She was no longer important. Politely, just like that, she had been asked to leave. She knew the decision had nothing to do with the American government.

"It's over, Linda. Max Green wants to see you. All the American glitz and glamour is over for the both of us. Back to good old London."

"You know the old saying. When you're bored with London you're bored with life. When are we going?"

"Any time before Christmas."

"Give me more than enough time to wear out Mark. Don't look so glum. Now you'll find out quickly if that apartment is yours or Finn's. But don't take bets on it. Look on the bright side. A couple of years' free rent. What more can a gal want?"

"At times like this I wish I'd stayed with Bobby in Africa."

"If you know the reality of what's going on in Rhodesia at the moment you wouldn't. Think ahead, darling. Never think back. The past has always gone. There is only the future... Back in a minute. This won't take long with starchy old Max."

"Who is it tonight?"

"Johnny Cartwell. Or is it Cartwright? Cheer up. We're going home. It's been fun. A whole lot of fun. That's how you got to look at it. We'll always look back on our time in America with fond memories. You know the other old saying, Katie?"

"What's that?"

"A change is as good as a holiday. We're going on holiday. What's the lease on your Shepherd's Bush flat?"

"The tenant has another year."

"Then we really will take a holiday. I've never been to the Caribbean. We'll go home slowly. Very slowly... See you later, alligator. Got to see Maxy boy. You could always go out with Anton. Didn't he ask you to go on safari? The world is our oyster, Katie. Let's enjoy it. Three months we've got. We're going to squeeze the last bit of fun out of it. Shake all the fruit off the tree. And the best for you, my Katie, is, for three months in our luxury apartment you won't have Finn on a Monday. You never loved him. This is everyone's best way out."

Strangely, Katie thought, she felt nothing. Not a twinge of regret. Not a murmur of sadness. Nothing.

THE FOLLOWING EVENING, back from a pleasant day's work, Katie visited the supervisor of the building. The ownership of her apartment was registered in the name of a corporation. The directors of the corporation were F and B Cousins. Back at the flat, still laughing at herself for being so damn naïve, she found the flat unserviced, with no sign of the Filipino maid. In the modern world a man's word was worth nothing. 'Whatever had happened to the days when a gentleman's word was his bond?' Katie asked herself. Now everything had to be in writing, drawn up by a smart, expensive lawyer. She phoned Finn on his private number to find the number had changed. Next morning when she phoned his office she was asked if she wished to leave a message.

"Please tell Mr Cousins, the Misses Frost and Gaskell will be vacating the apartment on the thirty-first of December unless we're told to the contrary."

Katie asked the girl to repeat the message, together with her name. For the rest of the week there was silence; every night coming home from work she was expecting there to be a new lock on the door of the apartment.

She phoned Finn's office again.

"This is Miss Frost. Did Mr Cousins receive my message?"

"Oh yes, Miss Frost. The thirty-first of December will be fine. Have a nice day."

Feeling dirty, used and wretched, Katie walked home through the streets of New York. Not even a phone call after three and a half years. Not the slightest sign of a courtesy. By the time she reached the apartment she was feeling better. A good walk always made Katie feel better whatever the problem. The next day the Filipino maid turned up at the door before Katie had left for work. Neither of them mentioned her absence. As the girl on the phone had said, the end of December was fine. Linda was sitting with her at the breakfast table, eating a slice of toast covered in marmalade.

"You could sue him for breach of promise, Katie."

"I wouldn't lower myself."

"He inferred in front of me the flat was yours. In America, they sue for everything. He'd pay you to shut up. And that's another idea. Tell your story to the newspapers."

"That kind of thing never pays. Anyway, I'd be making a fool of myself. No, we leave it as it is. Another three months' free rent with a maid thrown in. Not to be sneezed at. You know, it's a load off my mind. I've never been good at dumping people whatever the reason. I still feel terrible about Bobby."

"You were trying to convince him to come back to England before it was too late. They call that tough love. Not dumping."

"I hurt him terribly."

"You probably did. Bobby had feelings. Unlike our Finnie. Why Bobby married on the rebound."

"You think it was on the rebound?"

"I'm sure it was."

"I hope they're happy. You think Blanche knows she's a director of a corporation that owns this apartment?"

"Doubt it. Don't they by law need at least two directors of a corporate company? You should give Anton a call at his office. Ask him out. Now Finn's out of the picture you can ask him round for dinner without worrying Finn will walk in through the door. No, I have another idea. We'll throw a party. You remember that first one of Finn's? We'll do another just as splendid. Send Finn an invitation. Cock a snook at him.

There are more ways than one of skinning a cat. That'll piss him off. Invite his stuck-up friends."

"They won't come."

"Doesn't matter if they don't."

"Linda, you're wicked. Wicked and nice. We'll get a band. Make some noise. The neighbours can complain to Finn. No, a better idea. We'll invite the neighbours. Linda and Katie's coming-out party. Everyone loves a good party. People from work can come. Thank them all for having us. A coming-out and farewell party they'll never forget. We're going to rip the ring out of it. It's what it's all about in America. Getting everything you can out of life before you're too old to enjoy yourself. We'll start a list of who we want to invite. What a brilliant idea. You're incorrigible, Linda."

"I know I am. But isn't it fun?"

By the time they left for work, Katie was feeling flat, all the bravado in the idea of throwing a party had left her. She was back at the beginning. Starting all over again. Nothing in her life ever seemed permanent. One minute she had a life and then it was gone out of the window, the great unknown beckoning. Heavy hearted, tired, mentally drained, Katie walked into the office to begin work at her desk.

Like so many brilliant ideas, the idea of the party came and went. Who were they anyway without Finn? People came to a Finn Cousins's party because he was rich, hoping to mingle with the rich and famous. Katie and Linda were computer programmers of little significance, two a penny in the great big world of New York money. People wanted the glamour, not the ordinary. If Finn Cousins had the power to get them thrown out of the country, he had the power to make their business associates boycott a party. Most of her other friends had been met through Finn. Would any of them jeopardise their friendship with Finn for a couple of has-beens on their way back to good old England? Katie doubted it. Money ties were more important to people than friendship. Katie couldn't be sure, but the look from people was different ever since Finn severed their relationship. It made Katie sad to realise how the power of money ruled over all of their lives. Without money, prestige and the position it bought them, people were small and insignificant. Katie, quietly amused at the thought, had become mostly invisible to other people, the reflection of Finn's money no longer providing her with an aura.

Three weeks after she had been given her marching orders the doorbell rang in the flat. Linda was out as was usual. Katie had still not plucked up the courage to invite Anton round for dinner. Expecting one of Linda's numerous boyfriends, Katie opened the door.

"Miss Frost. Are you Miss Katie Frost?"

Her stomach sank, the man looked so official. Glasses, wearing a dark suit and carrying a black briefcase.

"What's this all about?" The feeling of insecurity being in a country other than her own flooded over Katie.

"Would you mind if I came in? My name is Izak Budman of Prescott, Cohen and Rothman, attorneys."

"Now what have I done wrong?"

"Nothing. It's what the owner of this apartment did wrong."

"What's Finn done, Mr Budman?"

"Call me Izak. May I come in? October's cold in New York."

"Of course. Come in. How may I help you?"

"May I say your British accent is most interesting."

"You may if you wish. Now, what can I do for you?"

"Let me explain. I share an apartment with Mark Bloom. You met Mark and Anton three weeks ago at Jimmy's. Mark and your friend Linda have become close."

"Putting it mildly," said Katie, smiling now the fear had gone out of the moment.

"Linda explained in detail your predicament. All confidential, of course. Now, it seems to me your rights have been infringed by the recent actions of Mr Cousins. Putting it mildly, he has unilaterally had you thrown out of your home and this country without thought of the pain you're suffering. I and my law firm would be most happy to represent you against Mr Cousins, to ensure you receive your rightful financial compensation. Or, in Linda's words, stop the bastard getting away with using her friend in a semi-formal relationship, I think you would call it. You have given him three and a half years of your life, for which the law says he must pay."

"Please, Izak. I don't have the money to sue Finn Cousins. He and his lawyers would walk all over me. The little I have saved would go straight down the drain."

"It won't cost you a penny, Katie. If I may call you Katie?"

"You can call me what you like but it won't help. I don't like lawsuits. Or anything to do with them. I've had a good time in America, a lot of it at Finn's expense. I shall be travelling home to England at the end of the year. Three days before Christmas, to be exact. I wish to spend Christmas in Dorking with my parents. A good old traditional English Christmas with a Christmas tree in the hall, presents under the tree, villagers in the street under the streetlight singing Christmas carols. All my old friends at matins in the Norman church that has stood for eight hundred years where many of my ancestors are buried. I'm rather looking forward to it as a matter of fact. In some ways, Finn has done me a good turn."

"He'd do you a better turn if he placed a million dollars in your London bank account."

"How much!"

"We'll try for ten million of course. Five million for you and five million for us. In the end, we'll settle for a couple of million, money Mr Cousins won't even notice. But for you, Katie, it will change your life."

"I don't believe it."

"But you should. It's how America works. I'm certain Mr Cousins expects it. All he's done so far is try and keep the final settlement as small as possible."

"Do I have to do anything?"

"Well, we'll need every detail of your relationship with Mr Cousins. After that I will haggle over the amount of the settlement. You have nothing to lose. Everything to gain."

"And that's how it works in America?"

"That's how it works."

"I would be able to pay off my mortgage on my flat in London? Never have to work for the rest of my life?"

"Something like that. When you rub shoulders with money some of it rubs off, if you'll excuse the expression."

"It won't affect my work at IBM?"

"Why should it? They won't know anything. The argument is between you and Mr Cousins. It's how it works in America."

"If it gets nasty it will boil over."

"We doubt it. I spoke to one of our partners who suggested I make this call on you. Mr Cousins is a married man with a position in business and society. He won't want a scandal. They never do. All he'll want to do is haggle over the price."

"Well, I'll be buggered."

"I wouldn't quite have suggested going that way."

They both laughed as Izak Budman opened his briefcase.

"Now what are you doing?"

"Getting myself ready to go into detail... Do we have a deal? Whatever we get from Finn Cousins we split fifty-fifty. And you don't have to risk one cent."

"Sounds too good to be true."

"It's how it works in America." Again the man smiled. "Now, where was I? Let's start right at the beginning. Isn't it true to say Mr Cousins enticed you to come to America?"

"You could probably put it that way."

"Then we will, Katie. Then we will."

"Would you like a cup of coffee?"

"I'd love one."

To Katie, it was almost obscene. But a million bucks was a million bucks. The kind of money she'd never save in a lifetime. She knew what Linda would say: 'Don't be a bloody fool, darling. Go for the money. Always go for the money. When you're rich, you don't have to be polite to people. Only money gives a gal security. The rest is hope and not much glory.'

A week later, Anton phoned. Katie wasn't sure his invitation was prompted by the thought of her or the money, her naïvety having done an about turn. After all, it was a month after their meeting each other in Jimmy's. The previous day, Prescott, Cohen and Rothman had sent her demand to Finn Cousins, precipitating an immediate response of denial. Katie thought it all over when Izak showed her the letter, hand-delivered to Izak's office by the Cousins' attorneys.

"This doesn't look any good, Izak."

"On the contrary, Katie. In law-speak they are opening the bidding. Our reply has been delivered. If our demands are not met by tomorrow we will take Mr Cousins to court. By tomorrow I will get a phone call to stop any lawsuit. Oh, don't worry, Katie. Everything is on track."

"Do you enjoy your job, Izak?"

"I love it. It will give me considerable satisfaction to give you a piece of Mr Cousins's not so hard-earned money."

"Do you hate a man so rich? Or do you envy him?"

"When someone makes his kind of money from scratch there are always losers. All those policy holders who find out a large percentage of their hard-earned savings went to pay the man who sold them the policy his commission. To say nothing of the insurance company's overheads and profits for processing and investing the money."

"Finn said if they didn't save the money they'd drink it."

"He would, wouldn't he? But that's how it works in big business. Millions of consumers making the system work while the few make most of the profit."

"Won't Finn delay the process, knowing I'm out of the country by Christmas?"

"Oh, if he doesn't pay up, we'll blow it sky high long before then."

"Well, I wish you luck. It's your money you're spending to sue him, not mine."

The following Thursday evening, while Katie was watching television with a worn-out Linda, the phone rang in the lounge.

"How are you, Katie?" It was Finn. "What's this all about? You were quite happy with our arrangement. Did rather well out of it as a matter of fact."

"Why didn't you say you wanted to end our affair instead of going behind my back? A simple explanation would have been quite sufficient."

"I made a mistake."

"You made an expensive mistake, Finn. I had no idea how expensive until the jackals of your law system came calling."

"Can I come round?"

"You can always come round, Finn. When I bothered to look I found out my apartment belongs to you and Blanche. I suppose you want me out so you can move in the new girl. Poor Blanche. I'll bet she has no idea what you get up to. If they don't get a response to their liking, Prescott, Cohen and Rothman will be serving you tomorrow while calling a press conference or whatever they do to make your life uncomfortable."

"I never thought you were such a bitch."

"I never thought you would be unable to ask me to my face to vacate the apartment. I rather thought we understood each other. Up till my awakening in the office where I'm told my work permit now expires after Christmas, I thought you were a gentleman. Have a nice day."

"So you still want my money?"

"Not me, Finn. My attorneys. These attorneys in America are a bloodthirsty lot. You should be careful. You see, they're not charging me a penny. Enjoy your life, Finn. I hope the new girl's nice. And please don't hurt Blanche more than you have to. She's been through enough."

"You can have the apartment."

"I thought it was mine already. Please have your people talk to mine. I'm sure they will sort it out without any fuss. We don't really want an argument, do we? What a shame you weren't honest with me. It's made an otherwise pleasant relationship end in acrimony. So silly. It's always better in life to be straight. So, when are you coming round to apologise to my face, Finn? That would be nice."

"Oh, go to hell."

"Now that does make me sad. Goodbye, Finn. Have a good life. Sadly, I won't be missing you. You've left a nasty taste in my mouth. Poor Blanche. I really, really feel sorry for her."

Gently, Katie put down the phone.

"That went well," said Linda. "He'll have to live with that. What a shame. The end of a beautiful friendship."

"Wasn't that Humphrey Bogart in *Casablanca*?"

"It probably was."

"He offered me the flat."

"Then he's going to negotiate... When are you going out with Anton?"

"Saturday night. To a show. A musical... You think Anton is after my new-found money?"

"They're all after money. And if the girl comes with a ton of money, he shouldn't complain. Enjoy yourself... Do you want a cup of tea?"

"I'd love a cup. My parents are so excited I'm coming home."

"So are mine. Parents have a hard time. All that money and effort bringing us up and we fly the coop. You think Dorking will have changed?"

"Probably not. Why should it?"

WHEN KATIE REACHED the theatre with Anton on the Saturday it was raining. The cab had dropped them outside the door. The board in sparkling neon lights above the entrance told Katie they were going to see *A Chorus Line*, which had become the biggest smash hit in years. Katie smiled, not daring to mention to Anton she had gone to the prestigious opening night with Finn the previous summer. Happy to see the show again, she followed Anton inside. Afterwards, the songs ringing happily in both their heads, they went out to supper. During the interval, Katie had avoided the question uppermost in her mind. When the food was put in front of them, she asked him outright.

"Did Mark tell you or Izak Budman?"

"What would Mark or Izak wish to tell me? Haven't seen Mark since the night we all met in Jimmy's."

"Why did you wait a month to phone me?"

"What's this all about, Katie? I've been on a roadshow this last month with one of our account executives making presentations across the country. Not all the big clients are in New York. Chicago, Denver, Kansas City, Vancouver, Los Angeles and a few stops in between. I think we may have landed the Hallmark account in Kansas City. They make greetings cards. Izak Budman? I barely know him. Mark and I are casual drinking friends. We meet in the bars. It's better to hunt in pairs." He was grinning. "And it worked. Here we are, while your friend Linda is going out with Mark. So, what would Mark or his friend Izak want to tell me that's so important?"

"It wasn't important. I enjoyed the show so much. Why does good theatre so lift our hearts?"

"Any good art lifts the spirits. Takes us into the artist's world. I would love to have written a musical. All the creative arts give you the same deep satisfaction. Making up ads to sell greetings cards is not so uplifting. But it pays the bills. So, what have you been doing since we met at Jimmy's?"

"My work permit has been terminated."

"Was that what Mark was going to tell me?"

"Sort of. Linda and I are going home for Christmas. To stay."

"Then we'll have to take in a lot more shows before you go. I've never been to England."

"Finn Cousins dumped me."

"That's a relief to hear. He was far too much competition for a commercial artist. So, Katie. Why don't you tell me all about your time in Rhodesia? Africa has such a magic. Hemingway spent months in the African bush. On safari. Though he was shooting the animals. Back then we thought differently. There was so much virgin Africa. Did you spend much time in the bush? Did you see the Victoria Falls? How long did you spend in Africa? How's the wine? Now that would be a wonderful scenario. Painting wild animals in Africa."

Happy she wasn't being wined and dined because of the money that was coming to her from Finn Cousins, she went back to 1967 and her months in Africa, her eyes on fire, the pictures flooding back again as she talked. By the end of the evening they had made a pact to go on safari together when Anton had saved up enough money.

"We could go Dutch, Anton?"

"No, I want to take you, Katie. Kenya. You'll love Kenya if you don't want to go back to Rhodesia now there's a war going on. It's so sad. In the end they'll destroy each other. Why can't people live together in harmony? Why do they always fight?"

"I've been asking myself that question recently... We could meet up together after Christmas."

"Sorry, Katie. I won't have enough money by then. It's expensive living in New York even on my kind of salary."

"But I can afford it. Why should the man always have to pay? I thought Izak or Mark had told you. This morning, Finn Cousins agreed to pay me a million and a half dollars. Izak's firm earn the same. I was his mistress, Anton. They call it severance pay. It was Mark and Linda's idea to get Izak to sue Finn Cousins on my behalf. There was more to Jimmy's than a good night out... Why are you laughing?"

"You thought I was after your money?"

"I wouldn't have put it exactly like that."

"Wow. That is a lot of money."

"I feel like a whore."

"Divorced women don't feel like whores when they screw their husbands."

"Then they should. I feel dirty. So, do you want to come to Africa?"

"I'll think about it, Katie. I'm an artist, not a gold-digger. What a shame. All that money has soured my evening. I can't compete with that. Be careful. That kind of money can ruin a person's life. And you're right. People will look at you differently. You'll never know if they're looking at you or your money. Money attracts the wrong kind of people. The conniving, manipulative type who are only interested in getting at your wealth."

"But it gives me security for the rest of my life."

"Yes, it does. But there's a price for everything. Being stinking rich in a city can have its benefits. But give me a shack in the hills and a paintbrush any day in preference. Money taints people. Oh, well. I've enjoyed our evening. Never been out with a millionaire before. What are you going to do with it?"

"I have absolutely no idea. It's all a bit new to me. So you think having a lot of money isn't worth it?"

"Never had any capital myself. Most of what I earn I spend. I don't really know. It all sounds glamorous. I hope it doesn't turn round and bite you... You want some coffee?"

When Katie got home she could only think of Bobby, all the talk of Africa bringing on a drenching sadness. Anton was right. Did all that money really matter if people were happy? Having to save up to go on safari made the trip all the more exciting, all the more valued. Linda had not come home and probably wouldn't. She thought it was better to build up memories, the only thing she said she had that was permanent.

"Men come and go, Katie. So does money. Only your memories stay with you forever."

In bed, lying awake, Linda's words in her mind made her smile. She would always have Bobby and Africa in her memory. No one could take that away. She let her days on Hopewell Estate float through her mind, bringing back the smells and sounds and sights of the African bush. By the time she fell asleep she was happy, the images of Bobby having washed out the hard vulgarity of her new-found money. Her last thought was to give all the money to the cats' home. Then she fell asleep and dreamed she was back in Africa. With

Bobby. They were happy. Living in a shack. No farm. No money. Just the two of them.

When she woke, Linda had come into her room and turned on the lights.

"What time is it, Linda? I was dreaming so beautifully."

"So, have you heard anything from Izak?"

"I thought you were staying out for the night?"

"I was. Didn't work out. You can't win them all... So?"

"One and a half million in my pocket."

"Oh, shit! I told you. It worked. I can't believe it. You're rich, Katie. My old schoolmate is rich. Money, money, money... Now, how was your evening with Anton?"

"He didn't know. He had no idea I'd come into money. Thinks it's going to ruin my life."

"He's jealous. The only time you get ruined by money is when you lose it."

"Can I go back to sleep?"

"Of course you can."

Linda closed Katie's bedroom door and let out a whoop. Then there was silence inside the apartment. From outside Katie could hear the sounds of New York. She fell back into sleep and a dream where Bobby had his own body with the head of a hyena. The hyena's face had a sneer like Finn's when Finn wasn't getting his own way. For the rest of the night she tossed and turned, waking in the morning more tired than when she had gone to bed. Wearily, she got up. No feeling of elation at finding herself rich. She was flat. As if someone had taken the fun out of life. The challenge. The excitement of a future.

On the Monday afternoon Katie was called into Max Green's office. She had spent all day Sunday in the flat thinking about what she was going to do now that, as Anton had put it, she could buy people the same way as Finn did. Max, in contrast to their previous meeting, when he had told her she would have to go back to England, was all smiles, ingratiating himself to Katie by standing up when she walked into the room.

"Oh, Katie," he said, no longer 'Miss Frost'. "Please sit yourself down. There's been a big mistake. We've gone back to the people at immigration and made a plea on your behalf. It seems they are now happy to grant you a green card. You know these government departments. They are the same all over the world. They flip-flop. Anyway, you can stay with us here in America. Would you care for a cup of coffee? Oh, how silly, you Brits drink tea. Of course. How is your work going? Celeste Fox will be so happy we've sorted out the mess. Frankly, I don't know what happened. In a few years you can apply for American citizenship. I think that's how it works."

"It doesn't matter anymore, Mr Green."

"Please call me Max."

"Well, Max. I've made other plans. My mother and father were so happy to hear I was going home. Can't disappoint them. No, I'm going to live back in London."

"You'll be staying with IBM, I hope?"

"Maybe. Let me get home before I decide. Don't worry about the tea. We've both got lots of work to do. Thank you for your kindness. Thank you for your help."

"Thank you, Katie."

By the time Katie walked out of Max Green's office the man, to Katie's amusement, was literally wringing his hands. So, she thought, everyone has covered their bases. All day her phone had been ringing with invitations to go out. Some of the men, Katie barely remembered. From being excluded with the slam of a door by all of Finn's friends, she was back on the circuit. The change in people's attitudes because she had money made her sick. From somebody to nobody to somebody all in a month.

That evening, while watching television in the flat with Linda, the news came on. Katie had little interest in the upcoming presidential election. She was drinking her tea when a panning camera brought a picture of the African bush into her living room, instantly drawing her attention to the television screen, the dry bush just before the start of the rains happily familiar. As the camera focused on a reporter with a microphone in his hand both of them listened. Behind the man in khaki shorts was a fence stretching far into the distance.

We have been told today the Rhodesian security forces have crossed this border into Mozambique in hot pursuit of terrorists who have been attacking white-owned farms in Rhodesia with

> *rocket-propelled grenades. Casualty numbers on either side of this growing bush war were not given to us. The Rhodesian forces have gone deep into Mozambique where they are aligned with RENAMO who are fighting against the communist FRELIMO government of Samora Machel, yet another conflict in post-colonial Africa. It is believed the FRELIMO government are giving sanctuary to the Zimbabwe African National Liberation Army of Robert Mugabe in ZANLA's fight against the white Rhodesian government of Ian Smith. This morning we saw armoured cars and helicopters crossing this border in a major offensive. This is Scott Johnson for NBC news, reporting from the Rhodesian/Mozambique border.*

"What's a rocket-propelled grenade?" asked Linda. "Sorry. Just asking. Do you want me to turn off the news? I've never found the news in America that interesting except when they talk about England. I'm looking forward to going home."

"Would you like to stay in America? You can if you want. Max Green told me this afternoon I can get a green card if I want it. Eventually become an American. If he had helped Finn get our work permits cancelled the company might have a problem. Whatever it is, he's changed his mind. Everyone in this country is frightened of litigation."

"About you or about both of us?"

"I didn't ask him. It's all a bit fuzzy. We'd never get to the bottom of it. I suppose Finn was behind it all but who knows? Anyway, now it doesn't matter. I'm going home. The jobs are still open in London if we want them, that much I'm sure. We've learnt a lot in America."

"If you're going, so am I. Let's watch another channel. Back to good old England where most news is full of wars and other people's problems. Back to good old England where most of the problems are local. We're no longer a superpower. Just a small island off the coast of Europe. Much better. You can never sort out other people's problems. If you ask me, we're better off out of the colonies. Let them all fight with each other instead of blaming the British for their problems. The simple life. That's for me. I can't be bothered with arguments."

"So you're coming home with me?"

"Yes, Katie... You want a drink?"

"Why not? Poor Bobby. That picture of Rhodesia brought it all back again. Gave me a fright."

"Who the hell is Samora Machel?"

"Some revolutionary black politician. Says he's a communist. They'll say anything to get Russian and Chinese backing that gets them into power. I read in the paper that if you want to get rich in America you go into business but in Africa you go into politics. The likes of Machel and Mugabe. All this one-man-one-vote is a joke, according to the article. They call it one-man-one-vote once. After the first election there isn't one that allows the opposition to get into power. Once they lose power they lose their money and chances are they get themselves killed. So much for democracy in Africa. Not that I really know anything about it. Just what I read in the paper. It said the only choice for changing a government is a military coup followed by a dictatorship."

"Are you glad you didn't stay in Rhodesia with Bobby?"

"Most definitely. By the look of all that shit just now they'll be lucky to get out of Rhodesia alive. You mark my words, one day Bobby will be back in England with his tail between his legs. Men never listen to us women. Bobby and I would have had a perfectly good life in England. Not so exotic. Not so rich. But perfectly comfortable. Makes me mad now I think of it... Who's pouring the drinks?"

3

While Katie was pouring the drinks and wondering why her new money had created a barrier for Anton, preventing him from phoning her, Canaan Moyo was watching the rising sun pale the sky behind the Chimanimani mountains that dominated the eastern skyline separating Rhodesia and Mozambique. It was cool, the only cool part of the day as the heat and humidity of October built up for the rains. Like Jacob next to him, Canaan was exhausted. Unlike previous raids, when their equipment was handed in afterwards to Comrade Tangwena at Chiweshe, they were still carrying their guns and what was left of their grenades and ammunition, unable to sink back into the local population and make their way out of Rhodesia to Mozambique by bus. A week earlier, Canaan and his men had fought their way out of an ambush. The sun was almost down, the night ready to give them cover, when crossfire hit them as they entered the Centenary, killing two of his men. There was no escape up or down the bush road, the security forces having let them pass through the first ambush before opening fire. Those still alive had run into the trees and kept running, gunfire still coming at them, the light fading fast. Jacob and Canaan had hidden in a thorn thicket listening to the Rhodesians talking as they searched the bush, finally passing beyond where Canaan and Jacob were hiding. All night Jacob and Canaan had hidden in the thicket, with no idea what had happened to the rest of the cadre. In the middle of the night, with only stars giving light, they had heard more gunfire. Afraid to go back to Chiweshe, they stayed in the thicket all day and began their walk after dark, the stars pointing their way to Mozambique. For three weeks, only moving at night, they walked, crossing the Rhodesian border into Mozambique near the town of Umtali. They were still armed, hungry, sore of foot and still wondering what had happened to the rest of the cadre when they heard the thump of a helicopter flying south of them towards the Rhodesian border.

By the time the sun came up, red and hot in the morning haze, they were still a mile from the railway line where they intended boarding a train for Beira.

"You think we can win this war, Canaan?" asked Jacob in Shona. "Looks like they're following us into Mozambique. That must have been a returning Rhodesian helicopter."

"Apart from South Africa, the whole world is behind our fight for freedom."

"You think we can run the country? How are we going to know how to run everything when the whites leave?

"Of course we can. The land belongs to us, not a few whites out from England intent on getting themselves rich. I hate them for stealing our land. When the party gets into power, you and I will be rich. I don't want to spend my life working a farm for a white man who despises me and pays me a pittance. What kind of life is that for a man?... Those mountains are so majestic... Don't you worry, Jacob. In the end, we'll grind them down. We may not win the fight but we'll grind the bastards down. In the end, constantly in fear of us attacking their farms, they'll want to pack up and go home. They can't be having much fun not knowing if tonight is the night we are going to attack them. They don't know we are here. We might have stayed after the ambush, ready to go in and hit them again. It's a war of nerves and we're winning. We decide when to attack... I can't wait to get back to Mozambique where Grace and the kids are safe, living a normal life. That one trip home to Chiweshe for Grace was enough for me. When we attacked that farmhouse I was more worried about Grace and Joshua than about myself."

"Did you ever find out whose farmhouse it was?"

"Does it matter? We killed them. That's all that matters. The next time we go in I'm going to suggest we lay landmines on the roads away from the farmhouses so when they drive into town in their smart trucks they'll blow the whole family to pieces. Less dangerous than getting up close and firing rocket-propelled grenades over the security fences. Burrow under from the side of the new tarred road so they can't see what they're driving over. Come on. Last leg of the journey. On the train we can put our feet up."

"I hate this war."

"Don't say that, Jacob. It isn't finished."

"Have you got plenty of escudos to buy us food?"

"Of course I have... Just look at that sun. It's going to get hot. Did you know the whites call October suicide month?"

"When do you think they'll give in?"

"Soon. Very soon. You keep thinking about a month's leave. I love the beach. Grace loves the beach. The kids love the beach. That's how life will be when we win the war, Jacob. A life of love with our families and plenty of money."

"I don't have a wife."

"You'll have more than enough *lobola* to buy three wives when we win the war. Come on, old friend. Up on your feet. Not far now."

Wearily, they lifted their rifles onto their shoulders, the hot sun now burning their faces. One foot in front of the other, Canaan and Jacob began to walk through the open savannah towards the small siding next to the railway line, the one building clear in the morning sun. For the first time since crossing the border during the night, Canaan felt no fear. He began to sing his favourite song of the revolution, 'Bring me my machine gun'. They were almost at the railway line when the thrum of the rotor blades brought back his fear. The helicopter was coming over the low hill as Canaan and Jacob threw their rifles into the long grass. When the helicopter reached them, hovering overhead, the mounted swivel machine gun pointing down at them through the open door, the adrenaline pumped, clearing Canaan's brain and making him think. Smiling up at the helicopter, he waved. The white man behind the machine gun waved back. The pilot, no longer interested in them, flew on towards the Rhodesian border. Jacob had pissed in his pants, the front of his trousers wet with urine. They sat down, both of them shaking. Leaving their guns hidden in the long grass, they walked the last yards to the railway line. In the siding, one goods truck was standing full of maize bags waiting for the railway engine to hook it up.

At the small shop in the railway building, Canaan bought them each a Coca-Cola.

"When's the train coming?" he asked the man in broken Portuguese.

"Later this morning."

"What food can you sell us?"

With tinned food in a brown paper bag they climbed up into the railway truck and sat on the tarpaulin that covered the bags of maize, their feet dangling over the side. Jacob was looking at Canaan. He was smiling. With the spoons they carried in their knapsacks, the tin opener having opened the baked beans, they began eating.

"I thought he was going to shoot at us," said Jacob.

"He would have done if I hadn't waved."

When the railway engine hooked up the truck, Canaan and Jacob were hiding under the tarpaulin. The clanking and jolting over, the truck began to move, and they crawled out from under the tarpaulin to see what was happening. They were the last in a long line of trucks. Up front, rounding a curve, they could see the railway engine belching white smoke. The wind in their faces caused by the motion of the train was pleasant. Comfortable, lying between two sacks of maize, Canaan dozed off. Leaning forward, Jacob touched the back of his hand to Canaan's face.

"What was that for, Jacob?"

"For not panicking back there. I couldn't move I was so frightened."

"Real fear makes me think clearly... The breeze is so lovely lying here on my back... We'll look for those rifles when we return next month. I marked the spot... What I really want now is one of those very cold Portuguese beers."

Two days later at Beira they took the bus along the Indian Ocean to Maputo. When Canaan walked into the room he shared with his family, his son Joshua ran to him. Canaan felt tired, exhausted, drained of emotion. Grace was smiling with Rose in her arms.

"Was it awful this time?" she asked.

"Not so bad. Let's take the kids to the beach and buy some of those prawns."

"You want to tell me about it?"

"Not really."

"I'll get ready. You look tired, Canaan. When's the war going to be over?"

"Soon. Very soon."

"I heard the Rhodesian security forces came deep into Mozambique looking for our training camps."

"It's a big country, Mozambique. They won't find the bush camps. Don't you worry, Grace. Come on. Let's go and have a swim in the ocean."

4

Katie received the invitation to Mark Bloom's dinner party through Linda the following Friday, the same day she found a letter from Vince Ranger in her mailbox. Vince was thinking of going back to live in England and wanted to know how much longer Linda was going to stay in America. The situation in Rhodesia had deteriorated since his last Christmas card with its accompanying letter. The Centenary East club had been attacked by terrorists at dusk in the previous month, the club members at the bar ducking back from their barstools to their guns in the rack along the wall. Henry Scanlan had been drunk, his normal situation on an evening, and had run out of the club firing his automatic FN rifle at the attacking terrorists. When the terrorists fled, Henry Scanlan had run after them into the bush, incensed by the sudden interruption to his afternoon drinking. When he returned to the bar half an hour later he was stone-cold sober, according to Vince. The piece in the letter that most caught Katie's attention was the part about Bobby. Bobby had employed a young assistant, the son of his friend and one-time employer, Jeremy Crookshank. The boy, Randall, was turning nineteen in December and, unlike his older brother Phillip, who was studying history at Rhodes University in South Africa, wanted to be a tobacco farmer like his father. With Bobby away from Hopewell Estate three nights a week on night patrol with his police anti-terrorist unit, he needed help on the farm, someone to watch the gang when he was sleeping the next morning after a night on patrol. Vince was no longer in Bobby and Jeremy's PATU, going out on different nights to Jeremy, leaving one of them always guarding World's View.

While she was rereading Vince Ranger's letter, Linda had arrived home from work and given her Mark Bloom's invitation.

"Will Anton be there by any chance?" asked Katie.

"Of course. Just the six of us in Mark's apartment. Believe it or not, Izak Budman has found himself a girlfriend. You can look at Anton's paintings. Don't understand modern art myself. You judge for yourself... Who's written to you, Katie?"

"Vince Ranger. Wants to know when you're going back to live in England."

"Does he now? The poor man was besotted with me."

"Maybe it's love."

"What's love, Katie? No, more likely he didn't get enough. How it works with people. Once you've had enough of them sexually you want to move on. I get bored quicker than most. Poor old Vince. So he's going back to England with all those years in Rhodesia wasted."

"He'll have his memories."

"Is Bobby packing up?"

"Doesn't say. Why's the invitation from Mark and not from Anton?"

"Mark wants to talk to you. Business."

"What kind of business?"

"He wants to discuss what you're going to do with your money. You can't leave it on call at the bank, according to Mark. He's a good investment consultant. All you have to do is listen to him. Your lawyer will be present, darling. I'm sure Izak will keep everything kosher."

"Mark wants a piece of the action? Is that it?"

"Something like that. I mean, Mark did put you onto Izak and Izak got the money."

"And a fat chunk of cash for himself."

"How it works in America."

"What are Anton's paintings doing in Mark's flat? Anton has his own place."

"He's loaned some to Mark. Can't hang them all in his own flat I suppose."

"When's the dinner party?"

"Tomorrow. Six o'clock for pre-dinner drinks. We'll probably all go on to Jimmy's after we've eaten our supper. Money's a responsibility, Katie. You should know that. You've got to make it work for you properly or inflation will eat it away. Some say the most difficult part of money isn't getting hold of it but hanging onto it. You know the old saying, darling. Easy come, easy go."

"Can I trust Mark?"

"Who knows? Can you trust anyone these days? You pay your money and take your chances... Can I read Vince's letter?"

When Linda burst out laughing a moment later, Katie looked up from where she was reading the newspaper. Linda was waving Vince Ranger's letter.

"I don't bloody believe it. Why didn't you tell me? What a giggle. Hammond Taylor has recognised he's the father of Elizabeth Wells's two-year-old son. Miracles never cease. Most men run like hell from their illegitimate children. Too much responsibility."

"Some men do the right thing."

"Not very often. Believe me. At the beginning they'll promise you anything to get you in the sack. Why on earth wasn't stupid old Elizabeth using a contraceptive? There are some rules when it comes to elicit sex. A gal's got to look after herself... So you think Vince is still in love with me? Maybe he's just lonely."

The next day, on the way to Mark Bloom and Izak Budman's apartment, Katie was still sceptical as to why Anton was coming to dinner. A girl in her mid-thirties with flashing green eyes and a boy's haircut answered their ring of the doorbell.

"You must be Katie and Linda. I'm Eileen. Come in. The men are in the kitchen doing the cooking. Izak looks so cute in an apron. You want a drink? Mark, your guests have arrived."

Mark, smiling, came out from the kitchen followed by Izak and Anton.

"Hello. It's all prepared. What's it like outside? Let me take your coats."

"Cold... Which are Anton's paintings?"

"The ones signed Anton Dubov."

Katie walked round the big sitting room looking at the paintings. The strange rendition of leopards caught her attention. The three animals lay across branches of the same tree with a river in the background. All three of the animals' faces were human. At the bottom right-hand corner Katie saw the Anton Dubov signature. For a long while Katie stood in front of the painting.

"So, what do you think of my painting?"

"Why didn't you make it a normal wildlife painting? Their faces are so weird."

"It wouldn't have been so interesting."

"How are you, Anton? I was expecting you to phone me. Why did you come tonight?"

"To see you. If I asked you out you'd think I'm after your money."

"Aren't you, Anton? Everyone else seems to be."

"Mark wants to help you."

"And make some money for himself."

"How it works in a capitalist system. We help each other and the money goes round. The quicker the velocity of money, the richer everyone gets. The principle of advertising. Make them buy and the money comes back to you. How we create money."

"Does that kind of money have a real value? You never see it as anything but paper."

"It does when you spend it," said Anton, laughing.

"What's for supper?"

"My favourite Bombay curry I learnt in Kenya."

"I thought Mark was the chief cook?"

"Not tonight. Why they invited me. There's a motive for everything in life."

"What about friendship?"

"That also comes into it. Why it's often better to do business, Katie, with people you know."

"Are you making Mark's pitch?"

"Not really. Just trying to help... Do you like the apartment?"

"Very upmarket. Very rich. About right, I'd say, for a lawyer and an investment consultant. I'm sorry, Anton. All this money has made me cynical. I'm now a lady of leisure with nothing important to do other than talk about money. No challenge. What's the point of a job when you don't need the income? There's no incentive anymore. Being rich is boring... So Mark, what do you want to tell me about my money? Do you have a study? Let's get the business out of the way."

"It's all about spreading the risk," said Mark.

"Yes, I suppose it is. I'm listening. I never do business unless I am perfectly sober and free of any trace of a hangover. Come on. Don't look so serious. It's only money, the kind of money my schoolfriend Angela Tate would be proud of. In polite terms, Angela is a courtesan. Money for sex."

"You were his common-law wife," said Izak. "A man can't take the best years of a woman's life and not pay for it. Wouldn't be right."

"Thank you, Izak, for trying to make me feel better."

"Over half the marriages in America are going to end in divorce. The women have to be looked after. That's my job, Katie. In an older, better society we married for life. For better or worse. Once a woman married she knew she was going to be looked after for the rest of her life. We created families. Now I'm not sure what we are creating. If you think your case was acrimonious you should see some of the others. If anyone should be cynical about life it's me. When we first talked you didn't even want Finn Cousins's money. You were going home, period."

"Thanks, Izak. Now I do feel better. Let's go and get the business over with. Then we can all relax and have a drink."

Mark sat down behind a desk and pointed to a chair in front of Katie. Izak took an easy chair on the side. A sheet of typed paper was brought out from the drawer of the desk, turned round and put in front of Katie. From his inside breast pocket Mark took out a pen with a pointed tip and directed it at the top of the paper. Mark read upside down.

"A discretionary trust. Offshore in the Island of Jersey, Katie. The trust will be managed by Ernst & Young, a worldwide firm of auditors among the top five in the world. The money will belong to the trust with movements to you at your discretion. In the future, no predator will get access to your money other than in terms of your letter of discretion to the trust. Legally, you won't own the money so no one will be able to get at you and steal it. The trust laws in Jersey are some of the best in the world. This trust will protect both you and your money. There are also considerable tax savings."

"Where do you come into it, Mark?"

"The graph I am now pointing to is what I recommend you do with your money to keep it safe and earn a good return on your capital. Half a million dollars will be placed in first-class banks earning you the interest. Five banks to spread your risk. The remaining million I will invest on behalf of the trust in ten separate Global Equity Funds, again spreading the risk as far as possible. Each of the funds have top-class investment managers constantly watching the shares you're invested in through their fund. Some call these funds Mutual Funds. Usually a third of each fund is held in cash waiting for opportunities to invest. The rest is placed in government bonds in Europe and America and shares in listed companies like your employer IBM, companies listed on the New York stock exchange and the top bourses in Europe. We expect these funds to earn seven per cent per annum on your capital over a ten year period. Yes, the funds charge a fee for administering your money, but it's well worth it in today's complex investment market. Everything I point to is written clearly for you to take home and study. I recommend you phone your father in England and ask his opinion."

"How do I explain where the money came from?"

"Then ask your business associates in America. As an IBM computer programmer you must have come in contact with many people you would trust."

"I'm impressed, Mark."

"Thank you, Katie. There's no point in doing anything in life unless you do it properly. Each of the ten funds I have listed are well known in the market. Some funds will do better than others, that's how markets work. My intention is to grow your capital, which you will if you draw no more than five per cent of your investment each year. This trust will guard you against predator governments as well as predator men, one of which is definitely not my friend Anton who hates the idea of people thinking he is after your money. That side of your life you must now get used to... What do you think, Izak? Have I covered everything? Do you have any questions, Katie?"

"And if I want to buy a house?"

"The trust will buy it for you in the name of the trust. I understand you own a flat in London that is occupied by a tenant until the end of October."

"Could I pay off the mortgage?"

"Yes, if you transfer the flat into the name of the trust. The Katie Frost Trust."

"I'm swamped for the moment. Give me a week to think and I'll come back to you. Linda and I leave for England in the second week of December."

"When you tell Izak what to do with the money he will release it from the account that is presently earning you interest awaiting your instructions. Now, enough of money and business. Let's have a drink. Anton calls it a 'damn fine curry'. Learnt to make it from a fellow countryman of yours who lived in India at the time of the British Raj. Are we finished here?"

Carefully Mark folded the piece of paper, placed it in a white envelope and handed it across the desk to Katie who put it in her handbag. Katie smiled at Mark. Even though half of what he said had gone over her head, she felt more confident. By the sound of it, Mark Bloom knew what he was talking about. Back in the living room the faces in the painting caught Katie's eye. They seemed to be laughing at her. Or was it with her? She couldn't make up her mind. In their absence the side table had been covered in dishes. Dishes of chopped fruit. Chutney. Chapatis. Katie counted twenty different dishes. In the centre was a large pot on top of a hotplate.

"So that's a damn fine curry," Katie said to Anton who was offering her a drink.

"I hope you like it."

"Smells wonderful. All those Indian spices. Thank you, Anton. And you remembered what I drink."

"Don't all you English drink gin and tonic?"

"At home, most of the men drink pints of beer... So, Eileen. Where did you meet Izak? Do I detect a little of the Irish under your American accent?"

"Indeed you do. Eileen O'Shea. Me and my friends were having some trouble in a pub in Boston. The man was a sell-out. Said he was a member of the Irish Republican Army but my friend had found out he was working for the British government. It was my job to go round the pubs collecting money for the republican cause. You British have no right to be in Northern Ireland."

"Don't blame me."

"No, I shouldn't. But it's best for everyone the British let all of Ireland become one country."

"Isn't the problem to do with religion more than nationality?"

"It's to do with British imperialism. Like it is in Rhodesia. I marched with Josiah Makoni in '62 in Trafalgar Square. The 'Release Mandela' march."

"So, what happened in the pub, Eileen?"

"The man tripped over the pavement outside the pub, bumping his head and killing himself. Why I needed a lawyer. Wasn't it, Izak? Izak sorted out my little trouble."

"I just had a letter from Rhodesia. I was once engaged to be married to a Rhodesian tobacco farmer. So, you know Josiah Makoni? Bobby mentioned him. The farmer who trained my Bobby is married to a girl whose godfather paid for Josiah Makoni's education to school and university. What a coincidence."

"Josiah is in charge of the liberation army fighting the whites."

"How do you know this? I thought he was political, not military."

"We in the IRA have our contacts with all the liberation movements in Africa. From ZANU in Rhodesia to the ANC in South Africa. Some say Josiah will be prime minister of Zimbabwe when the blacks win the struggle. Josiah, not Robert Mugabe."

"I only pick up snippets. I loved Rhodesia. Wars are such a tragedy."

"But they have to be fought. One day we'll have a unified Ireland."

"I'll drink to that if it's peaceful."

"If he's still there, tell your ex-fiancé to get out of Rhodesia."

"I did, ten years ago. Didn't help. There's something about Africa that gets into their blood."

"They stole Rhodesia like they stole Ireland."

"I'm a simple working girl. Or at least I was. I keep well away from politics. So, did you kill the sell-out, Eileen?"

"The court said I didn't. That's good enough for me."

"What would we all do without a good lawyer. You'd be in jail and I'd be short of a million and a half bucks. Nice to meet you, Eileen O'Shea. Cheers. I admire people who stick up for their principles. It's just so sad when innocent people get hurt."

"The bastard wasn't innocent. Caused the deaths of a dozen brave Irishmen, assassinated by the British. There's nothing worse in the whole wide world than a sell-out. Selling out his own people. Now that's disgusting."

"She was charged, along with thirty others, of being an accomplice," said Izak, taking her hand. "Everyone was shouting outside the pub when the man fell over."

"Was he pushed?" asked Katie.

"Who knows? It was dark. The police couldn't prove anyone had murdered him."

"What a sad, sad world we live in. Makes you want to get away from everything. Bury yourself in the country. Anton wants to live in the hills and paint. He has a point. You've got to wonder where all the hatred will end. Why Bobby said he went out to farm in Rhodesia to get away from people. Now it's caught up with him like it's caught up with people in Northern Ireland. Seems to me, half the world is at war with itself... After what looks like a splendid supper are we all going to Jimmy's? Let's enjoy ourselves. Doesn't help making ourselves miserable."

From dead men outside pubs to wars in Rhodesia to a damn fine curry in a plush apartment in America, thought Katie. Everyone had their problems. The drinks went down, the food was eaten, the conversation stayed light and mostly trivial. A normal evening of entertainment, if one was rich. Even the Irish-American girl got down off her hobby horse after the third drink. In Katie's experience, people in comfortable circumstances took up causes to salve their conscience. Did a girl in America really care who was fighting who in the old country? The Irish had been doing it for centuries. All that money collected in American pubs and given to the Irish Republican Army to kill anyone who disagreed with their politics, their thirst for power. Was that good or bad, Katie wondered. The man dead outside the pub probably had a wife and children. Did Eileen O'Shea care about them?

After supper they took a taxi to Jimmy's. Linda's favourite singer was up on the dais, singing his heart out. To Katie's surprise Mark was more attentive to her than he was to Linda, their attraction to each other apparently faded. Mark's eyes wandered around the nightclub as it had the night they had met. Two other couples, friends of Mark, were invited to join their extended table. Giorgio sang and Mark invited one of the other girls to dance. Katie listened to the general conversation, watching her old friend Linda. Mark dancing with the other girl had made her annoyed. At a little after midnight the party broke up. Outside, Mark called up three taxis, putting herself and Linda into one. Anton said goodnight and got into his own cab. Mark, Izak and the Irish girl got into another. The other couples had gone off on their own. Since the meeting in his study, Mark had made no mention of money. In a matter of minutes they were all going their own ways.

"What was that all about?" asked Linda as they sat next to each other in the back of the cab. Outside it was snowing, the people on the pavements walking hunched into their coats, snowflakes drifting down on their backs. Inside the cab it was warm.

"Probably money," said Katie, still looking out the window.

"He didn't want to take me home and screw me."

"Isn't there an old saying you should never mix business with pleasure? How much do you think he'll make in commission investing my million bucks?"

"Not as much as Izak... That girl's a bitch. From what I understood they taunted the man who killed the sell-out. Goaded him on the kill. The whole bloody lot were as bad as the killer. I hate self-righteous people pushing their noses into other people's problems. What does that girl really know about the problems in Ireland? Activists. They make me sick. Self-righteous hypocrites, most of them, using other people's pain to make themselves look good. If they had to solve the problems themselves they wouldn't have a clue... You think at thirty-two I've lost it?"

"What do you mean?"

"In the past it was always me who did the dumping. That was the first time for me."

"You think he dumped you?"

"When they don't want to screw you every time, they've dumped you. I know from my own experience. The moment I don't want them to screw me I'm looking somewhere else. Giorgio didn't even look at me tonight. Despite my trying to get his attention after Mark danced with that girl."

"You'll find someone else. You weren't really interested in Mark."

"That's not the point. The bastard was using me this evening to get your business. Are you going to invest with him?"

"Probably. I like the idea of a trust looking after my money. How the hell would I know what shares to buy and when to sell them? Better to pay a professional. If he doesn't want to screw you anymore, screw him... Here we are. Our home sweet home of a couple of years. I'll miss America. I've enjoyed myself. But I won't be sad to get back to good old England. It's where we have our roots. Centuries and centuries of roots."

"When I get back I'm going to find myself a rich old man and marry him before it's too late."

"That's my girl."

"Both you and Angela have got a pile of money. I've got a bit saved up but it won't go far. A gal's got to look after herself. You're right, Katie. Screw Mark Bloom. He was only after your money. And what happened to Anton? Why did he come to the dinner if he didn't want to come after you?"

"To make up the numbers. He was doing his friend Mark a favour. I was set up, Linda. But it doesn't matter. When I have time and a clear head I'll study what he gave me in the envelope in my bag. Sometimes situations turn out different to what you expect. We're both thirty-two. I'll be thirty-three in a few weeks' time... I'm going to bed. I'm tired, in more ways than one. All the upheaval. The older you get, the less you like change. This time my travels are taking me backwards. A good night's sleep. A walk in the park tomorrow. That's what I need."

The cab had stopped outside the apartment. Katie paid the driver and took Linda's arm as they walked into the foyer of the building.

"It's not all bad, Linda. We still have each other. A pair of old spinsters but it doesn't matter. You take life as it comes. Enjoy what it offers. Who knows what's over the horizon?"

"One more drink before we go to bed? Tonight I feel lonely."

"Why not? It's so joyful to have a good friend."

Half an hour later Katie took herself off to bed, Linda watching her go. When she was alone, the room silent, Linda began to cry. The one thing she had in her arsenal, her ability to attract and hold men, was leaving her. In March, she thought, sitting alone with her drink, she was turning thirty-three. In a flash she'd be forty with nothing to show. No husband. No children. No money to speak of. And all on her own. She was lucky Katie hadn't gotten herself married to Bobby and then to a divorced Finn Cousins. Drying her eyes, she went off to her room, undressed and got into her bed. She leaned over and turned out the bedside light. With the curtains drawn, her room was dark, full of gloom, the noise of traffic outside somehow menacing, alien, not the usual sound of comfort that lulled her to sleep. So far from home, on the wrong side of the Atlantic, she lay awake feeling sorry for herself. Where was the future, she kept asking herself? The only comfort from the day was in Vince Ranger's letter to Katie. Well, she was going back to England. The strange idea of writing to Vince passed through her thoughts. But if they met again would she have the same power of attraction? Would he look at her and see a different person? She was losing it, of that she was certain. Maybe, looking back on all those men, she had missed a lasting opportunity. But which one? All of them had been temporary. Good fun at the time. None had ever kept her attention. Now the boot was on the other foot. Mark Bloom, bless him, was more interested in making money out of Katie than getting her into bed. It's got to be some old man with a pile of money before it's too late, she thought, drifting nearer to the softness of sleep. When the lights were out they all looked the same if a gal used her imagination. She might even try to get herself pregnant. That would make the old bugger marry her. When Linda finally went off to sleep there was a smile on her face...

When she woke the next morning, she felt her old self. She got up, cleaned her teeth in the adjacent bathroom, dressed and left her room. She found Katie in the lounge reading the morning newspaper, the central heating making the room nice and warm.

"Good morning, Linda. You slept well. It's eleven o'clock in the morning."

"I lay awake half the night thinking. Can you give me Vince Ranger's address? I think I'm going to write to him."

"You've never written a letter in your life."

"There's always a first time."

"The private bag number is on the letter you read. He's still at World's View working for Jeremy Crookshank. Can't be much fun anymore. I feel sorry for them."

"Last night I was feeling sorry for myself."

"That's bad... What shall we do today? Something exciting. Maybe we'll never come back to New York. Let's do everything we should have done but haven't. We'll go to the Broadway theatres. We'll go to the Met. Take a night at the opera. Listen to Bernstein conducting a Brahms symphony. Take a trip to Las Vegas. A trip to the snow slopes near Denver whatever they call them. I've got money."

"Be careful, darling. Neither of us can ski."

"Oh, they'll teach us. Let's be adventurous."

"What's got into you this morning, Katie?"

"I'm going home. Can't wait to see my parents and my grandmother in Dorking. See our old friends. One door closes, another door opens."

"What would I ever have done without you, Katie?... I wonder what he's doing right this moment?"

"Who are you talking about?"

"Vince Ranger."

"My word. You really do have a problem."

"He asked after me. No one ever asks after Linda. It was all physical."

"You want some breakfast? I'm starving. Bacon and eggs. Sausages. A couple of fried tomatoes."

"Sounds good to me. You know what they say? A good friend is often better than a good husband."

"Thank you, Linda. That's real sweet. Just don't get mushy... What's that for?"

"I wanted a hug."

The girls' reunion took place a week before Christmas in Angela Tate's plush Mayfair flat two blocks behind Park Lane and Hyde Park. Katie and Linda had flown in from America early in the evening, too late for them to take a train to their parent's homes. Before leaving New York Katie had phoned Angela saying they were on their way back to England. Hearing the time of their arrival Angela had offered them a bed for the night. Both Katie and Linda were sad to split up, having been together so long. Linda's short letter to Vince Ranger had yet to be answered, Linda having given Vince both her New York address and the address of her parents in the town of Dorking where all three of the girls had grown up and gone to the same school. A little miffed at not receiving a reply by return of post, Linda had hoped the problem was sending mail out of economically sanctioned Rhodesia.

Angela, looking more like a young duchess than a whore, met them at her door. All three of them gushed over each other, hugging.

"It's a bit like the three witches from *Macbeth*," said Angela, ushering them both inside with their luggage. "The 'when shall we three meet again' bit. So, meet again we do... Let's have a look at you. I'm so excited to see you both. Cancelled all my appointments. And Le Rififi is having to do without me tonight... Come in. Come in. Linda, you look fabulous. Not a day older. And Katie. Just look at you... How do I look?"

"You're still working?" asked Katie.

"Oh, yes. When they stop picking me in the club I'll retire. Bought myself a darling little cottage in Cornwall not far from St Ives. Five acres. Farmland all round. The perfect place to write. I've leased the land to a local farmer and an agent in St Ives lets the cottage to holidaymakers. That kind of rental gets a good return on my capital. So you're back in England. To stay? What you been up to, both of you? Oh, this is such fun. You remember those sleepovers we had as kids. Three of us in one room talking all night long, telling each other what we were going to do when we grew up. So, did you make any money in America? What's it like in New York? I want to hear everything. A restaurant round the corner is sending us supper. Never learnt to cook. So, did you bring back lots and lots of lovely dollars? The American dollar is so strong. Lovely when you convert them to pounds. And I should know. Some of my lovely clients give me their presents in dollars. You know what they want these days? Kinky. Two girls at once. My friend Darna and I pretend we're lesbians. Five hundred pounds each for our little performance. Only way some of the old buggers can get it up. Oh, I didn't tell you. I've written my first book. A novel set in the time of Oliver Cromwell. Luck was on my side, can you believe it. One of my long-time customers is a literary agent. He's sending *Clash of Passions* round the publishers, asking them to make us an offer. It's so important to have friends in the right places. By the time I go to live in Cornwall I'll be a famous novelist. No one will have any idea of what I got up to in London. I'll make a lady of impeccable character... So, what you been up to? Let's have a drink to celebrate... How does this look? Lots of Booth's gin and just a smell of French vermouth. They say Frank Sinatra shows no more than the cork of the vermouth bottle to the gin so as not to dilute it. So, my Katie. You start first. Tell Angela what you've been up to?"

"Some would say not much different to you. Cheers, Angela. My, that is a dry martini... I was a rich married man's mistress. Put me up in a flat much like this. Told me the flat was mine. When he kicked me out for a younger girl a lawyer told me to sue him for breach of contract. He'd said he was going to divorce his wife of twenty-three years and marry me. When the crunch came, what I thought was my apartment turned out to be owned by a company belonging to Finn and his wife."

"Did you get anything from the bastard?"

"He wasn't really a bastard."

"Did you get anything?"

"A million and a half dollars."

"Oh, Katie! That's wonderful. What are you doing with all that lovely money? You'll never have to work another day in your life."

"I've placed it in a trust in Jersey. Took some good advice."

"That's the best story I ever heard... And you, Linda?"

"Had a multitude of boyfriends but none of them gave me any money."

"Silly girl. You must have had proposals?"

"None I wanted to marry. I like men, Angela. That's my problem. Lots of them. Lots and lots of men."

"Why do you think they will accept your book?" asked Katie.

"It's full of sex. Lots and lots of sex. You got to know what you're writing about, Katie. You've got to have been there, had the experience. Sex sells books. Sells most everything else. First you got to live. Then you got to programme your brain to write to get your mind into the characters so the characters will get into the minds of the readers and take them down the rabbit hole into a new world away from the day to day drudgery of most people's lives. Let the reader escape into the kind of world where they really want to be. I've said I wanted to be a writer since the days when we were kids together. If this first one doesn't get accepted I'll write another one. And another one. Live in my own better world. The world of my imagination where people do exactly what I tell them. And the money doesn't matter anymore. I've got enough to live comfortably for the rest of my life. I don't have to be polite to people. To do what publishers tell me. I can write what I want and hope the readers like my story. I don't have to climb up anyone's arse. Oh, the power of having money. You must have found it, Katie. If you haven't, you will. We're independent. No husband to order us around. No husband to control the purse strings. It's our money. However we got it. For the rest of our lives we can behave exactly the way we want to behave. Not controlled by the whims of other people. That's how life should be lived. In control... You want another martini? The food will be here in an hour. So, Linda. What are we going to do with you?"

"I'm going to find a rich old man and marry him."

"Now you're talking. The older the better. A real old bastard and make him rewrite his will."

"A little more vermouth, Angela," said Katie, smiling. "That first one was almost pure gin. Do your parents know what you do for a living?"

"Of course not. It would kill my father. I'm his only child. The apple of his eye. I've told them I'm a model."

"And they believe you when they see this kind of luxury?"

"People believe what they want to believe."

"But a model would appear in advertisements. They'd see your picture."

"Often it's better not to ask too much in case you get the wrong answer. He'll be so proud of me when I'm a published novelist."

"Won't all the sex in it make him wonder?"

"I'll tell him every good writer needs a good imagination. That it's what the readers want. When I'm really successful, what's in my books won't matter. People aren't impressed with the book, Katie, they're impressed with how many books you sell. How much money you make. How famous you are. If everyone respects me as a novelist so will my father, whatever I write in the books. My daughter, the famous novelist. That sort of thing. And you, Katie. How are you going to tell your father where you got your money?"

"I'm not. Part of why the trust has been set up. Anyway, I want to go on working to have something to do. You always had a plan to write books, Angela. I'm a computer programmer, a one-time comptometer operator. That's all I know how to do. What would I do in a cottage in Cornwall all by myself? I'd go out of my mind. I'm not going to tell my parents about my money. It's there for a rainy day. Or when I'm old."

"Don't you want a family, Angela?" asked Linda.

"I can't have kids."

"I'm sorry. I didn't know."

"Anyway, I know far too much about men. Most of them are more faithful to a dog. The poor wives have no idea what their upstanding, socially acceptable husbands really get up to behind their backs. I see them without clothes. Both kinds of clothes. The clothes they wear on their bodies to cover themselves up and what they say in public to cover up what they think. I've seen some of those pillars of society grovelling on the floor, howling like a dog. Next day they cover themselves in that 'old school tie I'm educated' superiority and go to a board meeting, a business function or look like a bloody saint in parliament. No, the human race isn't quite what it likes to think it is. We call ourselves civilised. I know we are animals."

"That sounds like a book?"

"Wouldn't sell. People want to believe we all live in a beautiful world. The worst thing you can do in a book, or in life for that matter, is to tell them the truth. My father doesn't want to hear the truth. Neither does yours, Katie. If you told yours, Linda, you have had multiple partners he wouldn't want to hear either. They like to think we're saints. Pretend they are saints. Like my friend who the next morning, sweet as pie, sits on the front bench in parliament. We're all hypocrites. All after self-gratification. And why shouldn't they come to me for some fun? You want to see some of those stuck-up wives with their noses in the air to understand. For a lot of my clients, I'm all they've got. Lovely Angela who listens. Lovely Angela who gets them excited. Without me, half of them would die of boredom. We three shouldn't criticise ourselves. We're not the frauds."

"I'm looking forward to reading your books. They're going to be something," said Katie.

"I hope so."

"And what are you going to do for company? You can't live in your books all the time."

"Darna's about my age. She thinks she'll be out of it soon. She's saved her money. Maybe I'm being a bit of a hypocrite. Our little sessions together have sometimes gone on without the client. You should try it sometime. A woman really knows what another woman wants. And we get on together. Darna can type. I'll write and Darna can type and edit. Help me with the plot. We'll travel together. Have a whole new life without men."

"You've got it all worked out."

"I hope so. As far as you ever get life worked out."

"Doesn't Darna want her own children?"

"That's the beauty of it. Darna can have the children and we'll both bring them up. We'll have a family. Look how many girls are single mothers. What will be the difference?... So, when are you going down to Dorking?"

"Tomorrow," said Katie. "My dad's waiting for me to decorate the Christmas tree."

"They were good times, those Christmases growing up in Dorking. I miss those Christmases. Say hello to your folks for me."

"Aren't you going home for Christmas?"

"I'll be too busy. Christmas is a busy time. All those men in London for the Christmas holiday. Don't look so shocked. Christmas doesn't stop them. Far from it... There. How does that one look? Half gin, half vermouth. Cheers, girls. Lovely to see you. And don't get worried. I never fuck my friends. Well, not tonight." All three of them laughed, Linda and Katie nervously.

"Cheers, Angela... Now that is perfect... What's for supper?" asked Katie.

"Wait and see. Oh, and Darna's coming round. You'll like her. She's ducking out of Le Rififi for an hour to meet you. Told her so much about you both. How we all grew up together. She wants to meet my old schoolfriends."

"So you're really a couple?"

"Not exactly. Just very good friends. People don't admit who they really are. Even to themselves. Maybe they should more often. Everyone bare. No longer hiding. Now that would make it a different world."

"Maybe not a better one," said Linda. "Aren't we frightened of ourselves? Isn't that why we adopt the norms of society and take up religion? Let the wolf out of the sheep's clothing and all hell breaks loose. You see, I think I may have a problem with a really old man. However rich he is. Whatever he writes in his will. However much I use my imagination when the lights go off. If I saw him with his clothes off I think I'd vomit."

"You get used to it," said Angela. She got up, pulled back the curtain and looked out the window. "It's so drab and dark outside. Inside it's all familiar and warm."

"I don't know how you do it Angela."

"Neither do I, Linda, some of the time. Some of them are worse than animals. They steal what they want in business. Kill if they have to. Take a whole country to war. The good bit is, I'm nearly out. And I'm rich."

"Won't it stay in your mind?"

"Probably. Maybe I can let it out in the books. We'll have to see."

The supper came round and was set out for them on the table, compliments of the local restaurant which Angela recommended to her clients when they offered to take her to dinner. The quality of the food reminded Katie of Finn Cousins and the fancy restaurants in Manhattan.

"They'll send round to collect the dishes tomorrow. Enjoy."

"And it doesn't cost you a penny?"

"Not a penny. Cheaper than advertising. If I had the money in my pocket my clients have spent in the Magnolia Room it would run into tens of thousands of pounds. This is the way for the Magnolia to thank me. What's the basic cost of this food anyway? Peanuts in comparison. And when I order food, I order before the rush gets in. You scratch my back and I'll scratch yours."

"Doesn't Darna want supper?"

"She'll be taken out to supper most likely. Men like to keep everything normal. Pretend they aren't paying for it. The joke is every man pays for it. You ever heard of a good-looking bird picking up the dinner bill?... You must be tired after all your travelling."

"In New York it's still afternoon."

"When's your train to Dorking, Katie?"

"Eleven-fifteen from Waterloo station. Platform eleven. That much hasn't changed."

"What are you going to do, Linda?"

"I'm going to start looking for a flat in London. I begin my old job with IBM after Christmas. When I've got a flat I'll go down to my parents, if Katie doesn't mind going down to Dorking tomorrow on her own."

"Stay as long as you like," said Angela, getting up at the sound of the doorbell. "That must be Darna. I'll get the door... Hello, darling. Come meet my friends. We were just sitting down to supper. Katie and Linda, this is my friend Darna. Isn't she beautiful? Linda is looking for a rich old man so she can marry him. Got any ideas?"

"Dozens of them. You're welcome to all of them. So, here you are. Angela often talks of you."

"You're not eating?"

"Later. With a client. You can give me a glass of that wine."

"So how are tricks tonight?"

"Same as ever."

"Anyone missed me?"

"It's the usual City businessmen entertaining their overseas clients so they can offset the bill against tax. Everything goes on the credit card. Including my present. The British government picks up half the bill. Makes you think."

When Linda phoned her mother later in the evening, to tell her she was back in England and when she was going down to Dorking to see them, she was told a letter had arrived from Rhodesia that morning.

"Who's writing to you from Rhodesia, Linda? How are you? How is Katie?"

"We're staying with Angela Tate. School friends' reunion."

"Have you been drinking?"

"Just a little," lied Linda.

"Drink is no good for you, Linda. No good comes from drinking. Go to bed. It's late. I had to get out of bed to answer the phone."

"Goodnight, Mother."

Linda was smiling as she put down the phone.

"How's your mother?" asked Katie.

"Just the same. Hasn't changed one bit. She still thinks I'm ten years old. Wish I was. Life was a lot less complicated."

PART VII

JANUARY TO JUNE 1977 – "WHEN HOPE TURNS TO HATE"

1

Bobby Preston started reaping the tobacco on Hopewell Estate two weeks after Christmas. The season was late, the rains inconsistent. Bobby, more confident without a terrorist attack in the Centenary for months, no longer did night patrols more than once a week. With the army in hot pursuit, the terrorists had pulled back into Mozambique with mounting casualties. Stephanie and Deborah, seven years old, had started home schooling the previous year, taking their first small steps towards reading and writing. The Smith government was including blacks in the cabinet, opening prospects for the majority of Rhodesia's people. For the first time in five years, since the killing of George Stacy, Bobby had some hope back in his life thanks to his wife Wendy, the eternal optimist.

After four years there was still no sign of Welcome. With the last tobacco in the barn, Bobby walked back to the house. It wasn't the best of tobacco – lugs and primings from the bottom of the plant – but with good curing it would sell, the prime, highly prized middle leaves coming later. It was five o'clock in the afternoon, an hour before sunset and time for a swim in the pool. Both children ran to him as he reached the house. Hand in hand the three of them walked towards the house, the twins calling for their mother to come out for a swim. Over behind Chiweshe, far across the water of the dam, the mountains were coloured a deep mauve. Bobby smiled. Saturday afternoon and the week's work was over. Time to relax. Time to stop worrying himself. There was usually something to worry about in farming. It went with the territory. A constant vigilance to be ahead of the problems. Randall Crookshank, his new assistant, had helped. But the boy was young. The problems, when they came, were always Bobby's. One day, when Randall ran World's View with his father, it would be different. The boy was learning. Why Jeremy Crookshank had sent his son to Bobby. To be taught. To be made responsible. To take on the burden of his inheritance, the job of the employer, the one making decisions, no one to run to for help. Wendy appeared from inside the house wearing a bathing costume, a towel over her shoulder.

"Are we going to the club after a swim?" she asked.

"I don't see why not. Maybe the West club. I want to talk to Clay Barry and find out what's happening. He'll talk in the club. In the police station he's far too formal. Shows what a few drinks can do for a man. Loosens him up. You go on down to the pool with the kids and the dogs. I'll put on my bathing trunks."

"Did you fill a barn?"

"There was just enough ripe tobacco for one barn. The fire's in. I'll have another look at the barn temperature when we come back from the club. How was your day?"

"I'd hate to have been a schoolteacher."

"Did you teach them anything?"

"Not much... You think it's safe to drive after dark?"

"No sign of them in the last police report. Hopefully, the army's on top of it. Now we know what we're doing I'm much more confident. We'll take the guns. The new tarred surface stops them laying landmines in the road. No, we'll go. We can't stay frightened all the time. Just stay vigilant... See you in a minute."

Inside the house Bobby picked up the phone. There was no one talking on the party line. Below the telephone the Agric-Alert, connected to a car battery, was silent. Bobby wound the handle of the telephone... Three short rings and two long. Vince Ranger picked up the phone.

"We're going to the West club. Want to come along? Filled my first barn today."

"You won't believe it. Got a letter from Linda Gaskell. She's in England. They've left America. She's writing to me, Bobby."

"Have you heard anything about the terrorists?"

"All quiet as far as I know... She asked if I'm going back to England."

"Are you, Vince?"

"Probably. I don't know. Right now I'm looking out at the start of a perfect sunset. I love Africa so much. My own house. A good job. Boss I enjoy working for. How's Randall getting on?"

"We get along fine. He was a toddler when I first got to World's View from England. He was nineteen last month. So, are you coming to the club? I'm glad she wrote to you. Is Katie all right?"

"Staying with her parents in Dorking. She came into some money in America."

"Did someone die?"

"Linda didn't say. Just said it was a lot of money. Linda's started a new job with IBM in London. She's not sure if Katie is going back to work. See you later. The new tarred roads make driving a pleasure. Now takes an hour and a half to drive into Salisbury. The world's come closer. Something good had to come out of the war."

At the pool, Godfrey, who had taken Welcome's job after Welcome's disappearance, had brought down a tray of tea. The girls were splashing in the water, the dogs running round the pool barking. Bobby dived in the deep end, into a sensual pleasure of coolness after the heat of his day in the lands.

"That just feels so good. You coming in, Wendy? Gave Vince a ring. He's joining us at the club."

"Are we taking Randall?"

"Of course we are. The boy's bored stiff at night in the cottage all on his own. Don't I remember. I used to play that old wind-up gramophone to keep myself company. The same few records night after night. He's worked hard this week. The boy needs a break. We'll buy him a couple of drinks today to celebrate his birthday even though it's a bit late."

"I'm coming in."

Like Bobby, Wendy dived head first into the water. When she came up her hair was streaming wet, her small, protruding teeth smiling at Bobby.

"You know, you've got the most beautiful smile... Why are you blushing?"

"I'm a farmer's daughter. Not used to compliments."

"I'm sorry. That's my fault. The old boarding school upbringing. We were taught never to show our feelings. Stiff upper lip. All that crap. Next time you smile at me like that I'll bring you a bunch of roses... Five laps of the pool. I'll race you."

When Bobby let his wife win the race the whole family were laughing, the dogs barking. One of the cats had walked across the lawn and was meowing. Bobby, happier than he had been since the first attack, climbed out of the water, poured himself a cup of tea and looked out across his farm to the rich colours of the setting sun. The drums were playing in his workers' compound. They too were happy. Further away he could hear the drums from the village in the Chiweshe reserve. Like his own workers, the villagers were celebrating the end of the week. There would be maize beer and dancing, the drums playing well into the night, giving all who heard a feeling of comfort.

"I so love this place," said Bobby.

"So do I. So do the kids. This is just how life should be lived."

"And yet we end up having a fight with each other. And we never learn. Why can't we all enjoy what we've got?"

"Maybe they want what we've got."

"They wouldn't see what we've got if we hadn't come to Rhodesia. Before the first white settlers, all they saw was bush."

"Drink your tea while I change with the kids. We can all go to the club in the new Peugeot and eat at the club. Godfrey must be itching to get back to the compound now the drums have started... A bunch of roses? That will be something. Why can't men be romantic?"

"I think falling off a barstool in order to meet my future wife was very romantic. Don't be too long changing. I want to get to the club in daylight. It's going to be fun. A night out with my family."

With a towel over his bare shoulders, Bobby drank his tea. With Randall to help he was expanding the farm, diversifying where possible from his prime crop of Virginia flue-cured tobacco. The first to arrive of the animals was a small flock of sheep. Corriedales for meat and wool. The fresh water bass he had introduced to the dam were already providing protein for the labour force, most importantly giving the children nourishment. Some of the young children were learning to fish, sitting on the banks of the dam for hours with hand lines in the water and taking their catch back to their mothers, the sight of happy kids a pleasure for Bobby. Next to come was a herd of dairy cattle. For the first time Hopewell Estate was growing a surplus of maize, the extra bags to be sold to the Grain Marketing Board. For Bobby there was still so much to do.

He finished his tea as Godfrey came down from the house to collect the tea tray.

"You can go back to the compound and join the party," he said in Fanagalo to Godfrey. "We won't be needing supper tonight."

Godfrey, barefoot, dressed in a uniform of white shorts to his knees and a long white shirt, walked back to the house across the lawn as Bobby followed, the dogs running along on either side of them. The cat was still meowing, keeping its distance from the dogs. Pigeons and doves in the msasa trees that dotted the lawn were calling to each other in the softness of the evening. With dusk approaching, the perfume from the flowerbeds that circled the trees hung sweetly in the air. From near and far came the beat of the drums. Around the perimeter of the lawns, as a deadly reminder of the war, stood the tall security fence with its poles topped by Claymore mines that Bobby could detonate by pulling the wires from inside his house. Floodlights, square and incongruent, stood at intervals between the trees. Everything around Bobby was perfect except for the threat of attack, a constant nagging that fluttered in the pit of his stomach.

Inside the house Bobby pulled on his shorts and bush jacket, put his bush hat on his head and called for his family. Betty, the nanny, was waiting.

"You can go, Betty. We're going to the club."

The sun was sinking towards the horizon as Bobby drove his new car through the gate. He stopped the car and locked the gate before he drove into the sunset. The sky was blood red, the vivid colours splashed across the horizon above the mountains. Patches of pale blue sky still showed among the blood-red clouds. At the sheds, Bobby stopped and checked the temperature in the barn he had earlier filled with tobacco. The barn boy was smiling as always, his white teeth flashing as Bobby told him to stoke the fire that tunnelled through into the bottom of the barn. The smell of woodsmoke was rich in the air, which was vibrating to the beat of the drums, the drums from his compound and the far away Chiweshe village not missing a beat. Above, from the top of the chimney of the tall curing barn, the white smoke was rising straight up into the air, not a breath of wind to disturb it. Bobby could hear one of his dogs barking from inside the security fence at his house. For a moment he listened to the sound of the barking before getting back behind the wheel.

"Whiskey's barking because we left her behind. She's not barking at anyone."

The new car that had been on order for so long because of sanctions drove smoothly down through the avenue of jacaranda trees to the end of Bobby's farm where he turned onto the new tarred road. To the right would take him to the village of Centenary and the Centenary West club and round past Umvukwes to Salisbury. To the left the new tarred road went through Mount Darwin and Bindura and hooked back round to Salisbury. It was twenty minutes to Centenary.

"Why didn't we go to the East club?" asked Wendy.

"There are more people in the West club. I want to talk to our esteemed member-in-charge. A change is as good as a holiday, Wendy... Randall, you got your gun out the window?"

"With one up the spout and ready to shoot. Do you think Dad will be in the club?"

"I told Vince we were coming. When does Phillip go back to university?"

"He's gone. He likes it in South Africa. How many beers am I allowed?"

"We'll see, Randall. You know, I was exactly your age when I first got to World's View to work for your father."

"If I wasn't in the police reserve and working on a farm they'd call me up into the army... Just look at that sunset. Isn't it beautiful? Thank you for taking me with you tonight."

"It's my pleasure."

The light had almost gone when Bobby turned into the driveway of the club. The lights were on in the clubhouse. The scoreboard and sight screens were still visible to Bobby's left on the oval cricket field. At the back of the club Bobby stopped the car in the parking lot. Two men with their backs to them were walking towards the squash courts. The children burst out of the car. Bobby counted ten parked cars including the one he was looking for. It was the unmarked police car of Inspector Clay Barry, the member-in-charge of Centenary.

"Can't see Dad's car."

"Maybe later, Randall."

There was no sound of drums, only the bang of the squash balls hitting the side of the courts, a resonating wallop that echoed out into the surrounding bush. Wendy took the children out onto the veranda while Bobby and Randall walked into the bar. On the veranda Bobby had seen Elizabeth Wells with her two-year-old kid sitting with Hammond Taylor. At the bar, holding court, sat Inspector Barry. Down the end of the long bar, Noah the barman was sitting on a stool waiting for an order. When Bobby stood at the bar counter Noah looked up.

"Noah, give us two beers," said Bobby.

"Dad wants to know why all barmen call themselves Noah. There's another Noah in Meikles Hotel in town."

"There are plenty of Bobbys. Common name, I suppose... Evening, Clay. Randall turned nineteen just before Christmas so I'm standing him a belated celebratory drink."

"Happy belated birthday, Randall... Noah, put those two beers on my card. Seems only yesterday you were in a carry cot next to the bar. Your mother liked the club. That was all so sad."

"The lions killed her a long time ago. I don't remember my real mother. Phillip says he remembers her but it's more from the Livy Johnson painting of her that hangs in the lounge. I always think of Bergit as my mum... Have they been to the club today?"

"Haven't seen them, Randall. How's work on the farm treating you?"

"Just fine. I've only ever wanted to be a tobacco grower. To stop any problems, Dad sent me to Mr Preston for my first two years of training. Maybe three seasons. We'll see."

"Is anything going on?" asked Bobby. "It's been deathly quiet since the last attacks. Are we going out on night patrol next week?"

"There's always something going on," said Clay Barry, watching Noah.

"Can you tell us anything?"

"Why don't you and I go out and look at the last of the sunset from the cricket field, Bobby? Bring your beer. Randall will be all right for a few minutes. I've been sitting in my office behind a desk all day. Noah, if Boss Randall wants another beer put it on Mr Preston's card. Won't be long. Nice to have a chance to stretch my legs. Did you bring your guns? Of course you did. You've left them in the rack. Don't think they'll attack a club again after Henry Scanlan's performance in the East club. I think we're winning the war."

Walking from the bar through the veranda they stepped down onto the cricket field. The grass was newly cut, and the smell permeated the hot evening air, reminding Bobby of an English summer evening. From the swimming pool with its overhead lights on came the sounds of children playing. Bobby could hear Deborah calling to one of her friends. Bobby had waved at Elizabeth and Hammond on the way through the veranda. Clay walked out onto the field. Only when he had gone a distance did he stop and take a swig from his beer bottle.

"Beer gets warm so quickly in the summer. Why I never drink out of a glass. So, you want to know what's happening. Can't talk in the bar."

"Why not, Clay?"

"Noah is an informant for the terrorists."

"Then arrest him! He hears everyone talk. What an awful thought. I always hoped he was on our side. He's been serving me drinks for so many years."

"Well he's definitely not on our side, Bobby. But I use him. Why I've left him alone. When I want to give the terrs misinformation I come to the club. Like tonight. Why I spend so much time up at the bar."

"Thought you liked the drinking." Bobby was smiling, his face only half visible in the gloaming.

"Sergeant Goodson found out for us. You know he's the half-brother of Josiah Makoni. His father had four wives at the same time. That must have been fun. They both grew up on Elephant Walk down in Mazowe. The Harry Brigandshaw farm. Harry paid for Josiah's education. Much thanks he's got for that. Josiah's the brains behind all the attacks. Why we went into Mozambique and hit their training camps. You know the kill rate is twenty-three to one. One of us for twenty-three of them. One of the highest in history. But it's not helping. The world's against us, Bobby. The Americans and British think we'd be better off, all of us, under Mugabe. I hear at the lower levels we are talking to them. Why I didn't want to talk in the bar."

"Won't Mugabe take away our farms?"

"Not if we negotiate with him."

"So we can't win the bloody war?"

"We can win the war. It's the peace we can't win."

"So what you're saying is there's light at the end of the tunnel?"

"Something like that. Mugabe needs you farmers to keep the economy going. To produce the food for the exploding black population. Needs the whites in Salisbury and Bulawayo to keep industry up and running. If he kicks us all out of the country the place will grind to a halt. Then the people he says he's fighting for won't like him anymore. They want a better life, which they can't have without our skills. We built everything. That's Mugabe's problem. His people can all be taught to fire guns. What they can't be taught so quickly is how to run a modern country so that everyone prospers. Look at Randall. It's going to take long years of apprenticeship before he'll be capable of running World's View. Mugabe understands this. He's not a fool. He himself is well educated. They say he's got six university degrees. When Smith had him locked up all those years, Mugabe was studying by correspondence."

"Won't he let us carry on farming until his own people know how to farm? And then kick us out?"

"That's a chance we take. But going on fighting this war with the world against us is a dead end. The only friend we've got now the Portuguese have pulled out of Africa is South Africa. And I'm not sure how long four million whites can survive on their own in South Africa. Prepare yourself for a change, Bobby. We're going to have to negotiate ourselves out of the mess. It's the only way out unless we all pack up and bugger off like some farmers have done. Then everything we have done in Rhodesia will be worthless. Worthless for us. Worthless for them. Worthless for everyone. We have to find a compromise... Isn't the last trace of the sun over there so beautiful? I was born in Rhodesia. God knows where I go."

"Wendy says the same... Thanks, Clay. I'll remember Noah. Let me buy you a beer. Don't want to leave young Randall too long on his own. Vince Ranger is coming over later. You going to have some supper with us?"

"I promised Mary I wouldn't be late tonight. She worries about me."

"We all worry about each other. These are worrying times."

"You can say that again… How's the crop this year?"

"Looks all right in the lands. Depends on what the buyers are going to pay for it on the auction floors. My word, some kind of political settlement would bring back all the overseas buyers. Send the price of tobacco through the roof."

"Yes, it probably would. Most wars in history have ended in some kind of negotiation. Afterwards, we still have to live together. Have to depend on each other. Someone said war is just another arm of diplomacy. I don't think us humans have learnt much from history. When we can't get our own way we instinctively want to hit someone. Build it all up with our hard work so the other bugger can knock it all down again. I never did understand the human mind. We say we're civilised but underneath we're all a bunch of savages. Seems all so pointless. Anyway, that's how it is. It's my kids I worry about. What's going to happen to them. They don't have the right like you, Bobby, to live in England. They'll be the flotsam and jetsam when the tide goes out. Oh, I suppose they'll find a way… I'm playing cricket here tomorrow. All a bit incongruous don't you think? A few pockets of English culture in one great big sea of black people who must wonder where we came from. Or why. The British Empire's gone, Bobby. We're just the remnants. Forgotten, discarded, no longer of importance. Now it's all trade within the European Union. They don't need us. Or our tobacco they once liked so much because they paid us in sterling instead of forking out their precious United States dollars. I'm being silly. There's nothing more stupid than feeling sorry for oneself. I'm too bloody old to start again. The police and the army will be the first to go black."

"What happens to the likes of Sergeant Goodson?"

"Wouldn't like to be in his boots. I've heard there was a lot of sibling rivalry with Josiah when he was growing up. Goodson resented Josiah being sent to university by Harry Brigandshaw. Josiah is the son of Princess, his father Tembo's favourite wife. Tembo married her when he was old and she was young. The wives each had a hut in the compound for themselves and their children. Can't you just imagine that kind of rivalry? No wonder Josiah and Goodson hate each other. Or so I'm told."

"Has Josiah Makoni got a wife and children?"

"He never married so far as we know. There was a white girl in London when Josiah was running the ZANU office. She was Rhodesian.

One of those activists from a rich family who like to shout and scream for good causes. They were all involved in the 'Release Mandela' campaign back in the early sixties. Her name was Petronella Maple. Was often in London rallies demanding one man one vote. Her father was a tobacco farmer in Macheke and a Rhodesian Front member of parliament for Ian Smith's party. The girl dropped out of sight. Never came back to Rhodesia."

"Did Josiah want to marry her?"

"Wouldn't have done his political career any good... Still no sign of your man Welcome?"

"His family haven't seen hide nor hair of him since his disappearance after the first attacks."

"I told you he was a police informer. They must have killed him, poor chap. No one likes a sell-out whichever side it's on. Probably why Petronella Maple never came back to live in Rhodesia. She sold out her own people. Forget who was right or wrong, Smith or Mugabe. Families and people are meant to stick together. Especially when times are difficult. Don't mention Petronella to Randall. His father worked for Bertie Maple when Jeremy first came to Rhodesia from England. Though I did hear Jeremy liked the girl despite her radical politics. Being friends with a terrorist sympathiser isn't the kind of thing a young lad in the police reserve would like to imagine of his father. Not when both of them have their lives on the line. Wheels within wheels, Bobby. Everything keeps going round and round. No one ever gets to the end. Now they're terrorists, on the American black list. Tomorrow, when the world's politics change, they become world heroes. Depends if you win or lose. Some even say Adolf Hitler would have been a hero if he'd won the war for the Germans. And Winston Churchill would have been charged with war crimes for the incendiary bombing of Cologne and Dresden that obliterated so many women and children. Who knows? Here we are on a cricket field, for God's sake, in the middle of the African bush... Are the mosquitoes biting you?"

"Not yet. Can't imagine Churchill charged with war crimes after the German Blitz... We still take our anti-malaria pills."

"So do we."

"Let's go back inside. I've finished my beer. Randall will think we've run out on him."

"Isn't that Vince Ranger's car coming up the driveway?"

"I rather think it is... So, whatever happens this, for us, is all a bit temporary?"

"You can probably look at it that way."

"Vince wants to go back to England."

"What's he going to do?"

"That's the problem. For all of us. Some say we've made our bed and we'll have to sleep in it."

"England wasn't much fun during the war. Or for a long time afterwards. You pay your money and take your chances, old boy. You going to buy me that drink? Mine's also finished... Life just goes on. Only a little different. None of us are really in control of our own destiny. It's how it goes. Enjoy what you've got and hope for the future."

"Why I called it Hopewell Estate. Come on. That first beer didn't touch the sides. Thanks for the chat."

"It never happened."

"What do you mean, Clay?"

"I'm a policeman."

"Oh, I get it. I'll remember to be careful what I say in future in front of Noah."

"You do that, Bobby."

The sky above them was now studded with stars, the Milky Way a splash of light as if the gods had thrown a bucket of milk across the night sky. The bigger stars, the planets, were already twinkling. A faint blush behind the faraway mountains was all that was left of the day. There was no sign of the moon.

"A perfect time for a terrorist attack," said Bobby, nervously wishing he had brought out his gun. Whatever he did or said the war was always in his head, a constant nagging fear that had stayed with him all the past three years, a debilitating fear that niggled at any slight thought of hope. In such a moment in the cloak of darkness, Bobby wondered if it was all worthwhile, a hill so steep it wasn't worth the climb. Neither of them spoke as they walked from the field, the lights from the clubhouse beckoning, the voices of the children in the swimming pool crystal clear in the quiet of the night, the women sitting on the fly-screened veranda clearly visible. Just down from the veranda someone had started the *braai*, and the flames of the woodfire burned high in the stillness. Through the veranda and the inside window to the bar, they could see a line of people with their backs to them sitting on barstools up at the bar. Noah, now known to Bobby as an informer, was serving Vince Ranger a drink. Vince was sitting up at the bar next to Randall Crookshank, the second son of Vince's boss. And all those years Noah had been listening to their conversations and passing on the information to the people intent on killing every member of the club. When they were all gone, Bobby wondered what kind of job would be left for Noah. Would the terrorists reward their informer? Bobby doubted it. People used people when they were needed. Afterwards, the need gone, they were discarded. Forgotten. Bobby wondered if Petronella Maple ever gave a thought to any of them, including her mother and father. She most likely had some new cause, a new victim for her righteous indignation. There were people in the world who just loved pointing out other people's mistakes when the political moment took them. One day, when Africa sank into inevitable poverty with its fast-rising population, the likes of Miss Maple wouldn't brag about their part in the liberation struggle. She'd have another, comfortable life far away from the suffering people she had thought she was saving.

"Are we having the *braai* tonight?" asked Wendy as they walked through the screen door onto the veranda.

"I don't see why not. Order three packs. One will be enough for the kids."

"They're in the swimming pool with the other children."

"I heard them. If they're in the water they won't get bitten by the mosquitoes. You and Elizabeth all right? How are you, Hammond?... I'm going into the bar to join Vince and Randall."

"What were you doing out on the field?" asked Wendy.

"Having a chat with Clay. Took an evening stroll with our bottles of beer. See you in a minute. How's your son, Hammond?"

"He's just great. Two and a half years old and swims like a fish."

"I don't believe it."

"You should see him."

"Good for you."

After one beer in the bar Clay Barry left to drive home to his family, Noah as usual bringing their beers from the fridge under the bar, everything normal. Randall, happily talking to Vince, was on his third beer, already talkative.

"Four beers and you're done," said Bobby, smiling at his new assistant. If you want to eat the *braai* go and tell my wife to order the fourth pack... So, Vince, what's up?"

"Linda Gaskell. Can you believe it? A letter right out of the blue. I've decided. At the end of the season I'm going back to England to see Linda. You never know, I may even stay."

"Who's going to help run World's View for Jeremy?"

"Randall, probably. He'll have had one season with you."

"It won't have been enough."

"Anyway, don't let's get too excited. She'll likely take one look at me after all these years and make a run for it."

"How old is she now?"

"I worked it out. She'll be thirty-three."

"She too will have changed, Vince. At thirty-three they don't have the same power of sexual attraction."

"Women never went for me the way men went for Linda. Maybe not being quite so sexy will work in my favour. Not so much competition."

"You'd have to find yourself a job."

"I'll cross that bridge when I get to it. First things first. And the first step is Linda. Even thinking of seeing her again makes my knees go weak."

"You joining us for a *braai*?"

"Why not?... Noah, can you tell the cook to put out a *braai* pack for me? And give us another round. I've got Linda back in my life, so let's have a party."

"It's only one letter."

"Everything starts with a letter. Didn't you propose to Katie by letter?"

"But it didn't help. Anyway, I have my lovely Wendy and two beautiful girls. You hear all that noise on the veranda? That's Deborah and Stephanie. They've been in the pool."

"What were you two doing on the cricket field in the dark?" asked Vince.

"Talking about tomorrow's cricket. Having a look at the pitch."

"Wasn't it too dark to see?"

"Not really... Well, I'll be blowed. If it isn't my old boss Jeremy

Crookshank. Do you remember Petronella Maple, Jeremy? We were just talking about her."

"Haven't heard her name for years. She was a young girl when I first met her. I was just out from England and worked for her father... Hello, son. How many beers have you had?"

"This is my third."

"Good for you. Bergit's with Craig and Myra on the veranda. Go and say hello... So, what happened to Petronella?"

"No one knows."

"She never came back to Rhodesia. Last I heard she was living with a girl."

"You mean, as in 'living with'?"

"She's now a lesbian. Takes all sorts to make the world go round. I liked her. Far more than I liked her mother. That year in Macheke the mother didn't want to pay my bonus. The old man paid me round the corner. His wife controlled the purse strings. A real bitch. Their farm was bought with her family money. Isn't he now a Rhodesian Front MP?... Thank you, Noah. My usual. And put whatever they're having on my card. So, how are you, Bobby?"

"Just fine."

"And Randall?"

"All working out just fine."

"That's good. Vince tells me he's off to England at the end of the season. About time he got married. A man can't be happy all his life... Just joking. So, Randall, you may be working for your father sooner than you thought."

"How's the crop?" asked Bobby.

"Not bad. And yours?"

"First barn in today. The bottom of the plant. If I cure it properly it should sell."

"It's pitch black outside. Haven't been out in an evening this dark for a long time."

"Clay Barry has just gone."

"Are we out on patrol this week?"

"He didn't say, Jeremy."

"The patrols are a bugger. Buggers up the next day. I'm forty-nine this year. Too old for fighting wars... Thank you, Noah. Cheers, son."

"Bobby says this fourth one is to be my last."

"Good for Bobby. He's got more to teach you than growing tobacco. Take it easy with alcohol."

For a moment at the bar, everyone in the circle went quiet, all of them involuntarily thinking of Randall's mother Carmen who had driven into the bush drunk from the same club, ran out of petrol, tried to walk for help and was eaten by lions; Randall was two years old.

"Are you staying for the *braai*, Jeremy?" asked Bobby into the awkward silence.

"Of course we are. Pity Phillip isn't here. Spends most of his time in South Africa even when Rhodes is on vac. That way he avoids doing constant stints in the army. Most of the poor sods in Salisbury do two weeks in and two weeks out. How they do their jobs, God only knows. Wars wreck everything. Anyway, here we are, no more doom and gloom. Just keep your eyes on your guns in case they decide tonight's the night to attack the club."

"Clay thinks Henry Scanlan showed them what can happen when they attack a club."

"He was lucky to come out of that one alive. The man was drunk."

"He always is at that time of night."

2

By half past eight Bobby's family had eaten, the kids were back in the car, and all of them were ready to drive back to the farm. The three layers of stars in the heavens was giving some light. With Randall's gun pointing out of the window they drove home. Randall got out and opened the security gate, Bobby handing him the keys. From the compound the drums were playing a steady beat. Further away, Bobby could hear the drums from the Chiweshe village.

"Want to come in, Randall, for a nightcap?"

"Better not. Don't want to end up an alcoholic like my mother."

"She wasn't an alcoholic."

"People say so, Mr Preston. They don't think I listen or understand. In the end, I asked Dad. He said my mother, along with a lot of other farmers and their wives, had a drinking problem. She was from the city, my mother. Not used to the isolation of living on a farm in the middle of the bush. There wasn't much else to do but drink. Dad says everyone in the Centenary drinks too much. Especially now with the war. No, four beers is my limit. And I'm keeping to it. Thank you for taking me. I'll take the motorbike round to the cottage. Goodnight, everybody. Just look at them. The girls are both fast asleep."

Each with a child in their arms, Bobby and Wendy walked into the house. There was no sound coming from the Agric-Alert. Randall had closed the padlock after Bobby drove the car through the gate in the high security fence. They could hear the two-stroke engine of the motorbike take Randall back to his lonely cottage behind the main house with the gun hung by its strap over his back. They took the twins through to the nursery and put them to bed. The girls had barely woken up. Outside the fly-screened window the night was quiet apart from the drums, the crickets and the frogs, the sounds mingling together in harmony with the African night. Bobby and Wendy went back down the corridor between the bedrooms to the lounge, the dogs following them. There was no sign of the cats.

"You want a nightcap, Wendy? The cats must be out hunting mice."

"Poor Randall. He thinks more about his real mother than he lets on. Was she really a drunk?"

"She would have been if she'd gone on the same way."

"She must have been terrified."

"No one knows. Once a year Jeremy takes Phillip and Randall to her grave on the top of the escarpment overlooking the Zambezi Valley. Jeremy had planted a wooden cross where they buried her remains. There wasn't much left after the lions had eaten what they wanted. Are you having one?"

"You having a whisky?"

"I get so tired worrying. It's always in the back of my mind. Never goes away. A couple of whiskies helps me sleep... What are we going to do, Wendy?"

"Carry on, I suppose. What people did in England during the war. What else can we do?"

"We can run away. Clay says Smith is negotiating with the terrs by the gist of his conversation. With Clay, there's more substance between the lines."

"All wars eventually come to an end. When everyone has had enough of it life will go back to normal. If we run away to England we'll have no life at all."

Bobby poured two stiff whiskies from the decanter he had taken from the cocktail cabinet in the lounge. From the kitchen, Wendy had fetched them a tray of ice. Bobby went to the window and looked out over the lawn to the security fence and, beyond it, the bush.

"Cheers, Wendy," he said, not looking round.

"Cheers, darling. Thanks for a lovely evening. The only way to cook meat is over a fire. Come and sit next to me... You know, my only sadness was not being able to have more children. I know you would like to have had a son like Randall."

"I have two beautiful daughters. What more could a man want? I was so damn lucky to fall off that barstool."

"You were, weren't you?..." Wendy was smiling, both of them content in the moment. "Like a bad dream, the war will be over if Smith is negotiating. Who's he talking to?"

"Probably the British are mediating with Mugabe and Smith at a low level. It can't be that easy for the terrorists. They are people just like us... What I want tonight is one, long, uninterrupted sleep. When I wake in the night the worry hits me straight away and then I can't get back to sleep. In the morning, I'm often more tired than when I went to bed."

"At least the girls sleep."

"It must be wonderful to be so young and not have any worries. I've forgotten what it was like."

"You didn't check the barn temperatures when we passed the barns."

"I'll do it just before I go to bed so I only have to get up once in the night. The curing season sucks."

"Can't Randall check the temperatures?"

"Not tonight... Poor Randall. If the blacks finally take over the government, he won't have much of a future. The struggle, as they call it, was to get back their land now we've made it worth something. Before we got here it had lain fallow for all eternity."

"He'll have World's View."

"Not if they nationalise the farms."

"You think they will?"

"Why we're fighting, Wendy. Why we're fighting. Is your whisky all right? Not too much water?"

"It's perfect. Just come and sit down next to me. Relax. Stop worrying. There's nothing at the moment you can do about it."

"Except run away. The idea keeps gnawing at my brain. My mind keeps asking me if the hill is worth the climb."

"Of course it is. All hills are worth the climb when you get to the top... That's better. Now you can hold my hand."

"Randall isn't playing his gramophone. The four beers must have put him to sleep. That was so awful for him, losing his mother. You wonder if we wouldn't have all been better off staying in England. All that excitement of building an empire. And now look at it. Was it all worth it?"

"They say life is a journey, Bobby. We're all on a journey, some more interesting than others. We live in interesting times. Someone said that, not meaning it nicely. Maybe it was the Chinese. You have all these sayings in your mind and have no idea where most of them came from. I think the worst life to live would be a boring life. The same old routine day after day, year after year."

"You're right. Dad said he was never bored in the army."

"He must be very lonely living all on his own without your mother."

"Yes, I suppose he is. How selfish we are, always worrying about our own problems."

When Bobby checked the barn temperature before trying to get some sleep, the drums were still playing. At the barns, the barn boy was fast asleep next to the fire. The fire was going out, the temperature inside the barn dropping. Bobby woke the man and told him to stoke the fire. Curing the tobacco was not the man's problem. The problem was Bobby's. Why, without regularly checking the barn temperature for himself, the tobacco would lose half of its value. Sighing at life's reality, Bobby walked back to the house, the FN rifle over his shoulder. He had locked the gate and now unlocked the padlock and the chain that circled the gate, letting himself into the family compound. Everything up at the house was silent. When Bobby got into bed, Wendy was fast asleep lying next to him. The girls, by the light of his torch, had also been asleep when he checked them. His family was safe, tucked up in bed. Miraculously, Bobby himself dropped off to sleep.

When Bobby woke it was daylight and the birds were singing.

"Shit. I didn't check the bloody barn."

Wendy was still asleep next to him. Bobby pulled on his shorts and shoes and went outside. The drums had stopped playing, the compound and the Chiweshe village quiet in the first light of Sunday morning. At the barns, the barn boy was wide awake, the temperature in the barn exactly what Bobby had ordered. They smiled at each other.

"It's not all bad," Bobby said out loud as he walked back to the house.

Inside, Wendy and the children were still asleep. Bobby climbed back into bed. For a moment he lay awake thinking until he slept. The next thing he knew was Wendy standing close to him with the morning tray of tea. Outside, the pigeons and doves were calling. From the pool he could hear his children, something that once, before the girls could swim, would have sent him into panic. Whiskey dog was barking, answered by Susy dog.

"Good morning, lover," said Wendy.

"Wasn't much of a lover last night. That's the first time I slept through the night since the war started."

"Tea is served, master."

"Maybe, after tea, you would like to get back into bed."

"What's wrong with now? You always were sharp in the morning. When we first married we made love last thing at night and first thing in the morning. Then the twins were born."

"I told both Betty and Godfrey not to come in today. Let's make love and then I'll make all of us breakfast. Bacon and eggs. Sausages. Tomatoes. How does that sound?"

"I love you, my Bobby."

"And I love you, Wendy. Come on. Back into bed."

For the next half hour Bobby drew on his years of intimate experience with his wife's body to bring her to a screaming climax, then both of them fell back from each other, exhausted. Their cups of tea had gone cold when they drank them. Neither of them spoke to break the quiet moment of their contentment. Up on one elbow, Bobby poured from the pot kept warm by its woollen cosy. The milk went in last, neither of them taking sugar in their tea, for Bobby a legacy from growing up in post-war England when sugar was rationed.

"They sound so happy," said Wendy as she got out of bed.

"Where are you going?"

"To the lounge. Just to look at them."

Bobby waited in bed, drinking his second hot cup of morning tea. He was happy, despite all the problems. From the cottage behind the house

Bobby heard Randall start up his motorcycle and ride down to the padlocked gate. The clang of metal on metal told Bobby that Randall had opened the gate with the new, second key to the compound. On Sundays, Randall went home to World's View, to his father and stepmother and their two children. It was the boy's only recreation of the week. Bobby lay thinking of his own dead mother, his two older sisters, and his old father alone in the house in Epsom, his life spent. There had been happy moments growing up as children despite the aftermath of war and rationing. Reluctantly, he thought of Morris College and his five years in boarding school, the bullying, the beatings, and all the strict discipline that was meant to produce a man capable of playing his part in running an empire, a discipline that by 1960 was mostly irrelevant. All those cold showers in winter. All the team sports. All the rigid ranking of people. Bobby, wilful at eighteen, had not gone to the Royal Military Academy at Sandhurst like so many of his schoolfriends, breaking the Preston tradition and, thought Bobby, lying with his hands behind his head, his father's heart. All those generations of military Prestons broken by Bobby for a dream of owning a farm in the wilds of Rhodesia. Would he have been happier as a soldier? He doubted it. Anyway, the British Army was now largely irrelevant, much like the British Empire, overshadowed by the Russians and Americans. Maybe England was irrelevant, thought Bobby. Without the empire England was just another minor country in Europe, even its once proud industries falling into ruin, all its history and tradition unimportant to a growing number of immigrants. And here he was, drinking tea on his African farm, listening to the lovely sounds of his children, who knew nothing about England and all those military Prestons back in their ancestry, without any one of whom they could not have had an existence.

"What's all that faraway look?"

"You want some more tea?... They sound so happy."

"Both cats are down by the pool. Bruce has caught a field mouse with a long snout. The poor bloody thing is still alive. Bruce lets him go and when the poor mouse thinks it's got away, Bruce pounces on him. Why do cats like to torment their prey?... Yes, I'd love another cup of tea. Move over. You're hogging the centre of the bed."

"I was thinking of Dad. Maybe I should phone him."

"Make it worse for him, if you ask me. You came to Africa. He lives in England. That's how it is... Don't your sisters visit him?"

"Sometimes. They have their own lives to live. Their own families to look after. Once a girl marries, she belongs to another man."

"I don't belong to you, Bobby. I'm your wife."

"When did you last phone your father?"

"He's always out in the lands. On his birthday I suppose. I always phone him on his birthday. I didn't phone my mother this week. I forgot."

"So you see what I mean. Growing up we need our parents. Like the kids need us now."

"That's how life is. Nothing wrong with it."

"I suppose not..."

"Randall just left with the gun strapped to his back."

"I heard him. He hasn't quite flown the coop. We should try and find him a girlfriend."

"They find each other, Bobby. Nothing we can do about it... I'm so glad you fell off that barstool."

"So am I... What do you think will happen to us?"

"We'll get old and grey and I'll start nagging you."

"What are you going to nag me about?"

"I have absolutely no idea... You want to come for a morning swim?"

"When I've finished my tea. Of all the things I couldn't do without in life, tea in the morning would be top of my list. I can't imagine what my ancestors did before the Chinese brought us tea. It clears the brain. Relaxes me. Makes me think clearly. So, what's on the menu for later today?"

"A *braai* round the pool. Like we have every Sunday when it doesn't rain."

"We need some rain."

"We always need rain."

"If we don't get rain by the end of this week, I'll give the tobacco a cycle. Thank God for that dam. Takes all the worry out of growing tobacco. The irrigation system is real progress. I'm going to grow winter wheat this season. Totally irrigated. Give the farm an extra income. By the time I'm finished, I want every inch of Hopewell Estate to be productive. Intensive farming. That's the way to go. Maximise the use of the tractors and all the rest of the equipment. One big flourishing farm. What do you think of that?"

"I'll think more of it after my swim. It's going to be stinking hot again today."

The morning dip was followed by breakfast. They both did the cooking, the girls running round and round the kitchen, dogs barking, the cats down by the pool. Only when the food was put in front of the girls did they stop talking. Bobby served coffee on the veranda after their breakfast seated at the veranda table. The girls ran off back to the pool. The four dogs, fed in the kitchen, had flopped out on their sides, their tongues hanging out in the building heat.

"Dogs perspire through their tongues," said Bobby. "Where do the girls get all their energy? I'm going to take my book down to the chaise longue and read in the shade by the pool. There's something decadent about eating breakfast in a bathing costume, don't you think?"

"What are you reading?"

"Wilbur Smith's *When the Lion Feeds*. For the third time."

"I'd like to have been a writer."

"We all say that. Everyone thinks their own lives are so important they want to write about them. It's a way of boring a piece of paper instead of boring other people. I've met dozens of people who say they're writing a book. A couple of chapters and that's it. No, you need talent. Most of us don't have a creative talent."

"You never know until you try. I've got the title."

"And what would that be, Wendy?"

"*How Lover Fell Off the Barstool.*"

"You can't write about me."

"Can't think of anything else I know to write about. Finish your coffee. I'll get my book from the bedroom. What time are you going to light the fire for the *braai*?"

"Let's see how it goes. What have we got?"

"Lamb chops. Lots and lots of our own lamb chops. Why I never go down and look at the sheep. I prefer to buy my meat from the supermarket in cellophane packages. Not so personal."

By the time Wendy came out with her book, Bobby was stretched out in the shade of a msasa tree, deep in his book, the master storyteller taking Bobby straight into another world. Only when Bobby remembered to check the barn temperatures did he surface from the people in the book. For two hours the real world around him had not existed.

"It's one o'clock!"

"All you did was turn pages."

"How it should be with a good book. How's yours?"

"Not so good. Some detective story. I kept nodding off. You going down to the barns?"

"Running a farm never stops."

With all four dogs at his heels, Bobby walked down to the barns. The man tending the fire in the barn had changed, the night shift going off at ten o'clock. Bobby opened the door to the barn to check the thermometer that hung from the first line in front of him. The hot air thrust at him, pushing into his face. The leaves of tobacco were beginning to dry out, a process that would take days to complete. Everything was as it should be on the second day of curing. The man had waited behind the barn for Bobby's instructions, next to the cords of cut wood, the proceeds of last year's stumping of the new lands. The man had found a place in the shade of the barn with his back to the stack of wood. Bobby left him alone. There was nothing to say. With his wide-brimmed bush hat protecting him from the midday sun, Bobby went back to the house with the dogs following, their tongues hanging out as they panted, walking slowly like Bobby in the heat of the day.

At the pool, Bobby lit the fire. Godfrey had piled wood next to the *braai* Bobby had built in front of the pump that served the pool, circulating the water. He then jumped into the water next to his children. When the coals were ready, Bobby put the chops on the grill over the fire, letting the meat cook. Wendy had brought out bowls of salad which she placed on a table between their chaise longues in the shade of the tree. Neither of them wanted a beer after their previous evening in the club. It was a Sunday like so many Sundays. A family day. No pressure. No hurry. A day to enjoy each other's company.

"I want mine well done, Daddy."

"You shall have it, Deborah."

"And mine."

"Yours, Stephanie, will be exactly the same as your sister's."

The dogs had found the shade of a tree and were spread on the grass on their sides, panting in the heat, their pink tongues moving to the rhythm of their breathing. The head of the now dead mouse was under a nearby tree, next to Bruce who was asleep. When the chops were cooked, Bobby used the long fork to put them on a serving plate which he placed on the table.

"Lunch is ready, girls. Come and get it."

With his family seated up at the table in the shade, Bobby ate his lunch, happy and content, a life he wouldn't have changed for anything.

After their lunch they all went up to the house for their Sunday afternoon nap, the dogs following, leaving Bruce still asleep under the tree next to the head of the dead mouse. Within minutes of lying down on their beds, all four of them were fast asleep.

Bobby woke in the twilight from his dreams to the putt-putt sound of Randall Crookshank's motorcycle. He had not heard Randall close the gate.

"You want any supper, lover?"

"Maybe a sandwich later. I stuffed myself at lunchtime... You going to wake the girls?"

"Let them sleep. With luck they'll sleep on through the night."

"Mind if I go back to my book? Once you get started with a good book you want to finish it."

"You want to hear the six o'clock news?"

"Not really. Most of it's propaganda to make us feel better."

"The Agric-Alert has been so quiet these last few weeks."

"Long may it last. The last thing I want to do today is get into uniform and go out on patrol. I hate that damn gun."

"Can I bring you some tea?"

"That would be lovely. Oh, and do me a favour. Make sure Randall locked the gate. I'll only go down to the barns before we go to bed."

"You're in bed, Bobby."

"You know what I mean."

Outside, the garden was quiet, the frogs and crickets not having started yet. With the dusk, the birds had gone silent. From the workers' compound there was not a sound. After a night of beer drinking and dancing they were most likely exhausted, getting into their huts to sleep to rise for work with the first blush of dawn. Relaxed, Bobby fell back into the story he was reading in the book, the real world gone. Much later, he looked up from the page to find a tray of tea on the small table next to him, making him smile. He had not even heard Wendy bring in the tea. The book was finished, the story over. Pulling on his shorts and shirt, his keys in his pocket, Bobby went out to check the temperature of his barn.

3

While Bobby Preston was checking the barn, across at Chiweshe, Canaan Mayo and his men were checking their equipment, Canaan again taking them through their plan of action to dig under the tarred road between Mount Darwin and Bindura to lay the land mines in the path of the traffic, in tunnels just under the surface of the tar. Along with the Russian landmines he checked each man carried a trowel, a short-handled pointed pick and a canvas sack for carrying away the rubble. When the tunnels were complete there would be no sign of a disturbance for the farmers to see. As Canaan put it to Jacob, 'They won't know what hit them. One minute driving down the new road on their way into Salisbury, the next moment high in the sky and blown to pieces.'

Canaan had been in Rhodesia three months, letting the calm in the Centenary settle. The party the night before had been for them a send-off celebration, though only the cadre members knew what was going to happen. Canaan had danced to the drums all night, sleeping all day through the heat. When the light had gone completely, no moon, the stars still not giving their trace of light, Canaan led out his patrol. By sunup they would be back and integrated in the village, workers on the land, peasants like the rest of them. Only his cadre knew that tonight was the night. Canaan trusted no one, not even Comrade Tangwena. So far as

Tangwena's intelligence told them there hadn't been a police patrol at night in the Centenary for weeks, the whites imagining their army's incursions into Mozambique and the slaughter caused by them, had stopped the cadres crossing the Mozambique border into Rhodesia.

"Let's do it," he said in Shona when they were away from the village. "Good luck to all of you. Tonight will be the start of our victory, every one of you heroes of the revolution."

All together they raised their fists, softly calling the names of Comrade Mugabe and Comrade Makoni. In single file, ten yards from each other, they moved out, blending with the night, not a sound of footsteps, not a clink of metal against metal. They were trained soldiers. Veterans of the struggle. The night was theirs. The long walk had begun.

A mile from the Chiweshe village they regrouped, going forward as a military formation, pale shadows in the light of the stars. They trudged on, silent, everyone forbidden to talk, the heavy mines in the packs of their backs weighing them down with their AK-47 rifles. Far away, from behind the mountains, a black smudge on the distant horizon, Canaan heard the roar of a lion. The sound made him smile. It was fitting. The lions of Africa were about to roar so the whole world would hear them. 'Not long now, Grace,' he spoke in his mind. 'Just a little longer and you and the children will be coming home. To our grand job with the party. To prosperity. To the restoration of our dignity.' Canaan was happy, he had never been more happy. The future, with all its sunshine, was about to be his.

Taking his position again by the south-north pointer of the Southern Cross, Canaan knew exactly the direction he was going. He was cutting across country towards the new road, past grazing cattle, the property of the village, goats standing silently in the dark of the night. Far away he could see the lights of a farmhouse, hear music playing, the notes of the music floating in and out on the night, blown by the wind. A hyena called, the sound similar to a maniac laughing, the cruel sound fluttering Canaan's stomach with bad premonition. Praying to the ancestors for protection from evil spirits, Canaan walked on further into the night. When the hyena called again it wasn't so bad, the lack of surprise making the howl less frightening for his tensed-up nerves. Canaan changed the weight of his rifle from his left shoulder to his right, holding the gun by the end of the barrel. There was not a sound of man, other than the music, the song too far away for Canaan to recognise. It was Sunday night. Everyone but them was sleeping.

Half an hour on they came to a river, Canaan going in first to test the depth of the water. In the middle, up to his waist, he called them on, a soft imitation hoot of an eagle owl that was their signal. He could see his men on the bank of the river, shapes in the pale colourless light of the stars. Again, looking up at the pointer star, Canaan took his direction.

On the far bank they regrouped, taking off their military boots and emptying out the river water. The heat, hot and humid, would quickly dry their clothing. Not far away in a tree by the river an eagle owl had answered Canaan's call, the bird answered by its mate from a tree downriver. Canaan smiled. Wet socks chafing their feet, the cadre walked on. By the time the sickle moon rose in the sky they had found the road. Canaan looked along both sides of the road for the easiest place to tunnel. To build the road and stop it being washed away in the rains, embankments ran down on either side, the tarred surface six feet higher than the ditches. Canaan tested the soil, a compound of small rocks that had built the foundation of the road. The five men under his command had placed their equipment in the long grass away from the road. Nearer the road, down the embankments, the grass had been recently cut. They were to dig two tunnels from either side of the road, spacing the six land mines so wherever the farmers drove on the surface the pressure would trigger the mines. Taking it in turns, hot, sweaty, with dust in their mouths, they burrowed in under the road, filling the small sacks with rubble and passing them back to be dumped in the bush away from the road. When the tunnels were finished, Canaan, lying flat on his stomach, carefully laid the mines one by one, his small torch showing him the way. With the last bags, Canaan filled up the entrance to the holes, placing tufts of grass back into place. To anyone driving along the road there would be no sign of a disturbance. Happy with their work, they left the road, Canaan leading the way, the stars in the heavens showing him where to go.

By the first blush of dawn they were back in their huts, no one in the village knowing they had gone. Quickly, Canaan fell into an exhausted sleep, every muscle in his body aching.

. . .

By the time Wendy got up to drive the kids into Salisbury and the farm of her parents, an arrangement made when she had phoned them at Christmas, Canaan was dreaming of Grace and his children, Joshua and Rose, swimming in the Indian Ocean, all of them laughing, all of them happy. Outside Wendy's window the birds were calling, the *simby* clanging in the compound calling the gang to work. Godfrey brought in a tray of tea and put it on the bedside table. She could hear her children running round the house calling to each other with the renewed energy of a good night's sleep.

"Thank you, Godfrey." Smiling happily, Wendy watched the servant leave, closing the door behind him.

"You want some tea, lover?" she asked, prodding Bobby to wake him up.

"I was having such a lovely dream."

"You remember I'm taking the girls to my parents?"

"I had tried to forget. But no, I hadn't forgotten. Which way are you going? Through Centenary village or Mount Darwin?"

"It's quicker through Mount Darwin and Bindura. I'd better get going. I'm taking the Peugeot. We'll be back by the weekend."

"Do you really have to go?"

"My parents want to see their grandchildren. I'll give you a ring when I get to the farm. It won't be so bad. At least you'll have Randall. You can keep each other company."

"Take a gun, Wendy."

"Of course I will. The mornings aren't a problem. It's at dusk I don't like being on the road."

"You going to have breakfast?"

"I want to get going as soon as possible. I'll eat at Mum's. With the new road, I'll be home in a couple of hours."

"Isn't this your home?"

"You know what I mean. Enjoy your tea. Was the barn all right last night?"

"Fell asleep again. Next time he does it I've told him he can find another job. That'll keep him awake. It's a damn shame but sometimes you have to threaten people if you want the job done properly... I'll miss you."

"Miss you too. Just don't sit up all night drinking with Randall."

"Hadn't even thought of it."

"I'll bet you hadn't."

When the children stormed into the room they jumped on the bed, bouncing the springs and spilling Bobby's tea. Both girls were more excited than usual. Susy dog had followed them into the bedroom.

"We're going to see Granny and Grandpa. Can we take Bruce, Daddy? He can sleep in the back of the car."

"Bruce would much prefer to sleep on the windowsill."

"But he falls off."

"Come on, girls. We're going to go."

"Oh, goody."

"Did you pack your little bags?"

"Yes, Mummy. Let's go. Go, go, go. We're going to see Granny and Grandpa."

"Don't you want breakfast?" asked Bobby, grinning.

"Let's go, Mummy. We want to go."

"Get your bags. I'll meet you at the car."

"Oh, goody. Is Betty coming?"

"No, girls. She has her own family to look after. Granny will look after you."

Bobby, getting up, stretched his arms and let out a yawn.

"I'll see you to the car. Then I must go down to the sheds."

"I heard Randall go to the lands on the motorbike."

"He's organising the reaping gang. There's so much to do at this time of the year."

"Stephanie. Deborah. Give your Dad a hug goodbye."

One by one, Bobby pulled his girls up into his arms and hugged them, their bodies soft and warm.

"You two look after your mother, you hear? Now off you go. Say hello for me to Granny and Grandpa... I'll be back in the house at one o'clock for some lunch. You can phone me then. Just drive carefully. Some of our fellow farmers are maniacs on the road."

"There won't be much traffic during the height of the reaping season."

"You're right. You'll probably have the road to yourself. You got some money? Fill up the car at the barns. The tanker was here last week so there's plenty of fuel in the petrol drum."

The security gate was open, the padlock hanging on the end of the chain, the entrance having been opened by Randall. The Peugeot drove out, the children waving to him from the windows. Feeling flat, Bobby walked back into the house and their bedroom, poured himself another cup of tea and got back into bed. Suddenly, as if all the doors had shut, the house was silent and empty. He could hear the car, far away, stop at the tarred road and drive away with his family. Bobby finished his tea, threw back the sheet and dressed.

Closing the gate but not locking it, to stop the dogs following, Bobby got back into the truck and drove it down to the sheds. Most of the gang were out reaping. A tractor driver was changing the oil in one of the tractors, the tasks listed with their dates on a board at the back of the tractor shed. Every tractor on the farm had its own schedule. Maintenance kept Bobby's repair bill to a minimum. The barn temperatures came next. Bobby got back into the truck and drove to the lands where Randall was supervising the reaping. The workers were deep in the head-high lines of tobacco, the big leaves at the middle of the tall plants almost touching each other. The man in front passed the ripe leaves to a man behind him who twisted them together and tied them six leaves at a time to the top of a stick. As the sticks filled up a third man collected the hanging leaves of tobacco in exchange for an empty stick and brought them out of the line to be stacked on the waiting trailer. When the trailer was full, the tractor driver drove back to the barns where four men loaded the sticks of hanging tobacco high up into the tiers that rose at intervals inside the barn.

"How's it going, Randall? How was yesterday with your family?"

"Who drove out of the farm this morning?"

"Wendy and the kids. They're going to her parents' farm in Salisbury South. The girls were so excited. We've got the place to ourselves till the end of the week. Be careful with some of those leaves. They're too green. They won't cure properly."

"It's so difficult to tell when they're ripe."

"Practice, Randall. Practice. You'll get the hang of it."

"There's so much to learn. You'd think farming was simple but it isn't."

"Tobacco is weed but the most difficult weed to grow properly. I want you to start checking the barn temperatures tonight. Now, where did that stick of tobacco come from?"

Randall pointed to a line and Bobby walked in and up to his workers, passing the man loading the stick.

"You're reaping them green," he said in Fanagalo, walking along with the man and showing him which leaves to pick. "The ripe leaves have a faint tinge of yellow... You got it now?"

"Yes, boss."

"Good, or I'll have to take you out of the line."

Back with Randall, Bobby inspected each of the sticks as they were brought out of the lands, before they were stacked up on the trailer.

"Watch that chap, Randall. I think he's now got the hang of it. But watch him. The earlier stuff he sent out will fetch bugger-all on the auction floor. You bring a flask of tea?"

"I forgot."

"Go to the truck. Godfrey put some tea and some breakfast in a basket. Have the gang got clean drinking water?"

"I checked it before we left the sheds."

"Good. They get hot and thirsty... When the hell is it going to rain?... You got to check everything, Randall. Remember that. Getting it all right is our responsibility. And when you've checked what they're reaping you check it again half an hour later. It never stops. Your father says the reason why World's View gets the best price on the auction floor year after year is he tries to do every small job on the farm better than the rest of us. Drummed it into me when I was his assistant. Your father said it's all in the detail, being a successful farmer. And he's right. Probably applies to most other businesses. You can't afford to take your eye off the ball. Now go get some tea in you while I watch the gang."

"The crop looks good."

"Doesn't it? We're going to have to irrigate again. We won't be reaping tomorrow. Not enough ripe tobacco. Tomorrow we'll set up the irrigation pipes and give the tobacco a good sprinkle."

"How long's the cycle?"

"They'll need three hours by the look of it, especially the late plantings."

"It looks so good when it's all up high and even."

"That's the idea of it. This land will go two thousand pounds of dried leaf to the acre."

The day grew hotter as the trailer, loaded with tobacco, was taken back and forth by the tractor. With the crushing heat, the birds had gone silent. It was cooler in the lands shaded by the green leaves of tobacco. Standing in the farm road with the tractor and trailer, the heat was overpowering. Bobby and Randall's wide-brimmed bush hats kept the direct rays of the sun from their heads and necks but not the heat. By twelve o'clock, Bobby sent the gang back to the compound for a two-hour lunch, the gang sitting on the empty trailer smiling as they went, talking happily to each other. At the sheds, Bobby again checked all the jobs in the workshop and the temperature of the barn that was curing.

They drove up to the house, Bobby in the truck, Randall on the motorcycle, the dogs going berserk with excitement when Bobby pulled open the gate.

"My dogs are quite mad," said Bobby, smiling as he walked back to the open door of his truck.

"You know the old song," said Randall.

"'Mad dogs and Englishmen go out in the midday sun.' Noël Coward. He was probably right. You going to join me for some lunch? Without the kids the house is so empty. Wendy's going to phone me from her father's place at one o'clock... Another couple of hours of reaping and that barn will be full... Who's got the better crop, me or your dad?"

"You have, Mr Preston. Or should I say we have."

"That's the spirit. Everything is teamwork... Cold meat and salad. Sound all right?"

"Sounds good to me. I'm not much good at cooking on my own."

"Neither was I at your age when I first worked for your father. Were you playing music last night? I went to sleep early and slept through the night."

"One of Dad's old records. A London musical. *Half a Sixpence*. Played it to myself half the night."

"Wendy thinks you need a girlfriend."

"That would be nice. Trouble is, the girls don't look at nineteen-year-olds. The sixteen–year-old girls like twenty-year-olds like my brother. Now Phillip's going on twenty-one he's getting the girls. There are plenty of young girls at varsity."

"You'll find one."

"I hope so..."

"I drink a cold beer at lunchtime when it's hot like this. You want one, Randall?"

"What a pleasure."

With a beer in his hand and sitting on the veranda, Bobby looked at his watch, expecting a call from Wendy. By quarter-past one there wasn't a call and Bobby shouted into the house for Godfrey to bring them another beer. By half past one and still no call, Bobby became agitated and went to the phone, putting a call through the Salisbury exchange to his mother-in-law. The Agric-Alert on the floor under the phone was quiet, no crackling, nobody in the block having turned theirs on. Ten minutes later the phone rang with his sequence of long and short rings. Smiling, Bobby picked up the phone.

"How are you, Wendy?"

"She hasn't arrived, Bobby."

"She must have arrived. She left just after sunrise with the kids."

"Well, she isn't here. She's probably shopping in Salisbury. I'll get her to ring you when she gets here. How are you, Bobby?"

"I'm fine... Yes, she must have gone shopping."

"You know women. They love shopping."

At three o'clock, when Bobby heard the tractor take the gang back to the lands to continue the reaping, there was still no call from Wendy, making Bobby begin to wonder what the hell was going on. Randall had gone back to his cottage for a nap, Bobby hooting the horn of his truck to wake him. Randall came running out to open and shut the gate and get in the truck, the four dogs barking behind the shut gate. Passing through the barns, Bobby saw a police Land Rover coming towards them through his avenue of jacaranda trees. Clay Barry was at the wheel, Vince Ranger sitting next to him. The vehicles both stopped facing each other at the entrance to the sheds, the car doors opening, all of them stepping out onto the gravel road.

"Afternoon, Clay. This is a surprise."

"Not a good one I'm afraid."

"What's the matter? You both look terrible."

"Wendy took the full blast of a landmine halfway between Mount

Darwin and Bindura. I'm sorry, Bobby. Picked up Vince on the way here from the police station."

Bobby, white, cold, unable to speak just stood.

"They couldn't have known what happened. We think there was more than one mine under the road, it was a massive explosion. We only found the vehicle a few hours ago. I'm so sorry, Bobby."

"My family are dead," whispered Bobby.

"All of them. The blast was so bad it took us time to work out who was in the vehicle."

"Take me to it, Clay."

"You want to go?"

"Of course I do. They're my bloody family... Randall, take the truck back to the house and use your motorcycle... Why the hell wasn't I with them?"

"What do you want me to... I mean, what's the temperature meant to be in the barn?" asked Randall.

"It doesn't matter about the bloody temperature. Nothing bloody matters now. Vince, move over. I'm shaking so much I can't drive my own truck. I want to see my wife and children."

"You won't recognise them," said Clay.

"I'll recognise them... Randall! Bugger off and get your motorcycle... No, I'm sorry I didn't mean that."

"It doesn't matter, Mr Preston."

"How the heck did they put a landmine on a tarred road? She would have seen it."

"We think they created a tunnel in from both sides of the road. The army are going through the crater. What were they doing on the road?"

"Going to see her mother and father in Salisbury South. Her father has a farm."

Vince, next to Bobby, put his arm round Bobby's shoulder. In silence, Clay reversed, turned the Land Rover round and drove through the jacaranda trees and turned left at the tarred road, Hopewell Estate left behind them.

Seventeen miles from the farm Clay stopped at the Mount Darwin police station and picked up the member-in-charge. The man looked at Bobby but didn't say anything. Ten miles further down the road Bobby saw the vultures circling, the birds high up in the sky, slowly going round and round. Bobby knew their prey was his wife and children. Gripping his knees, his knuckles white, Bobby stared at the distant circling birds.

"We heard an explosion early this morning," said the man behind Bobby. "We thought it was the nickel mine blasting and took no notice. One of our chaps on patrol reported those birds circling and raised the alarm. By the time I got there the birds had landed I'm afraid. I'm so sorry, old chap. We took what we could find through to the church in Bindura."

"So my family are in Bindura?"

"We did our best."

When they reached the crater in the road the vultures were still circling overhead. Two black constables were guarding the site of the explosion. Fifty yards from the road, up against a tree, Bobby saw what was left of his Peugeot, the vehicle ripped open into mangled pieces. Clay Barry drove round through the bush to avoid the hole in the road and back up the embankment onto the tar and stopped the vehicle. Bobby got out, followed by Vince Ranger, Vince still with his hand on Bobby's shoulder. Bobby walked down the embankment to the wreck of his car where he stood, no tears, no feeling, totally numb. On a piece of tangled metal that looked like a piece of a door, Bobby saw Stephanie's tattered yellow sweater, Donald Duck still recognisable. There was blood and gore all over the tangled metal, the roof of the car unrecognisable.

"We collected what we could find. The vultures, you understand. The hyenas had found them, I'm afraid."

When Bobby turned round the man from Mount Darwin had come up and was standing behind him.

"We did our best."

"I'm sure you did... Oh God, they must really hate us."

"You never can be sure of a man's motive for killing. It's usually they want something."

"They want the country. Everything."

Bobby looked up at the vultures still circling on the thermals, biding their time. No longer shaking, Bobby walked back to the Land Rover, looking first in the hole. The crater was no longer than it was wide.

"We think there was more than one mine under the road. The car wheels set off one explosion which set off the rest. Never seen a landmine blast so devastating. They couldn't have known what happened. Quick. Very quick."

"My girls were seven years old."

"I'm so sorry."

"Did you know there were three of them in the car?"

"No, we didn't. We only traced you as the owner of the car when we found one of the number plates in the bush. Salisbury told us who the car was registered to so we contacted Inspector Barry. When he drove down and saw what happened he drove back to find you. The priest in Bindura is a Roman Catholic. I hope you don't mind."

They all got back in the Land Rover and drove onto Bindura. In the small Catholic chapel Bobby was shown the remains of his family. The police had collected, in sacks, small pieces of bone, pieces of flesh embedded with clothing, a small skull without any skin or eyes in the sockets.

"The vultures and hyenas, old chap," said the man from Mount Darwin.

"When do you want the funeral?" asked the priest.

"When I've told her mother and father."

"Do you recognise your family?" asked the man.

"No. But it's them. In these sacks is my family."

"We can take them out of the sacks."

"For Christ's sake don't be so fucking ridiculous... I'm sorry. I'm in a church."

The priest crossed himself. Bobby looked around the small chapel and up at the roof. Then he howled, his body rigid, his anger exploding. Bobby felt Vince's hand back on his shoulder, gripping him hard. Vince led him out of the chapel and back into the sun. Neither of the two policemen or the priest spoke.

"Are you a Roman Catholic?" asked the priest when Bobby had calmed down.

"Right now I'm an atheist. Tomorrow, next week, with luck, I'll be a Christian of the Church of England if that has any damn significance."

"I'll pray for you," said the priest.

"Thank you. All of you. Thank you. It's not your fault."

Only when Bobby got back to the farm, alone in the house, did he cry. Rudely, he had told Vince to leave him alone, not wanting anyone's sympathy. Randall came up to the house and was told to go to hell. For an hour, Bobby held the loaded FN rifle he had unlocked from the rack next to the Agric-Alert, the gun pointed up at him where he sat, the butt on the floor. Instead of shooting himself he put down the gun and went to the cocktail cabinet. The staff, Betty and Godfrey, were nowhere to be seen. The dogs, all four of them, had stayed away in the garden after Bobby had kicked out at Susy. He took the cap off a bottle of brandy and poured out a glass, his mind still raging, not yet feeling sorry for himself. He drank, trying to saturate himself in alcohol. When drunk, sitting in the dark, he lay back on the couch and passed into oblivion, all four dogs having crept back into the house and sitting in front of him, their eyes open and watching.

Bobby stayed drunk for three days, nobody daring to come near him, the phone ripped from its socket. On the fourth day, he repaired the telephone connection and phoned Wendy's parents. Clay Barry had already informed them what happened to their daughter and grandchildren. The next day Bobby drove his truck to Bindura for the funeral of his family. There was one large coffin and two small ones. All the faces of their friends from the block swam in front of him. There was no point in his life anymore. Instead of driving back to his farm, he drove to Lake Kariba. At the lake he hired a houseboat and went out alone on the water. After two days on the water, Bobby faced reality and drove back to the farm. With the help of Vince Ranger and Hammond Taylor, the farm had kept going, seven of the barns now full of curing tobacco. All through the reaping and grading season that ended in the first week of May, every night, Bobby drank himself into oblivion, the only way he could get some sleep. By the end of June, Bobby had sold the crop and was on his way to England to see his father, a bitter man full of hate.

PART VIII

JUNE TO DECEMBER 1977 – "IT'S ALL ABOUT THE MONEY"

1

On the Saturday morning Bobby Preston's plane landed at Heathrow Airport in London, Katie Frost was sitting on a wooden bench at Dorking Station waiting for the ten-twenty from Waterloo. She was five minutes early, the train not yet signalled. Katie was smiling with the happy thought of seeing Linda Gaskell. A few people were standing idly on the platform. The June day was warm, with a sweet smell of honeysuckle drifting over from the small garden behind the station; no wind, not a ruffle, a perfect English summer day. Katie, far away in her thoughts, was brought back to the reality of sitting on her bench by the clang of the signal box: the train was about to pull into the station. Katie got up, full of expectation.

The train rolled into the station, stopped, doors opened and Linda, not far from where Katie was standing, stepped out onto the platform looking around. When they saw each other they waved, then Linda turned back to the open door of the train where a man wearing a bowler hat handed her a suitcase, followed by a large, closed wicker basket. The two friends embraced each other. The man in the bowler hat walked away down the platform.

"You look wonderful," gushed Katie.

"So do you, darling Katie. It's so good to see you. I really do miss you now I'm living on my own."

"What's in that wicker basket? You want me to carry the case?"

"You carry the picnic basket. I'll carry the case. Did you bring a car? Of course you did... I've something to tell you. How are you, Katie?"

"Bored. That about sums it up. So? Tell me."

"In that basket is our picnic lunch. I made it all myself. Well, I made the tea and filled the flask. Bought the sandwiches on Waterloo Station. Anyway, we're going to take a little drive into the country to our favourite field, find our favourite oak tree where I'll lay out the rug and show you our sumptuous lunch. Oh, and there's a bottle of nice wine and two nice wine glasses wrapped in serviettes so they wouldn't break... This station never changes. It's been here forever. What a nice man to help me down with my luggage."

"Certainly since the middle of the nineteenth century... Why can't you tell me now?"

"IBM want to know when you're coming back to work."

"I'm still thinking about it... Is that it?"

"No, it isn't... You can't do nothing for the rest of your life."

"So, if you're not going to tell me, who's the latest boyfriend?"

"He's a bit younger than me and gorgeous."

"How old is he, Linda?"

"Twenty-three. Cute as a button."

"That's cradle-snatching."

"You only have one life. Make the best of it while you can, I say. Have you found a boyfriend?"

"In Dorking? You've got to be kidding. Anyway, I'm a bit out of it. The pubs are full of your twenty-three-year-olds."

"How was the Mediterranean cruise?"

"Terrible. The average age of the passengers was ninety. They sat in deck chairs during the day and played bridge at night. Half of them didn't even drink... This basket is quite heavy. What else is in it?"

"Well. I did put in three bottles of wine."

"There are drink and driving laws in England."

"Not in the country. Where are you going to find a policeman?"

"Don't you want to go home to your parents before we go picnicking?"

"Mother will only ask me when I'm getting married and having children... How are your parents?"

"Much the same."

"Have you told them about your money?"

"Not yet. Certainly not the full extent of it... Come on. I want to know what you've got to tell me. You're full of it. About to burst. I can tell just looking at you, Linda. Is it about Angela?"

"No. She's left London for Cornwall. Her book's coming out in the autumn, in time for her publisher to get it into the shops for Christmas. She got ten thousand pounds as an advance on royalty. She's going to be famous."

With Linda carrying her small suitcase, and Katie carrying the picnic basket with a rolled blue rug tied to its side, they walked out of the station. Katie had bought herself a Volkswagen Beetle, not wishing to flash her wealth. For English roads, the small car was perfect. With the case and picnic basket on the back seat, Katie drove out of Dorking Station.

"You remember how the three of us played under the tree as girls. Must have been nine years old when Dad first took us to a picnic under that oak tree. Those were happy, giggly times. Angela loved to braid my mother's hair while Mum was telling us stories. My memory tells me those days were always perfect, the blackbirds singing, cows in the field. Growing up in the country. What more could a child ever want? Can you remember where to find our oak tree?"

"Of course I can," said Linda. "In those days our parents were all on bicycles, us girls on tricycles with reins attached to our little bodies so our dads could pull us along the country lanes. There wasn't any traffic on the roads in the fifties and sixties. Now you can smell diesel fumes when the wind blows at you from the motorways. England's changed and it's going to change more. Dorking is now a dormitory town for London. England's getting so overcrowded. If it weren't for my job and friends in London I'd envy Angela writing away in Cornwall. Have you ever been to St Ives?"

"How's everyone at IBM?"

"The same as usual... When are you coming back?"

"When your private income in a month is more than your annual salary, what is the point of working? All my salary would be taxed at seventy per cent, or whatever the bloody top tax is these days."

"You should start enjoying your money. Why didn't you buy yourself a flashy car?"

"What's the point? The flashiest car won't get us to the oak tree any quicker or in any more comfort. It would just be showing off. Only the wrong type of people would be impressed. I don't see the point in having too much money. You can only eat one meal at a time whether you sit in the kitchen at home or eat in the Savoy. Chances are, the meal at home will be better than the restaurant. Nothing since has ever beaten my mother's cooking. Only people with inferiority complexes flash their money around."

"There were quite a few of those in Manhattan."

"Big cities attract that kind of person. London and New York are much the same, people trying to impress each other with their money. If you haven't got money, the rich look down their noses at you. You remember Finn. If they'd taken away his money, no one would have looked at him. And yes, I was impressed with his wealth."

"Never look a gift horse in the mouth, Katie."

"No, I shouldn't. It's just I'm not sure if I'm better off with all his money. I don't know who I am anymore."

Two miles down the road, Katie parked the car next to a four bar gate to the farmer's field. With the picnic basket they got out of the car, the morning sun dappling the gate through the branches of an old oak tree. In the field a bull was watching them as Linda climbed over the gate, turning back to Katie for the picnic basket. On the other side of the field, away from the road, was their favourite oak tree, which some had called the biggest in Surrey. Its trunk was so broad that four men could link their arms round it.

"You think that bull likes us, Katie?"

"We're about to find out. Thank goodness neither of us are wearing red... No, there he goes, more interested in eating the grass than chasing us girls... What a lovely summer's day. No people. No noise other than nature's."

Holding hands, the friends walked out into the field, across the tufted grass, both of them wearing sensible shoes. At the tree, Linda untied the small belt she had used to tie the rug to the picnic basket, unfolded the rug and laid it on the spongy green moss that grew between the giant roots of the tree, the few acorns pushed to the side. The girls sat down, their backs to their favourite tree. Where they were in the shade, the bull took no notice of them.

"You think it's the same old farmer who owns the land?"

"Probably not. Let's hope no one is around."

"You want tea or a glass of wine, Katie?"

"Depends on what you've got to tell me."

"Bobby Preston's in England. He flew into Heathrow this morning. Vince Ranger flew in on Wednesday."

"Why didn't they travel together? When we knew them they were the closest of friends."

"Vince says Bobby has become a bad-tempered drunk since his wife and girls were killed in January. Vince wants you to go and see him. See if you can help. Bobby's been lashing out at everyone."

"Where is he?"

"By now with his father in Epsom. Just up the road."

"Isn't now too early?"

"Maybe. That's for you to decide. Vince thinks you're Bobby's only hope."

"Won't his father be able to comfort him? He's a nice old man. The last time we met was at a Brahms concert at the Albert Hall."

"He's going to try. Why he persuaded Bobby to come to England rather than him go to Rhodesia where everything reminds Bobby of Wendy and the twins. Vince thinks if something isn't done, Bobby will kill himself. They stopped taking him out on patrol. In the one ambush Bobby broke cover too soon trying to get at the terrorists and nearly got Jeremy Crookshank killed. Took a bullet in his left hand. Bobby was screaming at the terrorists as he ran out of cover... His friends in Rhodesia think he should stay in England, according to Vince."

"He won't want me telling him 'I told you so'... How was Vince?"

"Much the same old Vince."

"Not cute as a button?"

"He says he loves me."

"But you don't think you could love him?"

"I don't know. Probably not. Maybe later as I get older."

"So he looked at you the same way?"

"Those same old sheep eyes. The poor man's besotted."

"That's not all bad in a man. He'll never stray. Always look after you, Linda."

"Are you going to visit Bobby? I've got the address."

"Let me think about it. It's only five months since his family were killed. No wonder he's bitter... Better make it a glass of wine... My poor Bobby."

"One minute you're sailing along nicely and then it happens. Your life stops."

"What are they going to do? Stay in Rhodesia?"

"Vince is looking for a job in England. Won't be easy. All he knows how to do to earn a living is grow tobacco. And you can't grow tobacco in England. He's thirty-five. A bit old to start again at the bottom."

"Has he got any money?"

"He got a bit out of Rhodesia before sanctions stopped him from transferring money."

"Couldn't he start a little business?"

"But what? He'd have to know what he was doing or he'd lose what little he's got. So far, all he can find is a menial job in security from his experience in the police reserve fighting terrorists. In a supermarket looking for shoplifters. From manager of a tobacco estate to standing around in a shop. Doesn't do much for a man's self-esteem."

"Better than getting himself killed... And Bobby? What will he do if he stays in England? One minute all that space and then you're in suburbia."

"Go and see him, Katie. Talk to him. Life changes. His life has changed. He's got to face up to it. Looking back, going out to Rhodesia was a big mistake. Vince says he's facing up to the reality. There's no longer a British Empire and never will be again. He thinks there's a lot of change coming. For everyone. Including the people in Europe."

"You'd better give me Brigadier Preston's address. Nothing ever turns out the way we want it to. You have to make the best of what you've got."

"Do you still love Bobby?"

"After ten years everything will have changed. It will be starting all over again."

"Vince says he would farm in England if he had enough money to buy a small farm. Both he and Bobby know about sheep and cattle... What are you giggling about, Katie?"

"I had a flash of a middle-aged frumpy Linda married to a sheep farmer."

"I'll never be frumpy. That's ridiculous... Oh, Katie. What are we going to do with the rest of our lives?"

The black bull came closer, staring at Katie, the horns, on either side of the white patch on its head menacing. Katie moved back against the tree, bringing up her knees, and stared back. A grey squirrel on the branch above her head twitched its tail, dropping the acorn it was eating, the acorn dropping into the open picnic basket. Katie turned her head and looked into the small wood behind them, looking for a place to run. When she looked back the bull was grazing the grass, no longer interested in them. The squirrel had gone up into the foliage of the spreading tree, the scents of summer pleasant again. Thinking of Bobby drinking too much, she put down her glass of wine. Stress made a man drink, that much she understood. Some people were happy drunks, some of them belligerent. Katie had no idea what it would feel like to lose her children, the thought of children making her sad. When she focused again on the field the bull was moving away.

"You're not drinking," said Linda.

"So many people these days are becoming alcoholics. Alcohol makes you depressed. It's a vicious circle. Men want to fight when their families are hurt, let alone killed. I can't even imagine his feelings."

"You want some of the tea?"

"And a Waterloo Station sandwich... Did you see that squirrel? They're not indigenous to England. The grey squirrel, when it was introduced to the island, chased out the indigenous red variety. There are a few of the red squirrels left in Scotland. The two are different species. The grey is a rat."

"A cute rat."

"I suppose so... Pass me the sugar... England's so peaceful."

"Wasn't so peaceful during the war."

"I feel so sorry for him. Did he say he wants to see me?"

"I don't know."

Katie, for a long time, watched a bee in the yellow flower of a dandelion, the stem undulating as the bee worried the heart of the flower. The bee flew off with the pollen sticking to its body and settled in another flower which it pollinated. Life went on.

"So, what are we going to do with the rest of our lives?" she said to Linda. "Without children, life becomes pretty pointless."

"Are you broody?"

"Just sad. At moments like this in a field, sitting under a spreading oak tree, it takes you out of the mundane routine of life and makes you think, 'why am I here on this earth?' What is the purpose of Katie? There has to be more to life than just getting through it day by day. I once asked a priest. He didn't know. Not when I asked him a direct question about life after death. He was just doing his job like the rest of us, earning his daily bread, giving what comfort he could... Yes, I'll go to Bobby. That's the least I can do. You only find out who your friends are when you're in trouble... Thanks for coming down to tell me. You're a true friend."

"All three of us, you, me and Angela, would have had a poorer life without each other. Most people don't give a damn about you unless they want something... How's the tea?"

"You made it perfectly, Linda. You're a genius. What's in the sandwiches?"

"Try one and see."

Later, side by side, the picnic basket at their feet, they lay back on the rug, the moss soft under their bodies, and both went to sleep. When they woke it was to the sound of a blackbird calling to them from above in their favourite tree.

"I'd better drive you to your parents and go and see mine. When are you seeing Vince again?"

"Tomorrow. I'm taking him to a posh restaurant for dinner now I'm a well-paid computer programmer. When I was a lowly comptometer operator in Salisbury, Vince did all the paying."

"What about the twenty-three year old?"

"He can wait."

"Do you also buy him dinner?"

"Of course I do. He's twenty-three. Doesn't have any money. You get what you pay for in life."

"Any sign of a rich old man you can marry for his money?" said Katie in jest.

"No, thank goodness... You're right. We'd better go."

Linda, rummaging in her bag, pulled out a piece of paper.

"Here, before I forget. The address of the house in Epsom. Do you remember that year when Taylor won the Epsom Derby? Dad won ten quid at the races. We were all so happy… Come on, let's go and see our parents."

THE NEXT MORNING, Katie drove to the address in Epsom without making a phone call. She hoped by mid-morning Bobby would not have started drinking, that it was better to surprise him than first talk to him on the phone. It was almost exactly ten years to the day since Bobby had sent her his letter of proposal. So much had happened to both of them. Good and bad.

The house was in a row of houses like so many others in England; a small front garden with a picket fence and a gate; flowerbeds on either side of the path that took Katie up to the front door. On the frame of the door was a small black bell with a white button, on the centre of the door a brass knocker. Katie chose to knock, sending the sound echoing through inside the house. Katie waited. Feet shuffled inside, increasing her apprehension, making Katie want to turn and run back to her car. When the door opened she had her back to it, her flight almost begun.

"Can I help you?" said a familiar voice.

"Good morning, Bobby. How are you?"

"Bloody awful since you ask. I've got a hangover. What are you doing here, Katie?"

"I came to see you."

They looked at each other, neither of them knowing what to do, both of them feeling uncomfortable.

"Then you'd better come in. Dad's gone to the shops. We had a bit of a falling out last night after I got myself drunk. It's my latest habit. Getting drunk every night… So. You've heard that I'm single?"

"And a nasty drunk."

"That about sums it up. I can't see the purpose of my life anymore. Anyway, at least here I'm under father's orders. He's poured all the booze down the drain."

"What are you going to do?"

"Fly home as soon as possible having done my filial duty. Dad having done his fatherly duty. With luck I'll avoid my sisters and their 'told you so' about going to Rhodesia instead of going into the army like all the other male Prestons. And you, Katie, are you going to tell me the same 'I told you so?'"

"I've come to try and help."

"You can't help me. Neither can anyone else. Have you ever seen your children in a sack? A small severed hand that yesterday had stroked the cat? A bit of thigh bone that was your wife? A child's skull with no skin and no eyes, picked clean by vultures? No, of course you haven't. Do you have children, Katie? Your own children?"

"No, I don't. I never married. Lived with a man but never married."

"Then you can have no idea. All I want to do is go home and kill as many as I can of the bastards who killed my family before they kill me."

"Can I sit down?"

"You can do what the hell you like."

"Please don't swear at me, Bobby."

"Then go back to your car and go home. I don't want your sympathy."

"You're self-destructing."

"Of course I am. My only regret is not having the guts to shoot myself. Bits of flesh and bone in a sack, blown to pieces by a Russian bomb. What was left of them picked over by vultures and hyenas. You remember that hyena outside the tent?"

"It ended in love, Bobby."

"Fat lot of good that did me."

"Please don't be hurtful."

"Then go home. Go away. Leave me alone... And don't start bloody well crying. I can't stand it. Two little coffins with bits of flesh and bone inside."

"Please stop, Bobby."

"How can I? For me it's never going to stop. They were seven years old, for God's sake. What have I ever done to anyone? I found a piece of useless bush and turned it into a flourishing farm. That's all I've done. Every Friday they line up for their rations of mealie meal, beans, sugar and meat because if I give them all their pay in money they drink it in the compound beerhall. I was looking after them. Looking after their families. Rhodesia, thanks to four thousand English and Afrikaans farmers, is the breadbasket of central Africa. Without us they'll bloody well starve. And what do they do for thanks? They blow up my family so Mugabe can become another African dictator in the name of communism while we're the stinking colonials. The Russians and Chinese are using him. It's just bloody politics. Mugabe doesn't care about the people. The likes of Mugabe and Makoni only care about themselves. About power. I'd rip their hearts out of their chests if I got my hands on them... And please stop that crying. Crying won't help. I've tried it. Nothing will help except killing the bastards who killed my family. My wife. My little girls."

"I'm so sorry."

"They'll be sorry before this is finished. The whole damn country. Black and white. But for me it won't make any difference. They're dead. Wendy, Stephanie and Deborah are dead."

"You want me to stay?"

"Not really. You were right, Katie. You were so damn right and now it's all too late."

"It's never too late. How long are you staying in England?"

"I don't know. I've fallen out with my father. I don't know."

"I'm sure he understands. He was a soldier."

"There's no point to anything. There probably never was... You'd better go, Katie. I'm no good to anyone. I just wish I had the guts to kill myself."

"Vince says they won't let you stay in the police reserve."

"I went berserk. You can't believe how much I hate."

"There are doctors who can help your pain."

"What the hell do they know about pain?"

"What's happened to the farm?" said Katie, trying to ignore Bobby's animosity.

"We've got the crop in, somehow. I don't remember much of it. Most of the time I'm drunk. What I want now is a bottle of whisky to get away from myself. When I'm really drunk I can't remember anything."

"Tell your father I called. That I'm staying with my parents in Dorking. Ask him to call me."

"Whatever for?"

"Because we love you."

"Pretty words. All I ever hear are pretty words."

"I'll see myself out."

"No one can help me, Katie. No one."

As Katie walked out through the hall she left her father's address and telephone number on the hall table.

BRIGADIER PRESTON ARRIVED at exactly eleven o'clock for his appointment. The old man had phoned Katie to make the time the previous afternoon. Katie's parents had both left the house, feeling their presence would make the visit more difficult.

"Is there anywhere we could go for a walk? I find walking clears my head when there's a problem."

"About two miles from here. Did you come by car?"

"No, I took the train. Pensioners like me can't afford to run cars. Anyway, I don't really need one. One of my neighbours takes me shopping. When I feel like a bit of company I stroll down to the Pig and Whistle. Walking is good for you."

"We can take my car. If you wait in the lounge I'll make us a flask of tea. I know just the spot for a walk in the woods... How are you, Brigadier Preston?"

"Not so good, I'm afraid, Katie. Not so good."

"How is he today?"

"His body is screaming for alcohol. Drunks find that. My son's a drunk... Please don't go to too much bother."

The black bull with the white blaze on its face was still in the field when Katie parked the Volkswagen next to the four bar gate. The sun was shining. White, fluffy clouds hung in the sky, all of them motionless. There was no one around.

"Can you climb over the gate? The farmer has a padlock on it to keep people out. I've been walking these fields since I was a child."

"You were lucky to grow up surrounded by such beauty. No, that gate's not a problem. I do a regime of exercises every morning. Legacy, I suppose, of my days in the army."

"Do you miss the army?"

"I miss the people, not the war. Bobby was meant to go in the army. At eighteen, he wanted an adventure. Rhodesia in Africa sounded exciting. At that age, who knows about politics and how it's going to affect a country and its people?... You think that bull's going to behave itself? I can't run as fast as I could in the old days. Have you been to the concert recently? Wasn't it Brahms's symphonies? I so enjoy good music. I hope I haven't inconvenienced you or your parents."

"They just popped out to see some friends."

"Yes, I'm sure they did."

"Over there, where we're going, is the biggest oak tree in Surrey. There's a lovely walk through the woods. As children, we collected blackberries and my mother turned them into blackberry jelly. Roast lamb and blackberry jelly. There's nothing better. Sometimes we found mushrooms in the fields. My aunt, who met a man one week and married him the next and went out to Sarawak, made wine from dandelions. Aunty Freda. She's quite a character. Her husband died in a Japanese prisoner of war camp. Have you ever heard of Sarawak?"

"As a matter of fact I have. I've been to Kuching, the capital. Sarawak is on the coast of Borneo. The British pirate – some called him a pirate – who took over the place in the nineteenth century and then handed it over to Queen Victoria was a chap called Brooke. Rajah Brooke. The white Rajah."

"Do you want to sit under the oak tree?"

"I'm avoiding the subject I've come to talk about, Katie. I've got a big favour to ask you. Yes, sitting down might be better. What a lovely place to grow up."

"Yes it was... Tea, Brigadier Preston?"

"Tea would be most pleasant. I remember the tea plantations in Darjeeling... But again I'm digressing. You see, I don't want Bobby to go back to Rhodesia. Ever. Or he'll kill himself. Or get himself killed. I don't want the tragedy of his wife and children to kill him as well. If he goes back, my son is finished. He won't listen to me. I want you to take him away somewhere. Into the country. Far away from any alcohol... Do you by any chance have the time?"

"I'm not working."

"I'm sorry to hear that. Well, I can afford a little money for you both to rent a cottage in the country. A little like you were ten years ago in Rhodesia when you were so happy. Look, I'm sorry. Do you have a man in your life? I see you don't wear a wedding ring."

"Not at the moment. And please, don't worry about money. I made quite a lot of money in America."

"Oh, good. The old army pension doesn't stretch far. One minute you have all the perks that give you a high standard of living, the next minute you're living on the bare minimum... Well, it's not so bad."

"What's he going to do with Hopewell Estate?"

"Give it to his labourers probably. It's no good to Bobby. Even if he could sell it with the war going on, he can't get the money out of Rhodesia. But that's a future problem. The first problem is weaning my son off alcohol so he can think straight."

"Who's idea is it to give the farm away?"

"Bobby's actually. In the odd moments he's rational he worries about his labour force. He talks about some man called Sekuru. Another man who's the teacher in the farm school... Then he rages on about Mugabe and wants to kill him and every other terrorist. He's not rational, Katie. It's the drink. He's saturated in alcohol. His body and his brain. You've got to take him away and talk some sense into him. He won't listen to me... You see, I've hidden his passport so he can't rush back to Rhodesia. He screams about vengeance. But that's not going to help anyone. Any more than your aunt would achieve anything by screaming at the Japanese."

"Can they really run the farm? Sekuru's the foreman but Bobby has to make all the decisions."

"That's their problem. It's what their politicians want. What the fight's all about. So give it to them."

"I have a friend near St Ives. I'll give her a ring. Angela will know where I can rent a cottage."

"You sure you've got enough money?"

"Quite sure, Brigadier Preston. Now, would you like some tea?"

"I'd love some. Oh, that really is a weight off my mind... When are you going back to work?"

"I'm not sure."

"You see, if his mother was alive she'd know how to handle the situation. It needs the soft touch of a woman. Not the orders of an old soldier. He never was very good at taking orders from his father."

"Have you really hidden his passport?"

"I've got it in my pocket."

The old man had a little smile on his face, the smile of a conspirator that reminded Katie of herself when she was a little girl.

After tea, they walked through the woods, the old man not bringing up the subject of Bobby. He talked of the trees and the birds in the trees, his job already done. Katie, feeling the new load on her shoulders, hoped he knew what he was doing. She had heard of special places for drunks staffed by professionals.

When Katie dropped the old man at Dorking Station he was quite chirpy.

"Are you sure you don't want me to drive you to Epsom?"

"And waste my return ticket?"

Wondering if the real reason was Bobby back at the house, Katie drove home. Her parents were back.

"Were you two watching the house?"

"Whatever makes you think that? How did it go?"

"It seems the problem is now mine."

"Do you mind, darling?" asked her mother.

"Not if it brings back the Bobby I used to know."

THE TELEPHONE CALL to Angela Tate went better than Katie expected.

"Oh, now that is lucky," said Angela down the phone. "Darna is bored to death with the countryside. You can have the cottage for as long as you like, provided you look after my cats. My publishers want me to prepare for a book tour now they're publishing *Clash of Passions*. And I've finished the new book... Why on earth do you want to bury yourself in the country? There's nothing to do here. Perfect to write a book but nothing else. I'll tell Darna. She'll be thrilled. How soon are you coming?"

The next day before breakfast Katie packed her clothes, said goodbye to her parents and drove the car to Epsom, expecting an argument with Bobby. When she knew what was happening she would phone Linda; she couldn't force Bobby to go with her to Cornwall.

This time both of them were in the house when Katie pressed the small white button of the doorbell, making a gong-like sound echo through the house.

"Pack a bag, Bobby. You and I are driving to Cornwall," said Katie when he answered the door, his father standing behind him.

"Whatever for?"

"Because I'm kicking you out of my house until you learn to be civil. And that's an order, son. Katie has kindly offered to help."

"Where's my passport?" said Bobby, turning belligerently back to his father.

"I have absolutely no idea. Now. Out you go. Get yourself straight. You're a grown man. Men of your education and breeding don't throw in the towel. They don't mope around the house feeling sorry for themselves. You're not the only one in the world to have lost a family. Be a man. Grow up… Now get out."

"Don't I need clothes?"

"Get in the car. I'll throw your clothes in your suitcase. You're a mess, son. Get yourself sorted out before you come back again. Can you imagine what your mother would have thought of you blubbering and drinking yourself to oblivion? There are other people in the world other than yourself. If you were in the army I'd have you cashiered, son of mine or no son of mine. And if you're abusive to Katie you'll have your father to reckon with."

"If you find my passport will you let me know?"

"Of course I will."

"Where are we going to stay, Katie?"

"In a nice little cottage. Just the two of us, Bobby. It will be just like old times."

Taking Bobby by the hand, she led him down the path and put him in the passenger side of the car. When he was seated, she kissed him on the cheek. They waited for five minutes in silence, both of them looking straight through the car's window. Katie still had him by the hand. When the old man put the suitcase on the back seat of the car she squeezed his hand, gave a wan smile to Brigadier Preston and started the car.

All the way down to Angela's cottage outside St Ives neither of them spoke. It was nine o'clock at night and the sun was still shining when they arrived. Katie rummaged in the pot plant full of geraniums by the side of the front door. A cat began to whine, pushing its back against a post, part of the walkway that led up to the house. There was a note from Angela on the door. Both of them had gone, Katie's phone call at the motorway service station warning Angela they were coming.

"Where's your friend?" asked Bobby.

"Gone up to London with her lover. Glad you can talk."

"Is there any booze in the house?"

"Shouldn't think so. I asked Angela to pour it down the sink."

"Is this going to work, Katie?"

"That's up to you. Let's go for a walk when we've put the cases in the house. Doesn't get dark till half past ten at this time of year. Then I'll make us some supper."

"Thank you, Katie." They looked straight at each other, both of them trying to smile.

Smiling her best, happy they were talking, Katie helped unload the car into the small, climbing rose-covered house, the scent of flowers on the soft evening air. When they were back outside Katie took Bobby by the hand and walked him down the path, out onto the lane with big elm trees on either side of the road. The twilight was building, the birds beginning to sing as they walked through the countryside, Katie hoping her best it was going to work. They were miles from anywhere, miles from a pub, miles from temptation for Bobby. Later, she was going to try and seduce him and see if that helped. For the first time in months she was happy; had something to do; something that was important. Not once on the journey down had it rained. Who knows, she thought, my life might be starting again; she had a purpose, a reason, a life worth the living.

"I'm so happy, Bobby."

"I'll try and behave myself."

"I know you will. We've both got to be patient. Each day at a time."

"Will the cat be all right?"

"There are two of them. We'll feed them when we get back."

"I love cats."

"So do I. Cats and dogs."

"You think my cats and dogs are all right on the farm? Randall said he'd feed them. They were all so lost without the children."

"I'm sure they're fine. It's only you I'm worried about. When you come right, all the rest will fall into place... Over there. Look. It's a rabbit."

AFTER AN OMELETTE and toast they both went to bed, neither of them having been hungry. There was only one bed in the house, a double bed for Angela and Darna. It was dark in the room. A nightjar called from the woods outside through the open window.

"Just like old times," said Katie, putting her hand on his leg. Both of them were dressed in their underclothes. Deliberately, Bobby removed her hand. The smell of the stocks growing outside the window was strong. For Katie, it was the first time a man in bed with her had refused her advance. If there was going to be seduction it was going to be later. Much later. Her body was hot, her mind ice-cold, a little annoyed. They lay awake, neither of them moving, both on their backs. Much later, when Katie had lost all sense of time, a dog-fox barked, the sound far away. There was a smell of salt in the air, the smell of the sea, the ocean quiet in the dark of the night. When Bobby fell asleep, making a soft, fluting sound that brought back happier memories, Katie relaxed. The light of morning was showing Katie the outline of the room when she fell into a troubled sleep. When she woke, sunlight pouring through the window, he was gone. In panic, she got up and looked out of the window, relieved to see her car was still where she had parked it. The door to the bedroom was closed. One of the cats had got in through the open window and was sleeping, curled up on the end of the bed. Katie was stroking the cat when the bedroom door opened and Bobby came in with the tea.

"There's something about us English, Katie. Wherever we live in the world we still drink tea in the morning."

"How are you this morning?"

"Still got the shakes. Withdrawal symptoms. I'll have it for weeks. The other cat's in the kitchen drinking milk... Who owns this house?"

"Angela. We were at school together. The three of us. Me, Linda and Angela."

"What does she do for a living?"

"She's a novelist. She's preparing for a book tour in London."

"She must be successful to afford all this. Most of the furniture is antique. What's her last name?"

"Tate."

"Never heard of her."

"She lives with a woman. Before she came here she was a high-class prostitute in London. A bit like me, Bobby."

"What do you mean?"

"I was a rich American's mistress. When he threw me out I sued him. Said he'd asked to marry me. He was married to another woman who'd lost her son in Vietnam. He really didn't propose. Just insinuated so he could put me up in a fancy flat in Manhattan. He didn't want a scandal. I had a good lawyer who also made a fortune out of him."

"How much did you make?"

"One and a half million United States dollars. Tax free."

"Blimey. That's twice what Hopewell Estate would have been worth before the war and sanctions. What have you done with it all?"

"Put it in a trust."

"You could buy a Rolls-Royce with that kind of money."

"My parents don't know. You see, Bobby, we all have our problems. Finn, the man in New York, lost his son and cheated on his wife... I'm sorry I tried to seduce you last night. It won't happen again. It was insensitive of me. An insult to your late wife."

"I don't want to talk about her."

"But you must. You can't keep it all bottled up or you'll burst. We were always able to talk to each other. We must talk, Bobby. Why we're here."

"Have some tea... You know, you can smell the sea from here."

"I thought you'd taken the car and pushed off."

"I thought of it. Where'd you hide the keys?"

"That's my secret. A bit like your dad and your passport. Now, get back into bed. We have the whole day in front of us."

"You know what I want right now?"

"I'm sure I do but you aren't going to get it. Not a drop. You're an alcoholic, Bobby. One drink and you're back on the slippery slide."

"I can control it."

"They all say that. To you, alcohol is a poison. Makes you depressed. Why you keep talking about killing yourself."

"We used to enjoy a drink together in the evenings."

"We used to enjoy a lot of things all those years ago. A lot's happened since, some of which made you turn to drink."

"We all drank too much. You never knew when an RPG rocket was coming through the window. Probably both of us were alcoholics."

"Well, you're not in Rhodesia. No one is going to shoot you through that window. Now, who's pouring the tea? It's on your side of the bed so you'd better pour."

"How long are we going to stay in Angela's cottage? Was your schoolfriend really a high-class whore?"

"As high class as you get them. Very expensive. She and her lover Darna did it in front of paying customers for mind boggling sums of money. How Angela ended up a lesbian. She and Darna fell in love with each other."

"Will it last, that kind of relationship?"

"Who knows? Darna was going to get herself pregnant by some unsuspecting man with the right genes. Angela can't have kids. A family in the English countryside was their dream. Trouble is, Darna got bored sitting around when Angela was writing. Why they're up in London. Who knows what will happen?"

"What happened to your American?"

"I hoped he would go back to his wife."

"Did he?"

"Finn had developed a predilection for young girls. I had become too old for him. He'd started screwing a twenty-three-year-old."

"They say you can always attract young girls with that kind of money."

"In America and England, life is all about money."

"But not in Rhodesia. Creating my farm wasn't ever about money. It was a lifestyle choice, living in the African bush. Creating something. Turning bushveld into a productive farm. You can only eat one meal at a time. I never understand all this money spending. Most of it is pointless. Showing off. Scoring points. Trying to be better than the next man. To me, that's a completely pointless way of using wealth."

"You have a big house and a swimming pool. Your labourers have very little."

"But they're never hungry. The kids have a school to go to. A football field to play in. And they were happy until this bloody war started. The ones that live through this war will pay for their leader's ambitions. Then you'll see a black elite on a spending spree like your friend in Manhattan. Left alone, we complemented each other. I did all the thinking and provided the skills to produce the crops, they provided the labour. It doesn't work, one without the other. Some of them will learn and go their own way. I hope so."

"Are you going to give them the farm?"

"Probably. Vince says they won't know how to run it in all its complexities. We'll see. He wants to know who's going to buy the fertiliser, buy tractors, pay the wages. Run a sophisticated commercial business. These days if you want to succeed in farming you have to run it like a business or you don't get the yields or the quality of tobacco. Your growing costs exceed your income. If I'm not to go back to Rhodesia as my father keeps telling me, I'll just give it to them."

"What will you do in England for money?"

"One day my sisters and I will have money from our maternal grandfather's estate. At present, it's in a trust with a small income paid to my father to supplement his army pension. Only when he dies will the trust be broken and the money paid out equally between the three of us. In the meantime, I'll muddle along somehow. With luck, my father will outlive me. No one wants a parent to die. It's all a bit pointless, my life. I've done what I wanted to do and it's all been taken away. I can go through the rest of my life sober and miserable or drunk and drive everyone mad. I can say my British passport has been lost and get myself a replacement. Go back to Rhodesia and pick up a gun. All of it's pointless from where I'm sitting up in this bed. Everything I ever wanted has gone."

"Didn't you want me, Bobby?"

"That was a long time ago. You only wanted me on conditions."

"There wasn't any point staying in Rhodesia."

"Yes. There you go. 'I told you so.'"

"Can I have my tea before we get into an argument? What's done is done. It's the future we've got to concentrate on."

"Maybe there was never a future. For any of us. For the whole of mankind. We just keep fooling ourselves. Time after time. Think somehow it's going to get better. No wars, no hunger, everyone being nice to each other."

"Are you hungry?"

"I could eat some breakfast."

"I just want you to be happy again."

"I know you do."

"Have you still got the shakes?"

Bobby held out his hands. Both of them were shaking.

THE DRIVE UP to the cliffs took them a few minutes. Breakfast had been eaten in the kitchen mostly in silence. The day was fine, no prospect of rain. The path took them along the cliff, up and down the dales. The sea was calm, there was the occasional cry of seagulls. Out to sea a yacht was making slow progress in the lightest of winds. The only sound of man was from an aircraft flying high and far away. The path was narrow, making them walk one behind the other. Katie led the way at a good pace. Somewhere she had read that a good walk lessened a person's depression, especially depression caused by drinking. On her back she carried a small pack, in the pack a flask of tea and a square plastic box filled with sandwiches, two boiled eggs and the sausages left over from breakfast. It was difficult to talk walking in single file. The big sun-hat, tied under her chin, kept the June sun from her skin. She was happy, the walk doing her good. After an hour, Katie found the path down to the cove and the small, circular beach, the waves from the calmest of seas barely brushing the shore. To their left, halfway up the cliff, seabirds were sitting on ledges with their chicklets, the big eyes of the birds watching their descent. The sand in the cove was rough, more pebble than sand, the small waves dragging the pebbles, making a soft clinking sound that blended perfectly with the cry of the gulls. Bobby picked up a piece of amber and gave it to Katie.

"Amber's the fossil of resin," said Bobby. "Keep it for luck. This is all so different from Africa. Nothing to threaten us. No lions or terrorists. It's so wonderfully peaceful."

"Why did you want to leave England?"

"For an adventure. You only get one life. I wanted to fill my life with as much as possible. I wanted to do some living."

"Hold your hands out... See? They're not shaking. It's the exercise... You want to go for a swim?"

"I don't have a bathing costume."

"Neither do I. There's no one around... Last one in the water's a chicken."

"What if somebody comes?"

"Then they'll have to arrest me for showing my tits and bum. Or we can just stay in the sea."

Pulling her clothes off, having placed the backpack on the beach, Katie ran naked down to the water, laughing as she ran. With the water up to her thighs, she plunged head first into the sea, the cold water knocking the breath out of her. Behind her Bobby had put his toes in the water as the sea lapped the shore.

"The water's bloody cold," he shouted. "I'm an African."

"Dive in, you pussy."

"Your nipples have shrunk."

"That's the way to go," said Katie as Bobby ran forward and dived into the water. "Now so has your ding," Katie giggled as Bobby stood up from the cold.

They were laughing as they ran up the beach, the sea salt water dripping from their naked bodies, the warm sun soothing their goosebumps, both of them oblivious to the old man high up on the cliff-path looking down on them. Bobby threw Katie his shirt.

"Use it as a towel and throw it back to me."

Katie dried herself, her back to the sea. To get the water out of her ears she shook her head.

"There's somebody watching us," she said, waving up at the man on the cliff. "Put your pants on."

"I'm sure he's seen it before."

"He's moving off. Now we've seen him, he's embarrassed."

"We really are a strange species. The only one that covers ourselves up. Not just to keep warm. So no one can see us. Why are we always hiding?"

"How we're brought up... Hold your hands out... See? No shaking... Here... Catch. Dry yourself... I'm impressed. You never put on weight."

"Neither did you, Katie. You know, for a short moment I didn't think of them."

Turning to the sea, Katie put her clothes on before bending down for the pack and taking out the flask of tea. Knowing Bobby was thinking of his family, she didn't want him to talk and bring them back on the beach.

"On our way home, we'll go into St Ives and buy two nice big mackerel for our supper. Mackerel has to be eaten the day it's caught... Here, have some tea... You think in the old days smugglers used this cove? I'll bet they did. Just the right spot to bring barrels of French brandy off a ship anchored in the bay. It was all about avoiding the King's tax. Now we avoid tax by putting our money in offshore trusts. Nothing really changes."

"And nothing stays the same."

"I hope so, Bobby. One day, I want you to be happy again. Really happy. The way you were when we lived in that tent."

Kicking herself for bringing back Africa, Katie drank her tea. The faraway look was back on his face, and with it the look of hatred. His hand, gripping the plastic cup, had tightened, almost crushing the cup. It was going to take time. A lot of time.

"You want a sandwich, Bobby?"

"Not just now... Sorry. I almost broke your cup."

"I understand."

"Do you? Do you, Katie? Have you any idea what's going on in my mind surrounded by all the nice manners and civility? I don't think so. I might look normal on the surface. But I'm not. And never will be."

Katie watched Bobby walk away from her, to the furthest end of the small cove where he stood, his back to her, looking out to sea. She let him be, opening the plastic box and taking out a sandwich and a cold pork sausage. In silence, brooding, she ate her lunch, willing him to turn back to her. A couple, hand-in-hand, were walking the cliff-path when she looked up. Both of them were young. And happy. They waved at her when they saw she had seen them. Katie waved back, envying them their innocence... Half an hour went by before Bobby came back to her.

"Let's walk back to the car," said Bobby. "Isn't there a pub in St Ives?"

"Not for you, Bobby. I promised your father."

"Why are you both bothering? I'm done. Well and truly done. Why the hell wasn't I in that damn car, all of us blown to oblivion, never again having to think."

Slowly, heavily, they walked back up the cliff, the day still young, Bobby not having eaten his lunch. Time hung over both of them. At the car, Bobby stood by the passenger side waiting to be let in. Katie, finding her keys, got in the car, leaned across and opened the passenger side door. The moment of happiness, when they ran naked into the water, had gone. Even the sun had gone in.

Katie drove to St Ives and parked at the top of the small quay. With nothing much to do they walked down the quay and sat on the ground, their feet dangling over the water, and waited for the fishing boats to come in. When they came, three of them, the seagulls were screaming, diving into the water. A man on one of the boats had thrown a bucket of entrails into the sea. They got up, the stone under Katie's bottom now warm from her sitting. They stood back as the fishing boats came alongside. The boats were tied up to the iron bollards. Boxes of wet fish were brought out of the boats and handed onto the quay, none of the fishermen taking the slightest notice of them.

"Have you got any mackerel? Can I buy some?"

"Take your pick, lady... Do you know what a mackerel looks like?"

"Not really... Two nice big ones... Thank you. Those look wonderful."

"How much do we owe you?" said Bobby.

"You've got a good tan, mate. Where've you been for your holidays? Don't get no tan like that in Cornwall."

"I live in Africa."

"Do you now? Give us a quid... You one of those white men exploiting the blacks?"

"I'm a Rhodesian tobacco farmer."

"So they chased you out. Read about it in the paper. Sooner you all get out the better, I'd say. Never stay nowhere you're not welcome."

"They killed my wife and children in a landmine explosion. Here's your quid. Thanks for the fish."

"I'm sorry, mate."

"I'm sure you are. They all are."

"Why don't you keep your quid?"

"Why don't you shove it up your backside?"

With a gutted mackerel in each hand by the tail, Bobby walked back up the quay to the car. Katie saw he was crying.

"I'm sorry, lady. How was I to know?"

"His twin girls were just seven years old."

"I've got a girl of five."

"Then look after her. Treasure her."

The man put out his hand and touched her arm. "You look after him."

"I'm trying to."

"You his sister?"

"Once, a long time ago, we were engaged."

"Didn't mean no harm."

"There's always two sides to a story. But you're right. He's best out of Rhodesia."

In the walk back to the car, Katie's day had just become longer. She had forgotten to lock the car and Bobby was sitting inside, the fish on the floor at his feet, no expression on his face, no more tears, just staring straight ahead through the windscreen at nothing. For a moment, Katie was prepared to say to hell with it, drive Bobby to the pub down the road and get drunk with him. Instead she drove straight back to the cottage, neither of them saying a word.

At the cottage, Bobby got out leaving the fish in the car. Katie picked up the fish, walked back down the lane and threw them over the hedge into the field.

"He didn't mean anything," she said, back at the small house.

"What did you do with his fish?"

"Threw them over the hedge into a field."

"Thank you, Katie."

When Bobby put out his hand in a gesture of thanks, it was shaking. Katie took the hand and pressed it before letting it go. Then she walked to the kitchen to start preparing the supper, leaving Bobby alone with his thoughts in the lounge. With the start of evening, she could smell the stocks. In the kitchen she remembered, wet the dishcloth, and went to the car. The rubber mat was still wet from the fish. Katie wiped it clean, not wishing to be haunted by the smell of dead fish when they got back in the car.

"One day at a time," she said to herself as she walked back up the garden path. In her trouser pocket was the piece of amber Bobby had given her on the beach. The amber was smooth and warm when she felt it, wishing, hoping for luck. When she passed the window, framed by climbing roses, he was just standing looking at the inside wall. Katie wanted to go in and hug him but knew it wouldn't do any good. She felt flat, unmotivated, drained by the words of the fisherman. At that moment she knew what it felt like not to have anything to do for the rest of her life. Unless Bobby came back to her, there was no point to it, herself and all her ill-gotten money. She sighed and went into the house. More than anything else, she could do with a drink.

2

Vince Ranger left them alone for a month before taking the train down to Cornwall with Linda for a long weekend. He was due to fly back to Rhodesia at the end of August in time to plant the seedbeds on World's View to start the new growing season. Katie met them at the railway station on the Friday evening.

"Where's Bobby?" asked Vince.

"At the house. He only leaves the house for walks. He's better. The shakes have gone. Said he didn't want to come into St Ives and pass the pub. Too much temptation. So, you are going back to Rhodesia. I thought you were looking for something to do in England?"

"I was. No luck, I'm afraid. A man has to earn a living so I'm going home. My boss is pretty happy. Can't live off Linda's generosity. I've got money in the bank in Salisbury but can't get it to England. Tight exchange control... Is he coming back?"

"I don't think so. Wants you to hand Hopewell Estate over to Sekuru and the farm labourers. Why I asked you to come down. He's instructing his lawyer in Salisbury to form a community trust. The farm and all the equipment will be transferred to the trust for the start of the new season. After that they're on their own. Bobby says they can either try and grow a crop of flue-cured tobacco or grow maize to feed themselves. They'll have the cattle and sheep."

"And Randall?"

"He'll get a year's salary in lieu of notice."

"Has he thought it through carefully?"

"Oh, yes."

"And what's he going to live off in England?"

"Our costs are small in Cornwall. Angela and Darna will come for holidays but Darna wants to live in London. She missed the theatre and all the excitement of people. I'm babysitting her cats... You know, one day he'll inherit from his maternal grandfather. He's numb, dead inside, doesn't care anymore. His only worry is the people left behind on his farm."

"He's going to give it all away?"

"He doesn't care anymore. Says his life is over."

"The farm will disintegrate."

"Says it will be their problem, not his. The war's all about regaining their land. Let them have it, is how he's thinking."

"He's not drinking?"

"Not a drop... How are you, Linda?"

"Oh, you know me. Take things as they come... IBM want to know when you're coming back to work. You can't bury yourself in the country for the rest of your life... Are you back with him?"

"Not in the biblical sense. He doesn't want to touch me."

"Everything and nothing?"

"Something like that."

"So there's no booze in the house?"

"Not a drop. I rather like it. Never felt better in my life. Regular sleep. Regular exercise. Lots of fruit and vegetables. My weight's under control. What more can a girl want?"

"A lover."

"I'm working on it. Biding my time."

"You still love him?"

"More than ever. We're going to get through it. The best things in life often take a little longer. Roast lamb and mint sauce for supper. Lots of nice roast potatoes. The mint and the vegetables out of the garden. What I want to do in the end is use some of my money to buy him a farm in England. Sheep or dairy. Something like that. A nice old farmhouse. You can come and visit us. Then I want to start a family."

"Have you told Bobby?"

"Not yet. It's a dream, Linda. Whether it works or not only time will tell... It's really good to see you."

"Damn. I thought you would come back to London. I miss you. No one to natter with. With Vince going back to Rhodesia it's going to be doubly lonely... Would you let me buy you a farm, Vince, if I had the money?" said Linda, looking at him wistfully.

"Any time you like. All I need is a job... That roast lamb sounds pretty good, Katie. Lead on... What a bugger-up. For a while in Rhodesia we really thought we were building something exciting. For all of us. Black and white. For all intents and purposes Hopewell Estate is going back to peasant farming. Not that there was any farming before Bobby opened it up. What a bloody mess. Wow, no booze for a whole weekend. That's a new one. You're not going to buy me a farm, are you, Linda?"

"Not really."

"By Monday you'll feel so good you'll wonder why you ever drank," said Katie.

"I hope so. I really hope so."

BOBBY WATCHED his old friend get out of the car, both of them looking at each other with not much to smile about. Linda and Katie were chatting away, Vince holding two small suitcases. The sun had gone down behind the elm trees, the countryside soft in the evening.

"You want to go for a walk, old friend? Let the girls talk. Katie needs some feminine company. I hear you're going back? How's the war going? We don't have television. Not even a radio. Lots of books. Haven't read so many books since my early days on World's View; books and a wind-up gramophone. Didn't have electricity. In some ways it's better not knowing what's going on in the world. My world has shrunk to the cottage and this garden; Katie and a couple of cats. All part of the therapy. It's a better world without people you might think. Anyway, here I am. I've written it all down what I'd like you to do with my farm. Will you do it for an old friend?"

"Of course I will... You look well. How's life treating you in England?"

"Different. Everything's different. The smells. The sound of the birds. A dog-fox has a different bark to a bushbuck."

"The army made a raid into Zambia. Came up on one of their training camps in the bush. The Selous Scouts led the way and caught them on the parade ground without their guns. Kept on firing until no one moved. Hundreds of dead terrorists. Some of our chaps were sick in the bush afterwards; couldn't face the carnage. Wholesale slaughter. Thought you'd like to hear."

"Not really. With the booze out of my system my level of anger has dropped. I only hate those who killed my family; their political masters; not every black man who calls himself a freedom fighter. Like me, their families will be grieving. People are just people... How is everyone in the Centenary?"

"Talked to Jeremy Crookshank on the phone a few times... I came over to England the same time as you, remember?"

"Of course... Roast lamb for dinner. Can't offer you a drink."

"You're not coming back?"

"They won't let me. My father confiscated my passport and won't give it back. Life goes on in a day to day way. You get up, have breakfast, go for a walk. That sort of thing. The worst thing in life is not having anything worthwhile to do. Nothing to achieve. Nothing constructive to think about... Give them all my regards in the club."

"You think Sekuru can run your farm?"

"Probably not. If they want us out they'll have to pay the consequences, the only winners will be their politicians. I'm sure there are plenty of Mugabe sympathisers in my compound. They'll have to learn the hard way so they might as well start on Hopewell Estate. Lovely name for it don't you think? Well, it was. Not much hope anymore. I'd give you my farm, Vince, if I thought it would do you any good. Some of the people here think we're just old colonial exploiters who've pillaged the resources of Africa. They'd love to see us all kicked out. Maybe they're right. Maybe it's jealousy. Who knows? Whichever, Rhodesia didn't work out and never will. Well, I've now got nothing. I hope they're all satisfied. When I've come to terms with myself I'll find something to do to keep body and mind occupied. Katie's been wonderful. The only thing I can't fathom is why she bothers with me now I'm a nothing."

"There's an old saying: they can take away your money but not your brains."

"I like that one. Trouble is, my brains have been scrambled by misery and alcohol... Can you smell the sea? We found a cove we go to. Katie thinks it was an old smugglers' cove. There's a lot of history in Cornwall... How you getting on with Linda?"

"We're comfortable together. I could settle down with Linda but she won't come back with me to Rhodesia."

"Sounds familiar... The meat's in the oven. We'll eat at seven... Have you noticed how everything is so small in England? The fields. The lanes. Everything close together... We can walk another half hour. Let them talk. What do they find to talk about?"

"Us, I suppose. Or someone like us... Isn't that a squirrel? Haven't seen a squirrel for years. Don't get squirrels in Africa."

"Good to see you, Vince."

"Good to see you, Bobby."

KATIE HAD LAID out a table close to the bed of sweet-smelling stocks. There was no wind, only the sound of the girls talking, the insects and the birds. Quietly, Vince and Bobby walked up the garden path.

"The house is very pretty," said Vince.

"Yes it is. A perfect English cottage in the country. Trouble is, you need a fortune to buy the place. Angela has two acres. All the rich investment bankers in London want holiday houses in the country. As much an investment as somewhere to enjoy. These days everything is about money. Making it and finding a place to invest the profit. No one in London has the time to savour the countryside. At cocktail parties they boast to each other about their estate in Cornwall or their place in the Algarve, according to Katie. The locals can't compete. Some of the new rich have a dozen houses around the world, the money made out of speculation sitting in their offices. They don't build up a farm that produces something that goes on year after year. They only create money, money that doesn't have any tangible value. What I want to know is what happens when the traders stop competing with each other pushing up the stock exchange and the price of property and all this paper money vanishes. A house can suddenly be worth double what it was worth five years ago: it's still the same house; the same bricks and mortar; the same garden. No one's done anything to improve its value as we did with our farms in Rhodesia. Last year, Hopewell Estate produced a million United States dollars' worth of tobacco, to say nothing of the maize that feeds the people. When I got the land ten years ago it had never grown anything. Just bush. Only now as it becomes worth something do they want it back again... Looks like we're eating under the trees out on the lawn. It's the time before supper when I really crave a drink. Sundowner time, the words that conjure up everything we enjoyed so much in Africa."

"Do you regret having gone out to Rhodesia?"

"I bitterly regret losing Wendy and the children. But not going to Africa. We had a lifestyle that will never be repeated. Great estates. Servants. Country clubs. Sunshine and all that wonder of the African bush. More like feudal barons living in the last part of the urbanised twentieth century. No wonder they all want to get rid of us. We're an anachronism. There we are, a few thousand farmers controlling an entire country we built from scratch. Think of it, Vince. Ninety years ago there wasn't a road in Rhodesia. No cities. No electricity. No infrastructure whatsoever. No one had heard of running water or an internal combustion engine."

"Must have been nice. A thatched hut by a river. Plenty of fish to catch. Game in the bush. The Garden of Eden. Mostly they hunted what they wanted. Didn't have to work for it; a patch of maize here, patch of maize there, a couple of cows to milk. There were only four hundred thousand people in the whole of Rhodesia. Not enough to want to fight with each other."

"What about Lobengula and his Zulu impis that conquered Rhodesia from South Africa? We British stopped the Zulus pig-sticking the indigenous Shona. There are always wars when someone has something. Someone will find you and try to take it away. Nothing changes. Or rather, everything changes and everything stays the same. Mugabe is a Shona. If he kicks us out and takes over the government it won't be long before he turns on the Zulus. People and tribes have long memories... Have you two girls got any tongues left?" said Bobby as they reached the table.

"We had a lot to catch up with," answered Katie. "How was your walk? Supper is nearly ready. Why don't you both sit down at the table? It's the perfect evening to eat outside. Are you hungry, Bobby?"

"Starving, Katie... What I wouldn't give for a drink."

"Sit you down. We girls will serve you if you'll carve the meat."

GOING BACK to the kitchen to take the roast leg of lamb out of the oven, Katie was happy. They were all so comfortable with each other. You couldn't make new old friends, she told herself as she used the oven gloves to pull out the roasting pan. The roast potatoes, parsnips and onions looked perfectly cooked. The steamed fresh beans, and broccoli on the top of the oven were also ready. Putting the meat and potatoes on the serving dish with the onions and parsnips, Katie poured the fat into a bowl, poured the water from the fresh vegetables into the roasting pan and made the gravy with a couple of spoonfuls of Bisto.

"Dinner is served, my lords," she said as she carried out the silver serving dish.

"You want some help?" said Linda, getting up from the table where Bobby and Vince were seated.

"The vegetables and gravy are in the kitchen. Don't forget the mint sauce. You can bring the plates. They're in the warmer at the bottom of the oven."

"What I wouldn't do for a bottle of good South African wine."

"Shut up, Bobby. Stop tormenting yourself."

"I was only kidding."

"I hope so... How does that lot look?... What a perfect evening. Not a breath of wind. The carving knife is next to you, Bobby."

While Katie was untying her apron behind her back, Bobby came across and lightly kissed her on the cheek, making Katie feel wonderful.

"Thanks, Katie. I promise never to mention alcohol again."

By the time they had eaten, the light was fading. Katie went back to the kitchen and made them coffee, carrying out the tray.

"Are the gnats worrying any of you?" she asked.

"After mosquitoes, gnats are pussy cats... Where are our two, by the way?"

"I've fed them in the kitchen. It's been a lovely day... Vince, your eyelids are drooping. Do you want to go to bed?"

"At home I'm asleep by half past eight. Farmers get up early."

"Just listen to the birds."

"They sing at dusk to tell each other which tree they're sleeping in."

"Is that how it works?... Your voice echoed, Vince. It only does that on a summer's evening in England... Have you all had enough food?... While you're having your coffee I'll clear away the things. Don't get up, Linda. You're a guest. Bobby and I do the washing up in the morning."

"That supper was perfect."

"Yes, it was. All of it. The food and the company. I can't remember when I've more enjoyed an evening."

In the kitchen, stacking the plates, she could still hear their voices mingling with the sound of the birds. Only then did Katie start crying, realising how much she had missed. By now they could have had a family far away from all the arguments. Gripping the side of the sink, she pulled herself together before going out into the gloaming to join him.

AT THE END OF SEPTEMBER, when Bobby's lawyer in Salisbury was implementing the community trust and the transfer of Hopewell Estate to his farm labourers, Bobby found himself a job on a building site in the City of London where all the investment bankers were making their millions. In developing Hopewell Estate and its farm buildings spread over five acres, he had always made sure he could do every job he asked others to do: the bricklaying, digging the trenches in perfect straight lines, cutting the timber, plastering, laying the roof. He was a builder created by practice. To ensure that nobody was uncomfortable with his expensive education at Wellington College, he had changed his British accent to that of a born and bred Rhodesian, so the cockneys would accept him as one of their own. He told anyone who asked that he had fled Rhodesia to get out of the army, not agreeing with Ian Smith's white supremacist politics. The daily rate of a labourer was just enough to live off: basic food, a rented room in Lambeth. When they asked him at the end of his first week to join them in the pub, Bobby declined, saying he didn't drink, causing a laugh. From then on they left him alone. Hard, manual labour made him tired and stopped him thinking of another life and his craving for alcohol. Only when he was alone in the room with its single plate cooker did he think of Wendy and the children, the craving for alcohol at its worst. He found a local library and began reading books of an evening to take him out of himself. Always, he made sure the books had nothing to do with Africa. He found a copy of Angela Tate's *Clash of*

Passions and took himself into another world, skipping the parts about war. Katie had gone back to her job at IBM for something to do. They had parted good friends, but still not lovers. For all intents and purposes Bobby was friendless, keeping to himself. At work, they began to avoid him, only the foreman happy with his work of plastering. His father still had his passport, removing any avenue of escape. Humping bags of cement and climbing ladders made him physically fit. The days went by, Bobby only thinking of the present. Katie and his father left him alone as he had asked them to do. He was alive but only in body and not in spirit, having turned off the engine of his mind. Days became weeks, weeks became months as summer turned into the cold of winter, his hands and feet so cold he couldn't feel them. He ate alone, slept alone and thought alone, never letting other people into his mind. For a whole day he didn't think of having a drink. Then a week went by. He was winning the fight, the only hope left for him. When a bricklayer didn't pitch up at work, Bobby did bricklaying. When they wanted a trench dug on a new site, Bobby dug the trench. He was a workhorse, like so many others through history.

"Where'd you learn how to do everything, Preston?" asked the foreman.

"Does it matter?"

"You don't have to be rude."

"I'm sorry. I'm not much of a talker."

"So it seems... Did you know, every now and again you lose your accent. Who are you, Preston?"

"A lost soul in need of a job. I'll try and do better with my accent."

"Are you really a Rhodesian?"

"Not anymore. There aren't Rhodesians anymore. When Mugabe takes over they'll be calling us Zimbabweans."

"Must be difficult losing your country."

"Yes, it is. I'd better get on. Will you excuse me?"

"You could do my job if you wanted to."

"But I don't want to, Mr Foreman. I enjoy what I'm doing. It keeps me occupied. Earns me a living wage... Now if you don't mind?"

"Get on with it. It's your business. It's just that most people I know want to get on in life."

For the first time in a while, Bobby thought of getting a drink as the man kept shaking his hand. Bobby stood still, waiting for the conversation to come to an end. Then he went back to his work, his mind fighting his body's craving for alcohol. When he picked up a steel girder, his muscles aching with the weight, the foreman had gone. One of the men was looking at him queerly, as if he had a bad smell under his nose. Only then did Bobby realise he had gone back to his upper-class accent.

"Sorry, old chap," Bobby said to the man. "That was a mistake. When a man doesn't have any money he does any work he can get."

"You're broke."

"Stony broke. Not a bloody penny other than what I earn on this job."

"What happened?"

"It's a long story. A very long story."

"You want to tell me? Maybe get a drink after work when the whistle goes."

"I don't drink."

"Good for you. It's bloody expensive. Where'd you learn the job?"

"The hard way. I taught myself. Trial and error."

"The bloke you worked for must have been after you when you made a mistake."

"He didn't mind. The first wall I built was crooked. So I knocked it down and built it again. Once I put the nails in a corrugated iron roof in the dip instead of the top. When it rained, the roof leaked like a sieve. I took it off, turned it over and put the nails back again, the nail hole in the iron now at the top. Never leaked again. A man learns by his mistakes. Or I hope he does. You want to grab the other end and help me lift this one up, Ted?"

"You're a queer one."

After that they were all looking at him, all of the looks unwelcome, the look people gave to an outsider who wouldn't join in and make friends. On the Friday, after the whistle, they cornered him, Ted holding back.

"You either join us for a drink in the pub, china, or you can bugger off. Find yourself somewhere else to stick your nose up in the air. We're a team. Join the team or get another job."

Bobby shrugged. There was no point in arguing. He collected his weekly pay packet and left.

"You coming back Monday, Preston?" asked the foreman.

"If I take one glass of beer I'm finished. I'm an alcoholic."

"You going to be all right?"

"Been through a lot worse altercations than that one."

"Come to the pub. Have a glass of lemonade. I always go with them on Fridays. Makes my job easier. How long have you been off the booze?"

"Since I got back to England. Five months and twenty-three days."

"It's almost Christmas. People make friends at Christmas. Treat it as a test. If you can stand in a pub and not drink, with everyone around you drinking, you'll know you've conquered your addiction. How long have you known you're an alcoholic?"

"Ever since the terrs blew my wife and twin daughters to pieces with a landmine planted under the road. Thanks for the advice, but no. On Monday I'll look for another job."

As Bobby walked off the job for the last time his hands were shaking, his teeth chattering, his body in panic. Every sense in his body was screaming for a drink, the sweet oblivion of drunkenness where he could no longer think. It was dark, a cold drizzle mingling with the fog. Step by heavy step, Bobby forced himself to the Bank Underground station and pushed himself onto the Tube, the doors sliding closed behind him, cutting him off from the nearest pub.

When he reached the small room in Lambeth with its single bed and threadbare carpet, Bobby put a shilling in the meter from his pay packet and lit the gas heater, holding his shaking hands to the building heat. When his hands were warm, he put the kettle on the single-plate gas cooker and made himself tea. With the tea mug in both hands he sat in a chair in front of the heater. Then he smiled. He had not gone to the pub, with the rest of them or on his own. One day, hopefully, he would stand in a pub and drink himself a glass of lemonade. Just not today.

On the Monday, having paid his landlady the extra month, Bobby took the train down to Epsom. He was smiling to himself: five months, twenty-six days and counting. When his father opened the door to the house they hugged each other, a new experience for both of them. Sons and fathers who had been to Wellington College shook hands, they didn't hug. Bobby's father had called his father 'sir'.

"Happy Christmas, son."

"Happy Christmas, Father."

"You look well."

"I feel well… Why's it so bloody cold in England?"

"Come in. There's a log fire in the lounge… You think we could put up a Christmas tree this year? Put a small one in the lounge next to the window. Turn on the fairy lights. Haven't done that since your mother died. The fairy lights and the decorations are in boxes up in the attic. Are you hungry? Mostly I eat sandwiches. Can't be bothered to cook for myself. There are some frozen chops in the fridge. A packet of frozen peas. We can make ourselves supper… You want a cup of tea, old chap? Outside it's as cold as charity. How's it been, Bobby?"

"Five months and twenty-six days."

"That's the stuff… Go and sit in the lounge. I'll put on the kettle."

Bobby took off his overcoat, which had got wet on his walk from the station, and hung it on the stand in the hallway next to his suitcase, then he went through to the lounge. First he warmed his hands at the fire before turning his back to the flames. When his father brought in the tea tray he was warm except for his feet.

"Took the chops out of the freezer. Should be all right."

"How long have they been in the freezer?"

"Six months. Maybe a year. One of the girls put them there on a visit. There's a good film on television tonight. All I do, really. Watch television. Seen it before, of course. Better to watch a good movie twice than a bad one once."

Deliberately, neither of them talked of anything important. They cooked, ate their food, watched the television and went to bed. All as if nothing bad had happened. After an hour of tossing and turning Bobby went to sleep. When he woke in the morning he had no recollection of what he had been dreaming about. He felt warm and happy. He got up and went downstairs in his dressing gown and put on the kettle. When the tea had had time to draw in the round brown pot he poured out a cup and took it upstairs and knocked on the door of his father's bedroom.

"Come in."

"Morning, Father. Brought you some tea. What you want for breakfast?"

"Make it a surprise. Like the tea. Your mother always brought me tea in the morning… You got anything planned?"

"Not a thing, I'm afraid. And you?"

"Nothing. You don't have much to do with your life at my age. Mostly I think back. Is it raining?"

"Not at the moment."

"We can always go for a walk. Don't have dogs anymore. Not be right to get a puppy. He'd be alive long after me. When Rufus died I left it at that. Not fair on the dog, you see."

"A walk will be nice."

"Jolly good... You slept well?"

"Perfectly."

"That's the stuff. Close the door when you go out. There's a nasty draught."

After breakfast Roland Preston handed his son a bundle of letters kept tight by a rubber band. Bobby had cooked the breakfast after walking to the corner shop to buy bacon and eggs. It was warm in the small kitchen, the sun shining through the window. Most of the letters were bills, the remnants of last year's growing season that Bobby would pay with the farm-cheque he had brought with him from Rhodesia. The statement from his bank made him smile. With worldwide sanctions against the Smith government in Rhodesia and the resulting exchange control, the money would not do him any good. The contrast between the money in his Salisbury bank account and the money in the brown envelope of his pay packet was ridiculous. Except the English money had bought them breakfast and the Rhodesian money was useless. Bobby opened the letter from Vince, glad to read of his labourers' jubilation at being given the farm and everything that stood on it. He wished them well. Like the money in the bank, the farm was no good to him unless he went back. As with the building site in the City, life would go on without him.

"You want some money?" asked his father.

"I had a job as a bricklayer."

"Winston Churchill was an amateur bricklayer. Did you know that? Soldier, graduate of Sandhurst, journalist, writer of books, painter of watercolours, politician. When they voted him out of office after he won the war for us he went into deep depression. He was a lieutenant colonel in the trenches in the first world war. Did everything right and they still rejected him."

"Why did he lay bricks?"

"Something to do, I suppose. The worst thing in life for an active person is boredom. We're not very good at doing nothing. Are you still working?"

"Got the sack. Didn't fit in. Wanted me to go to the pub."

"I see… Let's go for a walk while the sun is still shining. I enjoyed my breakfast. Where did you find the bacon and eggs?"

"In the shop."

Not even pleased by the mail from Rhodesia, Bobby went for a walk with his father. Later, he wrote out the cheques for his suppliers, walked to the post office and sent them to Rhodesia, his final job done for Hopewell Estate, the final cut-off, the final severance with Africa, the weight of burden lifting from his shoulders. They didn't talk much, happy to be with each other, glad of the company. On the way back, they bought a small Christmas tree. From the shed, Bobby brought out a large pot, filled it with earth and planted the Christmas tree in front of the lounge window, then he went up to the attic to find the old decorations in the boxes he remembered from his childhood. By half past four, with the light outside almost faded, they turned on the fairy lights, not drawing the lounge curtains. Like the houses opposite, they were ready to celebrate Christmas.

"Was there a letter from Katie?"

"I didn't see one. I said I would contact her first when I was ready. When the devil had left me. I've given her enough problems already without giving her any more. She's gone back to work."

"You mind if I play some music on the gramophone? She and I met at a symphony concert at the Albert Hall. I'm sure I must have told you. Brahms. Brahms's Third Symphony. I'll put it on now. You used to love good music."

"I still do."

"You'll be staying for Christmas?"

"If you'll have me. After Christmas I'm going up to Glasgow to get another job. That's if the Scots will tolerate an Englishman. Wasn't so long ago we English were fighting with the Scots. Why do we always end up in wars?"

"Not the right question for an old soldier."

"I hate wars."

"Good soldiers are meant to stop them. If you are powerful enough, your enemy won't pick a fight with you. That's the theory."

"Why do we have enemies?"

"Part of human nature. Built into us. We're all the product of rape and pillage, if we look back far enough. Only the strong survived. We only think we're civilised. Underneath the good manners of every gentleman there's a savage if you provoke him enough... The Christmas tree reminds me so much of your mother. When we were all so happy as a family. Those are wonderful memories for an old man."

"For the last few weeks I've been able to think of my children. See their smiles. Hear their happy voices. The distance helps. Posting those cheques has helped. It's all over. That part of my life is over. I can't yet think of Wendy. But that will come, I hope."

For the first time they both looked directly at each other, both of them trying to smile.

"You think our ancestors went through these kinds of problems?" asked Bobby.

"All of them. Every single one of them. How they survived. You'll have good times again. It's the pattern of life. How it goes. I'm proud of you, son. More proud of you now than I've ever been. Why don't you give Katie a ring and wish her a happy Christmas? I've got her new phone number. She and her old friend Linda are sharing a flat together."

"Maybe on Christmas Day."

"We'll get ourselves a turkey. Or a chicken. We'd be eating turkey sandwiches for a month if I bought a turkey."

"Nothing wrong with that. Save you all the cooking. Did either of the girls ask you for Christmas?"

"They both did. I go to one one year, the other the next. This year I'm spending Christmas with my son. They'll understand. Anyway, they have their own families to look after. I have a bad habit of falling asleep in the chair in front of the fire. The grandchildren exhaust me."

"This year we can both fall asleep in front of the fire after we've had our turkey."

The music flowed over them, the Brahms reminding Bobby of his first days in the tent, before any of the buildings had gone up on Hopewell Estate, before Katie had been frightened by the hyena and climbed into his bed, before that fateful time when he fell of the barstool, in Meikles Hotel, which brought him Wendy and his children. The music surged through his mind, both cleansing and hurting. They listened in silence, deep in the music and all the emotions it brought. By the end, Bobby was silently crying, his father staring at the Christmas tree not wishing to look. Maybe on Christmas Day, thought Bobby, maybe later when he was ready. When his father changed the record, the music of Beethoven flowed through the room, martial music evoking Wellington's victory at the Battle of Waterloo. Bobby got control of himself and smiled. The old soldier had gone back to his roots.

"'Wellington's Victory'," said his father.

"I know. Why I was smiling."

"The Prussians were on our side at the Battle of Waterloo. Mostly through history, we and the Germans were on the same side fighting the French. The two world wars in the context of history don't make any sense."

"Not a lot makes sense to me these days."

"No, I suppose it doesn't."

"Do you have *Half a Sixpence* or *My Fair Lady*?"

"I'll have a look. They were your mother's favourite kind of music."

"Don't put them on if it upsets you."

"Not with you here it won't... I don't know what I would have done without you children."

"Do you ever get over it?"

"No, Bobby, you don't. Any more than you get over going through a war and seeing your friends killed. After the fighting, you go back into the mess and half of them are missing, the room empty of them, never to fill up again. Some of the chaps I'd been with through school and Sandhurst. Fought right beside them. You never get over it. Every life has its ending. Sometimes now I envy them. They didn't have to learn about old age and loneliness. One minute they were alive, the next minute gone. Not this slow slide down the hill to oblivion. Maybe there is another life after this one but nobody really knows. Nobody is certain however much the priests reassure us... You want to go to church on Christmas Day? The old Norman church can be very comforting. Father and son kneeling in silence. Do us both good. You have to try and believe there is more to this life or it doesn't have a purpose. We can go to the eleven o'clock service having put the turkey in the oven. Don't you remember those Christmases when you were growing up? Presents under the tree given out when we came back from church and then the big lunch."

"Every one of them. Once, when I'd had a row with mother, I said I was going to the moon. Then I thought a moment and said I'd come back for Christmas."

"You were eight years old. Your mother had to fight to keep a straight face. What would we do without our families?"

"That's what I'm trying to find out."

"Sorry, son. Didn't mean to bring it all back to you."

"Church on Christmas Day will be good... That music is better. I used to listen to musicals on my old wind-up gramophone in my tent before there were any buildings on the farm... What a pity I don't drink anymore. We could have a drink together. Do you ever drink on your own?"

"Never. Never now. Never before. Drinking was purely social."

"Was for me until it caught hold of me. I'm getting through. One day at a time. We all drank too much on the farms in Rhodesia. Sundowners. It was part of our colonial culture. Sundowners at the club. That little part of England in the middle of Africa. Stupidly it made us feel secure. We only saw what we wanted to see. Ourselves and our culture even down to the cricket. No wonder we looked like aliens to the blacks. We could have come from Mars, we were so different. Some of them may have envied us. They had a perfect rural life until we showed them all the trappings that had grown from our science. Can you imagine seeing a car go along for the first time? This alien mass making noise and coming towards you and you don't know what it is. Poor sods. I'd have run a mile in the opposite direction. Maybe they should have done. For us in Europe the industrial revolution was a slow process. A telephone. A lightbulb. An internal combustion engine. A train. An aeroplane. For the blacks in Rhodesia it happened all at once. One minute they're cut off from the world, happy in their own way of life, and the next there is chaos. What had happened to us over generations happened to them overnight. We never integrated with them. Just lived our lives the way we would have lived in England. No wonder they grew to hate us. They could see our world but not be part of it. They walked our roads while we roared by kicking dust in their faces. I've had a lot of time to think on my own. Too often we only see life through our own eyes, never through the other person's. We don't see what they're looking at, which is us. No one can see themselves except in the mirror, fleeting images when we're having a shave. We're looking at the razorblade not ourselves. Too much time on one's own isn't good for us. We start questioning what life is about. The trouble is, I doubt if church on Christmas Day will be any help, except for the inner peace it brings to us and that feeling of belonging to society and with it the comfort. The church says God is in all of us. I just don't know. With all my heart I would like to believe what they taught me at school about our Christian religion. With the hard facts of evolution in front of me, I find it difficult... Where did you hide my passport?"

"In a safe place... You're starting to think deeply and that's good."

"Those good old days of escaping into alcohol with my friends are gone. The days now are so much longer. So much time to think... You mind if I go upstairs and have a bath?"

"You run along."

"Nothing like a hot bath in the winter. Thank you for helping me, Dad."

WHILE HIS SON was upstairs having a bath, Roland Preston phoned Katie.

"Would you like to come down to Epsom for Christmas? Bobby's with me. He's much better, Katie. I think he's ready to see you."

"Have you told him I'm coming?"

"Not yet. Make it a surprise. How are you, Katie?"

"Much better now I've had your call. Where's he been?"

"Laying bricks. Digging trenches. Not far from you in the city on a building site."

"He hasn't had a drink?"

"Not a drop."

"I'm driving down to Dorking for Christmas with my parents. I'll stop in on my way back."

"Whenever it suits you. Without you he wouldn't be where he is now."

"You still got his passport?"

"Still in my pocket. I've got something I want to talk to you about. You have financial connections in New York that may be able to solve his problem."

WHEN THE FRONT door bell rang a few days after Christmas, the old man went to answer it and ushered Katie into the lounge where they were having their afternoon tea in front of the fire.

"Hello, Katie," said Bobby, standing up. "I don't suppose this is a coincidence. Would you like a muffin?"

"How are you, Bobby?"

"Coping... I toast the muffins in front of the fire."

"I'm back working for IBM so I can't stay long. Christmas with my parents. Work again tomorrow morning."

"I'm sure you've time for a muffin."

"Your father said he has something to ask me about."

"Where are you living?"

"Back in my old flat in Shepherd's Bush. I'd given my tenant notice. Linda's staying with me. Thank you. I'll have one of those muffins. How was your Christmas?"

"I went to church on Christmas morning. So, Dad, what did you want to ask Katie about?"

"You left your bank statement open on my desk. You had converted the balance into United States dollars. The figure jumped out at me."

"How much is left in your bank?" asked Katie.

"Not that it's any good to me in Rhodesia. Exchange control prevents us from taking any of it out of the country. Just under nine hundred thousand dollars."

"Rhodesian dollars or American?"

"American."

"That's a lot of money."

"It was. And no, I'm not going back."

"Don't you have financial connections that could move Bobby's money, even at a hefty discount?" asked the old man.

"Izak Budman in New York would likely have a way. He's a lawyer. His friend Mark Bloom is in finance. Rhodesia still trades with the world, even if it is through the backdoor. I read somewhere that when the Americans applied sanctions they excluded chrome imports into

America. There are only two major sources of chrome in the world, Russia and Rhodesia. Chrome's a strategic mineral for American defence. There will be money passing between America and Rhodesia. If you got in the middle of a transaction you could pay the seller with a Rhodesian cheque and the buyer could pay you in pounds. They'd both make an extra profit on the transaction but you'd at least get some of your nine hundred thousand out of Rhodesia. I can give Izak a ring tomorrow. We still keep in touch. He handled my affairs in New York."

"Sounds very nice, Katie, but the transaction would be illegal. I couldn't break the law. Society makes laws for a reason. If we all broke the law when it was convenient, where would we be?"

"But you are no longer going to live in Rhodesia."

"Doesn't change Rhodesian law. Or the fact the money was made in Rhodesia with money I borrowed from a government bank to get me started. Now, do you want a muffin? Thank you for your help but no thank you. I would have to live with my conscience. My wife died because she loved Rhodesia and wouldn't come with me to England. I can't do something like that... Dad, have you ever broken the law?"

"Not that I know of."

"It was the way you brought me up... Isn't the fire lovely?"

"So you'll lose all your money?" said Katie.

"Probably."

"What are you doing for money?"

"Working. On a building site. Tomorrow I take the train up to Glasgow to look for another job. When I'm quite sure I have controlled my drinking, I thought I would start my own construction business. Use the balance sheet from Hopewell Estate to prove I know how to run a business to get some seed money. Start all over again. I like the thought of the challenge... There. How does that one look? You spread it with butter. The butter soaks right through the muffin. Quite delicious."

"Have you heard from the farm?"

"I don't want to, Katie. I don't want to even think of it. By now it will have reverted to subsistence farming... Go on. Take a bite."

"Quite delicious."

"I told you so."

"Better be off. Long drive in traffic to Shepherd's Bush. I've got some work to do before I get to the office. Nine o'clock meeting with a client. Have to do my preparation."

"I'll see you to the car."

"That will be kind of you. Sorry the visit is so short, Brigadier Preston. Did I answer your question?"

"So did Bobby... Drive carefully."

"I will."

Outside in the cold and gathering dark, Bobby walked Katie to the Volkswagen.

"Why are you crying, Katie?"

"You know bloody well why... Will I ever see you again?"

"Who knows? Who knows in this game of life? I hope so."

"So do I."

"Goodbye, Katie."

"Goodbye, Bobby. Look after yourself."

~

LEOPARDS NEVER CHANGE THEIR SPOTS (BOOK ELEVEN)

THE BRIGANDSHAW JOURNEY WILL CONTINUE...

One single bullet was all it took...

Terrified and heartbroken, Randall Crookshank packs his bags, a plane ticket purchased. Naïve as to where he's going, Randall is greeted with buzzing cars and hordes of people. It's Piccadilly Circus. Not the tranquillity of the African bush where the lions roar, the elusive leopard hides, or the fish eagle that haunts the skies. It's not Rhodesia.

Friendless and alone, reluctant to rely on Uncle Paul's charity, he finds lodgings in Notting Hill Gate. Eventually finding his feet, Randall makes new friends, including feisty, little Amanda Hanscombe. But there's more to Amanda than meets the eye...

Randall Crookshank's new life takes him far from home and not only to the hustle of London but to the magnetism of New York City. And there in New York, Randall meets up with the luscious Hayley Oosthuizen. She offers him a tempting proposal. But will it be enough to seduce him or will he find himself in jeopardy once again?

PRINCIPAL CHARACTERS

~

The Crookshanks
Jeremy — A tobacco farmer in Centenary
Carmen — Jeremy's late wife
Phillip — Jeremy and Carmen's eldest son
Randall — Jeremy and Carmen's youngest son
Bergit — Jeremy's second wife
Myra and Craig — Jeremy and Bergit's children

Other Principal Characters
Alice Swart — Wendy's friend and Blackie's wife
Andy — Linda's American boyfriend
Angela Tate — Katie and Linda's old schoolfriend who is a high-class whore
Anton Dubov — A commercial artist living on Madison Avenue
Bafana — Zulu doorman at the Meikles Hotel
Betty — Bobby's twin girls' nanny
Blackie Swart — A tobacco farmer
Blanche Cousins — Finn's wife

Bobby Preston — An English tobacco farmer in Centenary and owner of Hopewell Estate (central character of *Full Circle*)
Canaan Moyo — An African guerrilla fighter
Caroline Wells — Elizabeth and Stanley's daughter
Celeste Fox — Katie's supervisor at IBM, America
Clay Barry — Police member-in-charge for Centenary
Comrade Tangwena — Freedom fighter contact at the Chiweshe reserve
Darna — Angela Tate's girlfriend
Dave and Eric — Work friends of Katie and Linda
Donald Henderson — A Rhodesian policeman
Eileen O'Shea — An Irish republican sympathiser
Elizabeth Wells — Wife of Stanley Wells who has a string of affairs
Finn Cousins — Andy's business associate in America
Fred Rankin — Clay Barry's second-in-command
George Stacy — Tobacco farmer and man who shot the old lion in *The Best of Times*
Glynnis — Katie's supervisor at IBM, London
Godfrey — Bobby and Wendy's house servant
Grace — Canaan Moyo's wife
Hammond Taylor — Bobby's friend and fellow farmer
Hubert and Georgy —Two men that Linda and Katie go to a concert with
Hugh Quinton — Club Chairman of the Centenary East club and owner of North Ridge Estate
Izak Budman — An American attorney with Prescott, Cohen and Rothman
Jacob and Joshua — African guerrilla freedom fighters
Joshua Moyo —Canaan and Grace's son
Josiah Makoni — A revolutionary leader of ZANU
Katie Frost — Bobby Preston's fiancée
Koos Hendriks — An old Afrikaans's prospector
Linda Gaskell — Katie's best friend
Mark Bloom — Sells investment funds in New York
Michelle O'Reilly — Katie's roommate in America
Morris — The Centenary East club barman
Noah — Barman at the Centenary West club
Roland Preston— Bobby's father, a retired brigadier in the British Army
Rose Moyo — Canaan and Grace's baby daughter

Sekuru — Bobby's bossboy on Hopewell Estate
Stanley Wells — Tobacco farmer in Centenary East
Stephanie and Deborah — Bobby Preston's twin daughters
Vince Ranger — Jeremy Crookshank's farm assistant and Bobby's friend
Welcome — Bobby's camp cook and later his house servant
Wendy Cox — A young woman who Bobby meets in Bretts nightclub

HISTORICAL NOTES

~

Political Parties and Organisations

ZANU – Zimbabwe African National Union
ZANU was a militant African nationalist organisation that participated in the Rhodesian Bush War against the white government of Rhodesia. Due to a split in ZAPU in 1975, ZANU was formed but by 1976 it reformed again with the Patriotic Front, becoming known as ZANU-PF.

ZIPRA – Zimbabwe People's Revolutionary Army
ZIPRA was the military wing of ZAPU. Their camps were based around Lusaka, Zambia, training both regular soldiers and guerrilla fighters, concentrating their activities in the northwest and southwest of Rhodesia.

ZANLA – Zimbabwe African National Liberation Army
ZANLA was the military wing of ZANU. Their camps were based in Lusaka, Zambia and during the late 1970s the ZANLA fighters were deployed in the Matabeleland and Midlands provinces.

ZAPU – Zimbabwe African People's Union
ZAPU is a Zimbabwean socialist political party founded in 1961 until 1980 when it merged with Zimbabwe African National Union-Patriotic Front (ZANU-PF). ZAPU was founded by Joshua Nkomo who became their president.

PATU – Rhodesian Police Anti-Terrorist Unit
PATU was a tracker combat unit formed during the Rhodesian bush war by the British South Africa Police (BSAP).

BSAP – British South Africa Police
In 1889, Cecil John Rhodes's British South Africa Company formed a paramilitary force of mounted infantrymen from which it took its original name, the British South Africa Company's Police. It was renamed in 1980 to Zimbabwe Republic Police (ZRP)

FRELIMO – Frente de Libertação de Moçambique (Mozambique Liberation Front)
FRELIMO is the dominant political party in Mozambique that was founded in 1962, and begun as a nationalist movement fighting for the independence of the Portuguese Overseas Province of Mozambique.

RENAMO – Resistência Nacional Moçambicana (Mozambican National Resistance)
RENAMO is a militant organisation and political movement in Mozambique that was supported by the Rhodesian Central Intelligence Organisation (CIO). The anti-communist organisation was founded in 1975 in opposition against the country's ruling FRELIMO party.

Historical Characters

Joshua Nkomo
Nkomo was a Zimbabwean revolutionary activist and politician. Initially president of the banned National Democratic Party, he went on to found ZAPU in 1961. His party eventually merged in 1987 with that of Robert

Mugabe's ZANU. Nkomo was born in Matopos to a poor Ndebele family in1917, dying in Harare, Zimbabwe in1999.

Robert Mugabe

Mugabe was a Zimbabwean revolutionary and politician. From 1975 to 1980 he was the leader of ZANU during the Rhodesian Bush War. Mugabe was born into a poor Shona family in Kutama, Southern Rhodesia in 1924 and died in 2019, aged 95. Having won political power in 1980 from the white minority government, he led his party as prime minister and president of Zimbabwe until he was ousted in a military coup in 2017.

Ian Smith

Smith was a Rhodesian politician, farmer, and RAF fighter pilot who served as prime minister of Rhodesia from 1964 to 1979. He was born in 1919 in Selukwe, Rhodesia and died aged 88 in Cape Town, South Africa. Smith led the Rhodesian Front (RF) for almost fourteen years of international isolation that followed the unilateral declaration of independence from Great Britain (UDI).

Ndabaningi Sithole

Sithole was one of the founding members and chief architect of ZANU alongside Herbert Chitepo, Robert Mugabe and Edgar Tekere, even though he had first been an influential member of ZAPU. He was born in 1920 and died in the United States in 2000.

GLOSSARY

~

ANC — African National Congress
Braai — Afrikaans word for barbeque
IBM — International Business Machines – an American multinational technology and consulting corporation
IRA — The Irish Republican Army
Mokori — An African dugout canoe
RLI — Rhodesian Light Infantry
RMS — Road Motor Service: the road transport arm of the Rhodesia Railways
Simby — An old plough disc with a length of metal for a gong
Stoep — Afrikaans word for a veranda
Terr — A black insurgent in the Rhodesian Bush War
TTL — Tribal Trust Land
UDI — Unilateral Declaration of Independence

SELECT BIBLIOGRAPHY

~

You may wish to further your reading of the Rhodesian Bush War, and below is a list of a few non-fiction related books. Some of these books have been recommended by the members of Peter Rimmer's Band of Readers (our Facebook Group) and one that Peter himself owned and to which he probably referred.

African Laughter by Doris Lessing, ISBN: 978-0006546900

A Handful of Hard Men: The SAS and the Battle for Rhodesia by Hannes Wessels, ISBN: 978-1612003450

Mugabe by David Smith & Colin Simpson with Ian Davies, ISBN: 978-0722178683

Mukiwa: A White Boy in Africa by Peter Godwin, ISBN: 978-0330450102

Rhodesia by Peter Baxter, ISBN: 978-1726710626
The Rhodesian Civil War by John Frame, ISBN: 978-1789551853

The Great Betrayal: The Memoirs of Ian Douglas Smith by Ian Smith, ISBN: 978-1857821765

We Dared to Win: The SAS in Rhodesia by Hannes Wessels and Andre Scheepers, ISBN: 978-1612005874

Kamba Publishing

DEAR READER

~

Reviews are the most powerful tools in our kitty when it comes to getting attention for Peter's books. This is where you can come in, as by providing an honest review you will help bring them to the attention of other readers.

If you enjoyed reading *Full Circle,* and have five minutes to spare, we would really appreciate a review (it can be as short as you like). Your help in spreading the word and keeping Peter's work alive is gratefully received.

Please post your review on the retailer site where you purchased this book.

Thank you so much.
Heather Stretch (Peter's daughter)

PS. We look forward to you joining Peter's growing band of avid readers.

ACKNOWLEDGEMENTS

~

With grateful thanks to our *VIP First Readers* for reading *Full Circle* prior to its official launch date. They have been fabulous in picking up errors and typos helping us to ensure that your own reading experience of *Full Circle* has been the best possible. Their time and commitment is particularly appreciated.

Hilary Jenkins (South Africa)
Agnes Mihalyfy (United Kingdom)
Daphne Rieck (Australia)

Thank you.

Kamba Publishing

Printed in Great Britain
by Amazon